MAIN

All the Gold Of Ophir

All the Gold Of Ophir

David M. Drury

Five Star • Waterville, Maine

First Edition
First Printing: November 2005

Published in 2005 in conjunction with Tekno Books and Ed Gorman.

Set in 11 pt. Plantin by Minnie B. Raven.

Printed in the United States on permanent paper.

Library of Congress Cataloging-in-Publication Data

Drury, David M. (David Michael), 1951–
    All the gold of Ophir / by David M. Drury.—1st ed.
      p. cm.
    ISBN 1-59414-421-4 (hc : alk. paper)
    1. Gold mines and mining—Fiction.   2. Private investigators—Fiction.   3. Space stations—Fiction.
4. Drug traffic—Fiction.   I. Title.
PS3604.R87A79 2005
    813′.6—dc22   2005024284

This book is dedicated to my cats, Useless (now deceased), Midnight Sky, and TC. They not only introduced many interesting plot twists by walking across, jumping upon, or knocking objects onto my keyboard, but also gave up thousands of hours of playtime, cuddling, and cat-treat eating to let me write this book.

Chapter 1

Helene Asterbrook gazed at Jupiter Station through the viewport of the shuttle. Philip's e-mails hadn't done it justice. Helene's son had tried to describe its grandeur, its awesome beauty, its incomprehensible size, but nothing Philip had written had prepared her for the spectacle that filled the port and reduced the shuttle to insignificance. Jupiter Station was a kilometer in diameter and twice that in length. Helene had never seen an artificial structure that big. Nowhere else was there an artificial structure that big.

"Now I can understand what Philip wrote," Helene said softly.

"Hmmm?"

"About the Station," Helene explained to her husband. "Its majesty. The feeling he would get in his stomach."

Donald Asterbrook had not been thinking about Jupiter Station and did not reply. He was not a talkative man in the best of circumstances, and these were not the best of circumstances. He didn't like this business, but it had to be done. He wished it was over.

The shuttle approached the docking airlock on the end of the Station's hub. Helene could no longer see the entire Station through the port. The Station was rotating to produce artificial gravity, and she could see the spokes sweep past. They glistened white in the sunlight. In the distance, a quarter of a million kilometers away, was Jupiter itself, painted in swirls of orange and gray by its unending winds. Its Great Red Spot was not visible. Then the bow of the shuttle entered the docking collar and Helene's view was blocked.

Latches closed with a clang. The pressure increased slightly when the airlock was opened. The seatbelt light went out and the shuttle pilot announced, "Welcome to the Jupiter Station of the Conglomerated Mining and Manufacturing Company. Debarking Company employees should report to the Company desk just inside the airlock. All passengers can claim their luggage at the baggage claim area beside the airlock in the arrival lounge. We hope that you enjoyed your voyage on the *Planet Queen* and that you enjoy your stay on Jupiter Station."

Don Asterbrook unlatched his seatbelt. His wife was slow to follow suit. "Are you all right?" he asked.

Helene gripped her armrests to keep from drifting out of her seat. The docking airlock did not spin with the rest of the Station and there was no gravity. Helene had had trouble adjusting to zero gee when she had first left Earth. "I'm okay," she said. She forced herself to let go of her chair and join the crowd of people drifting lazily toward the bow of the shuttle. She steadied herself by holding onto chair tops and the convenient handholds attached to the overhead.

"What's holding up the parade?" called a voice from the rear of the shuttle. No one answered. The airlock at the bow was wide enough for only two people abreast. There were two hundred people on the shuttle. Debarkation was not going to be rapid.

The Asterbrooks approached the front of the shuttle. Through a grating above them Helene could see the pilots at their console. They wore headsets and microphones, and their features were bathed in the orange and green glow of the console displays. Helene felt a draft on her legs and pushed her dress back into place. She was wearing her best dress, made of heavy gray wool, but with no gravity to hold it down the hem had a mind of its own. Helene felt herself blushing and hoped that no one had noticed. She had known that there would be no gravity on the shuttle, but this was a formal occasion, and Helene Asterbrook had been raised to believe that on formal occasions women wore dresses.

The Asterbrooks passed through the airlock hatch and from the quiet, carpeted interior of the shuttle to the gray, metallic airlock of the Station. The airlock was only two meters long. Beyond it the brightly lit arrival lounge, a cylinder thirty meters in length and at least that in diameter, rotated with the Station. Glowing signs pointed to the Company desk and to Baggage Claim. Helene and Donald drifted slowly along the axis with the rest of the departing passengers, pulling themselves along the handrail provided for that purpose. The "bulkhead" of the cylinder was far enough off the axis of rotation to possess noticeable gravity and acted more like the deck than a bulkhead. There must have been thirty people seated in chairs on the "deck" that was simultaneously above, below, and to the side of the Asterbrooks. Helene looked at them in dismay. There was no way she could maintain a properly modest position in respect to all of them. Formal occasion or not, she should have worn pants.

Don Asterbrook could see luggage being disgorged through a hatch into the baggage claim area. Arriving passengers were pushing themselves away from the central handrail and diving toward their bags. The Asterbrooks were leaving for Earth on the *Planet Queen* in two days and had left their luggage in their cabin.

Helene pointed to the Conglomerated Mining and Manufacturing Company's arrival desk, along the bulkhead through which they had entered and opposite the lock from the baggage claim area. "Shouldn't we go there?" she asked her husband.

Donald shook his head. "We aren't Company employees." He nodded toward the Information Desk near the far bulkhead. "That's for us."

The Asterbrooks had to wait in line behind two salesmen on a business trip and a family of five moving to Jupiter Station, where the parents were joining an accounting firm, before it was their turn. The woman on the other side of the desk had artificially glossed blond hair and was wearing the latest in women's fashions: a blue and white dress that scarcely deserved the name, as it was ridiculously brief, worn over a pair of matching shorts that were, if anything, even shorter than the dress, and tights in the same blue and white pattern as the dress. Shorts, dress, and tights had a metallic gleam that was harsh enough to hurt the eyes in bright light. Helene tried to conceal her distaste. Back home, women didn't dress like that. At least, respectable women didn't.

A nametag on the woman's chest identified her as Jeri. She batted her artificially long lashes at the Asterbrooks and asked, "Can I help you?"

"Where can we find Mr. Egleiter?" Mr. Asterbrook asked.

The woman's smile was replaced with a puzzled expression. She scratched her head. Her hair was tightly braided and pinned in place, so that it would behave in low gravity. "The former Human Resources director?"

It took a moment for the woman's words to sink in. "Former director?" Donald said, with the emphasis on the first word.

"He transferred to Ceres four months ago," Jeri explained.

The Asterbrooks looked at each other. They had expected Egleiter to be at Jupiter when they arrived. They turned back to the woman. "We left Earth four months ago," Mr. Asterbrook explained. "We had exchanged messages with Mr. Egleiter before we left home."

"Oh, well," Jeri said, "then Ms. Jackson is probably expecting you. She's the new Human Resources director."

Donald nodded. He could deal just as well with Ms. Jackson. Still, they should have been informed. The Company could easily afford to send a message to the *Planet Queen*.

"Where can we find Ms. Jackson?" he asked.

Jeri smiled and switched on a holographic display of Jupiter Station. "You're right here," she said, pointing to a spot near the hub, at the end of the Station at the docking airlock. Jeri's nail polish matched her dress. "Take elevator number one." She indicated the shaft both on the display and in the arrival lounge. "Get off on level three. You'll be in the Main Plaza. The Company offices are directly across the plaza from the elevators. You can't miss 'em." She smiled again.

The Asterbrooks studied the display. Philip had described Jupiter Station as being large and complex, with many levels and crisscrossing corridors. Finding the Human Resources office couldn't be as easy as the woman claimed.

The woman sensed their hesitation. She had seen such doubts before. She reached beneath the desk and produced a flat black object the size of a credit card. "Or you could buy one of these Jupiter Station locators," she said. "It knows where it is no matter where you are on the Station. Just tell it where you want to go. It can find any address. Or

11

just tell it the name of the person you're looking for, and it will point you toward his or her home or office."

Donald took the locator from the woman's fingers. It was no heavier than a credit card, either. "How much?"

"Forty dollars. And it's guaranteed for life."

The guarantee didn't interest the Asterbrooks. They would need the locator for less than two days, maybe for less than one. But it would keep them from getting lost. Donald removed his wallet from his belt and counted out forty dollars. "How do I turn it on?"

"It's voice activated. Just tell it where you want to go."

Donald took the locator. "Thank you," he said. Jeri smiled again.

The Asterbrooks turned away from the desk. There were more people in line behind them. Donald suspected the woman in the gleaming clothes was going to do a brisk business with locators.

Donald held the locator in front of his face. "Company offices," he said. "Human Resources department. Ms. Jackson's office."

An arrow appeared on the surface of the locator, pointing toward elevator number one. The Asterbrooks headed in that direction, moving awkwardly in the almost nonexistent gravity in the Station's hub. The entrance to the elevator was below the level of the deck of the arrival lounge, down a flight of nearly useless stairs. They floated, rather than walked, down. A car had just arrived, and they joined the throng boarding it. The elevator car was large enough for fifty people, over half with luggage, to crowd aboard. Many of the people wore the gleaming metallic clothing that had become so popular in the last two years. Donald Asterbrook avoided looking at them. It was a free country; they had a right to look silly.

The car started downward very slowly because there was almost no gravity to hold the passengers in position, but its speed increased as it approached the rim and the gravity approached one gee. Three minutes and half a kilometer after leaving the hub, the car slowed with deceleration that would have felt normal on Earth. It stopped on level twelve, and a group of passengers made their way to the door and exited. More people left on levels ten and six. When the car stopped on level three the gravity felt like Earth normal, and the Asterbrooks stepped confidently through the sliding doors, then stopped so quickly that other debarking passengers bumped into them. They could scarcely believe their eyes.

The Asterbrooks were facing along the axis of the Station and the Company offices were thirty meters directly across the Main Plaza from them. To their left and right the deck followed the curve of the Station, so both directions seemed to be uphill. The overhead was several decks above them, and what appeared to be real, diffused, Earth-like sunlight came from the false sky. Trees grew through the deck from a lower level. And to their left was a waterfall— small, to be sure, but it was real water, cascading in an arc distorted by the Coriolis force, from three levels above into a pool, foaming and overflowing into another waterfall that plunged into another pool below. Their son had written of it, but it had to be seen to be appreciated or even believed. The Asterbrooks looked at each other silently. Jupiter Station really was one of the wonders of the twenty-first century.

The locator in Donald Asterbrook's hand pointed across the plaza to the main entrance of the Jupiter offices of the Conglomerated Mining and Manufacturing Company. Halfway across they paused to look over a railing, behind which a tree grew through a hole in the deck. Below them, on level one, a moving sidewalk carried people around the circumference of the Station. Other people hurried back and forth, dodging electric-powered taxis. They could have been in a shopping mall on Earth.

"I can see why he liked it here," Helene said.

"It's a city," her husband replied, glancing at the overhead far above. "An indoor city. There are no clouds, no blue sky."

"He liked cities," Helene answered.

The doors to the Company's offices were open—the air "outside" was conditioned by the same equipment that processed the air "inside," so there was no reason to close the doors. A uniformed security guard sat in the middle of a circular desk in the lobby. Donald started in his direction, but the guard was paying no attention to the Asterbrooks and the locator was pointing to the escalator, so he led his wife past the guard. The escalator whisked them up one floor. The locator pointed to the right, where signs marked the location of the Human Resources office. The door to that office was open, too. Behind the counter a woman sat at a computer terminal. For a second Donald thought she was the same woman who had sold them the locator in the arrival lounge, but this one's dress had a hint of purple, her hair was tinted metallic silver, and the tag on her chest proclaimed that her name was Samantha.

The woman looked up from her terminal. "Can I help you?" she asked with a polite smile.

Donald cleared his throat. "We, ah, we were supposed to see Mr. Egleiter," he said, "but we were told he had transferred."

"Yes," Samantha said. "Almost four months ago." Her tone implied that she didn't think anyone could be so out of date. "Did you have an appointment?"

"I don't know if you would call it an official appointment," Asterbrook answered, "but we did send him a message saying we were coming today."

"Your name is . . . ?"

"Asterbrook."

A holographic display on the counter glowed to life. Samantha barely glanced at it. She knew that no one by that name had an appointment with the Human Resources Director that day. "There's nothing here about an appointment, but if you could tell me the nature of your business I'm sure I could find someone who could help you."

Donald took a deep breath. "We are here to claim the body of our son."

Fred Zoldas smiled. The afternoon was scarcely an hour old, but his desk was clean and his electronic mail file was empty. Nothing requiring his attention ever occurred during the afternoon. He could take it easy until quitting time. Fred leaned back in his chair and grinned. His management methods had significantly improved the efficiency of the Human Resources office. His superiors would have to take notice. Before too many more months, a year at most, Fred Zoldas would certainly be promoted.

There was a light rap on Fred's office door and Samantha Steiner stuck her head into the office. "Ah, Mr. Zoldas . . ."

Zoldas scowled. The woman should have used her computer to contact him. Leaving the counter unattended was not only against the rules, but the time spent walking from her desk to Zoldas' office was wasted. "Yes, Samantha?"

"You remember the accident in the warehouse a few months back when those two guys were killed?"

"Umm, yes. Asterbrook and Mondragon. What about it?"

"Asterbrook's parents are *here*."

" 'Here,' meaning Jupiter Station, or 'here,' meaning in our office?"

"In the office," Samantha said. "They came to pick up the body of their son and take it back to Earth."

Zoldas stared at the woman. Nobody would come all the way from Earth for that. They could have had the body shipped back in half the time and for a fraction of the cost. "Wait a minute: didn't we bury him?"

Samantha nodded nervously. "They have the usual fax from Egleiter announcing that we would dispose of the remains as per wishes of the deceased unless we heard otherwise within seventy-two hours, but they have a copy of a fax they sent to Egleiter requesting us to hold the body until they arrived to collect it, at which time they would recompense us for any expenses incurred."

"Did we get the fax?"

Samantha shook her head. "There's nothing about it in the computer, and they don't have a reply from Egleiter to their fax. But they left Earth almost immediately after learning of their son's death, so they might have missed it."

"Did the deceased consign his body to us on his form nine?"

"Yep."

"Then we had a legal right to bury the body," Zoldas said, relieved.

Samantha hesitated. "Do you think you could explain that to them?"

Zoldas sighed. Ms. Steiner's lack of initiative would weigh against her during her next merit review. "All right."

16

He took a moment to call up the Asterbrook file on his own terminal to make sure Samantha hadn't overlooked anything. She hadn't. Philip Asterbrook had been buried, all right, and there was no request from anybody to hold his body for pickup.

Fred got up reluctantly. He was of medium height and stocky build, and he didn't exercise enough. Getting out of his chair was the last thing he wanted to do.

Zoldas led Samantha down the short corridor to the outer office. The two people waiting for him on the far side of the counter couldn't have been taken for anything but newcomers from some rural backwater. Their clothes had been out of fashion for a decade. The man was tall—a hundred and ninety-five centimeters, maybe—with a harsh, weathered face. The woman was a head shorter but her face was just as weathered. They looked somber and middle-aged, but with the development of youth drugs nobody looked old anymore. Philip Asterbrook had been twenty-eight when he had died; his parents could be anywhere from their mid-forties to their late sixties.

"Mr. and Mrs. Asterbrook? I'm Fred Zoldas."

The Asterbrooks didn't reply immediately. Helene deferred to her husband, and Donald was sizing up this new arrival. Zoldas had a pudgy physique and a high forehead. He was wearing the male version of the latest fashion: a glossy coat, glossy shorts, and matching tights. Fred's clothes had a silver tint, and looked ridiculous on an overweight office manager.

"Has this woman—" Donald started to say.

"Ah, yes, she has," Fred interrupted. He wanted to keep this short. "Let me extend my condolences and those of the Company to you and your wife."

Donald knew false sympathy when he heard it. "We are

here for our son's body and personal belongings," he said without emotion.

Zoldas wished he had paid more attention to the Asterbrook file; he wanted to know where these people had come from. Someplace you couldn't get to from here, someplace farther removed from civilization than was Jupiter Station. Only in such a place would people waste time by personally retrieving the body of a loved one for burial. Zoldas wet his lips. "There is a problem with that. We never received your message to hold the body."

Asterbrook stared at Zoldas. He produced his copy of the message he had sent to Egleiter. "We informed your Mr. Egleiter—"

"I know, I know," Zoldas said quickly, "but messages don't always get through. Every once in a while they get garbled in transmission, or just get lost in the system—this is a very large corporation."

"Where is our son?" Asterbrook demanded.

Zoldas swallowed. "We buried him."

Asterbrook's hard stare burned right through Fred's eyes and into his brain. Donald put his hands flat on the counter, leaned closer to Zoldas, and said, "Then dig him up."

Zoldas took a deep breath. "You don't understand. 'Buried him' is a figure of speech. We can't actually inter bodies on the Station. When we 'bury' someone, the body is taken in a shuttle and ejected on an orbit intersecting with Jupiter. The body burns up in Jupiter's atmosphere."

The Asterbrooks said nothing. Their expressions revealed nothing, not even anger. They didn't even look at each other.

"We want to speak with your supervisor," Donald said finally.

Fred Zoldas was suddenly aware that he was alone; Samantha had turned her attention to her computer terminal. "That would be Ms. Jackson, the Human Resources Director," he replied, stalling for time while he tried to think of what to say. "She's very busy at the moment, but I could arrange an appointment. . . ." Good idea: the Asterbrooks were probably returning to Earth on the *Planet Queen*, and it was leaving in two days. Get the Asterbrooks an appointment for tomorrow, postpone it at the last minute, and the problem would go away.

"We want to speak with your supervisor *now*," Asterbrook said firmly.

Fred's brain decided it was time for a coffee break and refused to function. Fortunately, Samantha came to Fred's assistance. "Here's something strange," she said from her terminal.

The Asterbrooks' attention was diverted from Fred to the woman. "There's an accounting flag in Philip Asterbrook's file," Samantha continued. "We must owe him some money."

"His last paycheck should have been sent to his parents," Zoldas said, puzzled.

"According to this, it was," Samantha said, "and the insurance company has taken over the payments."

"What payments?" Donald asked.

"Your son was killed on the job," Samantha explained. "Under the Uniform Employer Liability Act, we owe his survivors—according to his form nine, that's you—his regular wages until what would have been his seventy-fifth birthday or until his survivors are also deceased, whichever comes first. Our insurance carrier will be sending you regular checks, including all across-the-board raises for his job classification, until then."

Donald and Helene exchanged a brief glance. "We don't want the money; we have enough of that. We just want Philip's body so we can give him a proper burial."

"We can't give you his body," Zoldas replied, his exasperation beginning to show. "It's gone. It's burned up. We're very sorry about this snafu, but there's nothing we can do about it."

"You can take us to your supervisor," Donald insisted.

Before Zoldas could explain that there was nothing his supervisor could do, either, Samantha exclaimed, "Ah-hah! Here it is: we don't owe you money; we're holding your son's personal belongings!" She smiled.

Zoldas looked over her shoulder at the computer display. "That doesn't make any sense! If we didn't get the message to hold his body, we wouldn't have held his belongings, either! Surely they were sent to Earth!"

Samantha underscored a line in the display with her finger. "That's not what it says here."

Zoldas read it for himself, grimaced, and said, "That has to be a mistake. It says the personal belongings are *here,* in Human Resources." Even if the Company still had Philip Asterbrook's property, it would be in a warehouse someplace, not in the Human Resources Department.

"His belongings are not enough," Donald said. "We came a billion kilometers to take care of our son's affairs, pick up his possessions, and take his body home. We want our son's body, and if you can't provide that you had better provide your supervisor, *right now.*"

The situation was on the verge of becoming ugly. "I'll see if I can find the personal property," Samantha said, and darted down the back corridor.

Samantha's desertion had left Zoldas outnumbered. Fred needed immediate reinforcements. He hated to bother his boss, who would wonder why he couldn't handle the situation himself, but the Asterbrooks wanted to talk to his supervisor. Okay, he would see about that. "If you'll excuse me," he said to his visitors, "I'll see if Ms. Jackson is available."

To the surprise of Fred Zoldas, Clarisse Jackson came immediately after verifying the details of the case on her own computer. Her impression of the Asterbrooks was much like the one Zoldas had had: neat, formal, but out-of-date attire, somber expressions, a quiet dignity. They were farmers, most likely, from some conservative rural area—a religious commune, perhaps. They were not likely to make trouble. They were just upset, having come a long way at great expense to be greeted by very disappointing news. She would be able to placate them in no time.

Clarisse smiled. "Hello. I'm Clarisse Jackson, Human Resources Director here on Jupiter Station."

Donald Asterbrook didn't let his expression reveal what he was thinking. Ms. Jackson was tall and slender, and was wearing the business-suit version of the modern fashions that the Asterbrooks found so repulsive. More of the same glittering fabric—silver, like Zoldas's, but which actually looked nice against Ms. Jackson's black skin—the matching tights and shorts, the skirt so brief as to be nothing but non-functional decoration, and, on top of everything, a suit coat that extended lower than the skirt and had boxy shoulders that made Clarisse look like a football player. The Human Resources Director could not have made a worse first impression on the Asterbrooks no matter how hard she had tried.

"We sent a message to Mr. Egleiter, informing him that we would be arriving on the *Planet Queen* and that he should hold the body of our son for us," Mr. Asterbrook said. "Now we are told that has not been done. We would like to know why."

Clarisse found her mouth going dry. There was a firmness, a sense of purpose, in Donald Asterbrook's tone that she had not expected. She understood why Fred Zoldas had summoned her; Zoldas had been out of his depth. The Asterbrooks would not be placated easily.

"Ah, I'm really not sure," Ms. Jackson began. "There's nothing in the files concerning your message. Perhaps it never reached us."

"Perhaps you could ask Mr. Egleiter."

"Mr. Egleiter transferred to Ceres four months ago," Clarisse explained.

"Don't they have radios on Ceres?"

Clarisse was searching for an answer when Samantha returned. "Guess what I found!" she announced cheerfully as she came down the corridor that led past Fred Zoldas' office. She was carrying a medium-sized packing case. Perspiration glistened on her forehead. She pushed past Fred and Clarisse to the counter and deposited the case heavily on it. "Look at this," she said, pointing to a hand-written message taped to the side:

HOLD FOR D. ASTERBROOK ARRIVING ON PLANET QUEEN 8 SOL 2054.

Fred Zoldas looked away so that his face would not betray his thoughts. Stupid woman! What the hell was she thinking? More than likely, she wasn't thinking at all.

Ms. Jackson forced herself to smile. The foolish girl had ruined everything. Why had Zoldas put the idiot in charge of the counter? "Where did you find it?" Clarisse managed to say in a level voice.

"I came across a janitorial robot and asked it if it had seen a box containing someone's personal belongings,"

22

Samantha explained. "It directed me to the utility closet at the end of the hall."

Donald and Helene read the message and looked at each other. "Didn't get our message, eh?" Donald said. "Then how could anyone here know that we were coming on the *Planet Queen*?"

"Obviously, your message was received," Ms. Jackson conceded. "Whoever collected your son's personal belongings was told to hold them for your arrival. However, the undertaker was not told to hold your son."

"Why not?"

"I don't know why not," Clarisse replied, mildly flustered. "Some sort of breakdown in communication. This is a big corporation; these things happen sometimes."

"I want to know why," Asterbrook insisted.

"I don't know why."

"Then take us to someone who does!"

"I don't know who does!" Ms. Jackson was starting to lose her poise.

"Then take us to your supervisor!"

Ms. Jackson took a deep breath. "My supervisor," she said haughtily, "is Mr. Edwin Warshovsky, the general manager of this station."

Asterbrook nodded. "He'll do."

Clarisse stared at him in disbelief. "But Mr. Warshovsky is a very busy man! His entire day is scheduled! He sees no one without an appointment!"

Asterbrook picked up the case containing his son's property. "Our son told us that you have almost no crime here. Your police shouldn't be very busy. I don't suppose we need an appointment to see them." He turned to his wife. "Let's go."

"Ah, just a moment," Ms. Jackson said quickly. "You

misunderstood. I didn't say you *couldn't* see Mr. Warshovsky. It's just going to be difficult to fit you in. You'll have to be patient. If you'll take a seat," she indicated a row of chairs along the wall, "I'll see what I can do."

Donald Asterbrook nodded again. "That's better," he replied.

Edwin R. Warshovsky sat in his leather-covered chair behind the broad, polished surface of his executive desk. His elbows were propped on the arms of his chair, and his chin rested on his hands. He was staring across the expanse of his office, the largest office on Jupiter Station, to the far wall, on which hung the portrait of his predecessor, Arnold Lang.

Warshovsky and Lang were opposites in almost every respect. Lang had been short, blond, wiry, and overflowing with energy. Warshovsky was tall, dark-haired, broad-shouldered, and quiet. The management styles of the two men also contrasted. It was as though the Board of Directors of Conglomerated Mining and Manufacturing had deliberately chosen someone who reminded them as little as possible of Arnold Lang to clean up the mess that Lang had created.

Arnold Lang had conceived the idea of Jupiter Station fifteen years earlier, when asteroids were presumed to be rich in gold and other precious metals. People had expected them to be the source of mankind's minerals for thousands of years. But the initial surge into the asteroid belt had dissipated in the emptiness and vast distances. Most asteroids were small and, in the void between Mars and Jupiter, very hard to find. Even after the asteroids were located, the mining companies discovered that they contained very little precious metal. They consisted mostly of iron, nickel, and aluminum, and it took far too long and cost too much to move them to the smelters. Asteroid mining quickly centered on the large, locatable planetoids, which were too large to be fed whole to the smelters and had to be mined in the conventional, expensive fashion.

Enter Arnold Lang. Warshovsky's predecessor had seen Jupiter for what it was—a large vacuum cleaner, collecting planetesimals from the asteroid belt and storing them where they could be easily found and readily exploited. Lang's energy and enthusiasm had convinced the Board of Directors to mine the Jupiter system while everyone else thought that the giant planet was too far from Earth. The board had put Conglomerated Mining in hock to the banks in exchange for the forty billion dollars that Lang had estimated would be required to get started, and Jupiter Station had been born.

Lang had built Jupiter Station with materials shipped at great cost from Earth, Mars, and Ceres. When precious metals had been found in concentrations even lower than those in the asteroid belt, Lang had put the Company into base metals like iron and aluminum, which had very low profit margins. He had shipped partially processed ore at great cost back to Earth. Lang's enterprise had lost money at a rate that not even a government could afford, but to write off Jupiter Station was to write off the Company. The Board of Directors, faced with the greatest commercial disaster in history, had replaced Lang with Warshovsky.

Ed Warshovsky had convinced the Board that the problem with Jupiter Station was that it was too small to take advantage of the resources with which it was surrounded. To make the Station bigger, more money—much more money—was required. The members of the Board had swallowed hard, closed their eyes, and borrowed money on all Company property not already mortgaged. Warshovsky had made Jupiter Station ten times larger than what Arnold Lang had envisioned. He had obtained the raw materials to expand it from Jupiter's satellites. He had fabricated the parts right on the scene in manufacturing facilities built in orbit around Jupiter. He had increased the value of the materials sent back to Earth by smelting ores into pure metals and manufacturing the metals into finished products. Warshovsky had put Manufacturing into the Company name, and had put black ink back into the Company's books.

The Jupiter operation had grown so big that support companies had moved in to provide the needed infrastructure. Now the Station had stores, hospitals, saloons, theaters, churches, and banks. Warshovsky had made money by renting space on the Station to those companies and apartments to their employees. The support companies had to import materials from Earth, materials that were transported at a profit in ships owned by Conglomerated Mining and Manufacturing. The trade had increased so much that more ships were needed, and Warshovsky had built them at Jupiter. Everything Warshovsky had done was earning money for his company. Arnold Lang had been right: Jupiter was a gold mine, richer than the biblical Ophir.

Jupiter Station was the only asset that Conglomerated Mining and Manufacturing owned outright—no bank had been willing to take such a long shot, located so far from Earth, as collateral. Everything else—the African and Martian diamond mines, the Siberian uranium and gold mines, the North American gold and platinum mines, the aluminum mines on Ceres and Earth's moon—was mortgaged to the hilt. But after fifteen years, Jupiter Station was profit-

able. Oh, was it profitable! It was the largest, most automated, and most efficient mining and manufacturing
complex in the solar system. It was a city owned by a corporation that collected fees on all the business transacted in
that city. It had cost one hundred and twenty billion dollars, but in five more years it would have paid for itself and
paid off all of the Company's debt. The value of Conglomerated stock had doubled in the last year. Jupiter Station
was *the* commercial success story, and Edwin Warshovsky
was happy to take the credit for it. He would be the Company's next president. He would be the most powerful industrial magnate in the solar system.

And he owed it all to Arnold Lang's original vision.

Warshovsky rose from his chair and turned to face the
window in the back wall of the office. It was a real window,
not one of the computer-generated holograms that substi-
tuted for windows in most of Jupiter Station's offices. It was
made of a transparent ceramic that was a hundred times
stronger than steel and almost a thousand times more expensive. It would cross polarize automatically when it
pointed at the sun, and was specially treated to cut down
the radiation that abounded near Jupiter. Through his
window Warshovsky could see the *Planet Queen* less than a
kilometer away, rotating to provide its passengers with
gravity. Beyond the *Planet Queen* Warshovsky could see
other artificial structures—smelters and factories where ore
was refined and goods manufactured. Warshovsky could
take credit for all of them.

The intercom chimed softly.

"Yes?"

"Ms. Chadwick is here, sir," his office manager announced.

"Send her in."

Wendy Chadwick was the director of Jupiter Station's Legal Department. She was of medium height and build, and had the prettiest red hair that Ed Warshovsky had ever seen. Unfortunately, she had succumbed to the latest fashions, and wore the shiny tights and short skirt that Warshovsky thought belonged in a circus. Ms. Chadwick had added a matching coat with square shoulders that was intended to make her look strong. At least she hadn't spoiled that beautiful red hair by tinting it to match her outfit, the way so many women did. Warshovsky had a far more conservative taste in clothes. His suit was a dull brown and sloped naturally at the shoulders. He set a good example for his staff, but it was obvious that the example was not being followed.

Warshovsky skipped the preliminaries. "Well?" he asked as he slipped into his chair.

"They have a case," Wendy replied as she took a seat across the desk from her boss. "Asterbrook filled out a form nine, giving us authority to dispose of his body if he died here, as usual. Also as usual, Egleiter sent a message to his parents after Asterbrook's death, asking if they wanted the body shipped back at their expense. They usually don't go for that."

Warshovsky nodded. "I know."

"But the Asterbrooks replied that we should hold the body *at their expense* until they came here to take it back. That's the important legal point: we benefited by their action, since we were relieved of the burial cost. They in turn incurred costs by coming here *in response to our offer*. The result is a legally enforceable contract. And with that note in Egleiter's handwriting on that packing case down in Human Resources, they have proof that we got their acceptance of our offer."

The general manager considered the information silently. "I suspected as much. How much are we liable for?"

"Their round trip fares, for a start. Any loss of income incurred during their trip. Then there's the mental anguish they suffered when they discovered that their trip had been for nothing—that can be a very big box of cockroaches."

Warshovsky didn't need a lawyer to tell him that. He could imagine a jury listening to the story of two grieving parents, traveling a billion kilometers to collect the body of their son, only to learn that their instructions had been disregarded and the body had been destroyed. The bad publicity that would result from fighting the case in court would be incalculably costly. "Offer them a fair settlement. A fair settlement," Warshovsky stressed. "Don't worry about the accountants. Imagine they are your parents, and make the offer accordingly."

Wendy nodded. "Okay. When do you need it?"

"They're leaving on the *Planet Queen* in two days."

"That means tomorrow morning at the latest," Chadwick replied. "Can do."

"Don't run off," Warshovsky said. "You'll meet them in a few minutes; Clarisse is bringing them up here now."

Warshovsky leaned back in his chair. Ms. Chadwick could be trusted to do as she had promised. She was young—early thirties—and lacked the experience expected of the Station's legal director. Ed had made her acting director when her boss, the previous director of the Legal Department, had accepted a partnership in a prestigious New York law firm. Chadwick's appointment was to last only until a qualified replacement could be sent from Earth. But Wendy had impressed Warshovsky by reorganizing and revitalizing the Legal Department. She had seemed to care about what Warshovsky had accomplished in Jupiter Station, and that counted for much more than years of legal experience. So Chadwick had been promoted permanently, a move that Warshovsky had never regretted.

"This foul-up spoils Egleiter's excellent record," Warshovsky said.

"At least now we know why he took that job on Ceres," Chadwick replied. Jupiter Station was the Company's crown jewel; a transfer to any other site that did not include a promotion was effectively a demotion. "As soon as he heard Asterbrook had been buried, he realized he'd goofed cosmically. He probably would have taken the Human Resources Director's job in Hell if it had been open."

Warshovsky shook his head. "And deleted all the records while leaving that box of belongings with his handwritten note in the Human Resources Department? No, there's more to it than that. Besides, Ceres needs serious help— their human resources department is so snafued that people who never worked for the Company are collecting retirement pensions from them. It's number one on the Company's list of trouble spots. If he gets it straightened out, he has a priority orbit to corporate staff." Warshovsky paused. "At least, he would have, except for this blunder."

The intercom chimed again. "Ms. Jackson, Mr. Zoldas, and the Asterbrooks are here, sir."

"Send them in."

Warshovsky rose to greet the new arrivals. He liked the Asterbrooks immediately: quiet, sensible clothes and a look of solemn dignity. Mr. Asterbrook was carrying the cardboard packing case containing his son's personal belongings.

Since Donald Asterbrook's hands were occupied, Warshovsky extended his hand to Mrs. Asterbrook. "I'm Ed Warshovsky, general manager of Jupiter Station. I'm sorry to have to meet you under these circumstances." The Aster-brooks didn't reply, so Warshovsky nodded at Chadwick and said, "This is Ms. Wendy Chadwick, the head of our legal department. You can put that box down on the corner of the desk. Take a seat."

But Asterbrook didn't put down the box and ignored the offer of a chair. "Where are our son's journals?" he demanded.

Warshovsky looked confused. "Huh? What journals?"

"Our son has kept a daily journal since he was a Cub Scout," Donald explained. "There are none in this box."

The top of the packing case was not sealed; the Aster-brooks had examined the contents. Warshovsky glanced at Jackson and Zoldas, but they were as surprised as he was.

"I really don't know anything about the journals," Warshovsky said. "Are you certain he continued the prac-tice after moving here?"

"He mentioned in his e-mails that he had written certain things in his journal," Mrs. Asterbrook said. She had a pleasant voice, even under the circumstances.

Warshovsky shrugged. "Maybe there's more than one case of personal belongings," he suggested, glancing at Jackson and Zoldas.

Fred saw an opportunity to redeem himself in the eyes of his supervisors. "I'll check," he offered, and dashed from the room before anyone could stop him.

"His clothes aren't in here, either," Donald said.

"His clothes were recycled, as per instructions on his form nine," Ms. Jackson said. She knew Zoldas wouldn't find another packing case. Jackson had seen the form nine: everything listed thereon—including, she remembered, books and handwritten documents—would have fit in the packing case now resting on Ed Warshovsky's desk.

"Where are the journals?" Donald Asterbrook repeated.

Philip Asterbrook had been an L3, Warshovsky recalled from the files, and L3's couldn't afford to live alone. He had roomed with Jonny Mondragon, the other man killed in the accident. "What happened to Mondragon's personal belongings?" Warshovsky asked.

Jackson shrugged. "Sent home, probably."

"Some of Philip's belongings might have been mixed with his," Warshovsky suggested. "Track down Mondragon's things and find out."

"They're probably still in space," Jackson pointed out.

"Then contact the ship and have them check," Warshovsky ordered. "I want an answer and I want it today."

Clarisse took a deep breath. "Right, chief." She left the room without much hope. The people who took care of the belongings of deceased Company employees were too careful about things like that.

Warshovsky turned to the Asterbrooks. "We'll know by tomorrow morning where your son's journals are." He could understand why they wanted them. Their son's last thoughts, his dreams, his hopes for the future, were probably written in them.

"I hope so," Donald replied.

"Now, we would like to offer you a settlement."

Asterbrook looked askance. "A settlement?"

"You have incurred costs and personal anguish due to our mistake," Warshovsky explained.

"We are legally liable for those costs," Chadwick added.

The Asterbrooks looked at each other, then at Warshovsky. "I know what you take me for," Donald said, "but I'm not as stupid as you think. You have no record of our message to Mr. Egleiter, but our son's belongings—except for his journals—are kept for us right in your Human Resources office. How could you manage to keep them, but not our son's remains? And Egleiter has been transferred— to a less important facility. Why? Because he failed to hold our son's body for us? Or because he knew too much? Now you're offering us money. A settlement, you say. Or to make us happy so that we'll go home and cause no trouble? What are you hiding, Mr. Warshovsky? What did our son write in his journals that was so damaging that you had to destroy them? Why did you have to destroy our son's body? What are you trying to cover up?"

"We're not trying to cover up anything, Mr. Asterbrook," Edwin said soothingly. The Asterbrooks were more distraught than they looked. "We have made a mistake. An embarrassing mistake. That happens sometimes. This company is run by human beings who occasionally make mistakes. When we make mistakes for which we are liable we are required by law to compensate the injured parties. That's what we're trying to do."

Asterbrook did not believe him. "Nice words, Mr. Warshovsky, but lies. You are hiding something. We don't want your money. We want our son's body. If we can't have it, we want to know what happened to him. What really happened. What he wrote about in his journals. What you are trying to hide."

Asterbrook turned to his wife. "Let's go." They headed for the door.

"Mr. Asterbrook!" Warshovsky pleaded, but the door closed behind them.

Warshovsky and Chadwick looked at each other. Wendy said, "That is an unexpected complication."

Warshovsky sighed. "They're distraught. This has been a trying day. They will have calmed down by tomorrow," he said confidently. "In the meantime, get to work on that settlement."

"Okay, chief. Will you be doing anything concerning this case about which the Legal Department should be aware?"

"I'll contact Egleiter," Warshovsky replied. "He hasn't reached Ceres yet; it's on the other side of the sun. He'll deny everything, of course. He'll claim he arranged to store the body. He'll claim somebody else fouled up, somebody else deleted the computer records. He'll claim he knows nothing of this."

"That's easy for someone a couple of billion klicks away to say," Chadwick said.

"Oh, we'll straighten it out. We'll do what's right for the Asterbrooks. If this makes the press, we'll come out smelling like fresh air when the public sees what we're doing to make amends." Warshovsky waved his finger at the lawyer. "Always do what's right, if for no other reason than it's good business."

Chapter 2

Donald Asterbrook was burdened by the packing case containing his son's belongings, so he let his wife lead the way with the locator. Helene proceeded along what was called a street but which looked like a broad balcony. It fronted a row of apartments on the Asterbrooks' left; on their right were a railing and a precipitous drop to a real street one story below.

"Are you sure you know where you're going?" Donald asked.

"No," Helene answered. "I'm just going where this little forty-dollar box tells me to go."

"This doesn't look like a business district."

Helene silently agreed with her husband. Suddenly the arrow on the locator turned and pointed to the apartment door they were passing. Helene stopped abruptly and her husband almost bumped into her.

"What's wrong?" he asked.

"We're here, I think."

Donald rested the packing case on the top of the railing, just above a row of potted plants. The light was dimmer than it had been; it was almost nineteen o'clock on Jupiter Station and the computer-controlled lamps were simulating evening. The number on the door glowed brightly with its own light. "It's the right address," he admitted. "Go ahead: try the bell."

Helene pressed the button next to the door and a chime sounded softly from the interior of the apartment. The

Asterbrooks heard nothing else.

"Maybe he's not in," Helene suggested.

The door slid sideways into the frame and the Aster-brooks were bathed in light. They squinted as they tried to make out the human silhouette in the doorway.

"Can I help you?" the silhouette said.

"Mr. Flynn, the private investigator?"

The man's demeanor brightened. "Michael Flynn, at your service. Step inside, please."

Flynn stood aside and let the Asterbrooks into his apartment. The floor was carpeted. To the right of the doorway a flight of stairs led to a second level. Flynn pointed past the stairs to the living room, where a couch and cushioned chair crowded around a desk. Bookshelves lined the walls. The living room was barely large enough for the furniture. The adjoining kitchen was even smaller.

In the glare from the lamps around the desk, the Aster-brooks got their first good look at their host. Flynn was wearing a T-shirt with casual slacks and shoes. He was handsome enough to be a movie star, of average height but lean and well muscled, and with the dark hair that Helene always found so attractive. Philip had had dark hair.

"I'm Donald Asterbrook," Mr. Asterbrook said, "and this is my wife, Helene. We apologize for bothering you at home."

"It's my office, too," Flynn answered. "Put that box down and make yourself comfortable. Drinks?"

Donald felt his wife's eyes on him. She hadn't been in favor of the idea. The last thing they needed to do was to waste their money on a drunken investigator. "No, thank you," he said politely.

Flynn could recognize newcomers to Jupiter Station when he saw them. This pair had to be very new. They probably had come that day on the *Planet Queen*. It hadn't taken them long to get into enough trouble to require a professional investigator's assistance. "Well, sit down," he said. "Tell me: what do you think of Jupiter Station?"

Flynn took his seat behind the desk as the Asterbrooks sat on the couch. Donald and Helene looked at each other.

"It's not what I expected, what we expected," Helene said. "Despite our son's e-mails. It's . . . bigger. The trees, the plants—sometimes you catch yourself thinking you're outside."

"That's one reason why they're here," Flynn replied. "They also help regenerate the air—convert carbon dioxide back into oxygen."

Helene continued, "Then there are the shops, the churches, the gymnasiums . . . it's like a city on Earth."

Flynn nodded. "We have everything here: churches, schools, taverns, hospitals, doctors, lawyers, accountants, dentists, rich people, poor people, working people, prostitutes. Just like any city on Earth," he agreed.

Donald Asterbrook said, "Ah, what do you charge for a consultation?"

Flynn crossed his arms. "Consultations are free. If I'm working, I get twelve hundred a day, plus reasonable expenses."

The Asterbrooks didn't look at each other but Flynn could tell they were thinking the same thoughts.

Donald cocked his head. "What constitutes 'reasonable expenses'?"

"Cab fare, when necessary," Flynn answered. "Normally I walk, but sometimes I have to move fast. I buy my own meals, unless I have to take people to dinner to pump them for info. Bribes are always on expenses. The cost of sending messages to other planets goes on expenses. Things like that."

Donald nodded. It sounded reasonable. "You might be able to help us. Our son worked for Conglomerated. For one month he worked for them. Then he was killed in an accident—"

Flynn raised his head. "Ah! *That* Asterbrook!"

"When we were notified," Donald continued, "we decided to come out here ourselves, to wrap up Philip's affairs. He didn't have any really close friends here, none that could be expected to do that." He meant that there were none that the Asterbrooks would trust to do that. "And Philip had wanted us to visit him here. This was going to be our only chance to come out. So we informed the Company—a man named Egleiter—that we were coming. Asked him to hold Philip's body and personal belongings for us. But when we got here this morning, we were told that Philip had been 'buried.' The Company had taken care of his affairs. Egleiter had transferred to Ceres. They had never received our communication." Donald scowled and pointed to the box of Philip's belongings that was resting on Flynn's desk. "A lie! Philip's belongings were in a closet in the Human Resources office with this—" he fished Egleiter's handwritten note from his pocket and showed it to Flynn "—taped to it!" Asterbrook shook his head. "Just because I'm a farmer doesn't mean I'm stupid, Mr. Flynn. I know when I'm being given the runaround. They saved all his books, *except* for his journals! What did Philip write in them that the Company wanted to keep secret, eh? No, they're covering up something. And when we didn't give up and go home quietly, they offered us a 'settlement.' Hah! They're trying to buy us off, and we don't want it. We want to know what happened to our son."

Flynn remembered the news accounts of the accident that had killed Philip Asterbrook. It had been thoroughly investigated by government—not Company—officials. He didn't see how he could help.

"We went to your police—marshals, they're called," Asterbrook continued.

The police were called marshals because they were just that: United States marshals. They had provided law enforcement on Jupiter Station for four years, ever since the Congress of the United States had made Jupiter Station American territory, leaving Company security personnel to police those parts of the Station where only Company activities took place (which was most of the Station).

"They were as useful as teats on a bull. Claimed there was nothing left to investigate, and gave us this—" Donald opened the packing case and removed a file folder "—as proof." He handed the folder to Flynn.

The folder contained the report of the marshals' investigation into the deaths of Philip Asterbrook and Jonathon Mondragon. Flynn thumbed through it quickly. "Statements from witnesses, the reports of the forensic experts . . . medical examiner's report . . ." The marshals had found nothing suspicious. "I don't see anything I could use as a basis for an investigation," Flynn said. Then he did a double take, and looked closely at the ME's report. "Of course, some people don't like to talk to cops. I might be able to learn something they didn't."

"Then, you'll take the case?"

"Tell you what I'll do," Flynn said as he slapped the file closed. "I'll ask around, see if there are any rumors. If I find nothing, there's no charge. If I do, my usual rates apply. Deal?"

Asterbrook nodded. "Deal."

Flynn flourished the folder containing the police report. "Mind if I keep this for awhile?"

"Please do. It does us no good. How long will your investigation take?"

"I'll know by tomorrow if the investigation is worth pursuing," Flynn said. "You're staying at the hotel?"

"We're on the *Planet Queen,* cabin one twenty three," Donald answered. "She's leaving day after tomorrow."

"I'll call you there no later than tomorrow afternoon."

The three stood up. Donald and Flynn shook hands. "Thank you, Mr. Flynn."

"Don't thank me now. I haven't done anything yet."

Flynn showed his guests to the door and watched them walk down the balcony until they disappeared down the staircase to the street. Flynn had met strange people in the course of his business, but the Asterbrooks might well have been the strangest—coming all the way from Earth to take care of their son's affairs and take the body home! He shook his head, then retreated into his apartment. He dashed upstairs, donned a clean shirt and a sport coat, picked up his computer and the folder containing the marshals' report, slipped his telephone into his pocket, and darted out the door. He heard the latch lock behind him.

The Marshals' Office was on Government Plaza, at the opposite end of the Station from the Main Plaza and the Company offices. Flynn took the moving sidewalk, reading the marshals' report on the deaths of Asterbrook and Mondragon as he went. The pair had been L3's—unskilled laborers, the Company's lowest grade. They had worked for Conglomerated Mining and Manufacturing for only one month when they had been killed on the job. Their foreman had left them cleaning metal cuttings from around a massive metal frame in a warehouse. Asterbrook and Mondragon had apparently violated their instructions and had tried to turn the frame over. The cable they had used to lift the frame had broken and they had been crushed underneath. It had happened so quickly that they had not had time to cry out; the warehouse security camera programmed to respond to cries for help, screams, et cetera, had been pointing in the wrong direction and had not swiveled toward the accident scene. It appeared to be a simple industrial accident, with no evidence of foul play, but Flynn could tell from the report that the marshals hadn't looked for any.

The time was nearly twenty o'clock when Flynn reached the Marshals' Office. There were few people in Government Plaza at that time of the evening and the marshals had no customers. Sid Feldstein had the desk.

"Michael Flynn, as I live and breathe!" Feldstein exclaimed as Flynn walked through the door. "I haven't seen you in a Jovian year!"

It hadn't been that long but Feldstein liked to exaggerate. He was shorter than Flynn, but had broader shoulders and had shaved his head. He was wearing his blue marshal's uniform, complete with laser pistol.

"I thought that if I was careful, I'd never have to set eyes on your ugly face again," Flynn said, "but nobody told me you were working nights."

"Hey," Feldstein replied, "I *run* the evening shift now. All this," he gestured with his hands, "is under my direction."

"I wish you hadn't told me that, Sid. Now I won't be able to get to sleep until the graveyard shift comes on duty."

"Very funny, Michael. Very funny. Did you drop in on business or just to socialize?" He looked over his visitor carefully, trying to spot the whiskey flask that Flynn had been known to carry.

41

Flynn dropped the folder containing the marshal's report on the counter. "Recognize this?"

Feldstein glanced at it and made a face. "Yeah. I gave it to a couple of newcomers right after I came on duty. The Asterbrooks. They wanted to know how their son had died. Seemed to think the Company was covering up the facts. They didn't have a computer so I made that hardcopy for 'em—reports on closed accident cases are not confidential. They wanted us to reopen the investigation. I tried to convince them that there was nothing more to investigate. We had found nothing suspicious. OSHA's investigation proved that the accident occurred exactly like we thought it had, and they had three engineers on it for almost a month." Feldstein eyed the man across the counter. "Since they went to you, I guess I wasn't too convincing."

"Well, I tried to convince them, too. But then I noticed that the ME on the case was Vasquez." Flynn opened the folder and showed Feldstein the doctor's report. "Isn't he the one who O.D.'d?"

Feldstein backed away from the counter. "Whoa, Michael! Not so fast! He didn't O.D. He was using polymethyl two four. You can't overdose on that stuff."

Polymethyl two four dibenzolacetate was the short name for a chemical compound with a complete name that occupied two long lines of fine print. It directly stimulated the pleasure centers of the brain. Users of the drug described its effect as being like a two-hour orgasm. It was *very* addicting psychologically. Although chemically complex, it metabolized completely without toxic byproducts and left no residue to turn up in drug tests, so its use was hard to detect. It was unstable at body temperature, so large doses broke down before being absorbed, thus an overdose could not occur. For most people in good health, it produced no long-term ill effects aside from psychological dependence. However, eighteen percent of the users of polymethyl two four suffered weakened arteries that eventually collapsed when the users were high on the drug—the fate that had befallen Dr. Vasquez. Having a medical examiner die from the use of an illegal drug was embarrassing enough, but when the ME also worked in the drug testing department of one of Jupiter Station's hospitals, specializing in the detection of users of polymethyl two four, the news people had had a field day.

"Okay, okay," Flynn conceded. "He didn't O.D. But he died from using an illegal drug. And he must have been on the stuff for quite awhile to die from its effects."

"At least two years. It takes that long for the arteries to degrade."

"So he was using the stuff when he autopsied Asterbrook and Mondragon," Flynn said.

"He was using it before he moved here," Feldstein replied. "But he wasn't actually high during the autopsy. People on polymeth don't do anything but lie back and orbit. Believe me, I've seen it. So he didn't botch the autopsy."

"Accidentally, no."

Feldstein stared at the investigator. "What are you driving at, Michael?"

"I understand that polymethyl two four is extremely difficult to synthesize."

"Oh, very."

"And that there are no labs capable of making it here on the Station."

"None that we know of," Feldstein agreed.

"Vasquez left behind his connection when he came here. An addict wouldn't have done that unless he had known he could get polymeth at Jupiter. Where was he getting it?"

Feldstein shrugged. "If I knew that, I'd get promoted and be in charge of the day shift."

"If it's not made here, it has to be imported," Flynn continued. "Most of the ships that come here are Company ships."

"So?"

"So, what if the Company is importing the stuff? What if they were supplying Vasquez and the other polymethyl two four users? What if Asterbrook and Mondragon found out and had to be eliminated? The Company would want to make it look like an accident. Vasquez would want to protect his supply."

Feldstein shook his head. "You're way off base. Sure, the drug's expensive and pushers make a lot of money, but until Vasquez went belly up we didn't know that there were *any* users on the Station. We still don't know of any others."

"You wouldn't mind giving me a copy of the official report on Vasquez's death, would you?"

Feldstein started to reply, stopped, and then said, " 'Fraid I can't do that, Michael."

Flynn squinted. "Why not? Drug overdoses are considered accidents, aren't they?" Then Flynn caught himself and added, "Unless the investigation is still in progress! The doctor croaked two months ago, and you guys haven't closed the case yet! Are you treating the doc's death as a homicide?"

Feldstein wet his lips. "I'm not free to comment on an ongoing investigation. You know that."

"The cops think the doc who autopsied the accident victims was croaked," Flynn said to no one. "Of course, the cops aren't smart enough to see the connection."

44

Feldstein glared at Flynn. "Are you trying to wear out your welcome around here, old friend?"

"Oh, never, Sid. Never. Besides, I was just leaving. But before I go, I see that the appendices are missing from this file that you gave the Asterbrooks."

"You know we never release the appendices. They contain photos of the victims and the autopsy. Stuff the next of kin wouldn't want made public."

"I'm working for the next of kin. They want me to see them."

Feldstein hesitated. He had a feeling in the pit of his stomach that somehow, some way, he was going to get into trouble over this. "Okay, but don't go showing them to anybody. Especially not to the press!"

Flynn nodded. "Sid, I'm a *private* investigator."

Feldstein made hard copies of the photos for Flynn. The investigator looked at them and winced. The bodies had been crushed into irregular, blood-sodden forms, outlined on the steel deck by trickles of blood. He could understand why the marshal hadn't given them to the parents of one of the victims.

"That frame weighed two hundred tons," Feldstein explained. "They were squashed like bugs. Fortunately, one hand on each body remained intact enough for fingerprints, or we would have had to wait for the DNA sequencing to confirm the ID's."

"This Deputy Marshal Kytel who ran the investigation," Flynn said, pointing to the cover page of the report, "is he still working nights, or might I find him at home?"

Feldstein shook his head. "I doubt he's working nights. Not in his new job."

Flynn raised an eyebrow. "New job?"

"Yeah, he got a Company job about two months ago.

45

Just before Vasquez went terminal. Director of security at a Company diamond mine in Africa, for three times what he was making as a marshal." Feldstein sounded envious.

"What the hell does a deputy marshal know about security at a diamond mine?"

"Beats me." Feldstein shrugged. "But he'd been applying for Company jobs since the day he arrived here. He finally got one. Of course, he always thought that if the Company did hire him, it would be for a position here on the Station. He didn't mind going back to Earth, though."

Flynn nodded. "Thanks, Sid. After I've cracked the case, I'll be sure to mention your assistance to the press."

"Well, ah, thanks, Michael, but I won't be holding my breath waiting."

Flynn left the Marshals' Office and stepped into the reduced lighting that passed for evening on Jupiter Station. Richard Kytel had become the investigating officer of the incident by virtue of being the cop who responded to the report of the accident. Flynn had planned to start his investigation by interviewing Kytel, but since the former marshal was out of reach, Flynn decided to talk to Roger Ajanian, the Company foreman who had been in charge of Asterbrook and Mondragon and had discovered the bodies.

Flynn took his telephone from his pocket and asked for Ajanian's number as listed in the marshals' report.

"That number is no longer in service, sir," the switching computer responded.

That brought Flynn up short in the middle of Government Plaza. "Then connect me with Roger Ajanian," he directed.

"There is no listing for Roger Ajanian, sir," the computer answered.

Flynn was starting to get irritated. "How about Mrs. Ajanian?"

"There are no listings for anyone named Ajanian, sir."

Flynn snorted and put his telephone back in his pocket. Ajanian must have obtained an unlisted number. No matter—his address was in the police report.

Ajanian's apartment was in a block occupied mostly by Company employees. The corridor leading to the apartment opened onto a playground where children were roller-skating. Flynn preferred ice skating himself, but there were no ice rinks on the Station.

Flynn rang the bell and the door was answered by a short, attractive black woman wearing a lounging shirt and no shoes. "Can I help you?" she asked with a puzzled expression on her face.

"I'm looking for Roger Ajanian," Flynn replied.

The woman shook her head. "No one by that name here."

Flynn double-checked the number on the door. It matched the number in the marshals' report. "How long have you lived here?"

"Over a month now. We moved in as soon as the place became vacant. It's two bedrooms, and we needed more space."

"Do you know what happened to the previous tenant?"

The woman shook her head again. "Promoted, probably, so he could afford a bigger place."

Flynn thanked the woman and left. He was annoyed. Although Jupiter Station looked big to newcomers, it wasn't so big that Flynn should have had trouble finding anyone. He paused outside the corridor in the glare of the playground lights. Ajanian had been a foreman. He wouldn't have done his drinking in a swank nightspot on one of the plazas. He would have used a neighborhood bar, or perhaps a place near the docks frequented by Company underlings. Flynn knew such a place.

The bar that Flynn had in mind was called The High Vacuum, and was located in a corridor just off the elevators to the cargo docks. Flynn had been there before, and the bartender knew him.

"Well, look what the street sweepers blew through the door!" the bartender exclaimed. "Michael Flynn, of the famous Boston Flynns!"

"That's *infamous* Boston Flynns, Dinky. *Infamous.*"

Dinky was as small as the woman with whom Flynn had been talking moments before, but he wasn't nearly as good-looking. "The usual?" Dinky asked, with a bottle already in his hand.

Flynn hesitated, then said, "Sure, why not." He produced a ten-dollar bill and slapped it on the bar. The bartender splashed two fingers of Irish whiskey into a glass and pushed it in front of Flynn.

The money disappeared into the cash drawer and Dinky asked, "What brings you down to this end of the Station? Business, or pleasure?"

"Business, Dinky," Flynn answered, and took a sip of whiskey. "I'm looking for a Company man named Roger Ajanian. Does he ever come in here?"

"He used to," Dinky replied, "before he retired."

Flynn almost choked on his whiskey. He set the glass on the bar and flipped open the file containing the police report. "Retired? Are you sure? The guy I'm looking for is only forty-five years old. How could a Company foreman afford to retire at that age?"

The man at the bar to Flynn's right put down a half empty glass of beer and said, "Bonuses, that's how. Bonuses. Roger wasn't just a Company foreman. He was the *best* Company foreman. He ramrodded all the jobs that were behind schedule or over budget, and he got them done on time, within budget, and without anybody getting hurt. For that he got bonuses. Big ones."

"Asterbrook and Mondragon got hurt," Flynn pointed out.

The man with the beer was much bigger than Mike Flynn, and had the arms of a person who lifted weights, either for a living or for exercise. He might have imbibed a lot of beer or he might have had a low tolerance for alcohol, because when he leaned close to Flynn the investigator was nearly overwhelmed by the fumes. "That was their fault!" the man said loudly. "He told those clowns not to try to move that machinery frame by themselves, but the damn fools were trying to impress somebody into promoting 'em. They exceeded their instructions, they didn't know what the hell they were doing, and they got themselves squashed. Ruined Ajanian's perfect safety record. And how do you think he felt after he found 'em? He had to come down here that night and drink until the marshals closed the place."

Flynn edged away from the man. "Seeing it your way, I can feel real sorry for the man."

"You'd better!"

The man turned back to his beer, and Flynn turned back to Dinky. "Do you know to where Ajanian retired?"

"Someplace in Arizona, I think."

Flynn sighed. Ajanian was almost as far out of reach as Dr. Vasquez. He finished his drink, put another ten dollars on the bar and said, "Get this guy here another beer." He pointed to the man on his right, then left the tavern.

Mike was running out of good witnesses. Fortunately, two government paramedics had come with Dr. Vasquez to the accident scene. Their names and addresses were in the marshals' report. Flynn opened his telephone and said, "Connect me with Mitchell Anderson."

"There is no listing for a Mitchell Anderson, sir," the computer replied.

Flynn stopped in his tracks and shouted, "What? Again?" into the phone.

The computer couldn't decipher the tone of Flynn's voice. "There is no listing for a Mitchell Anderson, sir," it repeated.

Flynn consulted the report and said, "How about Derek Yu?"

"There is no listing for a Derek Yu, sir."

Flynn stared at the telephone. It wasn't possible. In just four months it wasn't possible for everybody connected with the case to have died or moved away.

The investigator hurried to Anderson's address, which wasn't far from the docks. The new tenants had lived there for three months. They hadn't known Anderson, but had heard that he had been offered a job in a Company hospital on Mars. The tenants in Yu's apartment didn't know what had happened to their predecessor, but a neighbor revealed that Yu was on his way to taking charge of emergency medical services at the Conglomerated Mining and Manufacturing Company's facilities on Ceres.

Flynn was ready to believe that there was no one left on Jupiter Station who had been at the scene of the accident. However, the next name on the list—a man who had helped lift the machinery frame from the bodies of the victims— was still at the address given in the police report. In less than half an hour Flynn had confirmed that all nine men in the crew that had moved the machinery frame from the victims were still on Jupiter Station.

Michael needed to think. He went back to his own apartment block, to the bar on the corner where he liked to hang out. The bar was small, so patrons who wished to dance had to do so in the street. There were a dozen people dancing in the street that night. Flynn picked his way through them and entered the bar. He signaled to the bartender and said, "Betty, my love, I need a double. And don't let my glass go empty."

Betty had dark red hair. She was almost old enough to be Flynn's mother, but in an age of youth drugs she didn't look it. She smiled at him and said, "Sure thing, Mikey. What's the matter? Barbara not talking to you again?"

"It's the other way around," Flynn replied. "I'm not talking to Barbara." He took his whiskey to an unoccupied table in the corner, pushed aside some empty glasses, and sat down. The Asterbrooks had been right. Those silly newcomers, who had made a wholly unnecessary billion-kilometer journey to collect the body of their son, had stumbled onto a cover-up of galactic proportions. All of the people at the accident scene who were likely to have known or deduced what had happened were gone—dead, or moved far away. Three of them had received coveted and hard-to-get Company jobs. The Company foreman had found himself with enough money to retire thirty years early. The former Human Resources Director, to whom the Asterbrooks' message to hold the body had been sent, had been transferred to Ceres. The doctor who had supervised the removal of the bodies and had performed the autopsies was dead, and two months after his death the police were still investigating it. And the bodies of the victims—the best evidence of what had happened—had burned up in Jupiter's atmosphere. Only the unskilled laborers—people who would have been shocked into an unthinking catatonic state by the grisliness

of the accident—were still on Jupiter Station, within reach
of an investigation. That could not be a coincidence.

Flynn opened the folder and looked at the accident
photos again. The first showed the massive machinery
frame with only two arms—one from each victim—protruding and a few trickles of blood seeping from underneath. The others were close-ups of the victims after the
frame had been lifted from the deck. Flynn couldn't see
anything suspicious in the photos, but there had to be
something fishy about the accident scene or the first witnesses to arrive wouldn't have been hustled away from the
Station. The Company was trying to hide something. And
not just the Jupiter division of the Company, either. The Jupiter division couldn't get jobs for people on Mars or Ceres.
No, the Company's board of directors had to be involved,
which meant that the Company was concealing something
very, very big.

Mike drained his glass and Betty appeared with a refill.
"Why don't you tell Betty what's bothering you, honey,"
she said.

Flynn didn't look up from the file. "Don't bother me tonight, Betty. I'm working."

"Working, like you're getting paid?"

"That's right."

Betty shook her head. "I wish I had a job where I got
paid to drink," she said as she walked away.

"You do," Michael said while continuing to read the file.

According to the medical examiner's report, Asterbrook
and Mondragon had died instantly of massive physical
trauma. All internal organs had been crushed. Their bones
had been crushed. There had been no traces of alcohol or
illegal drugs in their systems. Of course, polymethyl two
four left no traces in those users who did not suffer arterial

degradation, but the Company would scarcely be concealing illegal drug use on the part of the victims—if Asterbrook and Mondragon had been using illegal drugs, the Company would have been exempt from any liability under the Uniform Employer's Liability Act.

If Company negligence had contributed to the accident, Conglomerated Mining and Manufacturing would be liable for much more than the victims' salaries until their nominal retirement ages. That could explain a big bonus and an early retirement for Ajanian, the foreman, but it couldn't account for the suspicious death of Dr. Vasquez. Accidental death was accidental death, and an autopsy couldn't show whether or not the Company had been negligent. But if the deaths had been accidental, why had the cop and the paramedics been bought off with Company jobs? What could the deputy marshal and the paramedics have noticed that the laborers had not? And why hadn't the medical examiner been given a high-paying Company job? Had the Company been paying him under the table? Or had he tried to blackmail the Company for more money, and been paid off in a fashion he had not anticipated?

Flynn decided to stop asking questions for which he had no answers and to catalog what he knew or could deduce. First of all, the government probably wasn't involved in the cover-up, or the lowly deputy marshal wouldn't have been the only one to become a well-paid Company employee. Second, whatever the foreman, the cop, and the medical people had seen, it had to be something that untrained laborers would not see, or at least would not realize its significance if they did see it. Lastly, the Company had moved very fast—the autopsy had been completed within hours of the accident, and by that time the doctor had been persuaded to keep quiet.

Flynn read the marshals' report again. Roger Ajanian's outcry had activated the security camera and alerted Company Security Control to the accident at fifteen forty-five. If the ME's office changed shifts at the same time as the police, that was just fifteen minutes after Dr. Vasquez had gone on call. Could that be a coincidence? Or had Ajanian delayed in reporting the accident until a medical examiner that the Company knew could be bought was in position to handle the case? Now that was an interesting idea! How could the Company know that Dr. Vasquez, who was not their employee, was an illegal drug user?

"Ah, excuse me, but this is our table."

Flynn looked up to find two women standing next to him. One was tall and big-boned, while the other was short and slight. They wore matching outfits in the latest style— very short, shimmering pink dresses over dark-striped shorts, pink tights, pink shoes, pink fingernails, and pink-tinted hair. Flynn blinked. "I think I would have noticed the two of you if you had been sitting here."

The taller of the two took a determined stance. "We were dancing!"

"Then you weren't sitting here."

"This is still our table!"

"Not if you weren't sitting here," said Flynn, smiling.

"Those are our glasses!" the woman persisted.

Flynn looked at the glasses, then back at the women. "The glasses are empty," he pointed out.

"So?"

"So, the table was abandoned." Flynn turned back to the marshals' report.

The women looked at each other. The taller one said, "Let's go, Rhonda. The men in this place are just like the rest of the guys on this station—all jerks."

Drugs had to be involved. Dr. Vasquez had been a drug user, and Dr. Vasquez was the key to the case. He had performed the autopsy. If he had found no evidence of foul play, then there was none to find, and no need of any cover-up. Since something was being covered up, the doctor had known about it, but he had not been sent far away to a nice Company job. The Company had bought him another way. It had to be drugs.

The cops hadn't known about any polymethyl two four users on Jupiter Station until Dr. Vasquez had stopped breathing, but Dr. Vasquez had done most of the testing for polymethyl two four use by people who didn't work for the Company, and the Company tested its own employees. But what if there were no polymeth users on Jupiter Station? What if the Company wasn't importing the drug? *What if Conglomerated Mining and Manufacturing was producing polymethyl two four on the Station and exporting it to the rest of the system?*

Flynn closed the file and stared blankly across the table. Jupiter Station was supposed to be the most profitable manufacturing facility in the solar system due to the latest equipment, the relaxed labor laws, and an inexhaustible supply of cheap raw materials. But what if all that were a cover for its real purpose? Who, besides trusted Company employees, had seen all the Company facilities on the Station? The manufacture of polymethyl two four required a large, complex, expensive laboratory, but no polymethyl two four lab had ever been found by the police anywhere. Yet somebody was making the drug someplace, and Jupiter Station would be the perfect place—remote, inadequately policed by the government, and from it a parade of Company ships went forth to the rest of the solar system.

Mike tapped the tips of his fingers against the folder

holding the police report while he planned his investigation. This wasn't going to be like one of the background checks that constituted most of his work. This was a serious case, probably criminal, the kind of case that fictional detectives handled. The kind of case that could make him famous. He could either solve it himself—and if his suspicions about illegal drugs were correct, all the police forces of the United Nations hadn't been able to do that—or he could prove that the investigation into the deaths of Asterbrook and Mondragon had missed something important, so that the authorities would have to reopen the case. Flynn decided to pursue the second option.

He took his telephone from his pocket. The hour was late, and the Asterbrooks looked like people who went to bed early, but he didn't think they would mind being disturbed with the news he had for them. The liability of Conglomerated Mining and Manufacturing in this case went far beyond the bounds of the Uniform Employers' Liability Act. The Asterbrooks were going to be very rich.

Chapter 3

United States Marshal Ben Wofford, a twenty-three-year veteran of the Marshals Service, was a by-the-book professional with a reputation for incorruptibility. At one time he had been so highly regarded by his superiors that he had been sent to the FBI's Hostage Rescue and Anti-Terrorist courses. But that had been before he had risen high enough in the Service for incorruptibility to be a handicap instead of an asset. Jupiter Station, his home for only one year, had been his second choice as a duty assignment. His first choice had been anyplace else. Everyone in the Marshals Office and many people out of it knew that Wofford's assignment to Jupiter was punishment for his refusal to do unofficial favors for too many important people when he had run the Miami office. Since his arrival on the Station, his top priority had been to earn a transfer back to Earth as soon as possible.

Mike Flynn had seen Wofford on the Station, but until the morning after the Asterbrooks' visit he had never met the man. Their first meeting impressed neither party.

"The odds," Flynn said for the third time. "Calculate the odds. Don't take my word for it; calculate them yourself. With the Company's known hiring and rotation rates, the odds that everybody—"

"Not 'everybody,' " the marshal argued. "Just five of 'em. Five out of fourteen, counting the nine men in the work party that moved the machinery frame off of the bodies."

"The nine men in the work party don't count," Flynn argued. "L2's and L3's, every one of 'em. How many had ever witnessed a fatal industrial accident, eh? Did you check? Not a one, I'll bet. They wouldn't have noticed anything out of the ordinary because the whole affair was out of the ordinary to them. But the other five—"

"Wouldn't have noticed anything because there was nothing to notice," Wofford insisted. "Egleiter wasn't even there. We investigated thoroughly. OSHA had three engineers on it for a month and they didn't find anything, either. It was an accident, pure and simple."

"No," Flynn replied, "it only *looked* like an accident. And that's the source of the problem. Everybody *assumed* it was an accident and tried to find out how the accident occurred. Nobody investigated the possibility that a crime had been committed and the 'accident' had been arranged to cover it up."

Wofford shook his head, disgusted. It was a large head, topped with thick black hair, and had bushy eyebrows on the front of it. "You've been watching too many videos, Flynn. This is the real world, where real accidents—like the one that killed Mondragon and Asterbrook—happen."

"Then why did the Company dispose of Asterbrook's body after his parents asked them to hold it for them?"

Wofford sighed. "Maybe you've never screwed up, Flynn, but the rest of us aren't so lucky. Somebody made a mistake, that's all."

"Another 'accident'?" Flynn said sarcastically.

"Yeah. Another 'accident.' "

"And the ME on the case just coincidentally was a drug user."

"Ah! I'm glad you managed to figure that out for yourself!" Wofford said. His patience was wearing thin. "Coincidences happen, Flynn. So stop taking the Asterbrooks' money under false pretenses and go earn an honest living."

Flynn pointed his finger at the marshal's face. "I was thinking of letting you guys take some of the credit when I broke this case, Deputy Feldstein being so helpful and all, but I've changed my mind. I'll just tell everybody who'll listen—and everybody will be listening—what bumbling bozos you are."

Wofford turned away from Flynn and back to his computer. "I'm a busy man. I'm so damn busy I don't have time to breathe. So get out of my office before I have the watch commander impound you for loitering."

Flynn was glad to go. He hated dealing with idiots.

The Government Plaza had a waterfall, smaller than the one in the Main Plaza where the Company offices were located, which reflected the relative importance of the Company and the Government in the operation of the Station. Michael had seen the waterfall too many times to appreciate it that morning, especially when Marshal Wofford had just put him into a bad mood. Flynn strode angrily across the plaza to the OSHA office. Only one of the engineers who had investigated the Asterbrook accident was in the office and he was no more persuaded by Flynn's arguments than Marshal Wofford had been. The OSHA report on the accident was over two hundred pages long and not available in hardcopy. Flynn had to pay twenty dollars for a copy of the report on a memory disk. He stopped at his apartment to pick up his notebook computer so he could skim the report while walking to the warehouse where the bodies had been found.

The warehouse was on a public corridor on level one, at the end of the Station where the spaceship shuttles docked but out at the rim instead of near the axis. The warehouse was locked. Flynn stared glumly at the hatch.

"Can I help you?"

Flynn turned and found a short man in blue Company coveralls standing behind him. The man had a round, friendly face. His ID badge introduced him as James Bagnini. Flynn gestured at the locked hatch with his thumb. "Is this the place . . . you know, where the accident happened?"

Bagnini frowned. "What it is, is Company property, and off-limits to you."

"I just want to see where it happened."

"There's nothing to see. It's been cleaned up."

"Look," Flynn said, reaching for his identification, "I'm an investigator." He showed Bagnini his license. "The parents of one of the victims asked me to look into the accident, to see if there was anything that the official investigations missed."

"Yeah, so they can sue the hell out of the Company," Bagnini said.

Flynn shook his head. "I don't think so. They're not the type. I think they just want to know for sure how their son died."

"Well, you'll have to look elsewhere," Bagnini replied. "Like I said: this place is off-limits to all except Company personnel."

Flynn put away his identification and took out his wallet. He extracted a hundred-dollar bill and offered it to Bagnini. The man glanced nervously up and down the corridor. His fingers started to reach for the money, then drew back quickly. "I'll get into trouble," he said, shaking his head. Flynn took out another fifty. Bagnini looked around again. The corridor was empty and the red lamp on its security camera was off. "Oh, hell," he said, taking the money. "If it was my kid, I'd want to know for sure, too. Come on."

The lock responded to Bagnini's handprint. Bagnini let Flynn go through the hatch first, then took one last look to make sure they had not been observed before closing the hatch behind him.

The warehouse was entered through an airlock. A light on the bulkhead above the airlock came on automatically when Flynn and Bagnini stepped through the inner hatch. Bagnini flipped a switch, circuit breakers closed with a series of loud clicks, and the entire warehouse was illuminated. The far bulkhead was forty meters away and the overhead was seven meters from the deck. A large cargo hatch was set into the bulkhead to their left—the warehouse had a direct connection to space. The warehouse was empty except for several packing cases in the far corner.

"It was over there by the outside hatch," Bagnini said, leading the way. His footsteps on the metal deck echoed from the bulkheads. "We were assembling the frame for a big metal press. It's in Satellite Juliet right now." He stopped near the large hatch. "It was right here. The machinists had made all the assembly holes and notches in the topside of the frame. We had to turn it over so that they could do the same thing to the bottom side, but first we had to clean up the metal cuttings so they wouldn't get caught under the frame—it massed two hundred tons, and the gravity on this level is ten percent over normal, so those cuttings could have scratched the deck as well as getting imbedded in the frame. All those two guys had to do was sweep up the metal cuttings. We don't know exactly what happened, because the security camera there," he gestured toward the lens above the hatch through which the two men had entered the warehouse, "was pointing toward the center of the warehouse. Apparently, they thought it would be easier to sweep if the frame wasn't in the way. So they moved that overhead crane—" he pointed to a crane suspended from the overhead at the far end of the warehouse, "right here, ran a line to the end of the frame, and tried to tilt it up on its end."

"I thought they were trying to turn it over," Flynn said.

Bagnini shook his head. "If that's what they'd been trying to do, they'd still be walking around—they would have had no reason to get under it. But they lifted it just enough so they could sweep beneath it. The cops found Mondragon's fingerprints on the crane controls over there." He pointed to a control panel on the bulkhead near the large hatch. "Only they didn't know how to work the crane—hell, they were just L3's. Mondragon's thumbprint was on the emergency stop button. The investigators figured that they lifted the frame too high, tried to let it back down, and hit the emergency stop when it started going too fast. The line was a ceramic composite, dozens of times stronger than steel, but it was looped through that small pulley there on the crane, and when that big load was stopped almost instantaneously the line was overstressed due to the small pulley radius. It gave way when both of them were under the frame, sweeping."

Flynn found the section in the report that dealt with the line failure. The safety engineers who had investigated the accident had calculated that the one-centimeter diameter line could not withstand the stress of suddenly stopping the heavy frame when it was sharply bent around the four-centimeter diameter pulley. "They used a one-centimeter line to lift a two-hundred-ton frame?"

Bagnini nodded. "It's a compound pulley," he said, pointing at the crane. "Besides, that ceramic stuff's unreal. Come over here." He led Flynn to several coils of ordinary-looking rope hanging on the wall opposite the large hatch. "Feel this," he said, handing a coil to Flynn. "Much stronger than Kevlar."

Flynn rubbed the line between his fingers. It was stiffer than Kevlar, too. "Provided you don't suddenly stretch it."

"No," Bagnini corrected, "provided you don't suddenly stretch it when it's pinched around a small radius."

Flynn looked up at the crane. He wished he had binoculars. "That pulley looks a lot bigger than four centimeters."

Bagnini squinted up at the crane. "You're looking at the outside," he explained. "It's a lot smaller on the inside, where the line goes through."

Flynn nodded but continued to stare at the pulley. "This report says there was no supervisory interlock on the crane controls."

"It's not required," Bagnini said. "This warehouse isn't open to the public, and Company personnel who work in here are either taught how to use it or warned not to use it. Mondragon and Asterbrook were warned. But it has a supervisory interlock now. The Company added it so they couldn't be held liable for future accidents. I can operate it, because the computer knows I've been trained to use the crane, but not even the power switch will respond to you."

The warehouse hatch opened and two men in orange coveralls with Company security patches on the shoulders came through it. Company security personnel had been known as goons since the days when the Company made all of its money from mining. (Miners were notoriously rowdy, so security people had been selected for their imposing physical appearances and their willingness and ability to break heads when necessary.) The Company still favored security guards of above-average size—the two crossing the warehouse were each half a head taller than Flynn—but at

least on Jupiter Station they were trained to exercise re-
straint. Both men wore pulsed-laser pistols in holsters on
their belts. (Although the marshals had taken over law enforcement on the Station, the Company still wanted its security guards to be armed, and they were legally entitled to
be when on Company property—which was all parts of the
Station not leased to the government or other firms.)

"Can I see your identification?" one of the goons asked
Flynn. His speech was courteous enough, but with his size
advantage he could speak politely while still being menacing.

Flynn indicated Bagnini with a toss of his head. "I'm
with him."

"I didn't ask who you were with," the guard said. "I
asked to see your identification."

Flynn reluctantly showed the guard his investigator's license.

"I thought so," the guard said. "You're not an employee.
You're trespassing."

"I told you I was with him!" Flynn repeated. "I am being
escorted by a Company employee!"

The guards glowered at Bagnini, who was thinking that
he should have held out for much more than a hundred and
fifty dollars before letting Flynn into the warehouse. "He's
not authorized to let non-employees in here," the talkative
guard responded. "You'll have to leave."

"Okay," Flynn said. "Don't get all hot and bothered.
I've seen everything I wanted to see, anyway. Lead on, gentlemen."

They didn't lead. They made Flynn and Bagnini walk in
front of them all the way through the airlock and into the
corridor. The guard who had been silent slammed the hatch
shut needlessly hard and checked to make sure it was

locked. He turned to Flynn and said, "And stay out."

Flynn turned to Bagnini. "Where do you do your drinking?"

"Oh, ah, The Top Spot, level eight—"

"I know the place," Flynn said. "I'll have a word with the bartender. Your next drink's on me."

Flynn was thinking about pulleys and overhead cranes as he followed level one around the circumference to the opposite side of the Station, to an airlock set into the deck. Below level one was the space known as the basement, which contained the pumps that re-circulated the air, the collection systems for refuse, and the large weights that moved under computer control to balance the Station as people and objects moved about. Because the basement formed part of the outermost pressurized layer of the Station, it was kept at a slightly lower pressure than the rest of the structure. An air leak from the Station proper to the basement was detectable as an increase in basement pressure, and a leak from the basement to the outside wouldn't endanger the rest of the Station.

The first person who was not an employee of Conglomerated Mining and Manufacturing to make his home on Jupiter Station had been Joe Aguirre. He had opened a scavenging business in the basement. Conglomerated had reduced its scrap and disposal costs by selling broken, obsolete, and surplus components and equipment to Aguirre. He made a living sorting the junk, reselling what he could, and recycling the rest. In the process he had learned almost as much about what the Company manufactured at Jupiter and how the Station worked as did the Company engineers. Joe's shop was just beneath the airlock to which Mike Flynn had walked.

Flynn had to wait for the airlock to come up to Station

pressure before he could enter it. He waited again while the air was pumped out of the lock until the pressure equaled that in the basement. Then he was able to open the lower hatch and descend the ladder. All around Flynn bits and pieces of broken and discarded equipment were arrayed on shelves or piled in heaps. In the center of everything a well-worn desk stood in a circle of light from an overhead lamp. Behind the desk sat Joe Aguirre.

Joe was shorter than Flynn. His forehead sloped backward sharply from thick, bushy eyebrows. His dark brown hair matched his eyes. A small mustache kept his upper lip warm.

"Well, if it isn't Michael Flynn," Aguirre said with a smile.

"If it isn't, I shaved the wrong face this morning. How have you been, Joe?"

Aguirre shrugged. "Business could be better," he admitted. "It's all those safety and maintenance programs—the Company doesn't break as much stuff as it used to. But look at this." Aguirre motioned Flynn to follow him behind a pile of surplus metal fittings to a cart laden with electronic test equipment. Aguirre swept his hand over the equipment in a grand gesture. "Agilent Two-hundred-thousand series testers. Good to one gigahertz. Only eight years old. The Ceramics Lab just replaced them with the Two-fifty-thousand series. I got these for twenty-four K apiece. They sold for a hundred and sixty K brand new. I can get forty-five K for them on Earth. Maybe fifty."

"Does that mean you can afford to retire?"

"It's not all profit, Mike. I have to pay to ship them back. And I got to make sure these still work."

Flynn nodded. "You have the test specs?"

"Hey, if the Company has 'em, I have 'em."

Flynn smiled. "Do you have the specs on a . . ." He switched on his computer and flipped through the OSHA report on the accident. "Manitowoc Model 1940B overhead crane?"

Aguirre wrinkled his nose. "Let me check." He walked back to his desk and switched on his computer. "What model did you say?"

"Manitowoc 1940B."

"Manitowoc 1940B overhead crane," Aguirre repeated to the computer. He smiled and turned the display so that Flynn could see it. "This what you're looking for?"

It was indeed what Flynn was looking for. He pointed to the full-color picture and asked, "What's the size of that pulley right there?"

Aguirre scrolled the display through the specifications. "That's the output pulley . . . thirty centimeters."

"Not the outside diameter," Flynn said, "the inside diameter. The part that the rope, er, line, actually runs over."

"Thirty centimeters," Aguirre repeated. "That's how pulleys are specified."

"Is there an optional four-centimeter pulley?"

Aguirre frowned. "I doubt it, on a crane of that size—it will lift three hundred tons." He skimmed through the specifications and shook his head. "The manual doesn't show any pulley options."

Flynn was silent, thinking. "Remember Asterbrook and Mondragon?"

"The two guys that got squashed?"

Flynn nodded. "They were trying to lift a two-hundred-ton machinery frame with one of those cranes, and according to the official OSHA accident report, the line broke because it got pinched around the output pulley of the crane. A *four-centimeter* pulley."

"That's about the only way you can break one of those ceramic-fiber lines," Aguirre agreed. "They're nearly indestructible. Everybody wants 'em. The Company charges a hundred and sixty bucks per meter for the bigger ones and they still can't make 'em fast enough to meet the demand. Hell, I can get thirty bucks a meter for short pieces."

"Conglomerated makes those lines?"

Aguirre nodded. "The technology was invented right here in the Ceramics Lab. They're manufactured in Satellite Echo." He got up from his desk and walked to one of his racks. He took a short coil of thin rope from a hook on the side of the rack and handed one end of the rope to Flynn. "Pull on that," he said. Flynn pulled, but even by putting all his weight on it he couldn't feel it stretch. "That's five-*millimeter* line," Aguirre said. "With the compound pulley on that crane, they could have lifted that frame with this. Got a knife on you? Just try to cut it. You can saw on it all day and all you'll manage to do is dull your blade. About the only way you can break one of these things is to wrap it around a small radius and give it a really sharp, really heavy, tug. And they're working on overcoming that."

"Then why put such a small pulley on that crane?" Flynn asked. "If they had left the original thirty-centimeter pulley in place, the line would never have broken."

Aguirre shrugged. "I'd guess the original one broke one day, and they replaced it with whatever was handy."

"What would they have done with the broken one? Sold it to you?"

"Oh, cripes, Mike, how the hell can I remember? That crane's been in warehouse twelve for years. The pulley could have broken a decade ago."

"You keep records of everything, Joe," Flynn pointed out.

"Yeah, but what did I record it under, eh? Scrap metal? Broken pulley? I might have listed the bearings, bearing housing, and pulley proper separately, depending on the condition. *If* I got it in the first place. An automated record search might not find it. I'd have to search manually."

Flynn sighed, pulled his wallet from his pocket, and offered Aguirre a hundred-dollar bill.

Joe looked at the bill and shook his head once. "I dunno . . . the search might take an hour, maybe two."

"I'll throw in a drink at your favorite bar. Two drinks. Three, if you can tell me where they got the four-centimeter pulley."

Aguirre smiled and took the hundred dollars. "I'll check my records."

"Today?"

"Ah . . . I'll try, but I got to get those two-hundred-thousands ready to go out on the *Planet Queen* tomorrow."

"Soon as you can will be good enough. I appreciate it, Joe."

"Glad to help, Mike. Even gladder for the hundred."

Flynn started for the ladder. "Stop in more often," Aguirre called after him. "It gets lonely down here."

Ed Warshovsky was a gentleman of the old school, so he opened the door to the executive meeting room for Wendy Chadwick and let her precede him into the room. The conversation in the room stopped abruptly. A glance told Warshovsky that all of his department heads were present. That was good; Warshovsky hated waiting for others. "Sorry I'm late," he announced as he walked to his chair at the head of the table. He was only three minutes late, but Warshovsky demanded punctuality from his underlings and thought he should set a good example. "We've been trying to negotiate a legal settlement."

Wendy Chadwick strode to the remaining empty chair along the side of the table, sat down, and opened her computer to record the meeting. She was wearing a stylish, shiny outfit that was pale green from the boxy coat, through the skirt, the shorts, the tights, and all the way to the matching shoes. With her red hair, Warshovsky thought she looked like a Christmas tree ornament.

Warshovsky took his seat. Lou Cheng, head of the Research and Development Department, occupied the chair to Warshovsky's immediate left. He was smiling a little half smile and Chadwick knew that meant he was bursting with good news. "We might as well start with your report, Louie," Warshovsky said.

Cheng wordlessly opened the folder on the table in front of him, extracted a thin sheet of sand-colored material, and flipped it onto the table in front of Warshovsky. Ed picked it up. It was very light and very hard. "The latest creation from the Ceramics Lab," Cheng explained. "A hundred times stronger than the best aluminum-lithium alloy of the same weight. That black mark in the center: elephant gun, three meters. Bullet bounced off that sample and went through the overhead and two bulkheads."

"It didn't hurt anybody, I hope!" Clarisse Jackson, the Human Resources director, said.

"It shows great potential as a structural material," Cheng continued. "We think we'll be able to mass-produce it. After another year or two of development, we'll be making ships out of that."

"Not satellite factories?" Warshovsky asked, only half facetiously.

Cheng shook his head. "Not necessary—don't need the lower weight. And I don't think it will be cost competitive with steel during this century."

"If it's anything like your other ceramic marvels, it won't be cost competitive with *gold* any time this century," said Marvin Chalmisiak, the head of Accounting. Laughter circled the table, although Chalmisiak had spoken with a straight face. He thought that the Research and Development Department was a waste of money at best and was trying to put the Company out of business at worst.

"Melting temperature?" Warshovsky asked.

"Over five thousand Celsius," Cheng continued. "Almost six."

"Then you're not going to weld it. How are we going to assemble these ceramic spaceships?"

"We haven't figured that out yet," Cheng admitted as he took back the sample. "The Lab's working on an adhesive."

Warshovsky cocked his head. "You're proposing that we *glue* spaceships together?"

"And if the adhesive doesn't pan out, the people in the laser lab are working on a new high-energy carbon dioxide laser that they say will cut through even this." Cheng brandished the ceramic. "We'll drill holes in it and bolt the ships together with ceramic bolts."

Warshovsky shook his head and sighed. "Here we sit, surrounded by billions of tons of iron, nickel, aluminum, and other useful metals that are literally ours for the taking, and my scientists want to replace the demand for those metals with a manufactured ceramic that everybody on Earth will be making as soon as our patents expire."

"This stuff is eighteen percent iron," Cheng replied. "Eight percent nickel. Eleven percent aluminum. All mined here."

"But if it's a hundred times stronger than steel, we'll

only need one percent as much of those metals," Chalmisiak pointed out.

"Which means the profit comes from value added in manufacturing," Cheng replied. "It's the process, not the raw materials, that becomes the source of wealth. Remember, *anybody* can come out here and mine the rocks. And according to the news, that's exactly what that Japanese-led consortium proposes to do."

"They need at least another twenty-five billion before they can start," said Ron Uhlman, Mining Director.

"They got it," Warshovsky announced. "A bank in Singapore came through for them yesterday. We can expect them out here before the year is out."

"There goes the neighborhood," Lisa Reisbach, Manufacturing Manager, said wryly, producing another sprinkle of laughter.

Chadwick was sitting next to Cheng, so Warshovsky selected her to make the next report. "Ms. Chadwick, would you tell the others what we've been up to?"

Wendy glanced quickly around the table. "It concerns that sad affair in warehouse twelve earlier this year." She paused while the others recalled the event. "The parents of Philip Asterbrook had requested Sam Egleiter to hold his body here until they could come out from planet three to take care of his affairs. They arrived yesterday on the *Planet Queen* and were very upset to learn that their son had been buried."

"It's not like Egleiter to screw up like that," Reisbach said.

"He claims he didn't," Warshovsky interrupted. "I contacted him yesterday, and he says that he had directed that the Asterbrooks' wishes be granted. Some of Philip Asterbrook's belongings, at least, were in a box in Human Resources, being held for the arrival of the *Planet Queen*. But

there are no records that we received any of the Asterbrooks' communications, no records that Egleiter had directed that Philip's body be stored. Egleiter claims that
someone must have inadvertently deleted them after he left
for Ceres."

"He had, what, thirty hours notice of his transfer before
his ship left?" Cheng said. "More likely *he* carelessly deleted
them when cleaning out his files." Cheng had never liked
Egleiter.

"How much are we into them for?" asked Chalmisiak.
He was looking at Warshovsky.

Chadwick answered the question. "They don't want a
settlement. Mr. Warshovsky and I spent all morning trying
to negotiate one with them. You see . . . some of Philip
Asterbrook's belongings are missing. He kept a journal
every day since he was a child, but his journals were not in
the box that was waiting for the Asterbrooks in Human Resources, and they aren't in the box of Mondragon's belongings that are on their way back to Earth. The Asterbrooks
think that we destroyed their son's journals to conceal what
Philip Asterbrook was working on when he was killed. They
are convinced we are covering up how he really died."

"*Are* we covering up something?" Reisbach asked,
looking toward the head of the table.

Warshovsky was rubbing the back of his neck. It always
felt sore when he was under stress. "It really was an accident," he said. "But because those journals have disappeared, the Asterbrooks don't believe it."

"So they have hired an investigator," Chadwick added.

"An investigator!" Chalmisiak squawked. "Investigations
reduce our efficiency." He saw everything from an accountant's point of view. "Our employees will be interviewed on
Company time and asked the same questions they've al-

ready answered for the marshals and OSHA, more Company time will be wasted while our employees talk about the accident again, this business of the missing journals might attract the attention of the news media, and that kind of publicity could prompt the marshals and OSHA to reopen their investigations and cause the value of our stock to drop."

Silvanus Drake, the Security Director, always sat in the chair to Warshovsky's right. He was of average height and build, with brown skin and a face as featureless and unrevealing as a snake's. He rarely spoke at the weekly staff meetings, and startled several people when he said, "Whom did they hire?"

"A Michael Flynn," Chadwick said.

Everyone around the table looked at each other, but none knew the name, except for Drake, who nodded slowly. "Five private investigators on this station, and they pick the only one who can make a nuisance of himself. I'll have my boys warn him off."

"Wait a minute!" Chadwick cautioned. "We don't need that stuff anymore! There's a Federal magistrate on the Station now. I'll get a court order to keep this Flynn character off Company property and to keep him from bothering Company employees in their homes. That will stop him from interfering with Company business. And since we're not hiding anything, he won't be able to generate any bad publicity." Drake did not seem to be convinced, so she added, "If you really want to help, find out what happened to Asterbrook's journals."

Drake looked at his boss. Warshovsky was smiling at Wendy. Chadwick was Warshovsky's favorite executive; the general manager was going to take her advice. Warshovsky would change his mind eventually—Michael Flynn was not going to be stopped by court orders.

"If no one else has anything to say on this matter, I would like to proceed," Warshovsky said. His eyes focused on the far end of the table, where Kevin McSheridan, the Operations Manager, sat beneath a pile of black, curly hair. "Kevin, it took half an hour longer to unload the *Planet Queen* than it took to unload the *Shasta* last week. The *Shasta*'s a much bigger vessel. I'd like to know what took so long."

Flynn wasn't expecting cooperation from Conglomerated Mining and Manufacturing's Public Relations Department, so he wasn't disappointed when he didn't get any. He requested, while wearing his most innocent countenance, a copy of the report on the Company's internal investigation on the fatal accident in warehouse twelve. Instead of shiny metallic tights and hair tinted to match, the woman behind the counter was attired in what Flynn considered to be sensible clothes—slacks of dark red corduroy, a white blouse, and naturally black hair—although Flynn's investigative eye led him to guess that her wardrobe had more to do with heavy thighs than fashion sense. The nametag on the blouse bore the name Alicia. She had blue eyes. Flynn had a weakness for brunettes with blue eyes. Alicia shook her head sadly and explained that internal Company documents were not available to the public, gave Flynn a copy of the statement the Company had issued after the accident (which regretted the loss of life and pledged the Company's cooperation with all public investigations of the tragedy), and wished him a good day. She smiled while she said it, and failed to cure Flynn of his attraction to blue-eyed brunettes.

The Company ran a free shuttle service from Jupiter Station to its satellites and any ships that called at the Station. During shift changes, or when a ship arrived, the shuttles used were large enough to hold three hundred passengers. At other times the Company used smaller vessels that could seat twenty or so, or even work boats that held as few as six. The shuttle that Mike Flynn boarded had twenty seats, but only six were occupied. Flynn had to wait ten minutes before the shuttle departed on its scheduled run. The shuttle lacked viewports (even at Jupiter, three quarters of a billion kilometers from the sun, direct sunlight was harsh stuff). Mike had been hoping for a Company workboat, so that he'd be able to look through the pilot's viewports, but the Company wasn't cooperating with him that day.

The *Planet Queen* was closer to the Station than any of the satellite factories, and so it was the shuttle's first stop. Flynn debarked into the free-fall world at the non-rotating axis of the vessel. He passed through an airlock into the rotating section of the craft and headed for the outermost level of the ship. He drifted until the gravity approached a quarter of Earth standard, when he had to resort to using the ladders. The Asterbrooks were in cabin one twenty-three, on the outermost deck, where the gravity was thirty percent greater than Earth standard but the fares were the lowest.

Donald Asterbrook answered Flynn's knock on the cabin door. "Mr. Flynn!" He seemed surprised. "You have something for us already?"

"Not really," Flynn replied as he stepped past his host and into the cabin. There was scarcely room for two people, let alone three. The cabin was crowded with a double bed covered by a tan spread, a tiny writing desk in the corner, and two chairs held to the deck with magnetic clamps. Helene Asterbrook was sitting on the edge of the bed. "I talked with the US Marshal this morning," Flynn said as he took a seat in one of the chairs. The Asterbrooks looked at each other, concern showing on their faces. "I told him what I told you on the phone last night, but he was not impressed and claimed to be too busy to reopen the investigation. OSHA wouldn't cooperate, either. That's to be expected—bureaucracies hate to admit that they've made mistakes. And the Company won't release their internal report on the accident."

"Mr. Flynn," Donald began.

Flynn stopped him with a raised hand; he wasn't finished with his report. "Oh, the marshals think there's something fishy with the ME's death," he said. "They're still investigating that—I suspect that's why the marshal claims to be so busy. But as far as they're concerned, the death of your son was a simple industrial accident. I'll have to come up with something hard before they'll believe otherwise, and that could take months." He paused. "I suggest you force the issue. The authorities can ignore my arguments. They can ignore you. But they can't ignore public opinion. Take what I've discovered to the media. A cover-up by a corporation as large as Conglomerated Mining and Manufacturing is big news. It will get system-wide coverage. The witnesses that the Company transferred elsewhere will be tracked down and interviewed. The authorities will have to reopen their investigations just to avoid the appearance that they're participating in the cover-up."

The Asterbrooks stared at Flynn. They turned and looked at each other, then turned back to the investigator. "Mr. Flynn," Donald said, "I'm sure that you've figured out . . . A private investigator like yourself must know that the Company might be trying to cover up some sort of illegal activity," he said reluctantly. "We want to know how

Philip really died, but if he was doing something unlawful at the time, we'd prefer that the entire solar system didn't know about it."

Flynn looked askance. "Do you think that your son—"

Asterbrook cut him off with a wave of his hand. "No, we don't. But he might not have known that he was engaged in an unlawful activity. However, if this becomes a big news item, people won't remember that he didn't know that he was breaking the law. They'll only remember that he died doing something illegal. Can't you use the *threat* of more official investigations to get the Company to tell you what happened? We don't want their money and we don't care if they're punished. We just want to know what really happened to Philip."

Flynn took a deep, slow breath. His clients had vetoed his best tactic. "Conglomerated Mining and Manufacturing is hard to threaten. They'll quickly figure out why we haven't gone to the media with what I've learned and they'll just sit tight. I'll have to break the case myself, and that could take months."

"We can't afford to pay you twelve hundred dollars a day indefinitely," Donald said.

"Ah, that might not be true," Flynn said. "The Company has gone to extreme lengths to cover up the true circumstances of your son's death. That means it must have the potential of costing them a huge sum of money. You'll be able to sue them for more cash than the annual budget of a third-world country."

Asterbrook pursed his lips. "We don't want their money! We want to know how Philip died! We want to know why they destroyed his body instead of giving it to us!"

"Oh, you don't *have* to sue them for billions," Flynn said, "but you'll be entitled to recover your costs—your round-trip fares to Jupiter, my fee, lawyers' fees, stuff like that."

Asterbrook looked down at the deck. "I don't like lawyers. Shakespeare had the right idea of what to do with them. The Company lawyer spent most of the morning trying to make us agree to a settlement. All we want from them is the truth."

Flynn tapped the tips of his fingers together. "I can continue to investigate, at twelve hundred a day. I can send you a daily account of my expenses. When my bill reaches your limit, you fire me."

"But if you haven't solved the case by then," Donald said, "our money will have been wasted."

Flynn sighed. "I'm sorry, Mr. Asterbrook, but I can't guarantee results."

"I think we should risk it," Helene said to her husband. "If we don't, we'll never know what happened to Philip."

Donald clenched his teeth. The features on his face became harder and more angular. "You're right, dear. The money's yours, too. If you want to risk it, we'll go ahead."

Helene turned to Flynn. "Continue your investigation, Mr. Flynn. And send us a daily accounting of your expenses as well as a summary of what you've discovered."

Flynn nodded. "Okay, I'll do that." He leaned back in his chair. "Did your son have any special friends on Jupiter Station?"

"Just Jonny Mondragon," Donald Asterbrook said. "They met on the ship that brought them here."

"I think he means girlfriends," Helene said. "Didn't you, Mr. Flynn?"

"Anybody in whom he might have confided," Flynn replied.

"He didn't have a girlfriend," Helene said. "At least, he

never e-mailed us about one."

Flynn was not surprised—the male-female ratio on the Station was almost two to one.

"He wasn't here long enough to get to know any girls," Donald added. "He was only on the Station for three months before he was killed."

Flynn raised his eyebrows. Philip Asterbrook and Jonny Mondragon had managed to get hired by the Company only two months after coming to Jupiter Station. Mike knew people on the Station who had been trying to get hired by the Company for more than two years. That was something else about the case that was suspicious. "Did he have a job here before the Company hired him?"

"Harrington's Restaurant Supply," Donald answered with what sounded like a touch of pride. "The food business—you can take the boy out of the farm but you can't take the farm out of the boy. Not completely, anyway."

Flynn nodded. "Was there anyplace he liked to hang out?"

"Our son didn't 'hang out,' " Helene answered. "He wasn't like that."

"There must have been someplace he went for recreation."

The Asterbrooks looked at each other. "He mentioned a gym in several of his e-mails," Donald said. "Our son played basketball in high school and junior college. He was always looking for a game."

"Did he name the gym?"

The Asterbrooks looked at each other again. "I don't think so," Donald replied. "He did say it was a very fancy establishment."

That sounded like the Gymnasium Club. Flynn stood up. "I'll check that out. He might have made friends there.

Do you have a photo of Philip?"

Helene arose from her seat on the edge of the bed and stepped to the cabinet mounted against the bulkhead. "I think I have one in here." She took her purse from the cabinet, opened it, and extracted a color photograph. She handed it to Flynn.

Michael took the photo and looked at it. Philip Asterbrook had had dark hair and thin, dark eyebrows. He took his computer from the pocket of his coat, scanned the photo into it, and handed the picture back to Helene. He smiled at his clients, and said, "And now, since you're paying for my time, I'll get back to work."

The visit to the Asterbrooks had cost Flynn the opportunity to talk with potential witnesses on their lunch breaks. The work crew that had lifted the machinery frame from the bodies of Mondragon and Asterbrook had been split up: seven of them were working on various satellites, and the two on Jupiter Station itself were laboring on opposite ends of the structure. Flynn needed most of the afternoon to track the two on the Station down. As he had suspected, neither had noticed anything that would make them believe that the deaths were not accidental. They remembered mostly the mangled state of the bodies. One said the appearance of the remains had given him nightmares.

The Gymnasium Club occupied an ideal location on levels six and seven, where the gravity was Earth normal. The basketball and volleyball courts needed two levels to get sufficient overhead clearance. The Olympic-size swimming pool needed two levels because it projected three meters below its surrounding deck. Amid the athletic courts and the pool was a two-level restaurant and bar where Club patrons could relax while watching others exercise. The son of Donald and Helene Asterbrook would not have been a

81

drinking man; Flynn was not surprised when the bartender did not recognize Philip's photo. The club manager, however, remembered Philip very well. He looked at the photo that Flynn showed him and shook his head.

"He had just started that job, too," said the manager, whose name was Delano and who had a physique appropriate for someone who ran an athletic club. He sighed. "And to think that I congratulated him when I heard that he'd gotten in with the Company. I wish they'd recycled his job application."

"Did he come here a lot?"

"Four, sometimes five nights a week," Delano responded. "Weekend afternoons, too. He was one hell of a basketball player—very quick, good moves, terrific outside shooter. I've never seen anybody learn to compensate for the Coriolis force as quickly as he did. He was in big demand for pick-up games."

"Anyone in particular that he played with?"

"He preferred the better players," Delano said. "But the only one I saw him hang around with afterward was . . . Oh, what the hell was her name . . . Maria something . . . Maria . . . Estaban, I think. About a hundred and seventy-three centimeters, at least as quick as Asterbrook, almost as good a shooter inside of six meters. A team with the two of them in the back court was just about unbeatable."

Flynn looked toward the basketball courts. One was in use, but the players didn't seem to be of the caliber that would have interested Asterbrook. "Is she here today?"

Delano looked at the court, then around the restaurant, which was sparsely populated at that time of the afternoon. "I don't see her. Come to think of it," he said thoughtfully, "I haven't seen her in awhile. Six weeks, maybe two months. She doesn't come in much anymore since Asterbrook was killed." Delano hesitated. "They played a lot of ball together. Maybe this place reminds her too much of him."

"Is she a Company employee, do you know?"

"Oh, yeah. Chemist, or lab assistant. Something like that. Works on one of the satellites. Never saw her here before the shuttles arrived after the day shift ended."

Flynn thanked the manager for the information, then ordered a drink at the bar as payment for the favor. Through the glass on the other side of the bar Flynn could see the gym's swimming pool. To the surprise of most newcomers, Jupiter Station had a lot of swimming pools. They provided water to fight fires, which were the biggest safety hazard faced by the Station—fire could consume oxygen much faster than any likely air leak could lose it to space. The pool in the Gymnasium Club was the largest on the Station. At that moment only two men were swimming laps.

Michael flipped open his telephone and asked to be connected to Maria Estaban. The computer reported no such listing, nor could it find a listing for a similar-sounding name. Flynn put his phone away with a blank expression on his face. The Company had transferred Philip Asterbrook's girlfriend someplace, just like everyone else who could have shed light on the accident.

Flynn finished his whiskey. He decided that interviewing the other seven members of the work crew that had moved the machinery frame would be a waste of time. The fact that they were still on the Station proved that they didn't know anything. Flynn needed to see the Company's records, and if the Company wouldn't let him do that officially, then he would have to do it unofficially. He smiled as he opened his telephone. "I need the home address for Missy . . . Adamly."

"Level four, fourteen twenty Fifth Street."

The corridors of the Station filled with people at the end of the day shift. Shuttles disgorged swarms of laborers from the satellite factories. Office workers poured from their cubicles and technicians from their laboratories. Flynn joined the throng and rode a moving sidewalk back toward the center of the Station, then took an escalator down to level four. The lighting was already dimming as artificial evening settled over the Station. Missy's new apartment was in a block that looked just like Flynn's. Mike pressed the bell switch and stood against the wall, out of the range of the security camera at the end of the apartment block.

The door slid open. The interior of the apartment was brightly lit. The woman who had opened the door was shorter than average and had dark hair. She was wearing a tee shirt over bare legs and feet. Because of the back lighting, Flynn couldn't see her eye color, but he knew they were blue. Flynn stepped in front of the door.

"Hi, Missy!" he said cheerfully. "How's married life treating you?"

The woman gasped and tried to slam the door shut, but Flynn had anticipated the move and blocked it with his shoe. The woman leaned on the door with all of her weight, straining to close it. "Dammit, Michael, get the hell out of here!"

"Now Missy, is that any way to treat an old friend?"

Missy glanced over her shoulder. "Mike, please, my husband's home—"

"Good! I'd love to meet him. His name's Jack, isn't it?" Flynn could hear the sound of a shower running inside the apartment. "Jack!" he called.

"Mike, please! You don't understand! He's very jealous!"

Flynn grabbed the door and slid it open, pulling it from Missy's hands. The woman backed into the apartment. Flynn followed. "I just need a small favor from you."

"Oh, like I owe you one!" Missy complained. "You need a favor, go ask Barbara what's-her-name, with the legs that go all the way up to the stratosphere!"

"There is no stratosphere on the Station," Flynn pointed out, "and besides, she can't do this one for me."

The sound of a deep male voice singing in the shower came from the bathroom. "Oh, why did you have to drop by when he was home?" Missy lamented. She pulled down the hem of her tee shirt. "Dammit, I'm not even dressed!"

"Aw, come on, Missy: I've seen you in a lot less than that."

"*Shut up!*" she hissed as she glanced toward the bathroom. "Jack's bigger than you. Much bigger. And he has a terrible temper that he loses whenever . . . whenever other men come near me."

"Sounds like trouble," Flynn said casually. "Why did you marry him?"

"Because he wasn't running around investigating people at all hours instead of being with me, that's why! And because he didn't dump me for someone else just because I'm too short!"

"Missy, you're not short," Flynn said soothingly. "You're petite."

"I'm short!" Missy insisted. "And Barbara's tall and has magnificent legs and you've always been a leg man and don't try to deny it because I've seen you look at other women and you're always looking at their legs!"

"Missy, I haven't even spoken to Barbara in two weeks!"

"Oh, really? Whom did you dump her for?"

"For my peace of mind."

For once Missy had no quick retort. She glanced again at the bathroom. The shower was still running. "Go, Mike. Please. Just because I'm mad at you doesn't mean I want to see Jack beat you till you're bloody."

"Hey, I'm already leaving. I just need you to look up some info for me."

Missy sighed. "Another investigation?"

"Another investigation. I need to see all the Company reports on the accident in warehouse twelve that killed Mondragon and Asterbrook."

Missy's eyebrows rose sharply. "Are you kidding?"

"Also the Human Resources files of Mondragon and Asterbrook. And the maintenance records of the overhead crane in warehouse twelve."

"I don't have access to that stuff!"

"Missy," Flynn said patiently, "you're one of only two systems analysts on this Station. You *run* the computer network. You have access to *everything*."

"But not official access!" Missy protested. "There are *laws* against what you're asking me to do!"

"This is not industrial espionage, Missy," Flynn argued. "You might get fired for giving me the info but you won't go to jail."

"Fired is right! The network has a two-level operating system. The supervisory level will spot my unauthorized access of those files and sound alarm bells all over the Computer Center."

"Missy," Flynn said with a pained expression on his face, "you *told* me that you built yourself a trapdoor when you installed that operating system."

Missy chewed her lower lip, silently cursing her big mouth. The sound of the shower stopped, and she glanced toward the bathroom. That helped her make up her mind.

"Okay." She began pushing Flynn toward the door. "Just go. Go now."

Flynn let himself be pushed. "Dump the info into my computer when you get it. Tomorrow, Missy; I'm in a hurry."

"Okay, tomorrow. I promise. Now leave!"

Flynn stopped at Wing's Chinese Restaurant and picked up one spicy garlic chicken dinner, with egg roll, to go. The chicken would be fresh, not frozen or freeze dried, because poultry was now raised on Satellite Bravo. Beef, pork, bison, and fish were still shipped from Earth and were considerably more expensive than chicken. Flynn had heard that when Satellite Juliet was completed, the factories from Satellite Delta were to be moved into it, and Satellite Delta would also be turned over to food production. Maybe then he could buy steak for less than fifty dollars a pound.

The computer in Flynn's apartment was monitoring the security camera's view of the balcony. It recognized him and unlocked the door as he approached. His dinner was still hot. He put it down on the table and checked the computer for messages. His broker recommended selling his Northern Semiconductor stock—the company's new factory was behind schedule and way over budget, and not even Northern's new optically switched logic transistors could keep the company from red ink that fiscal year. Barbara had called, to Flynn's chagrin. He started to listen to her message, then paused with his finger over the key. Barbara could play him like a harp when she wanted to, and then Flynn would forget, or at least overlook, that she was shallow and selfish and the best reason for celibacy that Flynn had ever encountered. He changed his mind and deleted the message.

Flynn's black cat, Furrball, had crawled out of his favorite sleeping place on the chair under the table and was sniffing at the bag of Chinese food on the tabletop. Flynn scratched the cat's ears as he walked past the table and into the small kitchen. In the refrigerator was a half-full bottle of plum wine, just what Flynn liked with Chinese food. He was pouring a glass when the door chime sounded.

Flynn's computer displayed the output of the security camera, and the image on the monitor caught Flynn's eye. The person ringing the door chime was a woman, someone with bright red hair and a very pretty face, someone he did not know. Flynn sighed. Clients always seemed to come in bunches. He slid open the door.

The woman was dressed in the latest fashion: pastel green tights and blouse in a metallic sheen, with a boxy coat in the same color. Topped with the woman's bright red hair, it gave Flynn the vague impression that he was facing a Christmas tree.

"Can I help you?" he asked.

"Michael Flynn?"

"At your service."

The woman handed him a folded piece of paper. "This is for you." She smiled.

Flynn recognized it as a legal document even before he read it. "What the hell is this?" he said as he unfolded the paper.

"It's a court order enjoining you from trespassing on the property of the Conglomerated Mining and Manufacturing Company and from harassing or otherwise disturbing the employees of said company in their homes." She smiled again. "It's all in the document. If you have any questions, I suggest you talk with your attorney. Have a nice evening, Mr. Flynn." The woman turned and walked away along the balcony. To Flynn, it seemed like she was almost skipping with joy.

Flynn stared at the court order. He could deal with Company goons, but he had not expected a legal injunction. Goons might break his nose, but if he violated a court order, his investigator's license would be at the very least suspended and possibly revoked.

Flynn looked down the balcony but the woman was gone. He wondered who she was. Court orders were usually served by deputy marshals. If they were too busy, private investigators might be hired to do the job—Flynn had served some legal paper himself. Flynn knew all the marshals by sight, and the red-haired woman wasn't one of them. There were only four other investigators on the Station besides Flynn, and Mike knew them personally.

Flynn slid the apartment door closed and walked back to the kitchen. He took the glass of plum wine, poured it into a large tumbler, then filled the tumbler from the bottle. Flynn sat down in front of his computer and accessed the public library. Furrball was pawing open the bag of Chinese food on the table. The Company might have had an employee serve the papers, so Flynn asked the library for any photos of redheaded female Company employees it might have. There was only one, from a Company information brochure that listed the Station executives. Her name was Wendy Chadwick, and she headed the Company's legal department on Jupiter Station.

She was also the woman who had delivered the court order to Flynn's apartment.

Flynn leaned back from the computer display. He took a sip from his glass but he didn't taste the wine. He didn't notice that Furrball was chewing open the container of garlic chicken. The Company's top lawyer had personally served the injunction. Flynn read the document again: she had also been the one who filed the motion for the injunction with the Federal magistrate. The Company was bringing the very best of its legal talent to bear on Michael Flynn.

Michael took the photos of the accident scene from his desk and stared at them. He still saw nothing suspicious, but the first four people to reach the accident scene were no longer on the Station and the doctor who had performed the autopsy was dead from drug abuse. The Company *had* to be covering up something big. They could have been trying to keep secret a new product, another brilliant invention of the R&D Department, but Flynn couldn't think of anything bigger—or more profitable—than illegal drugs.

Chapter 4

According to Flynn's legal advisor (a software package known as Counselor™), the court order obtained by the Company prevented Flynn from entering any Company facility without an invitation from a Company executive for any reason except emergency protection of life, health, or property. To secure an invitation, Flynn made an appointment with Ms. Chadwick the morning after he received the injunction. When he arrived at the Company offices, the security guard stepped out from behind his desk as soon as Flynn walked through the door. The guards in the Company's main lobby rarely showed such energy, so Flynn changed course toward him.

"Mr. Flynn," the guard said, as politely as any goon had ever spoken, "you are in violation of a court order. If you do not leave these premises immediately, I will place you under arrest and hold you for the marshals."

"That will discomfit the director of your legal department," Flynn replied.

The ID badge on the guard's orange coveralls bore the name Paul. Paul suppressed a smirk. "I think not."

"I think yes. She will have to leave her plush executive office and go all the way down to the jail for our nine o'clock meeting."

Paul hesitated. "Do you have an appointment?"

"Of course I have an appointment. Do you think I'm an idiot?"

The guard seemed sorely tempted to answer the question, but instead he indicated the floor beneath Flynn's feet with his finger. "Wait right here."

Flynn waited right there while the guard returned to his desk and consulted his computer. He returned to Flynn with considerably less enthusiasm. "You can take a seat over there," he said, pointing to a row of chairs along the side of the lobby. "Someone will come for you."

Flynn took a seat beneath a row of copies of paintings of nineteenth-century impressionists. Paul's eyes never left him. Flynn did not have long to wait before another security guard in orange coveralls appeared in the lobby. Paul nodded in Flynn's direction, and the new guard walked over to where the private investigator was seated and stood directly in front of him. "Mr. Flynn?" he asked unnecessarily. "Come with me, please."

Flynn stood up, but the guard still towered over him. He was the largest goon that Michael had ever seen and had the build of an Olympic weight lifter. The name on his ID badge was Roger Fong. He made Flynn walk in front of him to the escalator. They rode up two flights, then walked down a carpeted corridor and made a right turn into the Legal Department.

Ms. Chadwick's office manager informed her boss that her nine o'clock appointment had arrived. "You can go right in, Mr. Flynn," the office manager said. She had pale skin but was wearing a metallic yellow outfit and had tinted her hair to match. She looked like a Popsicle.

Fong opened the office door for Flynn. Ms. Chadwick looked up from her desk. "Come in, Mr. Flynn." She looked past him into the outer office. "Where is your attorney?"

Flynn brandished his computer. "Right in here."

Chadwick made a face. "You're *pro se*. You know what

they say about people who represent themselves?"

Flynn nodded. "The attorney has a fool for a client. But between this," he waved the computer again, "and this," he tapped his temple with the forefinger of his left hand, "this foolish client has a brilliant attorney. Besides, this software cost me less than four hundred bucks. That would get me maybe . . . one hour? . . . of an attorney's time."

"Is this going to take more than an hour?"

"I hope not."

Chadwick looked at Fong. "You can go. I'll show him out."

Fong protested, "Mr. Drake said that—"

Chadwick stopped him with a raised hand. "This is my office. Mr. Drake doesn't give the orders in here. I'll show him out."

Fong looked at the investigator with an expression intended to make Flynn behave himself, then nodded and left. Chadwick closed the door behind the guard and walked back to her desk. Her outfit was almost the same metallic yellow as her secretary's, except her blouse was shiny white. At least she hadn't tinted her hair to match. As she sat in her chair Flynn was able to confirm the impression he had received the night before: Wendy Chadwick had terrific legs.

"Be seated, Mr. Flynn."

"Thank you." Flynn took a chair across the desk from his host. He extracted the court order from the pocket of his coat, unfolded it, and spread it on the desk in front of Chadwick. "According to this, I have to appear before the Federal magistrate at fourteen thirty today to show cause why this injunction should not be made permanent."

"Oh, you don't *have* to show up," Chadwick explained. "If you don't, the injunction becomes permanent automatically, and you have to petition the court for a hearing."

"I know, but I thought we could negotiate an arrangement that we both could live with. You don't want me appearing in court."

Chadwick seemed amused. "Why not? You're no friend of mine, Mr. Flynn. I don't care if you make a fool of yourself in public."

Flynn smiled. "Ah! That's the point! This afternoon's hearing will be in public. Members of the press will be present when I testify as to why I think I should be allowed to proceed with my investigation." Flynn began ticking off his arguments on his fingers. "Do you really want the press to hear that Deputy Marshal Kytel, who investigated the accident, was given a plush Company job back on Earth? That Roger Ajanian, the foreman who discovered the bodies, retired to Earth shortly afterward at age forty-five? That the two paramedics who responded to the scene were both given Company jobs and transferred off the Station, one to Mars and the other to Ceres? Or that Sam Egleiter, who corresponded with the Asterbrooks and received their instructions not to bury their son's body, was also transferred to Ceres while all the records of his communications with the Asterbrooks were mysteriously disappearing? Or that Philip Asterbrook's journals have vanished without a trace, although the rest of his belongings were waiting for his parents in a box in the Human Resources Office? Or that Asterbrook's girlfriend was transferred from Jupiter Station after his death? Do you want the solar system to know that the ME who returned a finding of accidental death was shortly thereafter done in by polymethyl two four? And finally," Flynn said, having saved the best for last, "do you want it made public that according to the data in your own publicity brochures, the odds against those transfers, hirings, and retirements are more than eighty thousand to one?"

Ms. Chadwick had to swallow before replying. "Mr. Flynn, you are not an officer of the court, so at the start of the hearing this afternoon you will be sworn in. Your testimony will be under oath—"

"Oh, everything I said is true," Flynn interrupted. "Don't take my word for it." He pointed to the computer on Chadwick's desk. "Check the facts for yourself. Calculate the probability yourself."

"I don't have to," Chadwick said. "I know the facts in the case. I also know that we own the video facilities on Jupiter Station. The members of the press here are all our employees, and will be busy elsewhere this afternoon."

Flynn's forehead wrinkled. "Haven't you heard? SSN now has a correspondent here. I met her at a nightclub on level nine last month. She'll be there this afternoon. The story will be on news broadcasts this evening. And SSN has correspondents all over the system. They'll be able to interview all those people who conveniently disappeared from here. I suppose they've been instructed to say, 'No comment,' but to the average person in the street, that just makes them—and the Company—sound guilty as hell. I'll bet you a hundred bucks that the government reopens the investigation within a month. They might even send some hotshots from Earth to do it right this time."

Wendy was drumming her fingers on her leg, beneath her desk and out of Flynn's sight. She had not anticipated such complications. "You're saying that unless we drop the restraining order, you'll see to it that other people make even more trouble for us than you would?"

"Exactly. I'm a *private* investigator. I'm sure you—er, the Company—would rather have this matter investigated privately than publicly."

"Mr. Flynn, the odds against those facts you cited being coincidental might be very high, but they really are coincidences. There's nothing for you to uncover."

Flynn smiled. "Then why not ask the court to withdraw the restraining order?"

Chadwick pursed her lips. "I only work here, Mr. Flynn. I'll have to ask my supervisor. I'll call you before the court time." Chadwick stood up. "My office manager will escort you to the front door."

The guard in the lobby seemed surprised when Flynn came down the escalator with Chadwick's office manager instead of with Fong. Flynn smiled at the guard and waved. The office manager walked Flynn to the Main Plaza and wished him a good day. Flynn wasn't certain that he was going to have one. He knew he was being stalled while the Company lawyers formulated their next move. He wasn't going to waste time while they decided what that move would be. If the court order made it difficult for Flynn to investigate the Company, then Flynn would investigate Dr. Vasquez.

The marshals hadn't closed their investigation into the death of the medical examiner, and interfering with an ongoing police investigation would get Flynn's license suspended as quickly as would violating a court order. Interference, however, was not clear-cut like the violation of a legal injunction. It gave Flynn some room to maneuver, and Flynn could outmaneuver almost anybody.

Jupiter Station had two hospitals. The larger and older of the two was owned by the Company and run for the benefit of Company employees and their dependents (who still made up seventy percent of the Station's population). The newer and smaller hospital had been started by the Meditech Corporation in the belief that Jupiter Station was going to get a lot bigger. Dr. Emilio Vasquez had been hired by Meditech to run their hospital's trauma unit and, since Vasquez was an expert on polymethyl two four, to provide polymeth testing for non-Company employers.

The Meditech facility was known officially as the Jupiter Area Technical Hospital. It was on level twelve, where the gravity was only ninety-two percent of Earth normal (injured people recovered more quickly in lower gravity). The entrance to the trauma unit was on Sixteenth Street, a major thoroughfare with a moving sidewalk and lanes for electric vehicles. The trauma unit itself was brightly lit and decorated in hospital white and stainless steel. Just inside the door a woman sat behind a counter, reading *Medical Emergency News* in hardcopy. She looked up as Flynn came through the door.

"Can I help you?" she asked, putting down the magazine and looking hopefully at Flynn for signs of trauma.

Jupiter Station was a safe place to live; the trauma center in the Technical Hospital had little business. Flynn guessed that the woman was bored. "I hope so," Flynn said as he stepped to the counter. The woman's sensible white scrubs bore a black tag with white letters that spelled *Carla McDonald, RN*. Carla had dark brown hair, brown eyes, and a mouth that was too wide for the rest of her face. Flynn took his investigator's license from his jacket pocket and showed it to her. "My name is Flynn. Mike Flynn. I'm a private investigator."

Nurse McDonald's expression changed from hopeful to alarmed. "Jimmy's been seeing my roommate, not me!" she said. "Don't believe those rumors!"

Flynn suppressed a smile. "That's not why I'm here. Is this the place where Dr. Vasquez worked?"

The nurse almost breathed a sigh of relief. She glanced

at a vacant office. It had an empty slot on the door where a nametag had been removed. "He did, but we're not supposed to talk about him."

"Says who?"

"The management. And the marshals," McDonald added, guessing that Flynn wouldn't be dissuaded by Meditech Corporation.

"Oh, but you must have discussed it with your friends."

"None of who look like you," Carla pointed out.

Flynn took his wallet from his coat pocket and produced a hundred-dollar bill. The nurse looked at it but didn't move from her chair. Flynn took out another hundred. McDonald glanced into the trauma room to make sure they were alone, then stood up and reached out quickly to grab the money, as though it was about to get away. "Good thing I make friends easily," she said.

"What was Vasquez like?" Flynn asked.

"Polite. Professional. Didn't chase the female staff around the examining tables. Very competent."

"Married?"

Carla shook her head. "He had been, though. To another doctor. She's back on Earth. I can understand why she ditched him: polymeth users lose interest in sex."

Flynn nodded. "Tell me what you know about how he died."

"He died in the evening, probably around twenty. Didn't show up for work the next morning and didn't answer his phone. I was running the evening shift then—Dr. Vasquez ran the day shift—and they called me to fill in for him about nine. By the time I got here, management had informed the authorities. The marshals got no response at his apartment, so they had Company security override the door lock. They found him on his living room couch. They called the paramedics but it was much too late. An ambulance brought him here but he was already cold. Rigor was setting in."

"He worked as an ME, too, didn't he?"

McDonald nodded. "He did a year's residency in pathology before he decided he'd rather keep people alive than figure out why they died," she said. "That qualified him. All the ME's on the Station are part-time, and there aren't enough of them. Or I should say that the few there are have to spend more time on call than they would like. Not too many people drop dead here."

"Who did the autopsy on Vasquez?"

"Dr. Luk, the Company's medical director. A good doctor. I heard he was very surprised when he discovered why Vasquez had died. Vasquez was an expert on polymeth abuse. That's one of the reasons why he was hired by Meditech. In fact, Vasquez had applied for the Company's opening for a polymeth expert."

Flynn could not conceal his interest. "When was this?"

"Oh, about three years ago, when the Company advertised for an expert on polymethyl two four. But they hired Dr. Dornhoeffer. You know, the woman with the hair . . ." She held her hands above her head to describe Dornhoeffer's bouffant hairdo.

"Did he say why he didn't get the Company job?"

McDonald shook her head. "The Company didn't tell him. It didn't help his ego that Dornhoeffer was unknown, while Vasquez had published ten papers on polymeth. But Vasquez really wanted a job here on the Station, and he kept trying until he got one."

Flynn could think of only one reason why a polymeth addict would want to leave his source of supply and move to Jupiter Station. "Why haven't the cops closed the case?"

"Rumor has it that they're trying to find Vasquez's connection." Carla glanced around to make sure they were still alone, then leaned across the counter. "I heard that they found only a four-week supply of polymeth in Vasquez's apartment," she said softly. "Less than that, if he were a heavy user. And he had no plans to go on vacation—hell, you can't get anyplace in four weeks from here, anyway. A polymeth addict would have been going bonkers at the prospect of his supply drying up. Vasquez hadn't had anything shipped here, so he must have been getting his dope on the Station."

Flynn ran his tongue around the inside of his mouth. "Did he have one patient he saw more often than anyone else?"

McDonald shook her head. "Most of our patients are kids that hurt themselves." Again she glanced around. "They've checked out everybody who works here, though."

Flynn leaned toward the nurse. "Did they find anything?"

"They didn't tell me if they did."

Flynn pressed his lips together while he formulated a new line of questioning. "Did you like him?"

"Well . . . sure. I mean . . . Well, when he first got here . . ." Carla shrugged her shoulders. "I wasn't seeing anyone, and he was . . . good looking. And polite. But he didn't seem interested in me." She was toying with the fasteners on the front of her scrubs. "So I started leaving one more snap undone. And when that didn't work I left *two* undone." She sighed. "And when that didn't work I decided that I must not be his type." She shook her head. "It never occurred to me that he was using. The signs were there, but . . . All those papers he'd written . . . I know better now. Not only wasn't he interested in women, but his polymeth research, it had nothing to do with *detecting* addicts. It was all about finding the genetic factors that made polymeth dangerous to eighteen percent of users, or modifying polymeth so that it wouldn't be dangerous. Oh, he was hooked, all right. He became a polymeth expert because he was a polymeth addict."

Flynn rubbed his chin. "He did polymeth research here?"

Carla nodded. "In the testing lab, one level down."

"He wasn't making his own, was he?"

McDonald shook her head vigorously. "Polymethyl two four is *very* hard to manufacture. You'd need much more extensive facilities than we have here. He had only a few milliliters that he'd brought along for his research. The marshals took that; no one here had a license to possess it."

If Vasquez wasn't making it, he had to be buying it. Flynn asked, "Do you know where he did his banking?"

"Second National. I saw his debit card."

Flynn grimaced. He didn't know anyone at Second National. Bribing his way into the bank's confidential records could cost him a fortune and was far too likely to bring unwanted attention from the Marshals Office. "Were you working here the day that those two guys got killed in warehouse twelve?"

"When the big piece of machinery fell on them? Yeah. I'd just relieved Dr. Vasquez. He did the autopsy on those guys, you know."

"So I heard. Was he still here when he got the call?"

The nurse nodded. "Barely. His phone beeped as he was walking through the door there. I was standing right here. I heard him say, 'Fatal accident! Where?' And he grabbed one of our emergency vehicles and took off."

"Did he come back here after the call?"

She shook her head. "He did the autopsies right away, at the morgue."

Flynn could think of no other questions to ask, so he thanked Carla and left. If the nurse's information was correct, Vasquez really had died of polymeth abuse. The marshals hadn't closed the case only because they hadn't found the source of Vasquez's drug supply, not because there was anything suspicious about his death. He hadn't been snuffed by the Company to keep him quiet. There would have been no need: he had applied for a Company job, and the Company's pre-employment background check could have revealed that he was a drug addict. Conglomerated could have bought his cooperation with drugs or could have blackmailed him into falsifying the autopsy results. The marshals were unlikely to investigate the possibility that the Company had been supplying Vasquez—everyone knew that Marshal Wofford had been ingratiating himself with the Company, in the hope that the Company would use its political influence to get him reassigned to Earth.

But Emilio Vasquez had left his polymeth connection on Earth and had moved to Jupiter Station. He must have known that he could obtain the drug at Jupiter. The marshals hadn't found any other polymeth addicts on the Station, and no drug pusher would risk smuggling polymeth all the way to Jupiter for just one customer. No, Vasquez must have figured out that polymeth was being produced on the Station, something that none of the solar system's law enforcement agencies had been able to do.

Wendy Chadwick breezed into Ed Warshovsky's outer office. She pointed at Warshovsky's door as she asked his office manager, "Is he free?" The woman nodded, and Chadwick proceeded through the door while the office manager hastened to announce her.

Ed Warshovsky looked up from a report he had been reading. He suppressed a grimace at the sight of Chadwick's business suit: the metallic yellow made her look like a canary. "Ms. Chadwick!" he said, forcing a smile. "Have you seen this report yet?" he asked, tapping the document with his finger. "The major reason for not raising cattle on Satellite Delta is the amount of space that would have to be devoted to growing food for them. If we can't find more space for food production, I'll have to continue eating frozen and irradiated steaks." He closed the report. "What can I do for you?"

Chadwick took a seat in a chair across the desk from her boss. "I have a problem with the Asterbrooks' investigator."

"Flynn?"

Chadwick nodded. "He's going to challenge the injunction in court this afternoon."

Warshovsky raised his eyebrows. "He won't get it lifted, will he?"

"He might," Chadwick said. "If I had been aware of all the facts in the case, I never would have sought that court order in the first place. I knew about Egleiter's screw ups and the missing journals, but I didn't know about the suspicious-looking personnel moves until Flynn himself told me about them in my office this morning."

"What was Flynn doing in your . . . what suspicious personnel moves?"

Chadwick explained, "The paramedics that responded to the scene of the accident were both hired by the Company within two months of the accident. One had never even applied for a job with us, and according to his human-resources file he wasn't particularly well qualified for the job we gave him. And the deputy marshal who investigated the accident is now the head of security at one of our African diamond mines. The foreman in charge of Asterbrook and Mondragon retired at age forty-five. And Flynn claims that Philip Asterbrook's girlfriend has been transferred off of the Station, but since I can't find her name in any of the reports I can't confirm that."

"Now, wait a minute," Warshovsky said. "The foreman was Roger Ajanian, right? I went to his retirement party myself. He was our top ramrod. If I had earned the bonuses he had, I could afford to retire, too."

Chadwick conceded that point. "Okay, we can explain that one. But I'm going to have a hell of time explaining the others."

"Oh, it can't be such a big deal," Warshovsky said. "Conglomerated Mining and Manufacturing employs over fifty thousand people. We're hiring continuously."

Chadwick looked her boss right in the eye. "A statistical analysis based on our hiring, transfer, and retirement rates shows that the probability of those events occurring randomly in a three-month period is one in eighty-two thousand."

"Eighty-two *thousand?*"

Chadwick nodded.

"Why, that's almost an impossibility!" Warshovsky said, surprised. "I'd had no idea."

Chadwick nodded again. "It's still a coincidence, of course, and I will make that argument in court this afternoon. But if the magistrate doesn't buy it, he might not only lift the injunction, he might order the marshals and OSHA to reopen their investigations. And when it gets into the news, we are going to look guilty and our stock is going to go down."

Warshovsky leaned back in his chair. "So, we'll keep it out of the press."

Chadwick shook her head glumly. "SSN now has a correspondent on the Station. Flynn knows her—according to Drake, he knows a lot of women. She'll be there today, and no matter what the magistrate rules we are going to be on Solar System News tonight."

Warshovsky pushed his chair back from his desk. "Can you suggest a new course of action?"

Chadwick nodded. "Flynn doesn't want those coincidences getting into the news," she said, "or he would have leaked that info to his reporter friend already. If the official investigations are reopened, Flynn loses his lucrative job with the Asterbrooks—private investigators are prohibited from interfering with official investigations. No," the attorney said, "he just wants us to let him investigate on his own."

"That's out of the question!" Warshovsky said quickly. "We can't have him running through our facilities, asking questions . . . He'll disrupt operations and remind people of the accident, which was a very depressing event."

"We don't need a court order to keep him out of our facilities," Chadwick replied. "He can't trespass in the course of his investigation—that's against the regulations he has to follow as a private detective. Since he doesn't work for us, he can be in our facilities legally only if invited by one of our employees."

"So if nobody invites him in, he can't harass us."

Chadwick nodded. "Exactly. A court order is better—we can take action against him even if some friend of his who works for us lets him in—but we can live with a memo to all employees instructing them not to let him into our facilities. That way, no one has the authority to let him in. And in exchange for asking the court to stay the injunction, we get Flynn to agree not to release anything he learns or has learned to the public."

Warshovsky smiled. "I knew you could handle it. Is there any way we can stop him from harassing our people in their homes?"

"Legally, he can't harass anybody anywhere at any time," Chadwick replied. "Just state in the memo that no one has to cooperate with him."

"Can we phrase it more strongly? Can we instruct our employees not to cooperate with him?"

"On their own time? Just how suspicious do you want us to look?"

Warshovsky nodded. "Okay. Take care of it, Ms. Chadwick. Write the memo for my signature. Let's get it out this afternoon."

Chadwick got to her feet. "Will do."

"One in eighty-two thousand, you said?" Warshovsky shook his head. "That really is strange. If I didn't know those two had died accidentally, I wouldn't believe the reports, either."

"Mr. Warshovsky," the computer interrupted, "you asked to be informed when the *Planet Queen* was departing."

Warshovsky stood up abruptly and strode to his window. The Station was on the sun side of Jupiter, moving retrograde to the planet's revolution about the sun, and the *Planet Queen* was moving toward the Station as it accelerated to escape velocity. Its next stop was Mars. Warshovsky could see the gas plume from its engines. The *Planet Queen* had been the first ship built at Jupiter Station that the Company had sold to another corporation. Warshovsky had had trouble convincing the Board of Directors that there was more gold in building interplanetary ships than there was in the Company's Siberian mines. Now they believed him. "I never get tired of watching the ships come and go," Warshovsky said.

Chadwick walked to the window and stood to the right and slightly behind her boss. "The Asterbrooks are on the *Planet Queen*."

"And if Egleiter had done his job properly, our problems would be leaving with them."

"I'd better go and contact Mr. Flynn," Chadwick said. She disappeared through the door, unaware that her boss was scowling at her attire. Warshovsky grudgingly approved of the boxy coat, which provided some modesty, but the Paris fashion that was sweeping through the solar system did not convey the image of corporate responsibility that was necessary in top-level managers. Warshovsky would have to write a memo to the department heads and senior staff.

Wendy Chadwick didn't like Silvanus Drake and hated dealing with his security guards, so rather than arrange an escort for Mike Flynn she met him for lunch at a restaurant on the Main Plaza within sight of the Company offices. Flynn was waiting for her when she arrived. He had taken a small table by the window that separated the restaurant from the plaza. His notebook computer was open on the table next to him.

Flynn got up as Chadwick approached and pulled her chair back from the table for her. She wished he hadn't done that. It had been good manners in a time when women wore full skirts and needed help seating themselves. Women didn't need help from men anymore.

"Am I about to hear good news?" Flynn asked. He

walked around the table to his own chair and sat down.

"If you're prepared to be reasonable, I think we can reach an agreement."

Flynn switched on the menu, which was projected from an overhead lens onto the tabletop. "I'm the most reasonable person I know. I've never eaten in this restaurant. What's good here?"

"Everything's good."

"Everything's expensive," Flynn said, half under his breath.

"Put it on expenses. This is a business lunch."

Flynn considered that option. "I usually buy my own meals. I have to eat whether I'm working or not. Doesn't seem fair to charge the client. What are you proposing?"

Chadwick looked the investigator right in the eye. "If you agree not to publicize anything you learn or have learned in the course of your investigation, we'll drop the injunction."

"Hey, I told you this morning that I'm a *private* investigator," Flynn replied. "But, since I'm not working for an officer of the court, I am required by law to turn over any evidence of a crime to the authorities."

"No crime was involved," Chadwick said confidently.

"I also have to tell my clients what I discover."

"You'll be telling the Asterbrooks only that you didn't discover anything." The lawyer turned toward the intercom at the end of the table. "I'll have the pineapple salad," she said.

"Anything to drink?" the intercom responded.

"A glass of cranberry juice. A small glass."

"I'll have the hot ham and cheese," Flynn said, "and an Irish whiskey straight up."

Chadwick made a face. "Isn't it rather early for that?"

Flynn made a show of scratching his head. "How can lunch be too early for a breakfast drink?"

Chadwick sighed. "Do we have a deal?"

"Of course we have a deal."

A robot waiter rolled out of the kitchen and stopped by their table. Chadwick reached for her plate but Flynn beat her to it and placed it and her glass of cranberry juice ceremoniously on the table in front of her. He helped himself to a sip of whiskey before taking his own plate from the robot cart.

Chadwick pursed her lips. "This lunch is Dutch treat, but when you're through wasting your time and realize that there was nothing to investigate in the first place, you're going to buy me dinner—an expensive dinner."

"After I had found out what you're covering up, I had planned do that anyway."

Wendy looked amused. "That's very presumptuous of you. What made you think I'd agree?"

"My good looks, wit, and incredible charm."

"Too bad modesty isn't one of your virtues. You'd be a perfect man." She took a bite of her salad. "That girlfriend of Asterbrook's . . . what was her name again?"

"Maria Estaban," Flynn said around a mouthful of ham and cheese. "She worked in a chem lab on one of the satellites, probably Charlie."

Chadwick nodded. "Our files show that they weren't very close." Actually, the Company files didn't mention that Philip Asterbrook had had a girlfriend. Knowing how thorough Drake's security investigations were, Wendy assumed that the lack of information about a girlfriend meant that the relationship had been very casual.

Flynn was taking a sip of whiskey and smiled into his glass. "In that case," he said as he placed the glass on the table, "Asterbrook isn't likely to have told her anything, and there would have been no need to transfer her. But she was transferred." Flynn wasn't being honest, either. He knew only that there was no directory listing for Maria Estaban. "This sandwich is excellent. How's your salad?"

"Fine, thank you. It also has considerably less fat than your sandwich."

"Youth drugs help the body burn fat," Flynn replied. "Besides, I exercise daily. Did you know that Dr. Vasquez had applied for a Company job?"

Chadwick nodded. "The marshals . . . went through our employment files."

"He was very highly qualified," Flynn continued. "Why didn't you hire him?"

Wendy smiled. "Company employment files are confidential."

"Does that mean that you knew he was a drug user?"

"It means that I can't tell you what's in them. Why are you interested in Vasquez? We obviously didn't buy him off with a Company job."

"No," Flynn said casually, "but you might have bought him off with polymethyl two four."

Chadwick choked on her salad and reached for a quick drink of cranberry juice. When her throat cleared she glared at the detective and said, "That dinner you're going to buy me will be *very* expensive. And you won't be there when I eat it."

"The marshals found only a four-week supply of polymeth in Vasquez's apartment," Flynn continued, "but people who knew Vasquez didn't think he was acting like an addict who was about to run out of drugs. Therefore he had to have a supply here on the Station. Now, do you really believe someone could be pushing polymethyl two four around here without Silvanus Drake knowing about it?"

Chadwick started to reply, then paused to consider Flynn's question. "No, I don't. And since Drake doesn't know about any pushers, then there aren't any. At least, there aren't any pushers working for the Company."

Flynn finished his sandwich and set aside his plate. "So how did you buy off Vasquez?"

Chadwick took a deep breath to calm herself. She hadn't finished her salad, but she showed her debit card to the intercom and stood up. "A very expensive dinner, for me *and* a guest of my choice, which won't be you. Forgive me if I don't wish you a nice day."

She turned and walked away. Flynn sipped his whiskey and watched her leave. She had great legs, all right. If only she'd throw away the shiny tights and coat . . .

Chapter 5

The information that Flynn had requested from Missy Adamly still wasn't in Flynn's computer. He didn't want to return to Missy's apartment—Michael knew all about Jack Adamly's temper, and did not want to find out for himself if Jack could hit as hard as his victims claimed. Flynn hoped that it was Missy's workload that had delayed the information and not Missy's displeasure at Flynn's choice of girlfriends. Flynn put his notebook computer back in his pocket and proceeded to check on a different source of information.

The hatch to Joe Aguirre's workshop in the Station basement was closed and locked. Flynn glanced at his wristwatch; seventeen o'clock was unusually early for Aguirre to have quit for the day. Joe might have been celebrating the departure of the *Planet Queen*, carrying his recycled electronic equipment to Earth for profitable resale, so before Flynn made the long walk to Aguirre's apartment he decided to check out a tavern that Aguirre was known to frequent.

The Moonshine Bar was located on level two, almost directly above Joe's workshop. Michael recognized Aguirre's silhouette standing at the bar as soon as he entered the tavern. He walked to the bar and stood next to his quarry. The bartender, filling glasses at the other end of the bar, was fashionably dressed in a skin-tight metallic red jumpsuit with hair tinted to match. Flynn got his attention.

"Fill my friend's glass again and get me a beer," he ordered.

Aguirre turned and looked at him. "Ah, Michael, my friend! I was wondering when you'd show up! I was expecting you this morning. What kept you?"

"I've been working." The bartender returned with Flynn's beer and a shot of tequila for Aguirre. Flynn glanced at the shot glass and shook his head. "Vile stuff. Can't understand how anyone can drink it."

"At least it's a man's drink, not like that Irish whiskey you're so fond of." Aguirre tilted his head back and poured down the shot.

"You got anything for me?" Flynn asked.

Aguirre wiped his mouth on his sleeve. "I never handled any broken pulley parts from a Manitowoc crane," he replied. "That doesn't prove anything, though—those cranes have a twenty-year warranty; they might have returned the broken parts to the manufacturer for replacement, or simply melted 'em down—steel is steel."

Flynn motioned to the bartender to bring another shot of tequila. "And put on a four-centimeter pulley as a temporary replacement?"

"They must have—that ceramic line wouldn't have failed on a thirty-centimeter pulley. But it's easier said than done. A four-centimeter pulley is too small to fit on the shaft for a thirty-centimeter pulley, which is standard on those cranes. But they could have replaced the entire shaft-bearing assembly with one from a model 804—the bearings have the same outer diameter. And an 804 is a much smaller crane— rated at thirty tons. Standard pulley is four centimeters."

Flynn took a long drink of his beer. "The Company has a Manitowoc Model 804 on the Station?"

Aguirre nodded. "Warehouse seven."

"Where's warehouse seven?"

"Almost straight across the Station from warehouse

twelve," Aguirre answered, using his hands to draw an invisible station in the air over the bar. "Right below the Company offices on the Main Plaza."

Flynn stared at the bottles of liquor on the shelves behind the bar, thinking. "Does warehouse seven have access to the outside?"

Aguirre nodded again. "Same as warehouse twelve."

Flynn grinned. He slapped Joe on the back and said, "Thanks, Joe." He drained the rest of his beer and signaled to the bartender. He took forty dollars from his wallet and asked, "Will this cover everything plus one more shot for my friend?"

"You get five dollars in change," the bartender answered.

Flynn handed over the money. "Keep it." He slapped Aguirre on the shoulder. Joe had supplied a big piece to the puzzle. "See you around," he said, and left.

The workday was ending and the streets were filling with homeward-bound people. Flynn paid them little attention. He was trying to figure out how he could prove his hypothesis, and walked right past his favorite bar without noticing it.

"Mikey!"

Flynn stopped and turned around. Betty was standing in the door of her tavern, waving at him. Flynn glanced at his watch. Afternoon had not yet given way to evening; he had time for another drink. Flynn reversed course.

"Not talking to Barbara, eh?" Betty asked. "Because you're talking to Missy Russell instead?"

"It's Missy Adamly now," Flynn corrected. "She got married."

"She did indeed! And her husband is not one to trifle with, Michael. He hurts people."

114

"I'm not trifling with anyone, Betty. I've only seen Missy once since her marriage."

"Seen her where?"

"Her apartment, with her husband to chaperone."

Betty pursed her lips. "I hope you're not lying to me and doing something foolish with that girl, Mike." Betty glanced around, then took a memory disk out of the pocket of her blouse and slipped it into the pocket of his sport coat. She lowered her voice and said, "She was in here earlier. Left this for you. Told me not to mention to anybody else that she'd been here, and that I wasn't to let anyone see me give this to you."

Flynn fingered the disk, wondering why Missy hadn't sent the information directly to his computer through the Station's communication system. He glanced into the bar. It was less than half full. "Pour me a whiskey, will you, Betty?"

Flynn walked to an empty table in the corner, sat with his back to the wall, and slid the disk into his notebook computer. He accessed the disk and a flashing red warning message filled the display.

What are you up to, Mike? You're hotter than your home-made chili! There's a memo to all employees from the head honcho himself instructing us to keep you out of Company property. The goons have programmed the security cameras to watch you wherever you go and keep Company Security Control informed of your whereabouts. The communication system is routing a copy of all your messages to Security Control, too—that's why I put this info on disk. The files appear to be unaltered—at least, none were modified since the document dates and the checksums are okay. Don't let ANYBODY else see this! Don't ask me for any more info—you're so hot, I wouldn't help you even if we were still dating. So make do with this and LEAVE ME ALONE!!!!!!

Flynn suppressed a smile. This is what he had expected from the Company—goons in his hair, in his face, and under his feet. Goons breathing down his neck. Silvanus Drake using all of the resources at his disposal to stop Flynn. Drake was a formidable adversary; Flynn would have to be careful.

Betty appeared and placed a glass of whiskey on the table next to Flynn's computer. "On your tab, I suppose?" she asked. Flynn nodded. "So what's on the disk? A passionate love note?"

Flynn shook his head. "Nothing so interesting. Just stolen Company secrets," he said lightly. "Do you own any Company stock?"

Betty nodded. "Yeah, I got about fifty thousand-worth. Why?"

Flynn reached for the whiskey. "Sell it."

Betty started to smile, caught herself, and said, "Seriously?"

"Betty, when have I ever been serious?"

"Never with women," she replied, then turned and walked back to the bar.

In hardcopy the Company report on the fatal accident would have required two hundred pages, but it contained nothing that Flynn hadn't read in the marshals' and OSHA reports. Like their public counterparts, the Company investigators had not noticed that a four-centimeter pulley on a three-hundred-ton crane wasn't standard.

The human resources files on Asterbrook and Mondragon were more interesting. Both men had originally applied for Company jobs on planet four, then had moved to Jupiter Station because the Company had greater need of workers there. Both had been single. Both had been hired at the L3 (unskilled labor) grade when the construction of Satellite Juliet had fallen behind schedule and the Company had tried to catch up by throwing more people at the project. The work logs for both men showed that they had reported to warehouse twelve on over half of the days that they had worked for the Company, including the morning of the day on which they died. The form nines for both men had authorized the Company to bury their remains if they died at Jupiter. There was nothing in Asterbrook's file indicating that his body and personal belongings should be held on Jupiter Station for Donald and Helene Asterbrook, but in the financial section of the file, listed under *Owed the Employee*, was a note that Philip's personal belongings were being stored in Human Resources pending the arrival of Philip's parents. That was the only evidence that the Company had received the request from the Asterbrooks to hold their son's remains for them.

Flynn was about to move on to the maintenance records of the crane in warehouse twelve when he noticed—much to his surprise—that both Asterbrook and Mondragon had had their background checks done by Silvanus Drake. Flynn took a drink of whiskey and stared at the report. He could not imagine Drake leaving his office to clear prospective laborers personally, no matter how desperately the Company needed them or how busy Drake's investigators were. Flynn was willing to bet that none of the other people hired to help with Satellite Juliet were deemed important enough to warrant Silvanus Drake's personal attention.

The maintenance records on the crane in warehouse twelve were disappointingly brief. The only entries pertained to the periodic testing that OSHA required of all overhead cranes. There was nothing to indicate that the crane had ever malfunctioned. If the pulley had broken, nobody had bothered to record the fact. If the pulley shaft and bearing assembly had ever been replaced with the unit from the smaller crane in warehouse seven, the event either hadn't been recorded or the records had been altered.

Flynn finished his whiskey and removed the memory disk from his computer. He had not intentionally copied the information from the disk into the computer's memory, and he checked to make sure that no unintentional copies had been made. He wrote *Tropical Drink Recipes* on the disk, took it to the bar, and handed it to Betty. "Stick this with your other disks," he said quietly. "If anyone asks, you never saw it. Missy wasn't here today. *I* wasn't here today."

"I'll never get anyone to believe that last lie," Betty said dryly.

Flynn returned to his apartment. Furrball met him at the door, rubbing against his legs and acting like he was glad to see him. The cat usually acted that way when he was hungry, but Flynn had filled the cat feeder earlier in the week. He glanced into the kitchen and found, to his surprise, that the dish beneath the feeder was empty. Furrball could not have eaten that much food so quickly. Flynn found the problem as soon as he tried to remove the lid from the food hopper. The lid was cross-threaded and hadn't seated properly; the safety interlock switch for the auger hadn't closed. The hopper was half full. Flynn carefully replaced the lid and the safety switch closed. The feeder sensed the empty dish and immediately filled it. Furrball pushed past Flynn and nosed into the dish, purring.

Flynn stood up from the feeder slowly. If he had cross-threaded the lid when he had refilled the machine, Furrball would have run out of food earlier in the week. Somebody had been fooling with the feeder. Company goons could get in easily—the apartment was Company property; Security had override codes for the door lock. The goons had searched his apartment and had done such a thorough job that they had even looked into the cat feeder. Missy had been right: Flynn was hot.

Flynn checked the rest of his apartment carefully. Nothing was out of position by as much as a millimeter. There was a thin layer of dust on the tops of the frames of the inexpensive paintings that adorned the wall behind the dining table. Flynn stood to the side of the paintings and carefully eased the upper of the two paintings away from the wall. Stuck to the back, behind a tiny pinhole in the canvas, was a video microcam. Flynn left it there. He'd let the goons think that he wasn't on to them.

There were more paintings in the bedroom. Flynn climbed the stairs to the second floor of his apartment. The painting that hung highest on the wall also concealed a surveillance device. Flynn suppressed a smile while he wondered how much it would cost him to get Silvanus Drake's wife up to the bedroom.

Flynn had been thinking of making Mexican food for dinner, but dinner would have to wait. The Company wouldn't be trying so hard to derail his investigation unless there was still evidence that Flynn could discover. That evidence, Flynn now suspected, was in warehouse seven, where the smaller crane with the four-centimeter pulley was located, not in warehouse twelve where the bodies had been found. Flynn was ready to believe that Asterbrook and Mondragon had been killed accidentally when a line to an overhead crane had broken, dropping something heavy on them. But the accident had occurred in warehouse seven. What had the victims been hoisting with that crane? Why had it been easier for the Company to move the accident scene to warehouse twelve instead of moving the material that had been in warehouse seven?

Flynn didn't know anyone with access to warehouse seven who would be willing to risk his Company job in exchange for a bribe that Flynn could afford to give. What Flynn needed was somebody who had official, Company-approved access to warehouse seven and who wanted to get to the bottom of this affair as much as Flynn did. Flynn smiled; he knew just such a person.

Flynn took his stun pistol from the drawer in the bedside table, slipped it into the right pocket of his coat, and went downstairs. Furrball walked out of the kitchen. Flynn bent down and petted the cat. "You're on guard, Furrball," he said. "Let no strangers in here, okay? Slash them to ribbons with your talons." The cat purred.

Flynn confirmed that his notebook computer was in his inside coat pocket, then stepped out of his apartment and onto the balcony that gave access to all of the apartments on that floor of Flynn's building. He closed the door behind him and made sure it was locked. The security camera at the end of the balcony was pointing along the balcony and not at the stairs to the street below. Flynn went down the stairs to the first landing, took the stun pistol from his pocket, and removed the energy cell. The cell showed full, so Flynn had enough energy for ten shots, but there was a thin layer of grease on the electrical contacts. Flynn grunted; the goons had tried to disarm him surreptitiously. He wiped away the grease with his handkerchief. He had to fieldstrip the pistol before he could wipe the grease from the contacts in the gun. He looked around to make sure that no one was watching him, put the gun back into his pocket, then set off to weasel his way into warehouse seven.

★ ★ ★ ★ ★

Wendy Chadwick strained against the magnetic force fields in her exercise machine, and a bead of sweat trickled off of the bridge of her nose and into the corner of her eye. Blinking didn't stop the burning sensation, so she reluctantly released the handgrips and reached for a towel to wipe her eyes.

The door alarm sounded. Chadwick glanced at the clock on the wall, which showed nineteen twenty. She wondered who would be bothering her at that time of the evening. She considered ignoring the alarm, then thought better of it. She got up from the exerciser and walked to the door.

The image in the monitor was that of Michael Flynn, private investigator and painful thorn in Chadwick's side. Civilized people kept regular business hours; Flynn didn't. He probably wanted to talk about the Asterbrook affair. Wendy was tempted to tell him to see her in the morning, but according to the report that Silvanus Drake had compiled, Flynn could move very fast. If Chadwick didn't find out what he was up to, she could be hopelessly far behind by morning.

Wendy was reaching for the door latch when her reflection in the full-length mirror by the door stopped her. Her exercise suit was inappropriate attire for a business meeting. She started to go back for her robe, then stopped and studied her reflection again. According to Drake's report, Flynn was a womanizer. Chadwick would see how easily Flynn could be distracted.

Chadwick opened the door. She pretended to be surprised. "Mr. Flynn! What brings you here? I thought we concluded our business this noon."

"Ah! I'm interrupting your workout!" Flynn deduced. "Are you . . . almost finished?"

Wendy leaned against the door. "Why?" she asked suspiciously. "You're not going to pay off that dinner you owe me already, are you?"

Flynn shook his head. "I have something to show you."

"Something concerning the Asterbrook case, I suppose."

Flynn nodded. "Something you should know. Something your clients haven't told you."

If Flynn was dazzled by the sight of Chadwick in an exercise suit, he didn't show it. Wendy regretted not putting on her robe. "My clients are my employers," she replied, "and they've told me exactly what happened—an industrial accident. Two men died. Period."

"I can prove otherwise."

Chadwick sighed. "Eighty thousand to one might be long odds, but they are still a coincidence."

Flynn shook his head. "That's not what I meant. I'm talking physical evidence." Wendy did not reply, so Flynn said, "Get dressed. I'll show you."

Chadwick hesitated. She didn't know what she was about to get into. She should discuss it with Ed Warshovsky. She should take care of it in the morning. She needed time to *think*. Flynn was looking at her—at her face, not her body. He looked so sincere. "You might as well wait inside," she said impulsively. "I have to shower." Flynn stepped into the apartment and Chadwick slid the door closed. The apartment's living room was just inside the door. "Have a seat," she said. She tried to stay casual as she walked toward the kitchen and her bedroom beyond it, but she was suddenly embarrassed by how much her exercise suit revealed. She had behaved unprofessionally by allowing Flynn to see her in it. She held her breath until she turned the corner and disappeared from Flynn's sight.

"Dress casually," Flynn called after her.

The investigator chose not to sit; he preferred to check out the apartment. It was in one of the luxury blocks that had been constructed when Satellite Foxtrot had been built and the rolling mills had been moved from the Station to the satellite. Flynn guessed that it was a perquisite of Chadwick's position as the Company's top lawyer on Jupiter Station. It was twice as large as Flynn's apartment and, unlike Flynn's, was all on one level. The living room was carpeted, but the floors of the entrance foyer and the dining area were tiled. The attorney's exercise machine stood in the corner of the dining area. Flynn preferred jogging—two full laps around the Station every morning, mostly on level one, where the gravity was the strongest—to working out on a machine. Besides, there was no room in Flynn's apartment for an exerciser, even if Flynn could have afforded one.

Flynn heard the sound of a shower running. Chadwick's living room window was displaying a stabilized holographic projection of the satellites following Jupiter Station in its orbit. The paintings on the walls were brightly colored abstracts and did not look to be more expensive than the artwork that adorned Flynn's apartment. Unlike Flynn's paintings, none of Chadwick's were concealing miniature video cameras. One entire wall of the living room was devoted to books, some of which were famous works of fiction and all of which must have been shipped from planet three at considerable expense. The sound of the shower stopped.

Flynn moved into the dining room. The window there was displaying a twilight view of palm trees. Then Flynn did a double take and realized that it was a real window, and that the palm trees were right outside of the apartment. Flynn walked to the window and looked at the ground below. The palms sprouted from a small garden that bordered the apartment complex's swimming pool. Beyond the palms and the garden was the back of another apartment block.

The sound of a door opening caused Flynn to turn from the window in time to see Ms. Chadwick, wrapped in a towel, cross from the bathroom to the bedroom. Flynn trusted her because Silvanus Drake was known to dislike lawyers. Drake had to be running the cover-up, so Chadwick wasn't likely to be a part of it.

Flynn was studying Chadwick's exercise machine when he heard the bedroom door open. The lawyer was wearing a light-brown business suit of soft cloth instead of fashionably shiny fabric. It had calf-length slacks and no skirt. "I said to dress casually," Flynn said.

"We have a business relationship," Chadwick explained. "What you have promised to show me involves our business. Therefore a business suit is appropriate attire. Besides, this is at least three years out of style. I don't care if this escapade ruins it. I just hope nobody I know sees me in this."

Flynn shook his head. "Well, don't say I didn't warn you." He led the way to the door.

"May I ask where we're going?" Wendy asked. "Lights out till I return," she commanded as she stepped into the corridor.

"The accident scene, of course."

Chadwick looked askance at Flynn. "According to a security report I read this morning, you've already seen that."

"Ah-huh. Have you?"

The lawyer nodded. "The day after the accident, with bloody imprints of the bodies still on the deck."

"Don't worry about that," Flynn said reassuringly. "It's been cleaned up."

Like Flynn's apartment, Chadwick's was reached from a

balcony above the street, but the balcony was joined to the street by a ramp instead of a staircase. The bright overhead lights that gave the effect of a hazy sunlit day had been dimmed to simulate evening, but the streetlights had come on and the front of the apartment block, in the field of view of a security camera, was well lit. Flynn wondered what the goons in Security Control were thinking at that moment.

The investigator used his phone to summon a cab. The computer-controlled, electric-powered vehicle was on the scene in less than a minute. Flynn flashed his debit card to the video sensor and said, "Warehouse twelve." He turned to help Ms. Chadwick into a seat but the lawyer was too fast for him. Flynn took a seat next to her and the cab drove away.

The corridor leading to warehouse twelve was rarely used by the public, and the Company had not wasted money decorating it. The plain white walls gave the corridor the antiseptic appearance of a hospital. It was only one level high, but with the lights dimmed to simulate nighttime the low ceiling could be overlooked. At that time of the evening the corridor was deserted.

The cab coasted to a stop in front of warehouse twelve. Chadwick hopped out of her side of the cab before Flynn could offer to assist her. "Wait here fifteen minutes," Flynn ordered the cab. "Charge my card. If we're not back by then you can go."

Chadwick was looking at the airlock hatch that led to the warehouse. "It's locked," she said, in a tone implying that the trip had been a waste of time. She turned toward Flynn.

The investigator was unconcerned. "So? You're the Company's top lawyer on this station. You can't tell me that you don't have access to Company property."

Wendy sighed. She turned back to the hatch and placed

her open hand against the video sensor. "Security computer," she said. "Executive lock override: Wendy Chadwick."

The lock status light changed from red to green. Flynn reached for the latch but the lawyer preempted him. "It's our property," she said. "I'll open the door."

The airlock hatches opened outward, away from the warehouse, and the inner hatch was open as required by safety regulations (if the warehouse depressurized, anyone in it would not be able to open the hatch against the air pressure inside the lock). The warehouse was dark except for the splash of light that spilled through the hatch. Flynn reached past the lawyer to the switch on the wall that activated the rest of the lights. The warehouse was just as empty as when Flynn had visited it the preceding morning. Wendy stared at the vacant space and said, "Okay, where's the evidence?"

Flynn pointed at the crane. "Up there."

The crane had been moved to the center of the warehouse. Chadwick walked toward it, her footsteps on the steel deck echoing from the walls. She stood beneath the crane and looked up at it. "I don't see any evidence," she said sarcastically. She couldn't be expected to see anything: the crane was more than five meters above her.

Flynn was already walking toward the crane controls. He crooked his finger at Chadwick to indicate that she should follow him. He stood beside the controls until Wendy joined him. "Can you unlock these?"

Chadwick knew why the controls would not respond to Flynn; the proposal for the safety lockout had originated in her office. "Are you a qualified crane operator?" she asked.

"It can't be that hard. Asterbrook and Mondragon supposedly did it."

"Asterbrook and Mondragon are dead!"

Flynn smiled. He pointed to the overhead crane. "But they weren't killed by that crane. Can you unlock this so I can hoist you up there so you can see what you came to see?"

Chadwick took a deep breath. Her legal training told her to go home. Her instincts told her to cooperate. Attorneys learned in law school to trust their training and not their instincts. She turned to the crane controls. "Computer: safety lockout override. Wendy Chadwick."

A small green lamp glowed on the control panel. Flynn pressed the power switch and the crane came to life. He lowered the line with its cargo hook to the floor. "There's your elevator."

Wendy stared at the line hanging from the crane. She waved her finger in Flynn's face. "Don't *ever* tell anybody that I did something this stupid." She started walking toward the crane.

"Here," Flynn said, taking his computer from his pocket. "You'll need this."

"Why? Does it turn into a parachute?"

"Just try not to drop it. It's impact resistant but not idiot-proof."

Chadwick managed a small smile. "If I drop it just right, you might break its fall."

Wendy walked to the line hanging from the crane, tucked Flynn's computer into her coat pocket, placed her left foot in the cargo hook, and took a firm grip on the line. "Okay, Mr. Flynn: take me up slowly."

Flynn very gently moved the control lever upward. The crane could lift over two hundred tons, and Flynn's light pressure on the lever was almost too much. "Easy does it!" Chadwick warned. Flynn released the lever and the line stopped abruptly, leaving the attorney clutching the line and swaying four meters above the deck.

"Sorry," Flynn said. He pushed on the lever again, as gently as he could, and managed to raise Ms. Chadwick the rest of the way to the crane without further incident.

"What am I supposed to notice?" Wendy asked, staring at the crane which was now level with her eyes.

"Appendix II in the OSHA report; attachment four in the marshals' version."

Chadwick held on to the line with her left hand while she carefully extracted the computer from her pocket, flipped it open, and called up the OSHA report. "Great," she said, "a picture of the crane. Am I supposed to compare this with the . . . What's a four-centimeter pulley?"

"That's the sheave diameter," Flynn explained. "The part the line runs over."

Chadwick looked at the line coming out of the pulley. "This has a diameter of a lot more than four centimeters."

"Thirty, to be exact," Flynn said. "That's the standard size pulley for one of those cranes. That's the pulley that was on that crane when it left the factory. It's not the pulley that was on the crane the day of the accident."

The line supporting the attorney slowly twisted, turning her so that she faced Flynn. "So? Somebody switched pulleys."

Flynn shook his head slowly. "According to the maintenance records for that crane, that pulley was never changed."

Chadwick glared down from her perch. "How do you know what's in the maintenance records? They're confidential."

"Some of your employees have quite a thirst," Flynn lied. "They can't always afford to slake it. You really should pay them better."

"Is this all you dragged me down here for? To show me that some of our employees ignored standing instructions to document all equipment modifications?"

"They didn't record it when they removed the four-centimeter pulley and put that one back on, either. Very sloppy."

"Very inconsequential."

"Not for Asterbrook and Mondragon," Flynn said. "The line found hanging from that crane the day of the accident would not have been overstressed if it had been wrapped around a thirty-centimeter pulley."

Chadwick clenched her teeth. Some damn fool had changed a pulley and hadn't recorded it; the accident could have been due to the fact that somebody thought the bigger pulley was still on the crane. The Company had been negligent. "That's hardly evidence of a great conspiracy," Wendy argued.

"No? Wouldn't that depend on where the four-centimeter pulley came from?"

Chadwick had been wondering what had happened to the smaller pulley. "I suppose you already know the answer to that question?"

"Of course. Care to see it?"

"If I say no, will you walk away and leave me up here?"

Flynn grinned, but he lowered the lawyer to the floor, ran the cargo hook back up to the crane, and shut off the power.

The cab was waiting for them outside the airlock. Chadwick made certain that the hatch locked, which gave Flynn the chance to beat her to the cab and help her into her seat. "Now where to?" she asked.

"Warehouse seven," Flynn ordered the cab as he took his seat.

"Where's that?"

"Other side of the Station," Flynn explained, "right beneath your office."

The pair rode in silence. Chadwick wondered what kind of man would think it gentlemanly to help her into her seat right after hoisting her five meters from the deck with a cargo hook. She glanced at Flynn. He was staring straight ahead, brow furrowed, apparently deep in thought. She couldn't decide if she preferred him silent or talking.

Warehouse seven was also entered through an airlock because, like warehouse twelve, it had direct access to outer space. Chadwick's handprint and magic words unlocked the airlock hatch and Wendy led the way through it. The airlock was a carbon copy of the one leading to warehouse twelve. Wendy found the master light switch on the interior wall of the warehouse without Flynn's help, and the lights revealed row upon row of packing cases. In some places they were stacked halfway to the ceiling. The overhead crane was obviously smaller, and instead of being in the center of the warehouse it had been moved to a position closer to the large hatch in the side bulkhead that opened directly to outer space.

"It doesn't look like the same crane . . ." Chadwick's voice trailed off as she realized that the stacks of packing cases might have been distorting her perspective.

"Same manufacturer," Flynn said.

He led the way to the crane controls, then stood aside while Chadwick unlocked them. The crane was directly over a pile of packing cases, all of which were marked with the destination code for Satellite Juliet. Wendy started climbing the pile.

"There's no need for that," Flynn said. "I can move the crane."

"That's okay. I might not need a lift." She pulled herself

to the top row of packing cases and stood up, but she was still three meters below the crane. Chadwick stared at the crane, her head tilted back. She was too far away to be certain. "It's certainly smaller than the other pulley, but how do you know that this is the four-centimeter pulley that was on the other crane?"

"There's another pulley assembly for a Manitowoc crane on the Station?" Flynn asked. "I haven't been able to find one. Of course, with your access to Company records, you could confirm in seconds what would take me days of legwork, especially since so many old Company friends of mine aren't talking to me all of a sudden."

The lawyer's urge to smile vanished when Wendy realized that Flynn had neatly outmaneuvered the Company's efforts to thwart his investigation by getting her to show him everything he wanted to see. She decided to climb down the backside of the packing cases; she could do without giving Flynn another undignified view of her.

"The morning that Asterbrook and Mondragon died, they reported for work in warehouse twelve," Flynn said, "but then they were taken here." He pointed to the outside hatch with his thumb. "In a space shuttle, so that no one would see them, via these hatches. It wasn't the machinery frame in warehouse twelve that fell on them, it was a packing case like one of these. The bodies were probably moved back to warehouse twelve with a shuttle, too. The packing case was so hush-hush that whoever was here with the victims moved the accident scene to the other side of the Station rather than have government investigators look around in here. He had to change the pulleys, too: it was the small pulley that caused the ceramic line to snap. The maintenance records don't show the pulley switch because that would have given the game away."

131

Before Chadwick could reply, a noise from the entrance hatch caused Flynn to look in that direction. Two Company security guards stepped into the warehouse. Flynn was not surprised; he wondered what had taken them so long.

One of the guards looked at Flynn. "There he is!" he said to his companion. To Flynn's astonishment, both guards drew their laser pistols.

Flynn wasted no time assessing the situation. He darted behind the pile of shipping crates that Chadwick had climbed. A laser pulse missed the packing crates and blew metal particles from the hatch leading to the exterior. The superheated air produced a small thunderclap as it expanded.

Chadwick was still one packing case from the floor. She stared in disbelief at Flynn, then at the blast mark on the hatch. The odor of ozone reached her nostrils. "What the hell's going on here?" she said loudly. She turned and peered around the packing cases toward the entrance hatch.

"Get down!" Flynn ordered as he grabbed Chadwick's ankle and yanked her from the crate. She shrieked as she fell backwards into Flynn's arms, just as the corner of the crate around which she had been looking erupted in a shower of fragments and another minithunderclap echoed through the warehouse.

Chadwick pushed Flynn away from her. "Keep your hands off of me! I'll handle this!" She stormed around the corner of the packing cases and faced the goons at the hatch. "I am Wendy Chadwick of the Company's legal office—"

Flynn grabbed her arm and pulled her back as another laser pulse flashed past. "I don't think they care who you are."

Chadwick gasped for breath, then noticed the stun pistol

that Flynn had taken from his pocket. "Where did you get that?"

"McGuire's Shooting Supplies, Boston. Stand right here and don't move."

Flynn tiptoed back around the other side of the packing cases. As he had suspected, one of the goons was trying to sneak up on them from that direction. Flynn aimed his pistol. The guard stopped abruptly when he saw the gun, hesitated, then ducked behind a convenient crate just as Flynn fired. Flynn heard something clatter to the floor.

"Damnation!" came from the direction of the guard.

"What's wrong?" his companion called out.

"That stun pistol of his is working!"

"Did he hit you?"

"Hell, yes, he hit me!"

"Bad?"

"No. It's just my damn arm. My arm's not working. It . . . it tingles like hell."

Flynn muttered a dirty word. Nine shots to go, and his best chance to put one of the bad guys out of action was gone.

"Those pistols can be set to stun, but they're trying to kill us!" Chadwick said, her face revealing what she thought of the guards' intentions.

"Let's see if we can keep them from succeeding," Flynn replied. He peeked cautiously around Chadwick's side of the crates. The other goon had taken cover, but had his pistol trained on Flynn's position. Flynn pulled his head back just as another laser pulse flashed past. "Good thing they can't shoot worth a damn."

"Listen!" Chadwick called out. She was crouched against the side of the packing crate. "I am Ms. Wendy Chadwick of the Legal Office! We have a legal right to be in this warehouse! Put those guns away and—"

A laser pulse slammed into the front of the crates and Chadwick shut up. Flynn heard rapid footsteps near the entrance hatch and hazarded another peek. He glimpsed one of the goons at the light switch next to the hatch just as the overhead lights switched off.

"Now what?" Chadwick asked.

"We're lucky," Flynn answered. "Intelligence isn't a requirement to be a Company guard." With light still coming through the open airlock hatch and the glow of the *Exit* sign above it, the goons would be silhouetted while Flynn and Chadwick would be shrouded in darkness.

"Vinny!" came a voice from the door. "Get over here!"

"My arm still doesn't work!"

"It doesn't matter! Get over here!"

Then Flynn understood the goon's strategy. The crippled guard would stand watch at the door so Flynn and Chadwick could not escape while his colleague sneaked behind them in the darkness. Flynn took his telephone from his coat pocket but couldn't get a dial tone. "It figures."

"What?" Wendy asked.

"My phone's not working."

Chadwick took her phone from her pocket. "Emergency!" she said. "Emergency!" But she got no response. "What the hell's wrong?"

"If it were just my phone, I'd say they'd deactivated my account." That was easy for the Company to do; it ran the Station's communication system. "But since your phone's not working either, they might have shut down the repeater in this warehouse." Flynn handed his computer to Chadwick. "Try this," he suggested. He hazarded another peek around the corner of the crates but saw nothing.

"I can't get the network," Chadwick said.

Flynn took back the computer. The Company could have deactivated his computer account as easily as his telephone, but he guessed that they had shut down the repeater. If the repeater wasn't working, Silvanus Drake couldn't control his goons and keep them from making mistakes. "We have to get away from here. We can't let them get behind us." He felt, more than saw, Chadwick nod. "They seem to have a tendency to shoot high, so stay low. Follow me."

Flynn led the way to the side bulkhead, then along the large hatch that led to the Station exterior. He wanted to get to the back of the warehouse where the shadows were the deepest and where no one could get behind him, but a row of shipping crates blocked his way. He detoured away from the bulkhead, toward the center of the warehouse, until he reached a corridor between rows of containers that led toward the back. There was a bright red flash, a sharp crack that stung Flynn's ears, and a shower of sparks from a crate farther toward the rear. Flynn turned and darted behind another row of containers, dragging Chadwick behind him.

"How can they see us?" Chadwick complained. The goons had not been wearing low-light vision goggles.

"They can't," Flynn said. "They're shooting at shadows."

"Well, they almost killed a couple of shadows that time!"

"Almost only scores with hand grenades and H-bombs. Let's go." Flynn led Chadwick farther to the rear.

"Vinny! Can you see anything?"

"Yeah. A couple thousand tons of stuff for Satellite Juliet. Are you sure you didn't hit 'em with that last shot?"

"I'm not even sure I was shooting at them."

Flynn took advantage of his opponents' distraction with their conversation to make another break for the back of the warehouse. He and Chadwick hadn't covered five meters when a brilliant flash against the packing case to Flynn's left showed that the move had been spotted. Chadwick shrieked. Flynn pushed her rudely behind the container that the laser pulse had struck.

"I'm sorry," Chadwick said.

"For what?"

"Screaming."

"Maybe they'll think they hit us. Keep going."

Now Chadwick was in the lead. She stumbled and Flynn tripped over her.

"Ouch! Dammit!" she said.

"What happened?" Flynn asked as he pushed himself up from the pile that they had made on the deck.

"I barked my shin on something."

Flynn felt through the darkness for the deck, trying to discern the obstruction that had impeded their progress. He couldn't believe his good fortune. "Sonuvabitch. It's a basement hatch." It was locked, of course. "Can you unlock this?" he asked quietly.

The basement hatch didn't have a handprint scanner. "Security computer," Chadwick ordered, "executive lock override: Wendy Chadwick."

Flynn tried the latch again and felt it turn. "Get ready," he warned. "When I open this the airlock light will come on and we'll be perfect targets."

"Okay."

Flynn lifted the hatch and his dark-adjusted eyes were almost blinded by the light. "Go!" he ordered. Chadwick stepped over the hatch coaming and started climbing down the ladder.

"They're getting away!" someone shouted from the front of the warehouse.

Two laser pulses flashed overhead in quick succession. Flynn jumped through the hatchway, knocking Chadwick to the bottom of the airlock, and pulled the hatch closed on top of him. As he spun the latch shut he noticed that the rubber gasket around the rim of the hatchway was badly worn. It would be Flynn's bad luck if the hatch wouldn't seal. He flipped the switch to reduce the lock pressure to that of the basement, and breathed a sigh of relief as he felt the air pressure build behind his ears.

"That'll hold 'em," he said. "There's almost three kilonewtons of air pressure holding that hatch closed. Those two will never open it without tools. They'll have to find another hatch."

"Is there another one in this warehouse?"

Flynn shrugged. "I didn't know there was *this* one."

The lock pressure reached that of the basement. Flynn took out his telephone and opened the lower hatch. He got a dial tone immediately. "Emergency!" he barked into the phone. "Emergency!" There was no response. He shut off the phone and turned it on again, but there was no dial tone. "Damn! They *just* shut down the basement repeaters!"

"But, how could they know—"

"I'll bet a light flashes on a console in Security Control every time a basement hatch is opened. Whoever's on watch knew where we were headed as soon as the goons in the warehouse did. And he'll be sending more goons to head us off. Come on; we'll have to hurry."

"Damn that Silvanus Drake!" Chadwick said. "This time he's gone too far, and I'm going to hang him for it!"

Flynn shook his head. "It's not Drake. We're facing a

panic response, and Drake doesn't panic. He'd have had those two stun us, then arrange a fatal accident for us someplace else. We're fighting someone dumb enough to get stuck with the night watch until Drake can get there and take command."

Flynn led the way down the ladder, gun ready. The basement was dimly lit by emergency lights. Structural support members cast threatening shadows, but none of the shadows moved and none fired lasers. Flynn put his pistol in his pocket and helped Chadwick down the ladder. One of her pants legs was torn and her leg was bruised. Flynn left the lower hatch open so the goons couldn't pressurize the airlock.

"Which way?" Chadwick asked.

Flynn pointed to his left. "That's the end of the Station, so we go that way." Flynn indicated the opposite direction.

Chadwick pointed to a hatch-like object set into the deck behind Flynn. "What's that?"

"Hatch to the outside," Flynn replied. "Er, actually, to the radiation shield." The outermost two meters of the Station had been filled with loose rubble and mine waste to absorb the radiation that surrounded Jupiter. "But it's unpressurized. We can't get out that way. Let's go."

Flynn led the way, alternately stepping over structural beams or ducking under water and air pipes. A distant metallic clang reached his ears.

"What was that?" Wendy asked.

Flynn checked his pocket to make sure his pistol was still there. "Somebody just opened an airlock," he said quietly. "Keep your voice down."

They came to a bulkhead. The basement was subdivided into many airtight compartments; they would have to find a hatch.

"Now which way?"

"The noise we heard came from over there," Flynn said, pointing to his left, "so we'll try the other way."

"You don't know where the hatches are, do you?"

"Nope. Do you?"

Wendy had been in the basement only once, during her orientation tour when she had first arrived on the Station. She shook her head.

"Can Silvanus Drake cancel your lock override privileges?"

Chadwick shook her head. "Only Ed Warshovsky can do that."

"You mean, only Warshovsky can do that *officially*."

"What does that mean?"

"That means that I wonder just how much control Drake has over the Station's computer system," Flynn explained.

There was a flash behind them, accompanied by a shower of hot metal fragments from a laser pulse impact on an overhead beam. Flynn turned but saw no one. "Go!" he ordered. "I'll cover you!"

Wendy went. Flynn crouched behind a girder that held the deck—the outer airtight skin of the Station—in place and watched the direction from which the shot had come. There was another laser flash. The pulse went past Flynn and vented its anger on the bulkhead behind him. Flynn focused his attention on the point from which the pulse had been fired and saw a shadow separate into two parts, one of which moved to Flynn's right. He leveled his pistol at it but it was too far away for a shot. The shadow leaped lightly over a girder and moved in closer. It passed close enough to an emergency light for Flynn to get a glimpse of the orange coveralls worn by security guards. The goon was moving quickly, probably concentrating on glimpses of the escaping

Chadwick, and didn't realize that Flynn was lying in ambush. The investigator waited until the shadow showed a distinctive silhouette, put the red dot sight of his pistol on where the goon's chest should have been, and fired. The guard pitched forward and Flynn heard something skid toward him along the floor.

Flynn jumped over the beam that sheltered him and sprinted toward his victim. The man was sprawled on his face, stunned senseless. Flynn had scored a direct hit. Somewhere in the shadows was the guard's gun, a lethal laser pistol that would keep other goons much farther away.

Three laser pulses split the dim light. One hit a girder only a meter from Flynn's head and showered him with hot metal particles. Flynn hit the deck, cursing himself for forgetting that goons usually traveled in pairs. Flynn crawled to the bulkhead, got to his feet, and dashed after Chadwick. Another laser pulse slammed into the bulkhead behind him. Security guards rarely had to use their pistols; their marksmanship was abominable. Flynn took cover behind a beam and looked for his assailant. A shadow moved and Flynn snapped a shot at it. Seven left in his gun. He turned and resumed his hasty retreat without observing the effect of his shot.

Michael heard two more shots behind him but didn't see their effects. Ahead of him a shadow moved. It was Chadwick waving to him. She had found a hatch.

"It's not locked," she said as Flynn caught up with her.

"Very careless of someone," Flynn replied, catching his breath.

"No, I mean there's no lock, period."

Of course—the basement wasn't open to the public; there was no need to lock the hatches. Their only function was to limit the air loss in case of a hull breach.

"I didn't want to go through . . . unarmed," Chadwick said hesitantly.

"Well, if there's no one waiting on the other side and if that goon back there stays to take care of the one I stunned, we should make a clean getaway. Stand back against the bulkhead."

Flynn eased the hatch open. Its hinges squeaked. There was no airlock; Flynn could see directly into the next section of the basement. To his surprise, it was only four meters across. "What the hell . . . It's the balancing weight track!"

Jupiter Station rotated about its axis. To keep the Station's center of mass on the axis, three huge iron weights moved under computer control on the track which Flynn and Chadwick had encountered. Early in the Station's history the weight system had been a maintenance nightmare: the weights had jammed on small imperfections in the rail on which they rode. By the time the Station had been extended the engineers had gained more confidence in the Station's plumbing and had found sufficient water in icy moonlets; the Station's extension and all of the satellites were balanced by pumped water.

"I remember this from my orientation tour," Chadwick said.

Flynn glanced behind him; the pursuers must have been getting close. "Do you remember the fastest way out of here?"

Chadwick shook her head. "It was a guided tour. Without the guide I would have been lost down here in one minute."

There was another hatch directly across the track. Flynn led the way, looking in both directions for moving weights. It was an unnecessary precaution: at that time of the evening very little was moving on the Station and there was no need to reposition the weights to compensate. Flynn opened the hatch on the other side of the track. It squeaked on its hinges, too. He looked cautiously into the next section but saw only a duplicate of the section he had just left: more dim emergency lights and shadows everywhere. Flynn had to force himself to take his finger off the trigger of his pistol. He took a deep breath and darted through the hatch. Nobody fired at him. Chadwick came through the hatch and closed it as quietly as she could. The hinges squeaked again.

Flynn still couldn't get a dial tone on his telephone. "They must have shut down every repeater in the basement," he muttered to himself.

"Now which way?" Chadwick asked.

"The average goon has the IQ of a grapefruit. They'll expect us to keep moving along the Station axis. So we'll head around the circumference." He pointed to his right. "Let's go."

Jupiter Station was over three kilometers in circumference. Flynn wanted to move at least a kilometer in that direction before heading again along the axis, but an axial bulkhead blocked his path only one hundred meters from the hatch. He led Chadwick along that bulkhead, looking for another hatch. Then a laser pulse hit the bulkhead between them, missing Flynn's head by less than twenty centimeters and scaring the breath out of both of them. Flynn dove for the deck and Chadwick landed right next to him.

"This is not happening," she said, her eyes tightly closed. "I am asleep in my own bed. I'm just having a nightmare, that's all. Any second now I will awaken. This is just a nightmare."

"Then stop snoring," Flynn ordered. He raised his head

to look for his assailant and a laser pulse just missed his hair. Ozone stung his nostrils. He hugged the deck, submerging himself in the shadows, and crawled along the bulkhead. The deck was not cold—the heat the Station lost through infrared radiation was partially replaced by the eddy currents induced in the steel skin by the Station's rotation in Jupiter's intense magnetic field. Flynn looked back to make sure that Chadwick was following; she crawled very well for someone who was at home asleep.

"Hurry up!" someone said. "That way!"

Flynn wished he knew which way "that way" was. He assumed that a goon was being vectored to cut them off. Flynn kept crawling until he reached a vertical girder, behind which he could stand erect. He peered cautiously around the edge in the direction from which the shots had come but saw nothing. When he looked around the other side of the column, however, he saw a backlit silhouette moving quickly. It was definitely trying to get in front of Flynn and Chadwick, but it was moving as though it didn't know it was being observed. It became less of a silhouette and more of a shadow as it approached the bulkhead along which Flynn had been crawling. Flynn dropped into a crouch and rested his elbow on his knee to steady his aim. He put his sight on the next vertical girder in his path. The shadow reached the girder, hesitated, then peeked around the edge, right where the red dot of Flynn's sight was waiting. Flynn shot the shadow in the face. It managed a loud grunt before it collapsed.

"Roscoe?" the same voice called. "Roscoe! Is that you? Roscoe, where the hell are you?"

Flynn crawled to where Roscoe lay on the floor. His laser pistol had fallen from his grasp and was lying next to him. Even in the dim light, Flynn only had to glance at it to know that it couldn't be fired by someone who wasn't wearing an activation ring. Roscoe was wearing two such rings, one on each hand, but the rings fit tightly and Flynn couldn't pull them off of Roscoe's fingers. He chose the direction with the fewest obstructions and, mindful of the low overhead, threw the laser pistol as far as he could. It struck a support beam with a loud clang and clattered to the floor.

"Roscoe! Is that you? Dammit, Roscoe, they're getting away!"

Chadwick came crawling along the bulkhead toward Flynn and the unconscious guard. She bent down to remove the guard's ID badge. "I don't want them claiming that this never happened."

The hatch in the axial bulkhead was within sight. Flynn and Chadwick crawled to it. They could hear the other goon making his way toward where Flynn had thrown the pistol. The hatch squeaked when they opened it, drawing laser pulses from the remaining goon. They crawled over the hatch coaming and closed the hatch behind them.

Flynn stood up. His telephone still didn't work and he had only six shots left in his gun, but he was starting to understand the basement layout. The compartments had an airlock to the Station proper near the center and a hatch in each bulkhead. The security guards were moving swiftly through the Station's streets and entering the compartments through the airlocks. Either the watch commander had stopped panicking or, more likely, Silvanus Drake had arrived and taken command. Flynn didn't know how many guards were trying to corral him and Chadwick. It was time to change strategy.

"Come on," he said, and started toward the center of the compartment. He heard the sound of an airlock opening somewhere in front of him.

Chadwick heard the same sound. "There are more of them."

"But they're over a hundred meters away. We'll take cover here."

Flynn pulled Chadwick down behind a deck beam within easy view of the hatch through which they had just come. He couldn't see the hatch begin to open in the dim light, but he heard it squeak. He rested his gun on the beam and took careful aim. Roscoe's fate had taught this goon the virtue of caution. He opened the hatch just enough to slip through, and moved quickly along the bulkhead. Flynn didn't like his chances of hitting a crossing target in the bad light, but the goon was only fifteen meters away. Flynn's shot hit the guard in the side. The guard gasped in surprise and slumped against the bulkhead. Flynn shot him again and the guard collapsed. Four shots left.

"Let's go," Flynn said. He leaped over the beam and dashed for the unconscious guard. He scooped up the guard's pistol. His activation rings were also too tight for Flynn to remove.

Chadwick stepped to the other side of the guard and removed his ID badge. She put it in her coat pocket with the other badge she had claimed. "I'm going to stuff these up Drake's nose."

Flynn scratched his head. "Is that some sort of legal maneuver that I've never heard of?"

"Very funny." Chadwick glanced over her shoulder toward the sound of people hurrying in her direction. "We'd better move." She set off along the bulkhead.

Flynn grabbed the collar of her jacket and pulled her back. "Wrong direction," he said, and pushed her toward the hatch. "Back the way we came."

"But, the goons are—"

145

"The goons are in front of us."

The guard hadn't closed the hatch. Flynn followed Wendy through it. Roscoe was still on the floor but was moaning and trying to rise. Flynn thought of the four shots remaining in his stun pistol and decided he would have to trust in Roscoe's slow recovery. "Follow me," he whispered. "Quietly."

Flynn led the way toward the center of that section of the basement. He discarded the laser pistol he had taken from the guard in the shadow beneath a beam. Michael was hurrying and twice barked his shins on deck beams. In the bad light he went fifty meters too far before he realized that either the compartment was much bigger than he had thought or that he had missed the airlock. He doubled back, moving to the right of the track he taken. He still didn't recognize the airlock when he saw it, but he recognized the ladder that extended from the airlock to the floor.

"Here we are," he said, pointing out the airlock to Chadwick. "The goons have been waiting at the airlocks," he explained. "Up on level one. That way they can keep in touch with Security Control. Drake sends them down when he learns that we've entered a particular compartment."

"Here's somebody!" came a faint voice from the direction of the hatch. "Damn it to hell! He got Roscoe, too!"

"Here come the guards from the other section," Flynn said.

Someone shouted, "The airlock!" but the guards were too late.

Flynn followed Chadwick up the ladder. In the light from the airlock he could see that the left pocket and sleeve of her coat had also been torn during the evening's adventure. He had warned her, but she had not listened. That, Flynn knew, was one of the two problems with

146

women: they wouldn't listen to him.

Flynn closed the lower hatch and pressurized the lock. They were safe from the goons in the basement, who wouldn't be able to open the lower hatch against the air pressure. The real test would come when he opened the top hatch.

The lock reached station pressure. Flynn looked at Chadwick, his gun in his hand. "You ready?" She nodded. "If they're waiting for us, I just want to say it's been nice knowing you."

She closed her eyes. "I know I'm dreaming this, and that I'm about to wake up, so I can say it's been nice knowing you, too."

Flynn opened the top hatch. There was no one there.

He climbed out of the airlock and found himself at the side of a minor street on level one. A four-seat electric car bearing the logo of the Conglomerated Mining and Manufacturing Company stood next to the lock. Company maintenance shops, closed for the night, lined the street. Flynn extended his hand and helped Wendy out of the lock. He took his phone from his pocket, flipped it open, and heard a dial tone. He said, "Emergency!"

Chadwick grabbed Flynn's shoulder and pointed up the street. It ran around the circumference of the Station and curved upward out of sight in both directions, but in the direction Wendy was pointing an electric car had just come into view. It was traveling at high speed and bore two individuals dressed in orange coveralls.

Flynn didn't help Chadwick into the car. He jumped into the control seat while Chadwick leaped in beside him. He flipped the power switch. Nothing happened.

He looked at his companion. She was staring at the control console. "My executive override authority doesn't apply to Company vehicles," she said.

Flynn wanted to spew forth a stream of vulgar language, but a laser pulse flashing overhead made him shout, "Run!" instead. Just ahead was a side street. Flynn followed Chadwick in the dash for cover as laser pulses hissed against the walls along the street. They turned the corner just in time.

And ran right into a blue-uniformed United States marshal.

The deputy knew the sound of pulsed lasers and had drawn his own weapon. When he saw the stun pistol in Flynn's hand he leveled his gun at the investigator and said, "Federal officer! Freeze!"

Flynn and Chadwick slammed to a halt. Neither so much as blinked.

"Put that gun down!" the marshal ordered.

While Flynn was obeying, Wendy said, "Officer, my name is Wendy Chadwick and I'm the Company's attorney and—"

Chadwick was interrupted by the squeal of rubber on metal as an electric car skidded into the turn for the side street, and then stopped abruptly when the guards in the car saw the marshal.

"What the hell's going on here?" the deputy asked.

The goon sitting beside the driver had his gun in his hand. He pointed at Flynn and Chadwick and said, "They killed a couple of security guards!"

All of Chadwick's legal training was deleted as her temper boiled over. "Like hell!" she exclaimed. *"They* assaulted *us!"* She pointed at the Company guards while looking at the marshal. "I want them arrested!"

"Have the guard put his gun down," Flynn said calmly. "I don't want any 'accidental' discharges."

"Company security personnel are authorized to carry weapons!" the guard said.

The marshal disagreed with him. "This is a public street. You have no authority here. Put the gun away." The guard hesitated. The marshal directed his own laser away from Flynn and toward the security guard. "Put the gun away!"

The guard didn't move. "Do it," the driver said in a voice barely above a whisper. The guard reluctantly did so.

"As I was saying," Chadwick said, "I'm Wendy Chadwick and I'm the Company's legal director, and we have been assaulted and I want those men—"

"I don't care if you're the queen of England," the deputy interrupted. "You'll speak when I tell you to." He took his telephone from his belt while waving his pistol back and forth between Flynn and the two guards in the car. "This is Gunderson again," he said into the phone. "I still don't know what's going on, but you'd better respond a supervisor to my location."

"There are some stunned people in the basement," Flynn said.

The marshal sighed. "Better send everybody you can spare," he said into the phone. "I think I have only the tip of the iceberg here."

Chadwick pointed emphatically at the guards. "I want them arrested!" she repeated.

"Lady," the marshal said wearily, "you're all under arrest."

Chapter 6

There were government standards, based on psychological research, for the dimensions, lighting, furniture, and colors of interrogation rooms, to insure that suspects were not subconsciously made to feel threatened, uneasy, or in any way induced to confess or otherwise forfeit their rights. The interrogation room in the Marshals Office on Jupiter Station met the standards. The decor was almost cheerful, from the pastel colors of the walls to the warm lighting. The chairs were comfortable.

Flynn, Chadwick, and the two security guards arrested with them were seated on one side of the table in the center of the room. Marshal Ben Wofford sat in the middle of the other side of the table. U.S. Attorney Kyle Pierce was at his left and Silvanus Drake sat on Wofford's right. The table was bare except for Flynn's computer (which, with its legal software, was functioning as Flynn's attorney), Flynn's stun pistol with its power supply removed, and the ID badges that Chadwick had appropriated from two of the goons that Flynn had stunned. The clock on the wall behind Flynn had an analog display and both hands were pointing nearly straight up.

Wendy Chadwick leaned over the table, as if proximity to her audience would make her words easier to understand. "Do I have to spell it out for you?" she said, the energy in her voice belying the late hour. *"Arrested!"* she insisted, pounding her fist on the table. *"A, r, r—"*

"I know how to spell," Marshal Wofford said wearily. He

had been working long hours on the Vasquez case and he desperately wanted to be back in bed with his wife, from whose embraces Deputy Feldstein's call had dislodged him.

"The charge is attempted murder," Chadwick continued. "That's *murder: m, u, r—*"

"Attempted murder requires felonious intent," Silvanus Drake said calmly. "The two security guards who went to the warehouse were sent there to arrest a trespasser, who was the subject of a memo from Mr. Warshovsky issued . . ." Drake glanced at the wall clock. "This very afternoon, I believe with advice from our Legal Department." He was looking directly at Chadwick and smiling as much as he ever smiled, the corners of his mouth barely turning upward. "The fact that Mr. Flynn has a permit to carry a stun pistol is a matter of public record, so Security Control warned the two guards that Mr. Flynn might be armed."

"First of all," Chadwick replied, "Flynn was not trespassing. He was with me, which should have been obvious to the goons monitoring the displays in Security Control. And Flynn's stun pistol was in his pocket and out of sight until *after* your goons opened fire on him without even attempting to place him under arrest. And finally, the guns carried by those guards could have been set to stun, in which case nobody's life would have been in danger tonight."

Drake continued as though he had not heard the lawyer's words. "Under the stress of attempting to apprehend a man about whom they had been warned by the Company's general manager just hours before, in the poor light of the warehouse—"

"The overhead lights were all on!" Chadwick interrupted. "That place was lit up like a sports stadium!"

"They thought they saw a deadly weapon in Mr. Flynn's

hand and proceeded to defend themselves," Drake said calmly. "A stun pistol usually causes no permanent harm and has almost no deterrent effect; if you thought that someone was shooting a deadly weapon at you, you'd shoot back with the same, just to keep his head down."

"What did they think they saw in my hand?" Chadwick demanded. "Or when your goons feel threatened, do they simply try to kill everyone in sight, even after I had identified myself to them?"

Drake managed his small smile again. "Anyone can claim to be Wendy Chadwick."

"Good point," Flynn conceded casually. He was slouching in his chair, his feet extending so far under the table that he had to be careful that he didn't kick Mr. Pierce. He glanced at Chadwick. "Next time, try claiming that you're Silvanus Drake."

Drake ignored the investigator. He could see that Wofford didn't like Flynn and would not be disposed to believe him. Chadwick was the real problem. The Company's own attorney bringing charges against Company employees could not be explained away. He said, "Security Control informed the other responding personnel only that one of the guards in the warehouse had been hit. They assumed that he had been hit by a lethal weapon. As Mr. Flynn . . . disabled other guards, rumors distorted the incident into a case of multiple homicide of Company Security personnel."

"In which case the marshals should certainly have been informed," Pierce said. He was a thin man of average height, with a thin, pointed nose, black hair, and black eyebrows. Unlike Wofford, he had volunteered for the assignment to Jupiter Station—the colonization of the Solar System would soon create demand in the Justice Department for lawyers with space experience, and Pierce had considered the assignment to be a shrewd career move. He felt no need to ingratiate himself with powerful civilians. "But your security guards chased Mr. Flynn and Ms. Chadwick through half of the basement without even mentioning to the authorities that they were trying to catch murder suspects. I get the impression that they didn't want the marshals to know what was going on."

"The Company is in charge of security in areas of the Station not leased to the government or the public," Drake explained, "and the marshals don't have enough people to patrol the areas for which they are responsible. We expected no help from them and therefore requested none. They would have been informed at the appropriate time."

"How?" Pierce demanded. "By gunfire on a public street?"

Drake said, "Those were warning shots."

"Warning shots are unnecessary since their pistols could be set to stun," Pierce said.

"Our security guards rarely have to use their pistols," Drake explained. "Mr. Gutierrez and Mr. Maryk are obviously out of practice in their use."

"I trust you will remind them of the legal restrictions on the use of deadly force?" Pierce asked.

"Just teach them to shoot straight," Flynn advised. "You wouldn't want them shooting the *wrong* innocent person by mistake."

Pierce stood up. "I see no case against any of these four."

An angry Chadwick stood to confront him. "What do you mean, no case? They tried to kill us! We can prove it!"

"Wendy," Pierce said in the tone of a man who wanted to go home and go to bed, "stop thinking like a victim and think like a lawyer for a change. We can't find the goons that Flynn claims to have stunned—"

"Have you checked the Company hospital?" Flynn suggested.

"Or the laser pistols he claims to have taken from them—"

"Ruger Model twenty-one hundreds don't have transponders," Flynn explained, "and the lighting is terrible down there. It might take me hours to find the one I threw away. But I think I can lead the marshals straight to the other one."

"Even if we find that gun," Pierce continued, "and even if I excluded Company employees from the jury, do you really think we could find twelve people on this station who would vote to convict Company security guards of attempted murder after Silvanus Drake produces communication records of tonight's fracas that prove that the guards had reason to believe that they were trying to apprehend two killers? Besides, no jury is going to believe you or Flynn after they learn that you went to warehouse seven because Flynn has the addlebrained idea that two government investigations and one Company investigation were completely wrong when they found that Jonny Mondragon and Philip Asterbrook were killed in a simple industrial accident in warehouse twelve."

"If they were killed in a simple industrial accident, why were those goons trying to shoot us?" Flynn asked as innocently as he could.

Chadwick was taking Pierce's advice and was trying to think like a lawyer, but before she could argue that same point Pierce turned to Drake and said, "What were you doing while all this was taking place?"

The security director didn't bother to look at Pierce. "I didn't get to Security Control until after Flynn zapped

Santino. By that time the rumors had spread and the other guards thought that Flynn had killed some of their comrades. I didn't know my people were firing pulsed lasers until everybody was arrested."

Pierce stared at Drake and snorted. "I want a complete report on this incident from you by nine o'clock tomorrow morning. A *complete* report, including the video record from the security camera in warehouse seven." Pierce turned to Wofford and said, "The first two guards in the warehouse—"

"Kemper and Santino?"

Pierce nodded. "Kemper and Santino—have some explaining to do. They apparently started this, and, according to what I've heard tonight, without provocation and without instructions. I want to talk to them first thing in the morning. You should have no trouble locating them by then, especially with your friend Drake to help you." He glanced at the people on the other side of the table and then turned back toward Wofford. "Make sure these four have signed their written statements and then turn them loose."

Flynn had already signed his statement. He sprang to his feet, closing his notebook computer and reaching for his pistol in one motion.

Wofford reached across the table and clamped his hand on top of the gun. "The pistol stays," he said. "Your permit to carry a stun gun is hereby suspended."

"The hell it is!" Flynn protested. "Self-defense is *not* one of the reasons listed in the law for suspension of a gun permit!"

"We're still investigating your claim of self-defense," Wofford said.

"Marshal," Pierce said wearily, "give him his gun back."

"Huh? Why?"

"Because the magistrate will give it back to him in court

tomorrow when Flynn requests a hearing on the permit suspension, since he will be represented by an attorney—and I
mean *her* and not *that*." Pierce pointed first at Chadwick
and then at Flynn's computer. "And I will *not* be there to
argue against him."

Wofford reluctantly released his grip on the gun. Flynn
smiled at him and put the pistol in his pocket.

Drake reached for the ID badges, but Chadwick scooped
them off of the table. She waved her finger in his face. "Oh,
no. This isn't finished yet. I am *not* going to let your security guards try to kill me and get away with it unpunished. If
the authorities won't take action, I'll let Ed Warshovsky
handle it."

Drake sat back in his chair. "Warshovsky will back me
up," he said calmly.

"Hah!"

"I'd better show one of your deputies where I hid that
laser right away," Flynn said to Wofford, "because as soon
as your people leave the basement Drake will flood it with
Company guards and by morning there won't be anything
to find."

"I have the entire day shift on overtime right now because of you," Wofford replied. "I can't afford to keep them
on duty any longer."

"I don't need the entire day shift. Just send Deputy
Feldstein. He's on duty right now, anyway." Besides, Flynn
wanted to talk privately with Feldstein. His first altercation
with Drake had been a draw. Flynn wanted to make sure
that he won the next one.

The next morning, Flynn caught up with Kyle Pierce as
the U.S. attorney was leaving his office for the courtroom.
"Ah, Flynn!" Pierce said. "You should have been there this

morning when Santino and Kemper turned themselves in."

"I was watching the morning news report of last night's running gunfight," Flynn replied.

Pierce stopped in his tracks. He looked puzzled. "It wasn't on the news. The Company owns the broadcasting station."

Flynn smiled. "My point exactly."

Pierce shook his head. He resumed walking toward the courtroom. "Well, it's hard to believe that creatures as dumb as Santino and Kemper can walk on two legs without dragging their knuckles on the floor."

"Did they say why they shot at us?"

"They claimed that they thought they had seen a gun in your hand; Kemper, who fired the first shot, thought his gun had been set to stun and fired the first laser pulse by mistake; Santino reset his pistol from stun to kill because he thought Kemper's laser pulse meant that Kemper thought their lives were in extreme danger . . . Everything just got out of hand after that."

"Do you believe them?"

The attorney made a face. "The recorded video was worthless—the security camera was focused on the other side of the warehouse until the lights went out, and it's not a low-light camera. And Santino and Kemper had been coached, by someone who knew that I knew that you didn't pull your gun until after they'd opened fire. They were represented by Mitch Habruch, from Wendy's office, but I'd guess they'd been coached by Silvanus Drake. Wofford wanted to let 'em go; kept saying 'selective prosecution,' which it isn't. You're lucky that you had Wendy along last night, though, to confirm your story, or you'd be the one looking to make bail right now."

Flynn grunted. "Is that so? Funny: I thought I was confirming *her* story."

"Not funny, Mr. Flynn. I know Wendy Chadwick; I don't know you from Santa Claus. And I don't know how you managed to convince Wendy that there was anything suspicious about the deaths of Mondragon and Asterbrook."

"Aside from the fact that all of the important witnesses either retired at a suspiciously young age——"

Pierce cut him off. "I read the statement that you wrote last night. It's all coincidence. I reviewed the marshals' report and the OSHA report to see if there was any basis for legal action against the Company. Those were good investigations. *All* the evidence points to an accident."

"Those government investigations," Flynn replied. "The investigators *thought* that they were investigating an accident. They were only trying to figure out how the accident had occurred. They were *not* trying to figure out what actually happened."

"What do you think actually happened?" Pierce asked. "Why do you think that they were killed in warehouse seven and moved to warehouse twelve?"

"I think they were moving something the Company wanted to keep secret when they were killed, and that it was easier for the Company to move the bodies away from equipment than it was to move the equipment away from the bodies. I think that they were moving something so illegal—like the equipment for a polymethyl two four dibenzolacetate manufacturing facility—that the Company would try to kill us if we found out about it."

Pierce stopped and turned to face Flynn. "Self-defense is not justification for revoking a gun permit, but mental instability is. What the hell makes you think that the Company is manufacturing polymethyl two four?"

"Because somebody's making the stuff someplace, and

no law enforcement agency has ever found out where. No one's ever looked out here."

Pierce shook his head. "I repeat: how did you get Wendy Chadwick to believe any of this . . . this . . . nonsense?"

"Having the goons shoot at her helped," Flynn said. "Then there's the fact that the marshals haven't closed their investigation into the death of Vasquez. Is it true that they still haven't found his connection?"

Pierce pointed his finger at Flynn's face. "You even *look* in the direction of an open police investigation and I'll have your investigator's license suspended!"

"Rumor has it that Vasquez never had anything shipped to him here," Flynn continued. "So if no one was shipping it to him, where was he getting it?"

Pierce looked thoughtfully at Flynn, then turned and headed toward the courtroom.

"Are you going to charge Santino and Kemper?" Flynn asked.

Pierce stopped walking and turned around. He nodded. "Not for attempted murder, though—no motive for them to kill you. It will be conduct regardless of life or use of excessive force in performance of their security duties. Or maybe both."

"You implied that you didn't believe their story," Flynn said. "And you don't believe the Company is producing polymethyl two four. So why do you think that Kemper and Santino tried to kill us?"

Pierce reached out and took hold of the doorknob of the courtroom. "I think that your investigation has greatly irritated Company honchos. I think that Kemper and Santino knew that. I think that they were stupid enough to believe that if they put a permanent end to that investigation, they would be greatly rewarded."

"Isn't that a motive for attempted murder?"

"What I think isn't evidence that I can introduce in court. Good day, Mr. Flynn."

Pierce opened the courtroom door and stepped through it. As Flynn turned to go, he noticed that the security camera down the street was pointed in his direction. A security camera in a public area didn't have to show a red light when it was active, but Flynn still got the impression that the camera was focused on him.

The proposal was so shocking that Wendy Chadwick popped out of her chair as though it was spring-loaded. Her temper, brought under control overnight, boiled over again. She leaned across Ed Warshovsky's desk. "Get them *released?*" she said, her tone an equal mixture of anger and disbelief. "They tried to kill me!"

"No, not you in particular," Silvanus Drake said from the chair next to the one that Chadwick had occupied. "Kemper and Santino had never been shot at before. Under the pressure of the moment, they did not recognize you, and the guard monitoring the security camera didn't tell them who you were."

"Oh, so I should feel better because your goons thought that they were killing Flynn's latest bimbo girlfriend instead of the head of the Company's legal department?"

Warshovsky took a sharp breath. "How many times do I have to insist that the Company's security personnel are not to be referred to as 'goons'?"

Chadwick stared at her boss. "What would you call the thugs that tried to kill you?"

"Wendy, your job is to represent the Company's best interests. Our best interest in this case is to get those two employees released."

Chadwick hated it when Warshovsky started calling her by her first name. He did that whenever he became paternal toward her. She didn't want her boss acting like her father. "I cannot possibly represent them," Chadwick said. "First of all, I am one of the people bringing charges against them. Second, Kemper and Santino wouldn't want me as their attorney because the principle of attorney-client privilege doesn't apply if the attorney has been threatened by the client—being shot at with pulsed lasers qualifies as a threat—so I could be forced to tell the court anything they told me. Finally, why the hell are these two thugs still working for us? Why weren't they fired last night? Do you *want* attempted murderers working for you?"

"They won't be charged with attempted murder," Drake said, his face, as usual, expressionless. "They'll be charged with use of excessive force in the enforcement of the law."

"We shouldn't want guards who use excessive force working for us, either."

"We don't expect you to represent them," Warshovsky explained. "Mr. Habruch will do that. He's arranging to pay their bail right now."

Warshovsky was noticeably surprised by the effect that his words had on Wendy's normally pleasant features. *"We're paying their bail?"* she almost shrieked.

"That's only a short-term solution," Drake said. "We don't want this going to trial. But Kyle Pierce trusts you. If you withdraw your charges, we might be able to convince him that Kemper and Santino should not be prosecuted."

"Oh, I don't want 'em prosecuted," Chadwick replied. "I want 'em *persecuted!* They tried to kill me, and I want them tried, convicted, and sentenced to ten years!"

"Wendy—" Warshovsky began.

"Don't 'Wendy' me! I can't *believe* that two of our goons

161

would try to kill me and that you'd ask *me* for help to get them released!"

"It is Mr. Drake's opinion that if you don't withdraw the charges—"

"He probably told them to kill me!"

Drake closed his eyes. "I told them only to arrest the two of you and bring you to Security Control so I could be told why you were ignoring the instructions that Mr. Warshovsky had issued. The security records will show—"

"Oh, and you've never faked security records before?" Wendy protested. "You don't fool me, Drake. I've observed you ever since I came to Jupiter Station. The only rules you've ever followed have been your own. You always do whatever you damn well please. You've run over, outmaneuvered, or submarined everybody who got in your way. I *know* that you surreptitiously search the personal belongings of everybody that comes here. You have no respect for the civil rights of anybody. What kind of person is that to direct Station security?"

For the first time in the two years that she had known Silvanus Drake, Chadwick thought she saw his eyes take on a glimmer of steeliness. "Lady," he said, "you work in a world of rules, motions, and reversible errors. If a decision goes against you, you can appeal. But my adversaries are people who break rules. If I don't like the outcome of a confrontation, I can't petition anyone for a retrial or a new hearing. If I make a mistake, Company property is damaged or destroyed and Company employees are injured or killed. And don't think that can't happen! A hundred thousand people back on Earth are unemployed because the products they manufactured are now made here at lower cost. I've lost count of the number of firms that have gone out of business because we are producing better products than they did. There are a lot of people that would like to put us out of business by any means they can. Some of them have access to plutonium or enriched uranium, and if they can read at the eighth-grade level they can make a nuke big enough to destroy this station and kill everybody on it. So if I have to violate their 'rights' by inspecting *everything* and *everybody* that comes here, I'll do it. What kind of man am I, lady? I'm the kind of man who lets you sleep at night without worrying about dying before you wake."

Still sitting in his chair, Drake leaned toward Chadwick. His tone back to normal, he said, "What I'd like to know, Ms. Chadwick, is what kind of lawyer takes the side of her adversary against her own clients?"

"I am not taking Flynn's side!" Wendy protested.

"Then why did you let him into warehouse seven?"

"I let *myself* into warehouse seven! I was trying to find out what really happened to Asterbrook and Mondragon, because people around here," she glanced at Warshovsky, "haven't been giving me all of the facts. I did not want to learn them in discovery just before I went to trial, and I was getting very tired of getting them from Flynn. Everything Flynn has told me has checked out, so when Flynn told me that the pulleys on the overhead cranes in warehouse twelve and seven had been switched, I investigated, and—surprise, surprise—he was right again."

"Pulleys?" Warshovsky said with a puzzled expression on his face.

"The pulley on the crane in warehouse twelve right now is the pulley that the manufacturer put on it, but it's not the pulley that was on the crane the day of the 'accident,' " Wendy explained. "That pulley is on the crane in warehouse seven at this moment—I checked our records, and we don't have any other pulleys that will fit the crane in warehouse twelve. But we have no records that the pulleys were switched."

"Are we . . . Does that mean that we were negligent?" Warshovsky asked.

"That's what I thought at first," Chadwick said. "A simple foul-up: somebody switches pulleys because he needs a bigger one in warehouse seven or a smaller one in warehouse twelve, and he doesn't tell anybody about it, so somebody else runs a line that's too big through the pulley in warehouse twelve and Mondragon and Asterbrook pay for the mistake with their lives. But I stopped thinking it was anything as simple as that as soon as his goons—" she pointed at Drake, "tried to kill us."

"The action of the guards had nothing to do with the accident," Drake said. "They were dispatched to warehouse seven to arrest a trespasser."

"Like hell! We went to warehouse twelve first. We were there for . . . ten minutes. No goons showed up. You didn't care if we looked around warehouse twelve, because there was nothing there for us to find. But as soon as we went to warehouse seven, the shooting started. No, Flynn was right again: Asterbrook and Mondragon didn't die in warehouse twelve. They were killed in warehouse seven, and their bodies were moved to warehouse twelve where a fake accident was arranged because the Company didn't want government investigators seeing what was in seven."

"I ordered no action while you were in warehouse twelve because I was trying to figure out what was going on," Drake explained. "When you moved to warehouse seven I decided that I could figure out what was going on *after* I put a stop to the guided tour that you were giving Flynn. I would have done the same thing if you had let him into . . . oh, say, the air reprocessing plant. There's nothing special about warehouse seven."

"We'll see about that," Chadwick replied, "as soon as I get the results of the tests I ordered this morning."

Drake and Warshovsky exchanged glances. "Tests?" Warshovsky asked. "What tests?"

"Modern forensic science can detect microscopic quantities of blood," Chadwick explained, "and when blood traces from warehouse seven are DNA-matched to Mondragon and Asterbrook—who, according to their work logs, were never in warehouse seven—the marshals will have to take action. Now, before the authorities do that, would one of you like to tell me what really happened to Mondragon and Asterbrook so that I can prepare to defend the Company?"

Warshovsky's eyes were directed at the top of his desk. "I'm sorry to hear that you wasted Legal Department funds on those tests. There is nothing in warehouse seven to find. There never was."

Chadwick stared at her boss. It wasn't like Warshovsky to speak to her without looking at her. "I am your attorney!" she said, tapping her chest. "You can tell me what happened! I can't legally or ethically divulge it! But I can't give you the proper legal advice or a good legal defense if you don't tell me what occurred!"

Warshovsky looked up from his desk. "An accident occurred. That's all. Dammit, Wendy, I am not lying to you!"

Chadwick returned Warshovsky's gaze. "Then maybe you should consider the possibility that some of your employees are lying to you." She sat in her chair.

"None of this is getting the charges against Kemper and Santino dismissed," Drake said.

"The charges are not going to be dismissed," Chadwick replied. "And we're not going to try to get them out of jail, because they—and all those other trigger-happy goons that tried to kill me last night—are going to be fired."

"We can't fire people for doing what they think is their job," Warshovsky said.

"Who made them think that murder was part of their job?"

"We did, when we issued that memo banning Flynn from Company property and instructing our employees not to cooperate with him," Warshovsky replied.

"That memo said nothing about shooting on sight!"

"No, but . . . apparently we have not given our guards sufficient training," Warshovsky said. "Mr. Drake and I have already discussed the increase in his budget necessary to train his personnel properly. But it is our fault that those two guards—Kemper and Santino—in the warehouse last night were not properly trained. It is our fault that they overreacted. *Our* fault, Ms. Chadwick. It would be extremely unethical for us to fire Company personnel when the mistake was ours."

Chadwick was unimpressed. "I have no security training at all, and if the roles had been reversed last night I would have had no inclination to try to kill anybody. We are not dealing with a lack of training, but with a lack of character." When that didn't bring a response, Wendy said, "Let me put it this way: either they go, or I go."

Warshovsky considered his words carefully. "Ms. Chadwick, you had a very distressful experience last night. You probably got very little sleep. Why don't you take the weekend to think over what we've said here this morning?"

Chadwick stared at Warshovsky, unwilling to believe what she had heard. Finally she said quietly, "I see." She rose from her chair and left the room without looking back.

★ ★ ★ ★ ★

Kemper and Santino had attacked Flynn with deadly weapons in a Federal jurisdiction; Federal law required a minimum one-year prison sentence. They might agree to testify against their boss in exchange for having the charges dropped, but Silvanus Drake lived by the code of the professional security man, the professional keeper of secrets. He would go to jail rather than reveal what he knew about the deaths of Asterbrook and Mondragon. So unless Kemper and Santino knew something about the "accident," their arrest wasn't going help Donald and Helene Asterbrook learn what had happened to their son. Flynn would have to press on. He assumed that Asterbrook and Mondragon had been moving the polymeth fabrication lab from the Station to the brand-new Satellite Juliet. Flynn's next move, therefore, would be to persuade Wendy Chadwick to give him a tour of the new satellite.

Flynn, however, wouldn't recognize polymeth fabrication equipment if he tripped over it. That information was certainly in the library, but the goons were monitoring Flynn's communications and he didn't want them to know what he was doing. Not all of the information in the library was computerized, however; it had some hardcopy books. The public access point, from which those books could be checked out, also had computer terminals that were available to the public. The security cameras would reveal that Flynn had gone to the library, but the cameras were probably being monitored by computer, and Flynn hoped that the computer wouldn't consider his visit to the library to be suspicious enough to eavesdrop on the library's computers to see what Flynn was reading.

The library belonged to the Company, of course. The Company had created it when the Station was built, both because the Company's technical staff needed one and to provide recreational opportunities for Company employees. The government had leased public access to the library when it had taken over administration of civil authority on the Station. The library was on the Main Plaza, opposite the waterfall from the Company offices. There were twenty computer terminals in the lobby but only four of them were in use, all by children. The kids were staring intently at their holographic displays and ignored Flynn, who sat down in front of a terminal with a display that could not be seen by the security camera.

Polymethyl two four was the most abused drug in the solar system. Flynn was unprepared for the amount of research that had been published. The library had thousands of citations; there were sixty-four devoted to the drug's manufacture. Flynn started with the most recent.

Flynn had taken three semesters of chemistry in college and he considered himself to be chemically literate, but the papers in chemistry journals on polymethyl two four manufacture might as well have been written in Chinese ideographs. He wondered if the drug really was so hard to make, or if the instructions to make it were just too hard to read. He didn't make progress until he switched the library search to articles in the popular press. Then understandable information poured into his terminal so quickly that Flynn guessed that someone must have researched the same topic before, so that the library computer had the search on file.

Polymethyl two four was a large, complex molecule. It had been discovered in the byproducts of a chemical experiment, which had reposed in a refrigerator in a biochemistry lab at Cal Tech for two years until a curious graduate student had analyzed the contents and found traces of a very large molecule. Parts of polymethyl two four were electrically active and the grad student had managed to accumulate a milligram of the stuff by centrifuging followed by electrophoretic separation. After determining its chemical structure he had tested it on laboratory rats and observed startling effects. To test it on primates he needed much more of the drug, but repetition of the original experiment was not a feasible way of producing the many grams of polymeth needed. Fortunately, the method of optimal sequential synthesis had been developed during the preceding decade, and the grad student had spent the rest of his time at Cal Tech applying the method to the manufacturing of polymethyl two four. The successful synthesis of such a large molecule had done much to popularize the optimal sequential synthesis technique and had formed the basis of the student's doctoral thesis. The task of testing polymeth on primates had fallen on another grad student. It had had no observable effect on monkeys, but had seemed to have a strong analgesic effect on chimpanzees. The second grad student had then rashly taken the drug himself to see if it would relieve the pain of a sprained ankle, and within a month polymeth was the most sought after designer drug on the west coast of North America. It had appeared to have no harmful physical side effects and within a year the drug was in use worldwide. By the time governments had gotten around to making it illegal because it was so strongly addicting psychologically, the first deaths—due to the arterial degradation produced in eighteen percent of long-term users—had occurred. Law enforcement agencies had cracked down, but despite the complexity of the synthesis procedure not a single illegal polymeth fabrication lab had ever been found.

After four hours of reading and comparing, Flynn had a pretty good idea of how to make polymeth. The optimal sequential synthesis process involved one hundred and seventy-one separate steps, many of which had to be precisely controlled. Eight of them were laser-induced reactions, one of which had to be performed at a temperature of eighty-seven point two degrees, plus or minus half a degree. Eleven filtrations were needed. Half of the processing steps required heating (to different temperatures). Nine different catalysts were used. As far as Flynn could tell, the equipment required to manufacture polymeth would fill at least three standard shipping containers.

Flynn read on. Not only was polymethyl two four hard to synthesize, it wasn't easy to store. Such a large molecule with so many weak chemical bonds was unstable; its half-life at room temperature was only eighty-five days. It froze at two degrees and disintegrated rapidly in that state. It could be stored for months at five degrees, which was why addicts kept their supplies in refrigerators. Robot ships carrying manufactured products from Jupiter Station to the rest of the solar system could be kept at five degrees without discomforting passengers. Some of those ships went to planet three; others headed for Mars, Ceres, or one of the other asteroids. Jupiter Station, although seven hundred and fifty million kilometers from the sun, was actually an ideal polymeth manufacturing and distribution center.

Six hours after entering the library, Flynn leaned back from his terminal and glanced around. The children that had been using the other terminals when he had arrived were gone, their places taken by other children plus two men and a woman. Flynn checked the notes he had been making on his computer, made sure that he had downloaded all the files he wanted, and left the library. The workday was ending and the streets were filling with homeward bound people, all looking forward to an exciting weekend—the Station's eagerly awaited airball tournament was starting. Flynn wasn't an airball fan and intended to spend his weekend working.

A crowd had gathered at Betty's Bar. People were standing in the doorway and peering through the windows. Flynn could sense bad news. He stood next to a man who was craning his neck over the people standing in the doorway to watch the video monitor behind the bar.

"What happened?" Flynn asked.

"Mine blow-out," the man said without looking at Flynn.

"Here?"

The man shook his head. "Ceres."

"The Company operation?"

The man shook his head again. "European consortium."

"Casualties?"

"They think they lost the whole shift. Twenty, maybe twenty-five."

Flynn pursed his lips. He was taller than the man with whom he had been conversing and could see the video monitor without difficulty. Solar System News was showing the scene of the disaster. The rock to which the access and life support structures had been attached had given way, and the air pressure in the shaft had blown the structures right off of the surface and had spewed everything in the shaft into space. Flynn was looking at the reason why miners got paid twice as much as manufacturing workers. He did some mental arithmetic: Ceres was currently on the far side of the sun; the video, relayed through Earth, had to be at least an hour old.

"It's hard to believe," the man next to Flynn said. "Those European Union safety regs are so stiff . . . We out-

171

produce them easily. I never would have thought that they'd have a blow-out."

"Rocks know nothing about safety regulations," Flynn replied. There probably had been no fractures at that point when the access structure had been built and the shaft begun; the mining operation had weakened the rock. Nor did the rocks know that the European Union, despite its effort to insure a safe working environment, had mandated that there would be a surfeit of workers for the rocks to kill—EU job-protection laws had produced a work shift with three times as many people as the Company would have used (the American Job Protection Act did not apply to U.S. territories like Jupiter Station). Flynn wondered if the man next to him was a miner. Even if he wasn't, he undoubtedly knew many people who were.

Flynn returned to his apartment. Furrball met him at the door, rubbing against his legs and purring. The cat's dish was full. The microcam was still behind the painting on the wall. Flynn's broker had left another message. So had Barbara.

Flynn decided that he could go for a big bowl of chili. He took a container from the freezer and removed the lid. The door alarm sounded.

The image on the monitor was that of Wendy Chadwick. She was wearing a fashionable business suit in dark metallic orange that almost matched her hair. Flynn wiped his hands and opened the door.

"Ms. Chadwick!" he said cheerfully. He glanced at her empty hands. "No legal writs this time?"

Chadwick moistened her lips. "Could I . . . could I come in for a moment?"

Flynn stood aside. "Be my guest." He closed the door behind the attorney. "Would you like to join me for dinner? I'm making chili."

"Oh, no. I can't stay. I just wanted to tell you that—"

"Aw, come on. You have to eat something. And you're going to love my chili." Flynn returned to the kitchen. "Take a seat," he called over his shoulder.

"I really can't stay, Mr. Flynn. I just dropped in . . . well, I thought I should tell you in person that . . . The accident didn't occur in warehouse seven."

Flynn popped back out of the kitchen, disbelief on his face, certain he had misunderstood. "Huh?"

"I had warehouse seven tested for blood by an independent laboratory," Chadwick explained. "Radiometric resonance test for hemoglobin. It can detect micrograms—"

"I know about radiometric resonance," Flynn interrupted.

"We found minute blood traces from an accident two years ago—somebody's foot got run over by a forklift—and from another accident four years ago when somebody else cut his hand on a sharp object protruding from a packing case. But there was no trace of Asterbrook or Mondragon's blood. None. Zippo. Zilch. Being crushed the way they were, blood would have splashed everywhere. There's no way anyone could have cleaned that warehouse well enough to get rid of all of it. So they weren't crushed to death in warehouse seven."

Flynn turned and walked slowly into the kitchen. He couldn't have been wrong about that warehouse—Silvanus Drake had confirmed that part of Flynn's hypothesis when he had sent his goons to warehouse seven but not to warehouse twelve. "The chili will be ready in a minute."

"I told you, Mr. Flynn, I can't stay for dinner."

Flynn put the container in the microwave. "Sure you can."

Wendy wasn't sure what to say. Flynn was not behaving

the way she had thought he would. "Look, if you want to discuss this—"

"Dinner first," Flynn said. "Talk later. Can I get you something to drink?"

Chadwick hesitated. The chili smelled surprisingly good. Drake's report on Flynn had said nothing of the detective's culinary abilities. "Do you have any fruit juice?" she said impulsively.

Flynn scratched his head. "Orange juice okay?"

"That's fine."

"Take a seat. I'll be with you in a moment."

Wendy glanced around the tiny living room. She wondered how anyone could live in such cramped conditions, but she knew that many *families* on Jupiter Station lived in apartments no bigger than Flynn's. A black cat stepped cautiously from beneath the table and sniffed at her feet. She bent down to pet it. Wendy barely glanced at the Company-standard paintings on the wall. Her attention was drawn to the framed diplomas hanging behind the small desk. "You have a degree in . . . You have a *master's* degree in criminal justice!"

"Don't spread that around!" Flynn warned. "You'll ruin my reputation!"

"But, with these credentials, you could be working for a police department in a major city," Chadwick suggested, "or teaching in a junior college."

"I tried teaching," Flynn said as he walked from the kitchen, a bowl of chili in each hand. "Wasn't very good at it: half my students flunked. I see you've met Furrball." He went back into the kitchen for the orange juice.

Wendy glanced down at the cat. "He seems friendly. Has he been declawed?"

Flynn returned with a glass of orange juice for his guest

and a glass of plum wine for himself. "Yes, he is, and no, he hasn't," Flynn answered as he put the glasses on the table. He pulled a chair back from the table and indicated that Wendy should be seated.

"You really don't have to hold the chair for me, Mr. Flynn," Chadwick said. "Women learned how to sit down by themselves a long time ago."

"My father taught me that that was the proper way for a gentleman to treat a lady," Flynn replied as he sat down across from her. "You're going to love that chili. One of my college roommates was from Brownsville, Texas, the Tex-Mex capital of the universe, and he showed me how to make it. The secret's in the peppers and very slow cooking." He crushed some crackers between his fingers and strewed the crumbs across his bowl. He pushed the package of crackers across the table. "Crackers?"

"Ah, no thanks." Chadwick sampled the chili. "This is pretty good," she said, then quickly reached for her juice glass when the spices seared her tongue.

"Too hot?"

"No! This is fine." It was delicious, but much spicier than Chadwick was accustomed to. "Is this . . . real beef?"

"Bison, actually," Flynn answered before taking a sip of wine. "Less fat."

Chadwick eyed Flynn's wineglass with disfavor. "Do you drink at every meal?"

"Alcohol, you mean?" Flynn hesitated, as though trying to make an accurate estimation. "Not usually at breakfast."

"Not *usually?*" Chadwick shook her head. "You might have trouble getting clients if people start thinking that you're an alcoholic."

"Oh, no. Not me. My uncle was an alcoholic, so I know one when I see one. Besides, I've had the tests: I am neither genetically nor chemically susceptible to alcohol abuse. I have gone without for months at a stretch."

"Then why not give it up?"

Flynn took another sip of wine. "Because medical science has known for half a century that small amounts of alcohol lead to longer life for most people. It reduces triglyceride levels in the blood."

Chadwick fixed her eyes on the investigator. "You drink a lot more than 'small amounts.' "

Furrball interrupted the conversation by jumping onto the table and sniffing Chadwick's bowl of chili. "You want to resume flying lessons?" Flynn said sternly. The cat stared at him for a moment, then jumped from the table, dashed for the stairs, and disappeared. "He likes you," Flynn said.

"How can you tell?"

"Because he doesn't like chili. He wasn't checking out your dinner; he was trying to get close to you." Flynn shook his head. "First time he's ever shown interest in a lawyer, though. He used to be a good judge of character."

Chadwick suppressed a smile. "Oh, really?"

"Yeah. He didn't like Barbara. I should have paid attention to him."

"Who's Barbara?"

"A person who will someday make a great contribution to life on Jupiter Station by leaving it."

"May I, ah, have more orange juice?"

"Oh, it is too hot!" Flynn said apologetically.

"No! I mean, I'm just not used to it."

Flynn went to kitchen for the juice. "You shouldn't be worried about triglycerides," he said, "not with the way you exercise."

"I do that to maintain muscle tone."

"Synthetic steroids will do that," Flynn said as he returned with the orange juice.

"The less drugs you put in your body, the better off you are," Chadwick explained. "I would think your alcoholic uncle would have convinced you of that."

"He did."

"When was that?"

"At his funeral," Flynn said, scraping the last of his chili from the bottom of his bowl.

"Oh, I'm sorry. Did his drinking—"

"Yes. When his second liver gave out, so did he."

"His *second* liver!"

"Yeah, he ruined his original one; got a transplant and ruined that, too. His insurance wouldn't pay for another transplant. And if you're wondering how anyone could be so stupid as to ruin two livers with booze, my uncle did try to stop drinking once. Told me that it was the longest day of his life." Chadwick was aimlessly pushing the remnants of her chili around the bottom of her bowl. "Do you want more chili? I can microwave another bowl in no time."

"No, thank you, Mr. Flynn. I hadn't planned on staying this long. I really must be going."

"Are you going to your place? I have to go that way. Just a second and I'll join you."

Before Wendy could protest, Flynn had scooped the dirty dishes from the table and dumped them in the dishwasher. He grabbed his sport coat from the chair where he had tossed it and put it on. "Shall we go?"

Furrball was sitting on one of the steps leading to the second floor. Flynn looked the cat right in the face and said, "You're on guard again, Furrball." The cat was expecting to get its ears rubbed and looked miffed when Flynn walked by without petting it.

Flynn and Chadwick were walking down the staircase to

the street level and out of sight of the security camera before Flynn said, "We couldn't talk in there. Somebody put a microcam behind one of the paintings on the wall."

Chadwick looked at him. "By 'somebody' do you mean—"

"Who else?"

The lawyer scowled. "He can't do that!"

"Now, now, you're forgetting your grammar," Flynn replied. " 'Can' implies ability. 'May' implies permission. Silvanus Drake *can* do just about anything he wants."

"Well, he shouldn't be doing it. It's illegal as hell."

Flynn squinted. "They passed a law against hell?"

"Do your clients find you a bit facetious, Mr. Flynn?"

"On the contrary, they think I'm a load of laughs, even if I don't dress to look like a carrot."

Chadwick stopped walking. "Do you mean to imply . . . Are you saying that . . . I'll have you know that I'm wearing the latest Paris fashion!"

"I know," Flynn sighed. "It's the rage throughout the solar system. It also makes you look like a carrot."

"At least it's not six years out of date!"

"Seven, but who's counting if it's still functional?"

Ms. Chadwick resumed walking toward her apartment. "Thank you for dinner, Mr. Flynn, but I have to get home. I have a long day tomorrow."

Flynn took long steps to catch up with Chadwick. "Tomorrow's Friday. Since when do Company lawyers work on weekends?"

"I have to see what Warshovsky does with Kemper and Santino." Chadwick felt her companion's stare. "I almost quit my job today," she explained, looking straight ahead. "I wanted those goons that tried to kill us fired. Mr. Warshovsky and Silvanus Drake wanted me to drop the charges against them instead. I said, 'Either they go or I go,' and . . ." She shook her head. "They would rather keep two attempted murderers than me. I do not want to be the lawyer of a criminal organization. I had written my letter of resignation, giving two weeks notice . . . I was just waiting for the lab reports to confirm what I had already figured out. But then they came back negative."

"So you didn't quit?"

"No. Not yet, anyway. Those goons might have tried to kill us, but they weren't acting under Drake's orders. There was no need—there was nothing in warehouse seven for us to find, and Drake knew that."

"It does look that way," Flynn said thoughtfully. "There was no blood there, and it's unlikely that whatever Mondragon and Asterbrook were moving would still be in that warehouse—the Company wouldn't have left anything that important in there for four months. So there was no reason for Drake to get upset when we went there. But in that case, why did he send those goons to warehouse seven and not to twelve?"

"He claims it took him that long to decide to enforce Warshovsky's directive to keep you off of Company property, since I was accompanying you," Chadwick said.

"Do you believe him?"

"Not enough to drop the charges against Santino and Kemper. Even if Drake didn't order them to kill us, they shouldn't be running around with guns. But Warshovsky won't fire them. He feels that their overreaction was a result of the poor training we gave them and the atmosphere he created by sending that memo to all personnel instructing them to keep you off of Company property." Chadwick sighed. "He blames himself for what happened. He's like that. He has a very strong sense of personal responsibility."

She paused. "Could it have been something personal?"

Flynn squinted while he thought about that. "Not with me. I'd never met either Kemper or Santino until last night."

"Might you have met Santino's wife or Kemper's girl-friend?"

Flynn squinted as he thought about that. "I don't think so."

"For your sake, I hope you're right—the Company bailed them out this afternoon."

"I expected as much."

"If it wasn't personal, and since there was no evidence in warehouse seven to hide, then they overreacted," Chadwick concluded, "just like Drake said. I'll tell you what happened to Philip Asterbrook and Jonny Mondragon: they were cleaning warehouse twelve, where their bodies were found. They tried to move that machinery frame. But somebody had switched the pulleys on the overhead crane, the line got pinched, it broke, and the frame crushed them."

"Then why was the security camera in warehouse twelve pointing in the wrong direction to record the accident? Why the personnel transfers?"

Chadwick took a deep breath. "Coincidence."

"And Asterbrook's missing journals?"

The lawyer shrugged. "Whoever packed his belongings might have read them. Maybe there was something in them that Asterbrook wouldn't have wanted his parents to see. Maybe whoever disposed of them thought she was doing Asterbrook a favor."

Flynn looked at the lawyer out of the corner of his eye. "But you can't ask her, can you? She's been transferred," he guessed.

"To Earth," Chadwick admitted. "Three months ago."

Flynn said, "If the accident occurred as you described, the Company would have been negligent, right? How much are we talking about?"

"Average for such accidents is around six million. That's what I'm going to propose that we offer the families of Mondragon and Asterbrook."

Six million each. Twelve million dollars total. Petty cash to the Company—the cost overrun on Satellite Juliet was twenty-eight million. Flynn could not believe that such a small loss would prompt such a large cover-up. "Since you're working tomorrow anyway, could you do me a favor?" he asked. "You found blood from two minor accidents in warehouse seven. Could you find out if the people whose blood it was are still on the Station?"

Chadwick cocked her head. "You mean, you think that Drake had that warehouse sterilized to conceal the fact that Asterbrook and Mondragon were killed there, and then planted minute blood samples from previous accident victims, just in case anybody checked?"

Flynn smiled. "Never underestimate the resources or the cleverness of Silvanus Drake."

Chadwick sighed. "Okay, I'll check. But your scenario is getting more and more farfetched." She turned away. "One of these days, we'll have to figure out who owes who a dinner. I'll see you around, Mr. Flynn."

Flynn watched the lawyer walk away. He had thought that he would have good news to send to the Asterbrooks that evening. Now he had nothing. He had even lost his ally inside the Company. He decided that he could use a drink.

181

Chapter 7

The homeward-bound throng that had jammed Betty's Bar to watch the news coverage of the Ceres mine disaster had been replaced by the Thursday-night regulars. Most of the patrons were crowded close to the video display to watch the first game of the Station's airball tournament, which was about to begin. Flynn made his way to the opposite end of the bar.

Betty walked past two customers trying to get refills and stood across the bar from Michael, hands on her hips. Flynn had intended to order a double whiskey, but the lines of disapproval in Betty's face made him pause. "What's up?" he asked, as innocuously as he could.

"Don't play innocent with me, Michael!" Betty answered. "If you're going to carry on with women married to big, jealous husbands, you're going to wind up wishing those goons had shot you last night!" She slid a piece of paper across the bar to Flynn and stalked back to her customers.

Flynn unfolded the note. The handwriting was Missy Adamly's.

Our place in the park. 19:00. I'll fix the cameras.

Flynn glanced at the time shown on the bar's video display: he had fifteen minutes to make the appointment. But the park was at the far end of Jupiter Station, beyond the apartment block where Wendy Chadwick lived, and the place where Missy was waiting for him was almost directly across the Station circumference from Betty's Bar. He slipped the note into the pocket of his sport coat and turned to leave.

"Not so fast, wise guy!" The speaker, who was hurrying to get between the detective and the door, was shorter than Flynn, but he had the build of a man who did manual labor for a living, and he had a mustached companion who was a head taller and twenty kilos heavier. Each man carried a half-full glass of beer. Flynn had seen both men in Betty's on several occasions but didn't know their names.

"Yes?" Flynn said pleasantly.

"We want to talk to you!"

"I'd love to stay and chat," Flynn replied, "but I'm late for an appointment."

"You got an appointment with us!" The man stood directly in front of Flynn. His companion stepped around to Flynn's left side, then moved behind him. "I've been hearing things about you that I don't like! You don't go around Jupiter Station trying to kill Company security guards!"

Normally, goons were despised by Company employees—except when the goons had altercations with outsiders. "Who? Me?" Flynn protested. "When?"

"Forget already? Last night!"

"Ah!" Flynn said with a tone of sudden understanding. "There you go, now. How quickly rumors can get things mixed up! I was not trying to kill any security guards last night. The guards were trying to kill me."

"That's not what I heard!"

"From whom?" Flynn asked.

"From people who were there!"

"You've been talking to security guards, then." The man nodded. "Confidentially," Flynn said, lowering his voice and glancing from side to side, "I wouldn't believe anything a goon told me. Those security people have been known to spin tall tales from time to time."

"Hey!" the man behind Flynn said, "watch who you're calling a liar!" Flynn turned around to face him. The man held a glass of beer in his right hand and was tapping his chest with his left hand to emphasize the point. "I have friends who are security guards!"

Flynn gently took the man's left hand into his own. "I'm sorry to hear that," he said sadly. "You have my sympathies."

The man's features hardened and his mustache quivered, but he was right-handed, and as he transferred his beer glass to his left hand Flynn prepared to duck. The man had big hands that made even bigger fists, and the punch that he threw had all of his mass behind it. It would have done serious damage to Flynn's face if Flynn hadn't easily slipped it. Mike heard the sound of the fist colliding with flesh behind him.

"What the . . . what the hell did you hit me for?" the other man said.

Flynn stepped carefully over spilled beer while the punch-thrower protested, "I didn't hit you!"

"Like hell you didn't!" the first man said, and followed his words with a punch, or maybe it was the other way around. Flynn walked quickly to the door and did not look back as his two assailants redirected their anger at each other.

Taxis were like cops: there was never one around when Flynn needed one, even though Betty's bar was located at the intersection of two major streets. Flynn started walking briskly along the moving walkway on Denver Boulevard toward the far end of the Station while he summoned a taxi by phone. He had nearly reached the park before the cab arrived. Flynn rode it circumferentially around the Station and got out in front of a bar where he had frequently taken Missy when he was dating her.

The park cut a swath four levels high and almost two hundred meters wide around the circumference of Jupiter Station. It had been constructed because the psychologists had insisted that the overcrowded inhabitants of the Station needed some open green space. It also reduced the demands on the air processing system because plants converted carbon dioxide produced by people back into oxygen. The park was only seven years old, so its fast-growing flora still didn't reach to the overhead, which was shrouded in the darkness of artificial evening. The soil had come from tailings of the Station's mining operations, heavily fertilized by the organic byproducts of the Station's twenty thousand inhabitants. The walkways that meandered among the ferns and flowers were not brightly lit, with patches of shadow separated by islands of illumination. Because of the airball tournament there weren't as many people in the park as there would have been on a typical Thursday evening. Flynn felt conspicuous.

Missy Adamly was sitting on the ground, her back against a tree trunk, her knees clasped to her chest, in a grove of pine trees behind a clump of ferns. She was wearing a white tee shirt and dark shorts. She breathed a sigh of relief when Flynn appeared. "I was beginning to think that you hadn't gotten my note," she said.

Flynn glanced at his watch. "I'm only two minutes late."

"You're usually early. I was expecting you ten minutes ago."

Flynn decided that Missy could do without a detailed explanation of his tardiness. "What's up?" he asked as he took a seat on the ground, facing Missy, and leaned back against a tree of his own. The air was pungent with the smell of evergreens. "I thought you wanted me to stay away from you."

"I do. Even if my husband wouldn't beat you into a bloody pulp if he knew you had so much as looked at me. What the hell happened last night?"

"I thought I had this case all figured out," Flynn replied. "The pulley on the overhead crane in warehouse twelve had been switched with the one on the crane in warehouse seven. I concluded that the accident had actually occurred in warehouse seven and that the bodies had been moved to twelve because the Company didn't want the authorities seeing what was in seven. So I got the Company's lawyer to let me into warehouse seven. We were studying the crane when two goons—"

"Vinny Santino and Luke Kemper?" Missy interrupted.

Flynn nodded. "Know 'em?" Missy shook her head. "Well, Kemper and Santino walked in and started shooting at us with pulsed lasers. Lawyer Chadwick and I stumbled onto a basement hatch and got out of the warehouse, but goons started pouring into the basement through other hatches. I had to zap three of 'em with my stun pistol before we could get out. Then two more goons came roaring up in a Company car, just as a deputy marshal arrived on the scene. The deputy impounded all four of us; U.S. attorney Pierce kicked us loose."

"I heard Kemper and Santino were arrested, too."

Flynn nodded. "This morning. Pierce thought that they were the only two that he could prosecute successfully. But they're out on bail now. Why are you asking me about this? You have access to the entire computer system."

Missy took a deep breath. "I think people have been playing games with the computer system."

Flynn tilted his head to the side. "Meaning?"

"Well . . . some of the info I gave you the other day might not be entirely correct, but since you've cracked the case—"

"Whoa! Not so fast. I *thought* I had cracked the case. But Chadwick stopped by my apartment this evening to tell me that there wasn't a trace of Asterbrook or Mondragon's blood in warehouse seven. So they couldn't have been squashed in there. Which makes no sense at all because then why the hell did those goons try to kill me?"

"Well, maybe something I . . ." Missy's eyes narrowed. "Chadwick stopped by your apartment to tell you about the blood? Doesn't she know how to work a phone?"

Flynn could tell by the tone of Missy's voice that he was on very thin ice. "I didn't invite her. I suppose she thought that bad news should be delivered personally."

"Personally!" Missy said. "Now *that* I can believe! You dropped Barbara for your 'peace of mind,' eh? I've seen Chadwick in the gym: long, gorgeous legs! And a redhead, too!" She pushed herself to her feet. "I should have known! I don't know why I'm trying to help you!" She started to stride away.

Flynn jumped to his feet and reached out and grabbed her arm. "What are you complaining about? I'm not the one who ran off and got married!"

Missy pulled her arm away. "What was I supposed to do? You stopped calling me! Every night you were 'busy!' Every night!"

"I *was* busy!"

"You weren't that busy before you met Barbara! And in the seven months that we dated you didn't once bring me flowers! Not once! Jack brings me flowers every week!"

"I thought you didn't like flowers," Flynn said weakly.

187

"That doesn't matter! It's the thought that counts!"

Flynn was losing the argument, but Missy wasn't walking away anymore. Flynn took a chance and changed the subject. "You were saying something about people playing with the computer?"

Missy hesitated, but relented. "I told you the other day that none of the files that I gave you had been altered after the document dates. I'm no longer certain of that. The checksums are all correct, but in the data block containing Asterbrook and Mondragon's human-resources files . . . You see, the operating system periodically repacks the files to reduce fragmentation and free up memory space if any files have been reduced in size. A record is kept of all such memory-management activities. The data block containing Asterbrook and Mondragon's files was repacked about ten days after the accident. Two kilobytes were saved, so at least one file had to have been edited. But according to the records, none of those files had been accessed for three days. The automatic memory management takes place at least once a day. So on two occasions after the last official file access, the computer was unable to repack the data. Then, all of a sudden . . ."

Flynn mulled over Missy's revelation. "Two kilobytes is how much?"

Missy shrugged. "In a human-resources file, about a page. But not necessarily in Asterbrook or Mondragon's file!" she cautioned. "And only someone who knew how to recalculate and modify the checksums could have done it, and even then the change would show in the file records!"

"Even if the file had been modified from the supervisory level?"

"No, then it wouldn't," Missy admitted. "But it takes *two* people with supervisory access, working simultaneously on two different but *hard-wired* terminals—network access won't work—to pull it off."

"How many people have such access?"

"In addition to me, just Howie Ng, the other system analyst, and our boss, Bob Popolov, director of computing systems."

Flynn nodded. "No way someone could do it alone?"

Missy hesitated. "Well . . ."

"Could *you* do it alone?"

"Yes," she admitted, "through that trapdoor I built in when we loaded the operating system upgrade. But Ng and Popolov don't know about that."

"Could they have built in trapdoors of their own?"

"Oh, Howie *could* have," Missy said. "I've told you about him: Master's in Comp Sci from MIT; he knows more about computers than any other ten system analysts put together will ever learn. But he wouldn't. He's not a hacker. Computers are his religion; he'd never break into one. His only interest in hacking is in how to defeat it. I'm not sure Popolov is good enough, and even if he was, he's a Company man through and through. He'd never mistreat Company property that way."

"What about the managers of the individual systems?" Flynn asked. "In particular, the person who manages Security's computers."

"Romero?" Missy shrugged. "He *is* a hacker. I know, because I've caught him trying to get root access to our level of the system. And he knows enough about computers to redo the checksums. But you can't access the supervisory level through the network; you have to use a hard-wired terminal. Romero's too dumb to realize that."

Flynn pursed his lips. "How many of those hard-wired terminals are there?"

"Five. One in my office, one in Ng's, one in Popolov's, one in the room with the primary network server, and one in the room with the backup server. Romero doesn't have access to any of them."

"Security has access to everything," Flynn corrected.

"Physical access, yes. Computer access, no. Besides, we're running SOS nine point four. The last version of SOS that was hacked was eight point two."

Flynn took a deep breath. "You're telling me that the file fixing that you've discovered must have been done by Ng and Popolov working together."

Missy sighed. " 'Fraid not. You see, the video records of your shoot-out last night show some of the same anomalies, and Howie Ng's been on Satellite Juliet for the last two days, debugging the system there."

"So *nobody* could have done it?"

Missy nodded. "And I found other files that show the repacking anomaly. For instance, Sam Egleiter's computer files—at least, what was left of them—were repacked *three days* after he left for Ceres."

"Egleiter, the former human resources director?"

"The same. And remember that doctor that OD'd on polymeth?"

"Vasquez?"

"Did you know that he had applied for a Company job?"

The thought of Carla McDonald's brown eyes made Flynn hesitate. "I think I might have heard a rumor to that effect."

"Well, the data block holding his application file got repacked about two years ago during a period when there was no official access to any of the files in the block. Checksums are all correct there, too."

Flynn pounded his fist into the palm of his left hand.

"Vasquez! I *knew* he was involved in this!"

"Not in *this*," Missy said. "Asterbrook and Mondragon were killed four months ago. I said that the Vasquez records were tampered with two *years* ago."

"Yeah. They found out he was a polymeth addict when they did the background check for his job application. That's why he didn't get the job. Then, when he shows up here working for Meditech, they conceal that info so they can hold it over him if they ever need a favor, like when they need some autopsy results falsified." Flynn sat down against his tree again.

Missy remained standing and considered what Flynn had said. "I'll give you whatever help I can," she said. "Not because I owe you anything—I don't. I just want to find out how somebody penetrated my system."

Flynn looked up at Missy. "Speaking of penetrating computer systems, how did you fix the Security computer so that the cameras wouldn't track me here?"

"You know what the lighting's like in the park," Missy said. "I programmed the Security computer so that when you stepped into the first shadow it would automatically replace your image with whatever was behind you. You'd just vanish. When you leave the park the computer will let your image show on the monitors again, and my program will delete itself."

"How did you manage to vanish from Jack's sight?"

"Oh, one of the guys on his smelter is getting married tomorrow. They're giving him a party tonight. Guys only."

"I'm surprised he leaves you home without a chaperone," Flynn said.

"He doesn't," Missy explained. "Somebody told him he could program the door lock to keep track of whoever entered or left the apartment." She didn't have to add that she could easily reprogram the door lock to ignore her comings and goings. She took her telephone from the pocket of her shorts. "If he calls, I'll tell him I'm at home. I should be getting back, though, in case one of the neighbors drops in. I can't claim I didn't answer the door because I was in the shower all evening."

"Thanks, Missy. I owe you one."

"Oh, you owe me a lot more than one."

Flynn waited five minutes before leaving the park. He strolled back to Betty's Bar, his head bent in thought, trying to make sense of the information he had received that evening. Betty's was more crowded than when he had left, but the two men who had accosted him were gone. Betty brought him a glass of whiskey without being asked.

"Instead of serving you, I should be calling the deputies," she said. "What do you mean, starting a fight in my bar and then slipping away?"

Flynn pointed to his chest. "Me? I didn't start a fight. I didn't even participate in a fight, not so much as a single punch. Those two goon lovers started fighting. Each other. What happened to them, by the way?"

"Marshals took 'em away," Betty said, "along with the other eight that joined in the brawl."

"Ten men! Brawling! In Betty's Bar?" Flynn shook his head. "Wish I could have seen it."

Betty's gaze shifted from Flynn toward the door. "I thought you weren't seeing Barbara anymore."

"I'm not."

"Does she know that?"

In the mirror behind the bar Flynn could see the reflection of Barbara Olsen. She was in a silver mood—silver blouse, silver tights, silver miniskirt. At least she had left her black hair alone. She was tall to begin with, and wearing high heels she was statuesque. She walked from the door to the bar where Flynn was standing, swinging her hips in the manner that had first caught Flynn's attention. She smiled as she rested her arm on his shoulders, her graceful fingers massaging his left bicep. Her long fingernails were painted silver.

"Hi there, lover," she cooed in his ear. "Long time no see."

Flynn didn't look at her. "Hello, Barbara. How've you been?"

"If you'd return my calls, you'd know."

"I've been busy," Flynn explained. He took a sip of whiskey.

Barbara slid her hand down Flynn's arm. "Aren't you going to buy me a drink?"

"Barbara, you make as much as I do," Flynn said. "More, some months. I would think you could afford to buy your own."

Barbara's smile vanished. "I don't know whom you're seeing now, but someday she's going to want to kick herself for ever looking twice at you." Barbara turned and strode out of the bar. The seductive swing of her hips had disappeared with her smile.

The man at the bar to Flynn's right turned from the video coverage of the airball tournament and watched her leave. "You're letting *that* get away?" he asked in disbelief.

"And not a moment too soon."

The man didn't even finish his beer. He headed for the door, but he might have already missed his chance—men outnumbered women almost two to one on Jupiter Station, and Flynn had seen two other men follow Barbara from the tavern.

Flynn drained the last of his whiskey and put his glass

down on the bar. Betty, wet rag in hand, came to remove the empty glass and clean the bar. "I told you she was no good for you," she said. "Why you dumped Missy Russell for her, I'll never know."

Flynn was looking at the circle of moisture that his glass had left on the bar's surface. "If you must know, Betty, it was her language."

Betty stopped wiping the bar and stared at Flynn. "Her *language?* Missy? Not once did I hear a foul expression pass her—"

"She kept using the *M* word!"

Betty continued to stare at Flynn. Then she shook her head and walked away.

Flynn was still looking down at the bar. Flynn looked at the security camera on the wall at the end of the bar opposite the video display. The camera was looking back at him. Michael had the distressing feeling that Silvanus Drake was running him in circles. He didn't want his daily message to the Asterbrooks to make them think that they were wasting their money. Flynn, however, had been so confused by that evening's revelations that he was afraid that that was exactly what the Asterbrooks were doing.

Chapter 8

Flynn jogged two laps around the circumference of Jupiter Station every morning, before the streets became crowded with people on their way to work. That was less of a problem on Fridays, since fewer people worked on weekends, but Flynn still got up early for his daily exercise. He liked to be up and about while most of the Station's inhabitants were still in bed.

Three people who were not in bed that Friday morning were U.S. Marshal Ben Wofford and deputies Ross and Larmoretti. They were waiting on the balcony outside of Flynn's apartment when the detective returned from jogging. Flynn had trouble believing that he had so angered Betty that she would set the authorities on him. He had even more trouble believing that Wofford would personally handle a charge of disturbing the peace.

Flynn forced himself to smile. "Morning, gentlemen. To what do I owe the honor of this visit?"

Wofford didn't return the smile, nor did he waste time. "Where were you between nineteen and twenty last night?"

Flynn made a show of searching his memory. "Nineteen to twenty? I would have been . . . Betty's Bar, I think. Yes, Betty's." He pointed down the block. "Level three, Fourth and Denver—"

"There was a brawl in Betty's last night," Wofford interrupted. "Started a few minutes before nineteen. You weren't there. In fact, several witnesses say you left just before the fight started."

"What if I did? Are you charging me with *avoiding* a brawl?"

Wofford scowled. "I'm *asking* you where you were between nineteen and twenty last night!"

"Come to think of it, I did take a walk around that time," Flynn admitted. "Spotted this really curvaceous lady going by in a taxi. Summoned a taxi of my own to give chase, but by the time it arrived she had disappeared. Rode all the way to the park looking for her, couldn't find her, and walked back to Betty's. Why do you ask?"

Wofford smiled briefly. "Somebody killed Vincent Santino and Luke Kemper last night. Between nineteen and twenty—" Wofford was still talking but Flynn wasn't listening. Kemper and Santino murdered! The case was even bigger than Flynn had imagined. ". . . just after witnesses in Betty's Bar saw you leave without ordering—very suspicious behavior, considering your affection for malt whiskey. So where were you, Flynn? Anywhere near the weightless recreation area?"

Flynn's inhaled sharply. "I didn't even get on an elevator, let alone ride all the way up to the hub! I didn't get above level three until I went home! I took a taxi; check the records!"

Wofford seemed inordinately pleased. "Oh, I'll check your story, all right. But in the meantime, you'd better come down to the office with us."

Flynn looked carefully at Wofford's uniform and the hands hanging at his sides. "You wouldn't happen to have anything that looks like a warrant, would you, Marshal?"

"Oh, I'm not arresting you, Flynn. Not yet. I'm just bringing you in for questioning."

"According to the United States Supreme Court—*Gonzales v. California*, I think—any detention of a person by the authorities is effectively an arrest of said person," Flynn pointed out. "So, because you didn't catch me in the act of shutting down Kemper and Santino, you need a warrant to take me anyplace, even across the street. Since you don't have one, I'll be about my business. Forgive me for not inviting you in for breakfast, but my refrigerator's nearly empty."

"I can get a warrant!" Wofford said.

"For what? Zapping those two goons with my stun pistol and then kicking them to death?"

Wofford made a face. "According to your own statement, you took two laser pistols away from Company security personnel the other night. You were able to lead Deputy Marshal Feldstein to only one of them."

So Santino and Kemper had been shot with a pulsed laser. Flynn was tempted to thank the marshal for that information, but instead replied, "Nice try, but it won't hold up in court. I never held the other one by the grip. Any fingerprints of mine would be on the focus tube. Nor did I strip the unconscious goons of any of their activation rings, without which those laser pistols cannot be made to fire. See you around, Marshal."

Wofford glowered. "I can arrest you right now for failing to cooperate with a police investigation!"

"Wrong again, Marshal. Since I'm a suspect in this case, I don't have to cooperate with you—I have the right to remain silent. Have a nice day." Flynn opened his apartment door and stepped inside.

"You think you're so damned smart!" Wofford yelled after him. "It was *Gonzales v. Arizona*, you ignorant son of a bitch!"

Flynn smiled. "I'm still one up on you: I *know* who my father was." He closed the apartment door.

Michael leaned back against the door. He felt no sense of tragedy, although Vinny Santino had left a widow and small child. Whatever the Company was trying to keep secret had now claimed four lives. The killer of Santino and Kemper had hoped that Flynn would take the blame, or that the marshals would be busy for months investigating everybody the two goons had ever arrested, bullied, or harassed in the course of their security duties. But they had been killed to keep them from testifying as to why they had tried to kill Flynn, or maybe because they had failed to kill Flynn, or maybe for both reasons.

Flynn roused himself to action. His investigation was back at square one, and potential sources of information were dying like flies. Flynn needed to find out all he could about the murder of Kemper and Santino. He headed for the shower.

Wendy Chadwick flung open the door to Warshovsky's office and stormed into the room. Warshovsky was standing at his window, watching the arrival of the automated cargo ship *CMM-9*. Wendy strode directly to where Warshovsky stood. "What the hell is going on?" she demanded.

Warshovsky turned reluctantly from the window. Chadwick was casually attired in a loose-fitting blue jogging suit, and Warshovsky thought that she looked much prettier than when she wore those ridiculous skin-tight metallic fashions. He took a deep breath. "I assume that you are referring to the murders of Kemper and Santino?"

"At least you admit that these are murders! Or will our investigation reveal that a machinery frame fell on them, too?"

"Ms. Chadwick, that's no way to speak of this tragedy—"

"It wasn't much of a tragedy when those two goons were

trying to shoot me the other night!"

"Are we going to have yesterday's discussion all over again?"

"Somebody has made yesterday's conversation moot!" Chadwick retorted. "What I want to know today is how those two trigger-happy security guards wound up dead this morning!"

Warshovsky shrugged. "I only know what Silvanus Drake told me. A janitorial robot found them in a men's room near the weightless recreation area just before midnight. They'd been shot with a pulsed laser, apparently around twenty o'clock. The marshals think that investigator might have done it."

Chadwick looked askance. "Flynn? No way! I was at his place last night!"

"You were with . . . You were at Flynn's last night?"

Chadwick glared at her boss. "Not *all* night. Just around dinnertime. I'd gone there to tell him that the tests I'd ordered on warehouse seven had come back negative."

Warshovsky nodded. "I told you that those tests were a waste of money. Now that you know that I was telling the truth about Mondragon and Asterbrook, are you willing to believe that Mr. Drake and I *didn't* rub out Kemper and Santino?"

"I'm willing to believe that you didn't kill anyone," Chadwick said. "I can't say the same about Mr. Drake."

"Mr. Drake was at home with his wife last night," Warshovsky said, "so he couldn't have done it. Or do you think that we employ people who'll commit murder when ordered to do so?"

"Mr. Warshovsky, some of our employees were trying to murder me the night before last."

"But they were not ordered to do so. They were misinformed and overreacting. Besides, I told you that the marshals think that Flynn did it."

Chadwick made a face. "Flynn has a stun pistol, not a laser." She paused. "Or were Santino and Kemper armed last night?"

Warshovsky shook his head. "As a condition of their bail, we had to reassign them to duties that did not require them to carry pistols."

"So Flynn couldn't have done it. And since the only people on this station with pulsed lasers are our security guards—the same people who were trying to kill me the other night—one of our people is probably the murderer. Or was he simply 'misinformed and overreacting?' "

"Someone might have smuggled a gun onto the Station," Warshovsky suggested.

Chadwick winced. "Through Drake's ironclad security?" She shook her head. "It was one of our goons, and you'd better hope to high heaven that he was acting on his own and not on Drake's orders." Her attention was distracted by the sight, through the window behind her boss, of the approaching cargo ship. The *CMM-9* wasn't rotating—computers didn't degrade in the absence of gravity the way that human bodies did. Automated cargo ships had small engines and took very slow orbits. The *CMM-9* had been in transit from Earth for over a year.

Warshovsky noticed the change in Chadwick's focus and looked over his shoulder. "She's carrying enough frozen, freeze-dried, and irradiated foodstuffs to feed everyone on Jupiter Station for almost a month," he said, trying to change the subject.

Chadwick knew as much about the *CMM-9* as her boss did. It would take back to Earth steel and aluminum ingots and fertilizer. There were twenty-nine more ships like her in transit to Jupiter Station from Earth, and twenty-six headed back to Earth from the Station. Most of them had been built at Jupiter. If the Company could have afforded to put larger engines in them, they would have been faster, and fewer would have been required. Lou Cheng wanted to build hydrogen-reaction engines at Jupiter Station. If the Company built the engines instead of buying them it could afford to put bigger engines in the cargo ships. Chadwick said, "If we don't find out who's killing our employees, there won't be anyone left to eat all that food that's being shipped here."

The U.S. marshal caught up with Flynn on a main axial street on level six. Wofford took delight in waving the piece of paper in the detective's face.

"Recognize this, Flynn?"

Wofford was holding the paper so close to Flynn that Michael had to lean backward to see it clearly. "An arrest warrant? For me?"

"For no one else. Michael Flynn, you are under arrest for suspicion of the murders of Vincent Santino and Luke Kemper. You have the right to remain silent—"

"I know my rights, Marshal, and waive your recitation of them."

Wofford turned to the two deputies accompanying him. "Put the manacles on this wise guy. Carefully! He might be armed."

"And dangerous," Flynn added. "My pistol's in my right coat pocket," he said to the deputies. They also attempted to relieve him of his pocket computer. "Not so fast!" Flynn said. "That has my legal software on it. Taking away my computer is the same as denying me the right to counsel of my choice."

"Let him keep the damned computer," Wofford said.

"You're going to be in a lot of trouble, Marshal," Flynn warned. "You got that warrant under false pretenses."

"I got that warrant with reasonable cause," Wofford responded. "You had accused the victims of trying to kill you. You admitted having access to what might be the murder weapon. And you don't have an alibi for the time of the murders."

"Oh, really? That's not what Deputy Marshal Feldstein will tell you."

The deputies were leading Flynn to the patrol car. They stopped and looked to Wofford, who was staring at Flynn. "Feldstein had the desk last night," the marshal said. "He didn't say anything about you visiting him between nineteen and twenty."

"I didn't say I had, but if you take me in without checking out my alibi, and then discover that I'm innocent, that's false arrest. So say two different Federal appeals courts, including the one with jurisdiction over Jupiter Station."

Wofford hesitated. Flynn hadn't mentioned an alibi when Wofford had tried to question him earlier in the morning. The marshal hadn't misrepresented any facts to the magistrate in order to get the warrant. The warrant *had* to be valid, and Wofford was going to use it. "Put him in the car, boys. If he wants to invent an alibi, let him do it at the office."

Flynn took advantage of his arrest. Since he had been accused of the crime, he refused to talk until he had been informed of the evidence against him.

Santino and Kemper had been shot in the men's room just outside the ticket gate at the weightless recreation center. The medical examiner had placed the time of death at between nineteen and twenty. A game in the Station's airball tournament had started in the recreation center at nineteen thirty. The men's room had been crowded before the game started, but no witnesses had remembered seeing the victims, nor had the marshals found any witnesses to the shooting itself. Privacy laws prevented security cameras in restrooms from running continuously, and the camera in the men's room had not been activated, so the victims had not called for help. The bodies had been stuffed in one of the toilet stalls and had not been discovered until a robot cleaned the men's room just before midnight. No physical evidence had been discovered at the scene. The murder weapon had not been found.

Wofford concluded his narrative with, "You'll save everyone a lot of time and trouble if you confess. Hey, if they really tried to kill you the other night, maybe they tried again last night. You shot them in self-defense, right?"

"I didn't shoot them at all."

U.S. Attorney Kyle Pierce entered the interrogation room, bringing a frown to Wofford's face. Pierce skipped the amenities. "Has the suspect been informed of his rights?" he asked.

"I already know my rights," Flynn said as he got to his feet. "And since I now know as much as the marshal does about what happened to Santino and Kemper, I think I'll be going."

"Oh, you do, do you?" Wofford said. "It doesn't work that way when you're under arrest."

"False arrest," Flynn said, emphasizing the point with a raised finger. "False arrest."

"Oh?" Pierce said curiously. "How so?"

"Our overeager marshal refused to check out my alibi before taking me into custody," Flynn explained.

Pierce turned to Wofford. "He said something about

Deputy Marshal Feldstein, but it's a crock," the marshal said. "Feldstein had the desk last evening. And Flynn hasn't said anything about his so-called 'alibi' since we brought him in."

"What has he been saying?"

"Well . . . Actually, he's refused to talk, under advice of his 'attorney,' " Wofford glanced at Flynn's pocket computer, "until informed of the evidence against him."

Pierce squinted at the marshal. "So you arrested him, brought him here for interrogation, and he's been questioning *you*?" Wofford did not answer. Pierce suppressed the urge to shake his head; Wofford's desperation was greatly degrading the man's performance. He asked Flynn, "So just what is your alibi?"

"Ask Deputy Marshal Feldstein."

"We're asking you!" Wofford said.

"And I'm telling you to ask Feldstein," Flynn insisted.

"Better ask Feldstein," the U.S. attorney interrupted.

"Why?"

"Because if we hold him without checking out a reasonable alibi we leave ourselves open for a lawsuit for false arrest, that's why," Pierce explained.

Wofford chewed his lip. "Feldstein was on duty until after midnight. He's not here now."

"If Feldstein can run the night shift, he must be capable of working a telephone," Pierce replied. "Call him."

"But—"

"Call him now!"

The marshal left the interrogation room reluctantly. Neither Flynn nor Pierce spoke, and in the silence they could hear the marshal's angry voice through the supposedly soundproof walls. Flynn smiled. The marshal's voice died away, but five more minutes elapsed before Wofford re-entered the room. He scowled at Flynn. "You can pick up your belongings at the desk."

"Including my stun pistol?"

The marshal glanced at the U.S. attorney. "Yeah, including your gun." Wofford leaned across the table and said, "Maybe you can figure out how to get your buddy Feldstein out of the trouble he's in for wasting government resources."

"Trouble?" Flynn said with his best puzzled expression on his face. "I would think you'd be rewarding him. Because of his foresight, you were able to eliminate one suspect in a murder case. Now you can get on with finding out who really did it."

"Just what is the alibi?" Pierce asked.

"I expected the Company would try to get me off the Asterbrook case by framing me for some heinous felony," Flynn explained. "Actually, I thought they were going to have a woman accuse me of rape. I hadn't anticipated a murder charge, but then I didn't know their plans for Santino and Kemper. So right after Feldstein and I went looking for those laser pistols night before last, I had Feldstein put a security camera watch on me—perfectly legal, when done with the consent of the person being watched." Flynn knew that the Company also had the security cameras watching him; he had counted on the Company falsifying their video records, so that they could be caught lying when the marshals produced their own data. He had outsmarted Silvanus Drake this time.

"What do the cameras show?" Pierce asked the marshal.

"The camera data show him leaving Betty's Bar and going to the park just before nineteen last night," the marshal said. "The cameras lost him in the park—not unusual, with the lighting there—but picked him up when he left the park and returned to Betty's just before twenty o'clock. They don't show him anywhere near the weightless recreation area, and he wasn't off camera long enough to get there and back, anyway. There's no way he could have committed the murders." Wofford sounded very disappointed.

Flynn closed his computer and slipped it into his coat pocket. "Oh, Mr. Pierce, do I serve the papers for the false-arrest suit on you or on the marshal?"

Pierce was not amused. "Ask your legal advisor," he said, eyeing the pocket where Flynn had stashed his computer.

Flynn had no sooner stepped out of the marshal's office when his phone chirped. He answered it with a simple, "Flynn."

"Mr. Flynn, this is Carla McDonald."

Flynn kept walking. "Good morning, Nurse McDonald. What can I do for you?"

"I might be able to do something for you. I was watching the morning news . . . Did you hear about the murders last night?"

"Yeah, I just got an earful from the cops."

"Well, I just thought that you'd like to know: One of those murdered guys was in the hospital on Wednesday, right after you were there."

Flynn stopped in his tracks. The waterfall in the plaza in front of the Marshals Office was just to his right; the audio volume of the phone in his left hand had automatically increased to compensate for the noise. "Which one was it?"

"Santino."

"What was a Company employee doing in the Meditech hospital?"

"He wasn't very friendly," McDonald said. "Not nearly as friendly as you were."

Flynn sighed. "Are you at work?"

"Uh-uh. I don't work weekends unless there's an emergency. I'm at home."

"I'll be right there."

Nurse McDonald lived on the far side of the park. Her apartment was at street level, but her street was one level above that of the park, and a window in her living room gave a view of the park foliage. The park's overhead lighting created the illusion of a slightly overcast day on Earth. The apartment explained the roommate that McDonald had mentioned—an apartment in such a desirable location would be too expensive for a nurse.

Carla was wearing a blue-gray sweatshirt with matching shorts. Without her scrubs, she didn't look like a nurse. Flynn took two fifty-dollar bills from his wallet. "Are we still friends?"

McDonald folded the bills into her hand. "The best of friends. And as friends, we have no secrets."

"Tell me about Santino's visit."

Carla sat on the couch. "Right after you left Wednesday morning he walked into the trauma room and asked me if there were any supplies or test instruments in Vasquez's lab that Meditech didn't want anymore and would be willing to sell."

Flynn's forehead wrinkled. "Why the hell would a goon be interested in surplus lab supplies?"

Carla looked puzzled. "Santino was a goon?"

"Wasn't he in uniform?"

The nurse shook her head. "Civvies. I wouldn't have known that he was a Company employee if he hadn't been identified as such on the news this morning."

Flynn sat heavily in a chair against the living room wall and propped his chin in his hand. "That doesn't make any sense."

"I'm just telling you what happened."

"I know, I know." Flynn worked the problem in his mind every way he could think of, but ran into logical contradictions from every angle. Vinny Santino wasn't the type who would want to buy equipment or supplies from Vasquez's lab. He must have been acting under orders from Silvanus Drake. But why hadn't Santino been wearing the orange coveralls of the security force? And what was in Vasquez's lab that Drake wanted?

Flynn took a deep breath. "Are we friendly enough for you to let me into Dr. Vasquez's lab?"

McDonald shook her head. "Sorry. The marshals have it sealed. We can't even put the supplies that Vasquez ordered in there."

"Supplies?"

"Lab supplies. You know—chemicals and drugs. He ordered them months ago. They just came in on the *Planet Queen*. Company's still got 'em in a warehouse someplace because we don't know where to put 'em. I thought that Santino might take them off our hands for us, but when I asked our management, they decided to ask Vasquez's replacement if she wanted 'em. She hasn't replied yet."

"The chemicals: do you know what was ordered?"

"Not off the top of my head, but it's in the computer." Carla stood up and walked to the desktop computer in the corner of the room. Flynn rose from his chair and stood behind her while she accessed the hospital's database. He scanned the list of chemicals that Vasquez had ordered into his own computer and compared it to the list of ingredients of polymethyl two four that he had found in the library.

Only one of the chemicals on the Vasquez order was on the polymeth list.

Flynn looked at his host. "Do you know why he wanted this stuff?"

Carla shook her head. "Not specifically." She pointed to a seven-digit number on the computer display. "They're charged to his research account, so I'd assume he needed them for his research."

Unless Vasquez had been ordering one thing but an accomplice had been shipping him something else. Flynn smiled. "You find out anything else about the late Dr. Vasquez, we'll stay friendly."

Carla returned his smile.

Out on the street, Flynn called Wendy Chadwick.

"Mr. Flynn!" she said. "Are you in jail?"

"Nah. Our mini-brained marshal, probably with the connivance of Silvanus Drake, tried to pin the murders of Kemper and Santino on me, but I had an alibi. I just wonder what I did to him to make him suspect me in the first place."

"They did try to kill you the other night," Chadwick pointed out. "Some people would consider that a motive."

"They tried to kill you, too. And you weren't able to get them fired." Chadwick didn't reply, so Flynn said, "Do you have access to the victims' human-resources files?"

"Of course, but I can't share them with you. Human-resources files are confidential."

"Can you tell me if Santino and Kemper were working Wednesday morning?"

Chadwick hesitated. "Yeah, I guess that's okay. Just a sec . . . No, they've been working evenings."

"I'm trying to trace a shipment that came in on the *Planet Queen*," Flynn said. "Can your computer tell me what happened to shipment number 54-30-0930-0902?"

"Just what do you think I am? A file clerk?"

"I think you're the only person who can tell me what happened to shipment number 54-30-0930-0902. At least, you're the only person I can think of this morning."

"Does that shipment have something to do with Asterbrook and Mondragon?" Chadwick asked.

"I don't know. I won't know until I find it."

"Mr. Flynn, you had better be able to keep your mouth shut . . . Whoa! That shipment was ordered by Dr. Vasquez!"

"So?"

"So, the marshals are still investigating his death!"

"Yeah, tell me something I don't know," Flynn said. "Where is it?"

"You can't interfere in an ongoing investigation!"

"I'm not going to interfere. I just want to know where it is."

Flynn could hear Chadwick's sigh over the phone. "I don't know why I listen to you . . . It hasn't moved since it was unloaded from the *Planet Queen*. Meditech doesn't know what to do with it. It's in warehouse seven."

Flynn stopped walking. He stared at his telephone. Things were starting to make sense again. "Warehouse *seven?*"

"That's what I said."

"Are you busy at the moment?" Flynn asked.

"Yeah, I'm tied up on the telephone with a nosy and annoying private investigator. Why? What else do you need?"

"I need to get back into warehouse seven," Flynn said.

"I can't let you get at that shipment!" Chadwick protested. "It might be evidence in a drug-related death!"

Flynn considered his next words carefully. "Wendy, this is important."

"To what? The loss of your license and my disbarment?"

"If you want to find out what's going on, meet me at warehouse seven. Now." Flynn switched off his telephone.

Flynn splurged and took a taxi to warehouse seven. He should have saved the money. No one waited for him in front of the warehouse. He paced up and down in front of the featureless bulkhead, resisting the urge to kick the airlock hatch, for almost half an hour. There was no weekend traffic on the street. Flynn had his hand on the telephone in his pocket when he spied Wendy Chadwick walking down the street toward him. Flynn liked the way she looked in her jogging suit but refrained from saying so. He also forced himself not to ask what had taken her so long to get there from her office four levels above.

"Thanks for coming," he said.

"Don't thank me yet," Chadwick replied. "I'm not letting you through that hatch until you tell me what you expect to find."

"That's the warehouse where Kemper and Santino tried to kill us, right?" Flynn said, pointing at the locked hatch. "The same warehouse where a shipment of chemicals ordered by the late, drug-using Dr. Vasquez is being stored. It *officially* does not contain polymethyl two four dibenzolacetate, or even the ingredients required for its manufacture, but Vinny Santino was in Meditech Hospital on Wednesday, trying to buy it, and now Kemper and Santino are dead. Murdered. I know that you Company types believe in all sorts of coincidences, but isn't this one pushing things just a bit too far?"

Chadwick glanced at the locked hatch. "If what you're

assuming is true, then I certainly can't let you at that shipment. It would be evidence in not only a drug investigation but in a murder investigation as well."

Flynn gritted his teeth. "I don't want access to it. I just want to see if it's still there."

Chadwick stared at the investigator. She started to say something, stopped, then took her telephone from the pocket on her belt. "Company Security," she said into the phone. "This is Wendy Chadwick, legal director. I'm about to enter warehouse seven. I do *not* want to be shot at this time. There is no reason for you to respond anyone to this location. Do I make myself clear?" She flashed a brief smile at the response. Wendy re-keyed the phone. "Marshals Office . . . May I speak with Marshal Wofford, please? . . . How very dedicated of him. Are you the watch commander, Deputy Lopez? Good. This is Wendy Chadwick, the Company's legal director. Yes, that one. As a matter of fact, I'm about to enter warehouse seven again. I have so informed Company Security, so there is absolutely no reason for any violence this time . . . Thank you, Mr. Lopez." Chadwick put away the telephone. She turned to the airlock hatch and placed her hand on the scanner. "Security computer: executive lock override. Wendy Chadwick." The status light changed from red to green. Chadwick opened the hatch. "Follow me, Mr. Flynn."

The warehouse looked the same as it had Wednesday evening. Chadwick stared at the rows and rows of shipping containers. "Okay, Mr. Investigator: which one?"

Flynn shrugged. "You tell me. You're the one with access to Company records."

Chadwick made a face but took her computer from a pocket in her belt. "Well, I'm afraid this isn't much help. It just says grid location *A-6*."

Flynn noticed the yellow markings on the warehouse floor. "That's enough. Follow me."

Wendy followed, but couldn't keep from looking over her shoulder at the warehouse entrance, as though expecting trigger-happy security guards to appear. Row *A* was closest to the outside hatch. File *6* was right next to the pile of shipping containers on which Ms. Chadwick had stood to look at the overhead crane. The crane had been moved but the shipping containers, two of them showing pulsed laser impacts, had not.

The container marked 54-30-0930-0902 would retain air pressure to protect its contents if it was exposed to vacuum. Flynn, using his handkerchief to avoid smudging any existing fingerprints, began undoing the latches.

"Stop that!" Chadwick protested. She glanced over her shoulder again, this time at the security camera mounted over the entrance hatch. It was showing far more interest in Flynn and Chadwick than it had the night of the shoot-out. "You could be tampering with evidence!"

"No," Flynn corrected, "I'm just checking to make sure that the evidence is still here." He undid the last latch and eased open the end of the container. Light from the warehouse flooded into the interior. Flynn let the end of the container drop to the floor. "Huh. Empty."

Chadwick pushed him aside and stared into the container. Never had she seen a space that looked so vacant. She compared the number on the shipping container to the number shown on the computer, checking every digit, and then compared it again, reading the numbers in reverse. "There must be some mistake . . ."

"You mean, there had *better* be some mistake," Flynn corrected. "But there isn't. The chemicals that Vasquez ordered should be in that container. They're not."

"But, I don't see how . . . this warehouse is kept locked—"

"We left it open Wednesday night." Flynn glanced toward the security camera over the entrance hatch. "That camera doesn't work worth crap when the lights are out, *which they were* when Santino and Kemper were shooting at us."

Chadwick was still staring into the empty container, her legal mind concerned with possible Company liability. "There's no proof that it happened the other night . . . We don't know that Kemper and—"

"When you instruct the computer to unlock the hatch, *it records who gave that instruction*, right? So although Kemper and Santino could have used their Security jobs to gain access, as soon as the disappearance of those chemicals was noticed the authorities would check the computer logs to see who had been in here. Kemper and Santino would have been suspected immediately, *unless* they had a valid security reason for entering, *which we gave them* Wednesday night. And Kemper and Santino didn't follow us into the basement—I'd hit Santino in the arm, and Kemper stayed with him. They had this warehouse to themselves for quite awhile."

"But how would they know about the shipment?" Chadwick protested.

"Vasquez had to be getting his polymeth *someplace*," Flynn responded. "Kemper and Santino wouldn't have to be rocket scientists to bribe somebody at Meditech to tell them about any chemicals that Vasquez had ordered. They learn about this shipment and guess that the chemicals aren't what's shown on the shipping manifest, but are actually Dr. Vasquez's re-supply of polymethyl two four. They wait for an opportunity to grab the shipment. Wednesday night, they got it. But Santino had seen me in Meditech's Trauma Center that morning. He must have figured that I was trying to find out where Vasquez was getting his dope. When they came through the hatch and saw me standing next to this container, they probably thought I had beaten them to the drugs. No wonder they tried to kill us. So they spent yesterday in jail. Yesterday afternoon they got out of jail, retrieved the drugs from wherever they had stashed them, and tried to sell them to a third party. Or maybe they were going to split the shipment with a partner—the person at Meditech who had told them about the shipment, for instance. This third person liked a one-way split better than a three-way split. Exit Kemper and Santino."

Chadwick took her telephone from her belt. "Silvanus Drake, please . . . Mr. Drake, this is Wendy Chadwick. I'm in warehouse seven. You'd better get down here." She rolled her eyes toward the overhead in reaction to Drake's response. "In that case, I'll expect you shortly." She put away her telephone. "Drake's already on his way."

Flynn glanced again at the security camera. "He already knows what we found. Er, didn't find."

Chadwick leaned against the open shipping container. "I checked on the two people whose blood we found in here, like you asked me to: one of them has been on Earth for the last nineteen months, and he doesn't work for the Company anymore. So if you're right about the missing shipment, will you admit that our misadventure the night before last had nothing to do with the deaths of Mondragon and Asterbrook?"

Flynn bit his upper lip. "Yeah, maybe Drake wasn't thinking of Asterbrook and Mondragon when he ordered those guards to pick us up," he admitted. "Maybe Drake knew about the polymeth shipment, and ordered those guards to arrest us to get us away from the drugs."

Chadwick's eyes twinkled in amusement. "So our brush with death was coincidental to your investigation? I thought you didn't believe in coincidences."

Silvanus Drake stepped through the airlock hatch. Jogging suits could have been the Company's official weekend attire: Drake was wearing a gray one, with dark stripes down the sides. He walked to where Flynn and Chadwick were standing and looked into the open mouth of the empty container. "There were over thirty shipments in this container," he said. "We'll check to see if the Meditech order was delivered to the wrong address."

Flynn made a face. "You really think it was?"

"No, Mr. Flynn, I think it was stolen. Right out from under our noses. Probably the other night, when you were upsetting the calm and security of the Station." Drake shook his head. "We don't need another crime to investigate right now."

"This ties into last night's crime," Flynn replied. "Kemper and Santino were probably the thieves."

Drake started for the door. "Very foolish of them. The shipment wasn't worth stealing."

Flynn called after him, "Just because the manifest showed—"

Drake stopped and turned back toward the investigator. "This was the only shipment that Vasquez ordered in the two years he lived on the Station. The possibility that it contained another two-year supply of polymeth was obvious. Wofford didn't take the shipping manifest at face value. He had the shipment checked out on planet three."

Flynn squinted. "The shipment was exactly what the manifest showed?"

Drake nodded. "It was a legitimate shipment from a cut-rate chemical supply company, the employees of which were all investigated and found clean. So were the people who handled the shipment between the chemical supply company and here."

"But did *you* find the shipment to be legitimate?"

Drake cocked his head to one side. "Mr. Flynn, what good would it have done to have the authorities on Earth check out that shipment again?"

"You could have used the Station's electromagnetic scanners on this shipping container."

"I didn't have a warrant," Drake replied. "An electromagnetic scan for illegal drugs requires one." He looked at the empty container. "I should thank you for discovering why Kemper and Santino tried to shoot you the other night. If I had known this, I wouldn't have had to get them out of jail."

Wendy stared at him. "Mr. Warshovsky wanted them released because he thought your poor training program made the Company responsible for their overreaction."

"Mr. Warshovsky is the boss; he can feel responsible for their conduct if he wants," Drake replied. "I wanted Kemper and Santino released because they weren't going to lead me to whatever they were involved in while they were breathing the air in the jail."

Flynn looked thoughtfully at the security chief. "If you suspected them of wrongdoing, were you watching them last night?"

Drake nodded. "Security cameras lost them in the crush of people headed for the airball tournament. Are you done in here? If you're not, make sure you lock up when you leave." Drake turned and headed for the hatch.

"Don't worry, Mr. Drake," Chadwick called after him. "We'll make sure we lock the barn door after the horse has been stolen."

Flynn waited until Drake had left the warehouse to say, "Do you believe him?"

"About what?"

"That the shipment contained exactly what was listed on the shipping manifest."

Chadwick looked into the empty container. Her brow furrowed as she considered the implications. She knew that Drake scanned everything that came aboard Jupiter Station. If Drake knew that Vasquez's shipment was legitimate, then his only reason for sending his two goons into the warehouse to evict Chadwick and Flynn had to involve the deaths of Mondragon and Asterbrook. But Mondragon and Asterbrook hadn't been killed in that warehouse. That left only Vasquez's shipment . . . "But why would Drake lie about it? Wofford can confirm that the shipment checked out back on Earth."

"I don't know why Drake would lie about it," Flynn replied. "Maybe he has a psychological aversion to telling the truth. But the chemicals weren't found at the murder site. If Kemper and Santino hadn't brought the box of chemicals with them, they wouldn't have been killed—whoever killed them obviously wanted the chemicals. If they had brought the box but there had been nothing worthwhile in it, whoever killed them wouldn't have burdened himself with worthless—but incriminating—chemicals while making his escape." Unless the killer was either so dumb or so overconfident that he didn't check the contents of the box before opening fire. Flynn closed the container. "Either the killer is as stupid as Kemper and Santino, or that box really did contain polymeth."

Chapter 9

Jupiter Station had no weather, so Flynn couldn't blame a tornado for what had happened to his apartment. The books had been pulled from the shelves. The drawers of his desk had been removed and emptied onto the floor. The containers from the storage locker beneath the stairs were in the middle of the room, upside down amid their former contents. The Company-owned paintings had been stripped from the walls; the corner of one of them was peeking out from beneath one of the empty storage containers. Michael stood in the open doorway and surveyed the mess with a mixture of rage and resignation, knowing that the kitchen and the bedroom would look the same.

Furrball peeked cautiously from beneath the desk, then picked his way gingerly through the debris to Flynn's feet. "Some watch cat you are," Flynn said. He bent down to pet the animal. "At least we won't have to clean this mess ourselves, will we?"

Flynn stood up and looked around the apartment again. The item he sought was the only object left on his desk. He stepped over a heap of his books and picked up the copy of the search warrant that had been left for his benefit. Flynn scanned it quickly.

. . . The suspect admitted to having in his possession on the night before the murders a laser pistol that could have been used in the killings, and although he claimed to have thrown away said pistol, he had been unable to lead

Deputy Marshal Feldstein to the gun . . .

Michael made a face, but he resisted the urge to tear up the warrant and instead put it into the top drawer of his desk. He keyed his telephone. "Marshals Office." The call was answered by the watch commander. "Let me speak to Wofford," Flynn said.

"Marshal Wofford isn't in the office at the moment," the deputy said patiently.

"Then forward the call!"

"He's investigating a murder," the deputy explained.

"This is Mike Flynn calling. That empty-headed boss of yours executed a search warrant on my apartment this morning before he arrested me. There was nothing here to find, but Wofford made a mess of my place while proving that to his satisfaction. According to the Supreme Court, if a search does not turn up evidence, the premises must be returned to the condition in which they were before the search. That has not been done—"

"We're very busy at the moment, Mr. Flynn—"

"I don't give a damn! I want my apartment cleaned up *right now!* If you don't have a crew here in ten minutes I'm going to call U.S. Attorney Pierce *and* the reporter for SSN!" Flynn broke the connection.

Mike stepped carefully through his belongings and into the kitchen. The marshals had not plundered his liquor supply. He poured himself two fingers of Irish whiskey, set the chair behind the desk onto its casters, and sat down to wait for the clean-up crew.

The ten-minute deadline came and went. Flynn didn't follow through on his threat—ten minutes was a very short time for the watch commander to get a crew to Flynn's apartment. Michael pulled a painting from the mess on the floor and turned it over. The microcam that the Company goons had planted there was gone. Marshal Wofford hadn't asked him about it and Flynn guessed that Drake had reclaimed it before the search. Flynn inferred that Drake had known that the search was about to take place; the security chief had probably suggested to the marshal that Flynn had been the killer—Flynn couldn't investigate the Company while he was in jail.

Twenty minutes after Flynn's call, Sid Feldstein appeared in the open doorway. The deputy shook his head in disbelief. "Wofford must be madder at you than he is with me! Lopez said that he tossed your place himself. I've never seen a legal search leave such a mess!"

Flynn poured two fingers of whiskey into another glass and handed it to Feldstein. "He's probably out of practice."

"He was probably pretty exasperated, too," Feldstein said. "He had *everybody* up all night. We went to the apartments of the victims and interrogated Santino's wife and Kemper's girlfriend—high-percentage suspects—but they had alibis, so we got Kemper and Santino's work logs from the Company and checked every place they'd been for the day before they were arrested. That didn't turn up anything, either, and I suppose that's when he started suspecting you. What the hell was he looking for in here?"

"The pulsed laser that was used to deactivate Kemper and Santino."

Feldstein looked askance. "What good would that do? You can't link a specific pulsed laser to the wound made by one."

"No," Flynn answered, "but the Company won't let private citizens possess lasers on Jupiter Station, so if Wofford had found a gun in here that would have been pretty convincing evidence. But how did you get stuck with cleaning up? You said you were up all night."

Feldstein snorted. "So was everybody else. I'm working off the bad feelings that Wofford has for me for putting that security-cam watch on you that confirmed your alibi for the time of the killings. We don't get many murder mysteries on Jupiter Station, you know, especially ones where the marshal and half of the deputies were right next door when the crime occurred."

"Wofford was at the airball tournament?"

Feldstein nodded. "He was watching his people play. We constitute half of the Federal team."

"Then why were you beaten by the insurance agents?"

The deputy shrugged. "I wasn't there, but from what I heard, they had two guys who were so damned good they could almost play in the professional league back in Earth orbit."

"Silverberg and, ah, what's his name . . . Wang?"

Feldstein squinted. "You heard about them?"

"I did pre-employment background checks on 'em," Flynn explained. "They *are* good enough for the professional league. At least, they were. They both played professionally for a couple of seasons. Of course, that was nine, ten years ago."

Sid pursed his lips. "Why those . . . those damned insurance agents brought in a couple of *ringers!*"

"Terribly unsporting of them. But perfectly legal."

"It won't make Wofford any happier when he learns of it," Feldstein said. "He bet Kyle Pierce a hundred bucks that we'd win last night. So he was probably in a real bad mood when he got home. Then he gets called out of bed—for the second night in a row—and has to go right back to the hub, not a hundred meters from where he'd been watching the game, to investigate a crime that had occurred literally right under his nose. After we investigated all night and found nothing, you must have been the only person he could think of with a motive, so he picked on you. He figured he'd look like a genius if he wrapped this one up less than twelve hours after the crime occurred. Get himself transferred back to three before his wife leaves him and goes home alone."

"If he wants to look like a genius, why doesn't he just find out what the Company's covering up about the deaths of Philip Asterbrook and Jonny Mondragon?"

Feldstein suppressed a snicker. "Because there was no cover-up," he replied. "Kytel investigated it and he was a good investigator. If he didn't find anything, then there was nothing to find."

"And now he has a Company job in South Africa for three times what he was making as a marshal," Flynn said.

Feldstein's expression changed. "You won't make any friends in the Marshals Office if you go around accusing us of taking bribes, Michael, old friend."

"I'm not accusing any of you, Sid. I'm not even accusing Kytel."

Feldstein ran his tongue around the inside of his mouth. "Sounded like an accusation to me."

"Whatever's being covered up is so big that it would have been worth a lot more than a Company job to keep Kytel's mouth shut," Flynn explained. "Kytel was sent to Earth because there was something fishy about that accident, something he didn't see at the time but which might have occurred to him later. That's why all the personnel transfers were made. But I can't prove a damned thing." Flynn looked at the door. "When does the rest of the clean-up crew get here?"

"Hah! I *am* the rest of the crew!"

Flynn winced. "Sorry you got stuck with this, Sid. This mess isn't your fault."

"Yeah, well, I'm on overtime. Can you show me where this stuff goes?"

Flynn got up from the table. "Here, I might as well give you a hand—I'm out of leads and out of ideas of where to look for new ones."

"Aw, don't let it get you down, Mike. Only fictional detectives solve all their cases." From the look on Flynn's face, Feldstein could see that his friend wasn't in the mood to be cheered up. "It's time you took a break from investigating, anyway. I got an extra ticket to the airball games this afternoon—"

"How the hell did you get an extra ticket? The tournament games have been sold out for a month!"

"I was treating my family," the deputy explained, "but Rachel's not a sports fan. This morning she tells me that if I really want to treat her I should just take David and let her have an afternoon of peace and quiet."

"Sid, you could sell that ticket for a hundred bucks."

"Hey, old pal: did I say anything about *giving* it to you?"

Flynn had never been very good at airball, nor had he ever been interested in watching other people play it, so the airball mania that had swept through Jupiter Station since the airball cages had been constructed had passed him by. But with nothing better to do with his time, he found himself waiting with five other people for an elevator. The car was already half full when it stopped at Flynn's level, and it had to stop at every level above that until it was full and could proceed directly to the hub. It slowed as the artificial gravity decreased, finally creeping to a halt fifty meters from the Station axis, where the gravity was only one tenth of Earth normal. The other passengers on the elevator were fans of the airball teams that would be playing in that afternoon's tournament game, and they made their way toward the airball cage with much shouting and good-natured bouncing off of walls and ceiling.

Sid Feldstein and his nine-year-old son David were waiting for Flynn in front of the ticket machine, where a glowing display announced that the tournament was sold out. That close to the hub there was very little gravity and the floor covering had a tacky surface to improve traction. As Flynn walked toward his friend he passed through the intersection with a corridor that paralleled the axis and led the restrooms. Flynn couldn't resist glancing down the cross corridor toward the scene of the murders. The women's restroom was open for business, but on the other side of the corridor yellow tape with large black letters spelling *POLICE LINE DO NOT CROSS* had been stretched across the door of the men's room.

The door of the men's room suddenly swung inward, revealing U.S. Attorney Kyle Pierce and Wendy Chadwick, who ducked under the police tape.

Flynn paused at the corridor intersection. He waved to Feldstein, indicating that he'd only be a moment, then started down the corridor toward the restrooms.

Chadwick and Pierce were wearing the latest in leisure attire—tights, shorts, and casual coats—with a silver sheen. A matched pair of fashionable attorneys, Flynn thought. "I didn't know they had installed coed restrooms on this level," he said, taking them by surprise.

Pierce said, "I, ah, um, I just thought—"

"I asked him to show me the scene of the crime," Wendy explained.

Flynn nodded. "Would he be as helpful if I asked for the same favor?"

Pierce chewed his lip. "In her case, it was a matter of professional courtesy."

Flynn shrugged. "Can't you do me an unprofessional courtesy?"

"Mr. Flynn, that would be unprofessional."

"Oh, let him in, Kyle," Chadwick said. "What harm can it do? You're standing right here to make sure he does nothing wrong."

Pierce had a soft spot in his heart for Wendy. "Oh, all right." He stepped back into the restroom. "Come on in. But be careful! Keep your hands in your pockets and don't touch anything! You can guess what Wofford would do if he found your fingerprints in here!"

"The forensic team hasn't finished yet?"

"Oh, they finished last night," Pierce replied. "But at that time Wofford thought that you had done it. Now that he has no suspects he might send them back to look for more evidence."

Flynn ducked beneath the police tape and entered the restroom. There were five low-gravity urinals along the left wall and three low-gravity sinks and two toilet stalls along the right wall. In the mirror above the sinks Flynn noticed Wendy suppress a smirk. The security camera was on the wall above the door, its activity light glowing red to warn patrons that they were under surveillance. Flynn smiled at the camera.

Pierce pointed toward the back of the restroom. "The bodies were found in that last stall there. The door was closed. A swarm of people used this facility after the last airball game ended around twenty-two thirty and nobody noticed a thing. Janitorial robot found them around midnight."

Flynn walked to the back stall and looked in. There was no sign that Santino and Kemper had been killed there—pulsed lasers cauterized the wounds that they made and the victims hadn't bled. "How many times were they shot?"

"Twice each, right between the eyes. Must have died instantly. Neither made a sound that would have activated the security camera."

Flynn nodded. "Wofford told me that nothing else was found in here."

"That's right. The marshals even took the wastebasket to the lab and examined the contents in detail. Nothing related to the murder was found."

"And no box of chemicals," Flynn said.

Pierce gave Chadwick a puzzled glance. "Chemicals?"

"The shipment ordered by Dr. Vasquez," Flynn explained. "The one that disappeared from warehouse seven the night before last when Kemper and Santino tried to kill Ms. Chadwick and me in there. They—and whomever they met here last night—thought it included polymethyl two four."

Pierce shook his head. "You have a very active imagination, Mr. Flynn. Kemper and Santino were Company security guards. They'd probably bashed quite a few heads during their careers and made a lot of enemies."

Flynn flashed a smile. "But how many of those heads belonged to people with laser pistols?"

Chadwick diplomatically changed the topic of conversation. "I didn't know you were an airball fan, Mr. Flynn."

"I'm not. I prefer baseball. But there's no baseball field on the Station and a friend of mine had an extra ticket to the tournament this afternoon."

Chadwick blinked. "What's her name?"

Pierce ushered Chadwick and Flynn out of the restroom

in front of him. "We're here to cheer on the Bar Association," he said.

"The lawyers are playing this afternoon?"

Pierce frowned. "Didn't you know?"

"I told you: I'm not a fan."

The three headed for the airball cage. Pierce tried to walk in the middle, between Flynn and Chadwick, but Wendy outmaneuvered him and placed herself between the two men. As they turned the corner onto the corridor leading to the cage, Sid Feldstein was glancing impatiently at his watch. He looked up and saw Flynn. "It's about time!" he called. "What the hell were you doing down there?"

Flynn and the two attorneys were nearing the deputy. "Getting a guided tour of the murder scene," Mike said.

David Feldstein's eyes bulged open. He tugged at his father's sleeve. "Dad! Can we see it, too? Huh, Dad?"

"Ahh, I don't think so. I don't have the authority. Besides, the game's about to start."

"What do I owe you for the ticket?" Flynn asked.

"Twenty."

Flynn looked askance. "Sid, you only paid twenty for it!"

"Michael, I don't scalp my friends."

"Joey Yamaguchi's dad would have given you fifty bucks for that ticket!" David protested.

"I don't want to go to an airball game with Joey's dad," Sid said.

"The ticket wouldn't be for him!" David said, exasperated. "It would be for Joey!"

"I told you I didn't want you playing with him." Feldstein turned to Flynn. "Harry Yamaguchi's the Company's top biochemist," he explained. "His son Joey's always playing with chemicals. He's going to blow himself up one of these days."

A steep flight of stairs led past the robot that checked tickets and through a hole in the deck near the end of the airball cage. The cage was a cylinder of chain-link mesh, twenty meters in diameter and forty-five meters long, co-axial with the Station's axis of rotation. That close to the axis there was so little gravity that there were no seats. Instead, the spectators lay against the "walls" of the cylindrical cavity that enclosed the cage, some two meters from it, where the slight centrifugal force produced by the Station's rotation made the walls act like a floor. Chadwick and Pierce had prime positions near the middle of the cage and headed in that direction. Flynn, Sid, and David pulled themselves along the cage to their positions in the cheaper section at the end of the cage.

Just then the airball teams entered the cage through the hatch on the other end. The stalwart nine representing the Jupiter Bar Association were attired in bright red and white and tried to make a spectacular entrance, tumbling end-over-end in tight cannonballs from the hatch and along the length of the cage, but the team members slowly diverged as they crossed the cage and two of them ricocheted off the wall. That didn't stop their fans—mostly friends and family, as lawyers were not a popular breed—from cheering their lungs out. The team from the iron smelter was wearing bright blue and light gray and entered the cage casually. Most of the people in the crowd were Company employees, of course, and their cheers for the people who would defend the honor and reputation of the Company against the despised attorneys were deafening in the confined arena. Only two members of the smelter team were female, compared to four of the lawyers. Flynn wondered if the fact that he recognized both women on the smelter team and none of the women on the legal team revealed something about his social circle. In fact, Flynn recognized only one of the attorneys—Mitch Habruch, Wendy's colleague from the Company's legal department.

Substitute players and coaches of both teams entered the cage, followed by the referees in their striped shirts. "The game might depend on them," Feldstein said, leaning toward Flynn while nodding at the referees. "The smelters are big and muscular, but slow. The lawyers are smaller and faster. If the refs call it close, keep the smelters from pushing the lawyers around, the legals might pull it off."

Before Flynn could nod in understanding, David said, "The smelters will mop the cage with those bozos. They couldn't get the ball in the goal from a meter away, even with both hands and a funnel. You'll see."

The cage started rotating. That is, it looked like the cage was rotating, but Flynn knew that it was actually de-spun and that the Station was rotating around it, so that the players would be in free fall even when clinging to the wire mesh. The other two airball cages on the Station could not be de-spun. Flynn would have preferred to have the tournament played in one of them, so that the players would have to deal with the Coriolis acceleration due to the rotating reference frame, but airball in its purist form was played in free fall, and the tournament demanded the purist form of the game.

The game would start with the iron smelters defending the goal at the end of the cage where Flynn and the Feldsteins sat. Despite the name of the game, airball players tried to spend as little time as possible in the air, where they had little control of their motion and accurate passing and shooting were difficult. The players positioned themselves on the cage, the five forwards close to the center, the four defensemen closer to their team's goal. One of the referees placed the ball in the center of the cage. The crowd fell silent in anticipation. The other referee raised his arm, then dropped it sharply to his side as he closed the contacts on his electronic whistle. The crowd roared as the forwards from both teams launched themselves toward the ball.

One of the lawyers won the race for the ball, and tucked and twisted in the air to avoid colliding with a member of the opposition. The lawyers had a play going off the opening sprint: one of them had ignored the ball and had jumped for the goal. Now she was in the clear, and her teammate with the ball hit her right in the hands with a chest pass that looked straight and crisp to the free-falling players but which arced wickedly in the eyes of the rotating spectators. She was headed for the corner of the cage, crossing in front of the goal. The smelters' defensemen pushed off from the cage, aiming for the axis in front of the goal, trying to block the shot. The lawyer waited for their momentum to carry them past the axis. Two of them collided and went tumbling out of control. The lawyer took her shot, but the ball hit the back of the cage half a meter to the side of the goal opening. The crowd of Company supporters cheered wildly.

"I told you," David said. "Couldn't get it in with a funnel."

The ball rebounded toward the center of the cage. The smelters controlled it and formed a play of their own: one of their forwards launched himself through the knot of defenders in front of the goal, trying to make the resulting collisions look accidental. But the referees *were* calling a close game, and one signaled a delayed penalty. The shot went home and the crowd cheered, but the goal light didn't flash

231

and when the cheering died down the announcer gave the bad news: the smelter forward would do five minutes in the penalty box for blocking. The crowd responded with hisses and a barrage of plastic squeeze bottles that bounced off the cage.

The game did not settle down to the precise plays that Flynn liked to watch. Instead, it became a series of mad dashes from one end of the cage to the other as the lawyers tried to wear down their slower opponents. Their strategy worked, for at the end of the first half the lawyers had fifteen shots on goal to the smelters' seven. Their poor shooting skills offset their successful game plan, however, and they trailed two to one at the half, despite the fact that two of the smelters' starting players were in the penalty box and another had been evicted from the game for punching one of the referees in protest of a blocking call.

"It's not shots on goal that counts," David said sagely, "it's shots *in* goal."

The second half started out as a replay of the first, but with the lawyers trying to get closer shots. Flynn noticed that Habruch, the only attorney to score in the first half, wasn't in the cage. He scanned the crowd just in time to see Chadwick and Pierce headed for the exit. He poked Feldstein with his elbow and pointed to the pair. "What do you think? Rats leaving the sinking ship?"

Feldstein squinted at the departing attorneys. "Mmm, maybe, but more likely it's business. Wanna bet my boss has pulled in some goons for questioning about last night's murders?"

Flynn grunted. "It's about time he got his investigation going in the right direction."

The smelters took a two-goal lead before the lawyers' fast-break strategy wore down the Company team. The Bar

Association tied the game late in the second half, but lost it in the closing minutes when a desperation shot by one of the smelters from his own end of the cage sailed through the goal. The crowd, in higher spirits than ever after sucking beer from squeeze bottles for almost two hours, celebrated wildly.

Feldstein turned to Michael and shouted above the din, "If I had the beer concession for this place I could afford to retire before David gets to high school."

Flynn nodded. "Who's playing in the second game?"

"Satellite Delta Maintenance against Mining Crew Two. It'll be a helluva game."

Since both teams in the second game were composed of Company personnel, spectator loyalties were divided, with approximately equal numbers of fans for each team. Both teams played a physical game but the referees were still enforcing the letter of the rule book, so the penalty box was kept full and by the end of the first half three players had been ejected for fighting. The mining crew held a one-goal lead and their fans taunted the maintenance team throughout the break. The second half was even more unruly than the first and it wasn't long before another maintenance player was ejected for unsportsmanlike conduct. The crowd quieted enough to listen to the announcement and a fan to Flynn's right took the opportunity to get to his feet and shout, "Damn refs oughtta be flushed out an airlock!" The maintenance fans roared their approval, but threatening a referee with physical harm was against Company rules and two orange-suited security guards made their way toward the outspoken fan. He boldly faced the guards, thrust out his chest, and announced, "You going to kill me, too, like Kemper and Santino?" The crowd applauded him, and he gained courage, refusing to be evicted quietly. In the light gravity the guards had difficulty exploiting their advantage in numbers and physical size. The fan's friends came to his aid, more security guards hastened to the scene, and a low-gravity free-for-all broke out. It began to receive more attention than the game, distracting even some of the players, and one of the miners used the opportunity to score a cheap goal. The goons finally carried off four fans but the maintenance team was unable to overcome the two-goal deficit and went down to defeat.

Flynn was relieved when the game ended. He felt guilty watching airball games while he should have been working, even though he couldn't figure out what he should be working on. In a few hours he would have to send his nightly report to the Asterbrooks and confess that his investigation had led him in a circle back to his starting point.

"I'd invite you to our place for dinner," Feldstein said, "but I have to get to work. If the fans that watched the video coverage of these games are as well lubricated as these people—and they're probably worse—we're going to have a busy night."

Flynn was surprised. "You're working weekend shifts, too? And you worked this morning!"

"Everybody's been working extra shifts," Feldstein explained. "First with the Vasquez investigation, and now these murders."

"Well, thanks for the invitation, Sid, but I have to get back to work, too."

Feldstein raised an eyebrow. "Work on what? You told me that you were out of leads."

"That's where the work comes in: finding new ones."

The carousing fans were slow to leave the airball cage, and Flynn was able to catch the first elevator leaving the core. He ran through a mental list of the restaurants that were on his way home before he realized that he wasn't hungry. He walked without paying attention to where he was going, his mind preoccupied with depressing thoughts. He was inside Betty's Bar before he noticed where he was.

Flynn reached Betty's before the crowd that would come to celebrate the results of the afternoon's airball games and watch the evening ones. The video display above the bar was showing SSN's evening newscast—more scenes of the Ceres mine disaster—but the half-dozen patrons weren't paying attention. Jupiter Station had its own tragedy now, and with only twenty thousand people on the Station those that hadn't known Kemper and Santino probably knew someone who had. The airball tournament, which nearly everyone on the Station had been eagerly awaiting for weeks, had been supplanted as the principal topic of conversation by the murders.

"I heard that Wofford himself was going through every recycling bin on the Station, looking for the murder weapon," said a man at the bar as Flynn stepped next to him. The man was big and black-skinned and didn't seem to be in a good mood.

The man's companion contemplated his half-empty glass of beer and grunted. "Waste of tax dollars. Throwing away that gun is as good as confessing to the whole thing."

The residents of Jupiter Station didn't have to be trained criminalists to figure out that, aside from the marshals, the only people on the Station with pulsed lasers were the one hundred and forty goons that made up Silvanus Drake's security department. If one of them was missing his gun, he would instantly become the prime suspect.

"No need to throw away the gun, anyway," Flynn said, joining the conversation. "A specific laser pistol can't be linked to a laser wound." Betty walked over to Flynn's end of the bar. "Irish, my sweet," Michael said to her, "and don't let my glass go empty." He looked up just as the day's baseball scores chased each other across the bottom of the video display. "The Red Sox lost *again!* Two lousy runs, and Havana's pitching staff has a double-digit ERA!"

Betty poured three fingers of whiskey into a glass and placed it in front of Flynn. "No wonder you look depressed."

SSN's Science News of the Week was beginning. "Hey, Betty," the man next to Flynn said, "can't you put the local news on there? I want to see if they've made any progress on the murders."

"No," Flynn said. "I want to see this."

The announcer was a dark-haired Hispanic woman named Gabriella. She had big eyes and a bigger smile but was wearing the latest fashion in metallic red. She was saying,

. . . *when researchers at the National Institute of Standards and Technology in Boulder announced the results of their test of the theory of maverick physicist Patrick Marney, whose opposition to the gravitational theories of such noted physicists as Einstein, Wheeler, Dicke, and Yilmaz . . .*

Gabriella's image was replaced with a still of a man with a receding hairline and wearing a brown corduroy coat. Flynn didn't think that he looked like a physicist. Not like a real one, who spoke in invariant four vectors and didn't have the sense to come in out of the rain. If Flynn had seen him on a college campus he would have taken him for a literature professor.

. . . *The researchers confirmed that Marney's artificial gravity generator had changed the gravitational attraction in their Boulder laboratory by more than three percent. If confirmed by other laboratories, it would vindicate Senator Melissa Har-*

rington's insistence on funding an experimental test of Marney's theory with almost fifty million dollars at a time when other members of Congress are worried that the government won't be able to meet its payroll obligations by autumn.

To get another viewpoint on the results of the experiment, Solar System News went to Cambridge, England, and talked to Dr. Joseph N'Barubu, Nobel laureate of two thousand thirty-two and widely acknowledged as the world's greatest theoretical physicist . . .

The image on the screen changed to show a black man with a shock of unkempt graying hair, tweed coat, and a misbuttoned vest against a backdrop of what Flynn took to be Cambridge University. He could scarcely be anything but a physicist. The man said,

. . . I have too much work to do to concern myself with a silly experiment performed by some American technicians who are trying to keep their budget from being cut . . .

The man next to Flynn said, "Artificial gravity. Can you imagine a Jupiter Station that didn't rotate?"

"Three percent of normal isn't enough to keep the beer from floating out of your glass," Flynn replied. "Would you like to sip all of your suds from a squeeze bottle?"

The man's drinking companion said, "That kook Marney also says that it's possible to exceed the speed of light without using . . . what do they call it . . . negative energy. If he's right, the Company's next mining outpost could be at Alpha Centauri."

The man next to Flynn was less interested in superluminal travel than he was in Gabriella. "I love those fashions," he said.

"Makes her look like an overripe tomato," Flynn replied.

"Oh, but the way their legs show!"

Flynn swirled the whiskey around in his glass. "I watch

people for a living," he said. "Sometimes I have to watch women. Not all women have good-looking legs."

The man poured down the last of his beer and slammed his glass onto the bar. "Well, they should! With all that medical science can do these days, you'd think they'd be able to make women grow good legs!" He turned toward Flynn and squinted. "Say, wait a minute. You're that detective, Flynn, right? Well, we're not supposed to be talking to you—"

Michael was watching the video display. "Fine. Don't talk to me."

"But you can help me prove that it wasn't my fault."

Flynn sighed. He put down his whiskey glass. "What wasn't your fault?"

"My pressure suit! I wasn't the one who lost it!"

Flynn turned to look at the man. "How in the hell could you misplace something as large as a pressure suit?"

"I didn't!" the man insisted. "It was a couple of weeks ago. We were filling the radiation shield on Satellite Juliet with rubble. Got our suits all covered with dust, so the foreman says we should rack our suits in the airlock and not track dust all over the satellite. But then the next shift goes out, leaves the outer hatch open, and *my* pressure suit floats out into the vacuum and disappears. The foreman reads me the riot act the next day, but hell, accidents happen on the job. Then yesterday I check my pay deposit, and it's a thousand dollars short! I ask the foreman what gives, and he says they'd written off two suits on Juliet already, and they're looking to make an example of somebody, so they're docking my pay until it's paid for!"

Flynn understood why the man was in a bad mood. Pressure suits cost a third of a million dollars. The man would be paying for that suit until he retired. "What makes you think that somebody else was responsible for the loss of your suit?"

"I wasn't the last one out of the lock!" the man insisted. "It was that jerk Simmons—Thag, we call him. He's always had it in for me. If he racked his suit after I did, how come it wasn't his suit that drifted away, huh? I'll tell you how come: he pulled my suit out of the rack and stuck his in behind it, then left my suit unlatched on the end of the rack so any little disturbance would send it floating away. He thinks he's done it to me, but I'm gonna prove otherwise."

A lost pressure suit—something suited to Flynn's talents, not like a monumental cover-up or a double murder. "You said this was a couple of weeks ago?" Flynn asked. "So there won't be any fingerprints or other physical evidence left for me to find. The Company wouldn't be docking your pay unless they'd already investigated, and that means that there aren't any witnesses to back up your story. So I'll tell you what I can do for you: I can follow this guy Simmons around until he brags about what he did and I overhear him. That might take weeks. And I get twelve hundred bucks a day."

The man's eyes bulged open. The whites showed streaks of red. "Twelve hundred a day?"

"Plus reasonable expenses."

The man frowned. "Twelve hundred a day . . . for weeks, maybe?"

"Maybe. Of course, you could tail him yourself, or ask your friends to do it. Hell, he might have already bragged about it. Slip a hundred to the bartender at his favorite watering hole; you might get what you need cheap."

The man pursed his lips. "Yeah, sounds like a good idea. Thanks."

Flynn turned back toward the bar. "Don't mention it."

The man left. Flynn emptied his glass. Betty refilled it. He watched more of the evening news. Drake had outsmarted him; he would have to tell the Asterbrooks that he had failed. He finished the second glass of whiskey.

"You're not getting any happier," Betty observed as she prepared to pour Flynn another drink.

"Betty, do you know what I do?"

"Sure. You drink—whiskey, usually; beer, sometimes. And you chase women."

"I mean, for a living."

"You're a private investigator."

Flynn snorted. "I do pre-employment and premarital background checks. I listen to gossip to see if people are what they claim to be. I find out what happened to lost pressure suits. That's what I do."

Betty shook her head. "Case going badly, eh? Here, I have just the thing for you." She turned and stooped to open the cabinet along the wall behind the bar. "I've had something special on a shelf back here for years. I was saving it for when you get married . . . Ah, here we go." She stood up, blowing the dust from the bottle in her hand, and turned back toward Flynn. She placed the bottle on the bar in front of Michael. "Genuine Irish whiskey and very old. Bottled in County Cork before Irish independence."

Flynn shook his head. "You're wasting it on me tonight. I just want to get zombied."

Betty opened the bottle. "But you'll enjoy getting zombied more on this." She poured three fingers into Flynn's glass.

Flynn took a sip and smiled. "You're right, Betty: they don't make it like that anymore."

Betty smiled. "What did I tell you?"

Betty left to tend to her other customers. Flynn stared at

the amber liquid in his glass, marveling at how primitive chemical reactions could produce such a wonderful result.

Chemical reactions . . .

Of the many products that the Company produced at Jupiter, none were organic or biological. What was the Company doing with a biochemist like Harry Yamaguchi?

Flynn put his glass down on the bar. The chemistry labs were located with the rest of the research and development groups on Satellite Charlie, and the Company guarded its product development well. Satellite Charlie was harder to get into than a nuclear-weapons storage vault. Entrance was through computer-controlled hatches, and even most Company employees didn't have access. What better place for the secret production of polymethyl two four dibenzolacetate?

Betty was walking along the bar, looking for customers that needed refills. Flynn got her attention and asked, "Could I borrow your computer? I left mine in my apartment."

Betty made a face. "What do you think this is, an electronics supply store?"

"Okay," Flynn said, taking his wallet from his pocket, "I'll rent your computer."

Betty waved away the money. "Don't bother." She took a computer from beneath the bar and handed it to the investigator.

"Thanks, Betty. I don't know what I'd do without you."

Betty's nose wrinkled. "You'd drink someplace else, that's what you'd do."

Betty went back to work. Flynn used her computer to access the library. If Dr. Harry Yamaguchi was running a polymeth fabrication lab, he would scarcely have published that fact, and Flynn could find only one publication by

Yamaguchi in the preceding five years. That, however, was not unusual—Company research and development affected Company profits, and Company scientists were reputed to publish only their failures. Yamaguchi's work for the Company might be legitimate.

Flynn took out his telephone, then remembered that the Company was monitoring his communications. He used Betty's computer to call Joe Aguirre.

"You're lucky you caught me," Aguirre said. "I have a ticket to the airball tournament tonight. I was just on my way out the door."

"I won't keep you long," Flynn replied. "You have clearance to enter Satellite Charlie, don't you?"

"Yeah, but only for a few of the labs," Joe admitted. "Most of that place is locked up like CIA headquarters. But if you're looking for someone who can get you in there, you'll have to look elsewhere. My clearance is for me alone; I'm not allowed to escort anybody."

Flynn pursed his lips. He took a deep breath. "Thanks Joe. Sorry I bothered you."

"Hey, old friend, don't give up so easily," Aguirre replied. "Clearances for Satellite Charlie—for the satellite itself, that is; the labs are off limits to just about everybody—aren't all that hard to get. You could probably get one if you asked. Hell, that Meditech doctor who died from drug abuse last spring had one."

Flynn almost dropped the computer. "Vasquez? Emilio Vasquez had clearance to enter Satellite Charlie?"

"Must have," Aguirre said. "At least, I saw him there once last year, and he wasn't being escorted."

"Joe," Flynn replied, "I owe you another drink." Michael switched off the computer. He couldn't believe his good fortune. He had gone from having no leads to having a

242

great big one in just ten minutes and without working up a
sweat. What better way for Dr. Vasquez to get his polymeth
than by going directly to the secret fabrication lab?

Flynn restrained himself. There was a chance, a small
chance, that Vasquez had had legitimate business on Satellite Charlie. He switched on Betty's computer again and
called Missy Adamly. "I'm using a borrowed computer," he
said, since Missy knew that the goons were monitoring his
communications. "Where are you?"

"At work," Missy said disgustedly. "The computer
system on Juliet is AFU. Howie Ng's been over there full
time trying to fix it, so all our work here has fallen behind."

"Well, forgive me for taking advantage of catching you in
your office on a weekend, but could you use that computer
of yours to find out how Dr. Emilio Vasquez got clearance
to enter Satellite Charlie?"

Flynn could almost feel Missy's questioning stare over
the audio link. "What are you doing investigating
Vasquez?" she asked.

"Just following a lead." Flynn glanced at the security
camera at the other end of Betty's Bar. It wasn't pointed at
him. "Quickly, Missy. I don't know how long it will take
Security to realize that I'm not using my computer."

After a moment of silence Missy said, "Here it is: Satellite Charlie clearance for Dr. Emilio Vasquez, issued soon
after he got here . . . sponsored by Dr. Luk, our medical director." Missy sounded slightly surprised. "Security approval by Silvanus Drake . . . Ah-hah! Vasquez needed an
ultrabaric chamber for his research. We have an agreement
with Meditech to share equipment, and Meditech didn't
have an ultrabaric chamber, so he was entitled to use ours.
He got access to Charlie and room one eighty-two, where

the chamber resides, and used the chamber at three or four month intervals."

Flynn knew how the Company controlled capital equipment. "Who's in charge of it?"

"Ah, Dr. Lerman."

Flynn scowled. He had been hoping to hear that Harry Yamaguchi was in charge of the ultrabaric chamber. "Who's Lerman?"

"He's a metallurgist, or materials scientist. Something like that. He's head of the Ceramics Department. Most of our marvelous ceramic products are his inventions."

"Does Harry Yamaguchi work for him?"

Missy paused before replying. "Who's Harry Yamaguchi?"

"A biochemist."

"I doubt it," Missy replied, "but, just to be sure, let me check the accounting files to see what cases Yamaguchi's been charging . . . Uh-uh. Yamaguchi's been charging most of his time to his own case. He must be a department head. According to this, he's been working almost exclusively on that case ever since he got here . . . That's strange."

"What's strange?" Flynn asked. "That he should spend all his time on the same project?"

"No. About a month ago he started charging five to ten hours a week to another case, but it's not an R and D case. According to the number, it's a Security case, one that Silvanus Drake supervises personally."

Flynn's eyes narrowed. "Can you find out how many other people have been charging that case?"

Missy sighed. "Yeah, hold on . . . just two. One of Yamaguchi's assistants, and . . . This doesn't make any sense at all: Cynthia Dornhoeffer."

Flynn had to put his whiskey glass on the bar to avoid

spilling its contents. "The Company's polymeth expert?"

"Yeah. That's what doesn't make sense. She charges most of her time to a Medical case, but a few weeks ago she started charging time to the security case that Yamaguchi's been using, and the times correlate. They appear to be working on it together. Must be a rush job—they've charged most of the time on weekends."

Flynn drummed his fingers on the bar. "Thanks, I owe you another one."

"Yeah, well, I'm not holding my breath waiting for you to pay off."

Flynn switched off and stared at the shelves of bottles behind the bar. Vasquez might have been using the ultrabaric chamber for his legitimate polymeth research. Flynn would see about that.

With the aid of Betty's computer, Flynn found that Vasquez had published approximately one paper per year, eight before moving to Jupiter Station and two after his arrival there. None of the doctor's papers mentioned an ultrabaric chamber. If Vasquez had been using the chamber on Juliet, it wasn't for his published research. Flynn had a sudden thought, and directed the computer to correlate ultrabaric chambers with anything published on polymethyl two four: the only citations the computer could find stated that high pressures did *not* facilitate polymeth production.

A man pushed his way to the bar and jostled Flynn's arm. The intruder said, "If you're not going to drink, how about making room at the bar for someone who will?"

Flynn started to point out that there was lots of room along the bar, but then he noticed the noise level and turned to look at the room. It had magically filled with people who were talking and drinking and having a good time. Flynn glanced at the time display in the corner of the computer display and was surprised to discover that he had spent two hours studying Vasquez's publications.

Flynn picked up his glass and belted down the whiskey. He plunked the glass on the bar next to the computer. "Betty!" he called above the noise. He pointed to the empty glass. "On my tab!"

Flynn left the bar and headed for the ramp that would take him to his apartment. Yamaguchi and Dornhoeffer had been working on their mysterious project for Silvanus Drake on weekends. Tomorrow would be Saturday. Flynn would see what they were doing.

Chapter 10

Flynn didn't go jogging Saturday morning. He got up before six and headed for Yamaguchi's apartment.

Harry Yamaguchi lived at nine forty-three Eleventh Street, level ten, where the gravity was lower and the rents were higher than where Flynn lived on level four. Yamaguchi's apartment was reached from a walkway, twice as wide as the one in front of Flynn's apartment, one level above the street on level nine. Flynn stayed on nine, from where he could watch Yamaguchi's apartment inconspicuously. He need not have altered his morning routine: the lamps brightened, simulating daylight, and traffic on Eleventh Street picked up, but the door to Yamaguchi's apartment stayed closed.

Nothing occurred until after nine o'clock, when a woman wearing the latest fashion in metallic-sheened medical white walked up to Yamaguchi's door and rang the bell. The woman's head was surrounded by a mass of wildly teased blond hair. Flynn almost smiled—the exaggerated coiffure was Dr. Cynthia Dornhoeffer's hallmark. The door was answered by a man of less than average height, attired in tee shirt and casual tan slacks, and with a narrow, Oriental face and prominent eyebrows. He stepped out of his apartment and joined Dornhoeffer. The pair started walking toward the elevator that would take them to the hub and the shuttle docks. The morning rush of weekend-shift workers was over, and there were few people on the streets. Flynn followed at a distance, but Dornhoeffer and

Yamaguchi did not look around to see if they were being watched. They acted like they had nothing to fear. They didn't—they were working for Silvanus Drake.

Flynn watched the pair get into an elevator. He took the next available car, and reached the docks just in time to see Dornhoeffer and Yamaguchi board a shuttle. The shuttle's second stop would be Satellite Charlie. Flynn waited until the shuttle departed, to make sure his quarry didn't get off before it left. He assumed that Company Security was still monitoring his communications, so instead of using his phone he hurried to Wendy Chadwick's apartment. Michael could not afford to anger the lawyer, so he resisted the urge to lean on the doorbell and instead pressed the button only once. Chadwick must have checked the security monitor before opening the door because she didn't look surprised to see Flynn. She was in bare feet and was wearing a short, blue terrycloth robe.

"What now, Mr. Flynn?" she said, looking and sounding bored. "Are you taking me to breakfast?"

It was a tempting thought, but Flynn was after big game and he was in a hurry. "Ever see polymethyl two four manufactured?" he asked.

It took a moment before Wendy's bored expression was replaced with one of concern. "You actually found something? Where?"

"Satellite Charlie," Flynn replied, as though he was certain.

Chadwick drew back from the doorway. "How the hell did you get into Satellite Charlie?"

"I didn't, yet," Flynn said.

Wendy stared at him, then shook her head vigorously. "No way! I am *not* letting you into Charlie for one of your fishing expeditions! It's strictly off-limits to all except cleared personnel!" Chadwick could see that she hadn't dissuaded Flynn, so she added, "Besides, there can't be a polymeth fabrication lab on Charlie. Every square meter of space on that satellite is in use. We wish it was bigger."

"Including its basement?" Flynn suggested. "Fifteen minutes ago Dr. Cynthia Dornhoeffer, the Company's polymeth expert, and Dr. Harry Yamaguchi, the Company's top biochemist—the kind of person who would know how to make polymeth—boarded a shuttle to Satellite Charlie. This is Saturday, Ms. Chadwick. They shouldn't be working today."

Chadwick moistened her lips. "Those shuttles make the rounds of all the—"

"Dornhoeffer's office is in the hospital here on the Station," Flynn interrupted. "Yamaguchi's lab is on Charlie. Where else would they be going? Besides, Charlie is the most secure facility at Jupiter—the perfect place for a polymeth lab."

Chadwick contemplated Flynn's information. She had no knowledge of any project on which both Dornhoeffer and Yamaguchi would be working. Flynn might have stumbled onto something. Wendy stepped aside and motioned for Flynn to enter her apartment. "Come in, Mr. Flynn," she said with a sigh. "Let me get dressed."

Less than five minutes later Chadwick appeared from her bedroom wearing the latest fashion in women's business suits in metallic yellow—Satellite Charlie was continuously monitored by security cameras and she wanted to look her best. Flynn paid for a taxi to take them to the elevators, saving a few minutes, but they just missed the ten-o'clock shuttle and had to fidget away the time until the ten-thirty shuttle departed. The only other people on the shuttle were three maintenance workers. Company maintenance people wore yellow coveralls of almost the same shade as Chadwick's suit. Wendy was seated next to a viewport, and stared at gigantic Jupiter, down sun and illuminated, thinking that before she had met Michael Flynn she would never have believed that Conglomerated might be mass producing illegal drugs. Now she was spending her Saturday morning reassuring herself that Flynn was wrong.

Flynn interrupted Chadwick's reverie with, "You didn't stay for the end of the airball game yesterday."

Chadwick turned from the window. "No," she replied, "Kyle and I got to spend our afternoon convincing Marshal Wofford that his deputies couldn't pull in and question every goon with no better reason to suspect them than they carry laser pistols." She paused. "He wouldn't even talk to us in his office; we had to follow him all over the Station while he conducted his own investigation. He seemed desperate—his wife is rumored to be fed up with life out here and is returning to planet three; if he can't earn a transfer home, he'll lose her. I finally had to threaten him with an injunction. Kyle backed me up, so we got done in time for him to take me to dinner at the Martian Nugget."

The Martian Nugget was a new restaurant, located in the area beyond the Park and three levels above the one on which Flynn lived. It was not owned by the Company— Conglomerated Mining and Manufacturing would never have named anything after an incident that had nearly destroyed it.

"Well, at least you got a romantic evening out of it," Flynn said.

Chadwick hesitated. "Kyle got a romantic evening out of it," she corrected.

"Oh?"

"He . . . he likes me."

"But you don't like him?" Flynn asked.

"I don't *dislike* him. I'm just not attracted to him."

"Why not? He's not bad looking; you're in the same profession; I hear he has a great future in the Justice Department."

"He was married," Chadwick explained. "On planet three. To another government attorney—Environmental Department. Space law experience wouldn't do her any good—there's no 'environment' in space to worry about—so she didn't want to come here. An ambitious man like Kyle Pierce couldn't let a little thing like marriage get in the way of his career, so he divorced her. I won't start a relationship with a man who would leave me the moment our career paths diverged."

Satellite Charlie was just two kilometers ahead of Jupiter Station in its orbit and the shuttle trip took only five minutes. The shuttle left Flynn and Chadwick in the airlock and continued on its route to the other satellites. Michael grabbed a convenient handrail to stabilize himself in the negligible gravity of the docking airlock. He looked at the security camera, which was looking right back at him. Flynn smiled at the camera and waved.

Chadwick swallowed. "Executive authority," she said to the camera. "Wendy Chadwick escorting Michael Flynn into Satellite Charlie." She glanced at the inner airlock hatch, but its red light stayed red.

Chadwick pursed her lips. "Executive authority!" she said more loudly. "Wendy Chadwick! I *have* the authority to escort Mr. Flynn into Charlie!"

Nothing happened.

"The computer needs only a microsecond to make up its mind," Flynn said. "There's a human in the loop."

"Silvanus Drake," Wendy replied through clenched teeth.

Flynn shook his head. "It wouldn't take this long for Drake to reach a decision. They're calling Drake."

The computer suddenly announced, "Satellite Charlie is temporarily closed while its back-up air processing system is purged."

Flynn and Chadwick looked at each other. "It's a crock," Flynn said. "If Satellite Charlie was closed, the shuttle wouldn't have dropped us here."

Chadwick protested, "But I'm cleared to enter Charlie! All members of the executive staff are! We discuss R and D projects at our meetings! We know what's going on in here!"

Flynn raised an eyebrow. "You sure about that?"

Wendy's temper was approaching the boiling point. Flynn was right: the shuttle shouldn't have delivered them to a closed satellite. Chadwick bit her upper lip. "Computer," she said, "Wendy Chadwick entering Satellite Charlie alone. Mr. Flynn is staying in the airlock."

Flynn didn't bother protesting. The computer responded, "Satellite Charlie is temporarily closed while its back-up air processing system is purged."

Chadwick's temper boiled over. She kicked the hatch, bruising her toe and sending herself tumbling backward in the negligible gravity. She grabbed the hatch handle to steady herself.

At that moment the inner hatch opened, and Flynn and Chadwick found themselves face to face with Yamaguchi and Dornhoeffer.

The doctors were startled to find the airlock occupied. Yamaguchi scowled at the unexpected visitors. "Who the hell are—" The scowl softened when he thought he recognized Chadwick. He squinted at her and said, "Aren't you the head of the Legal Department?"

Chadwick took a deep breath to calm herself and extended her hand in greeting. "Wendy Chadwick. And this is . . . this is Michael Flynn."

Flynn also extended his hand but the chemist hesitated. "The same Michael Flynn who was suspected in the deaths of those two goons?"

"He didn't do it, Dr. Yamaguchi," Chadwick said impatiently.

The chemist relaxed. "No laser pistol, eh? Well, in that case, glad to meet you, Mike. Do you know if the marshals have any new leads?"

Flynn shook his head. "As far as I know, Doctor, they don't even have any old leads."

"Well," Yamaguchi said, "what are you doing on Satellite Charlie?"

"Actually, we were going to ask you the same question," Flynn replied. He pointed at a small bottle in Dornhoeffer's hands. "That couldn't be a bottle of polymethyl two four dibenzolacetate you have there, because Ms. Chadwick assures me that there's no room on this satellite for a polymeth fabrication lab."

The scientists looked at each other. Their expressions told Flynn the answer to his question. "Lucky for you it can't be polymeth," he said, looking at the bottle, "because what you have there would be worth, oh, about twenty years, if you get a lenient judge."

Dornhoeffer clutched the suspect bottle to her chest. "I have a license to experiment with polymeth," she said, as though that justified everything.

Chadwick had not recovered her patience after the dispute with the computer. "What's going on?" Her tone demanded an answer.

Dornhoeffer and Yamaguchi looked at each other again.

Neither wanted to take the lead. Yamaguchi finally said, "We were ordered not to discuss this project with anyone."

Chadwick's eyebrows lowered and lines creased her forehead. "Ordered by whom?"

Yamaguchi moistened his lips. "Silvanus Drake."

Chadwick thrust out her jaw. "I'm the Company's attorney and I'm on the executive staff. You can tell me."

Yamaguchi and Dornhoeffer both looked at Flynn.

"Mr. Flynn has agreed not to publicize what he learns," Chadwick said.

Flynn hesitated, then raised his hand to stop the scientists. "Ah, I should warn you that I am required to report any felonies I uncover to the authorities."

"We're not breaking any laws!" Dornhoeffer insisted. "I told you: I have a license to experiment with polymeth!"

Chadwick's phone chirped, interrupting the conversation. The lawyer took the instrument from her pocket and answered it with an abrupt, "Chadwick! . . . I'm just trying to find out what's going on . . . because I'm sick and tired of these things being kept from—" She sighed. "Yes, Mr. Warshovsky, I can do that." She switched off without saying goodbye. "Mr. Warshovsky wants to see us—all of us. Now. And he has requested us not to discuss this matter further until we get to his place." She glanced at Flynn. "Shall we go?"

"I'd advise waiting for the shuttle," Flynn quipped.

They rode back to the Station in silence. Dr. Dornhoeffer held the mysterious bottle in her lap with both hands, as though it was very valuable. Flynn estimated that it held about ten milliliters of a viscous liquid. That much polymethyl two four would have a street value of twenty-five thousand dollars.

Ed Warshovsky's apartment was on level twelve. It was

twice the size of the next largest dwelling on the Station, large enough to reveal the curvature of the deck and overhead. Artificial sunlight poured through the artificial windows. The living room window showed a mule deer grazing placidly in a mountain meadow. That window was an experiment: instead of the computer-generated holograms in the other Station windows, it was an actual video image that had been beamed to Jupiter from Company land in the Rocky Mountains. Fifty minutes earlier—the light lag between Earth and Jupiter that Saturday—that mule deer actually had been grazing in that meadow.

Warshovsky himself answered the door and escorted his visitors through the foyer into the living room. Seated on the couch was Silvanus Drake.

Warshovsky had not met Michael Flynn before that day, and looked the investigator over carefully. He was goodlooking enough to be considered downright handsome, but there was nothing in his appearance or demeanor to explain why Silvanus Drake would consider him such a threat.

Warshovsky's wife Mary appeared in the doorway to the kitchen. Youth drugs had been perfected too late to keep her hair from starting to turn gray. "Would anyone like coffee?" she asked pleasantly.

"Thank you," Flynn answered, "but the only kind of coffee I like is the Irish variety."

The others were not so particular, and Mary disappeared into the kitchen to fetch coffee and cups. As soon as she was out of earshot, her husband said, "Mr. Flynn, please explain why you were trying to gain access to Satellite Charlie this morning."

"I was looking for a polymethyl two four fabrication facility," Flynn said simply. "The late Emilio Vasquez wouldn't have left his supply source on Earth and come

255

here unless he had known that he could get polymeth, and since he wasn't getting it shipped to him, he had to be buying it here. He was visiting Charlie regularly, ostensibly to use the ultrabaric chamber, but since none of his research papers mention an ultrabaric chamber, that must have been an excuse for his real purpose—the purchase of polymeth."

Warshovsky looked at Drake, who barely glanced at his boss in reply. Warshovsky nodded toward the apartment door. "Mr. Flynn, please wait outside for a few moments."

Flynn suppressed a smile and shook his head. "Oh, no. You're not getting rid of me that easily."

Drake stood up. "Yes, we are," he said. "Wait outside."

Flynn didn't want to leave until he had been told what had happened to Philip Asterbrook and Jonny Mondragon, but Drake had a laser pistol and was reputed to be well trained in its use. An altercation that put Flynn in jail wouldn't help his investigation. "Don't take too long."

Flynn's admonition had no effect. The investigator paced up and down the corridor in front of Warshovsky's apartment, wondering what was taking the people inside the apartment so long. From time to time a raised voice—Chadwick's, by the sound of it—was barely audible through the door. The lawyer, apparently, was not happy with the course of the discussion.

The door to the elevator at the end of the corridor opened and two security guards stepped out. They headed directly for Flynn. Both outweighed Flynn by at least fifteen kilos. One of them had a short beard. The ID tag on his coveralls bore the name Shaw. He smiled and said, "Well, if it isn't the wise guy, Michael Flynn." He poked his companion with his elbow. "This is the PI who likes to use security guards for target practice."

"That's only because your orange coveralls make such splendid targets," Flynn responded.

Shaw's companion had Johansen on his ID tag. He looked at Shaw and said, "We're going to have fun throwing this clown in the klink!"

Both goons advanced on Flynn. Michael donned a look of injured innocence and said, "On what charge?"

"We can start with loitering," Shaw said, his eyes darting to the closed apartment door, "in front of Mr. Warshovsky's apartment."

Flynn held his hands in front of his chest to ward off the guards. "It's not loitering if Mr. Warshovsky—and your boss, too—told me to wait here."

The guards paused and looked at each other. "He's making that up!" Johansen said with a sneer.

"Why don't you call your boss and find out?" Flynn suggested. "If I'm lying, there are probably more charges you can bring against me."

The goons hesitated, then Shaw took his telephone from his belt. He keyed the instrument and said, "Connect me with the boss. Mr. Drake? Kurt Shaw. We're about to impound Michael Flynn for loitering in front of Mr. Warshovsky's apartment—But the security camera has shown him hanging out here for—Yes, sir. Will do, sir." Shaw switched off and put his phone away. He stared at Flynn, eyes narrowed. "Someday you're going to find yourself at the bottom of a recycling chute."

"Well, I won't worry about it," Flynn replied. "You'll be right under me, breaking my fall."

For a moment Flynn thought that Shaw was going to forget his orders and start a fight, but then Johansen grabbed his companion by the arm and said, "Come on, let's get outta here. Something in this corridor is making the air smell bad." The guards departed through the same elevator door from which they had entered.

Fifteen minutes after the goons had departed, the door to Warshovsky's apartment opened and Chadwick, Drake, Dornhoeffer, and Yamaguchi filed out. Dornhoeffer was still clutching the bottle that Flynn presumed contained polymeth. Drake led her directly to the elevator, with Yamaguchi following closely behind. The biochemist gave Flynn a smile and waved at him as he past. Chadwick stopped next to Flynn.

"Am I going to get some answers now?" the investigator asked as pleasantly as he could manage.

Chadwick took a deep breath and let it out slowly. "I'm going to tell you everything I am authorized to say at the moment. I'll be able to give you the rest of the story very soon."

To Flynn, that sounded like a delaying tactic. "Define, 'very soon.' "

"A week or two, probably. I doubt it will be more than a month."

"And if it turns out to be a year?"

Chadwick shook her head once. "It won't, believe me."

Flynn ran his tongue around the inside of his mouth. "Why?"

Chadwick searched for words. "I tried to persuade them to tell you everything now, but they're afraid of this getting out before . . . before . . . well, you'll see when I tell you. And I will tell you! I promise!"

Wendy's eyes were earnest, but lawyers were trained in the art of talking around a subject without actually lying. Flynn asked, "What *will* your clients let you tell me now?"

Chadwick almost breathed a sigh of relief. "First of all, there is no illegal polymeth fab lab on Charlie."

Flynn's patience evaporated. "The hell there isn't! I saw Dornhoeffer go over there, remember? She wasn't carrying her little bottle of dope at the time. Now, I'm willing to believe that she has a polymeth license—it's her field of expertise—but I'd be real surprised if Yamaguchi has one. Therefore that polymeth couldn't have been stored in Yamaguchi's lab. Ergo, they made it over there."

Wendy considered her reply carefully. "You have no proof that that bottle contained any polymethyl two four."

Flynn turned away in disgust. "This isn't a court of law, Ms. Chadwick." He turned back toward the lawyer. "You can forget your legalisms. We both know that bottle contained polymeth."

"Any polymeth that *might* have been in Dr. Dornhoeffer's possession was not manufactured in an illegal fabrication facility," Chadwick said.

Flynn looked askance. "Does that mean that there's a *legal* polymeth facility on Charlie?"

"No! It means that—"

"How does this tie into the deaths of Asterbrook and Mondragon?"

Chadwick gritted her teeth. "It doesn't!"

"Horse dung!"

"It doesn't!" Chadwick insisted. "You found out what happened to Asterbrook and Mondragon: someone switched the crane pulleys without recording the fact."

Flynn shook his head. "You might think that you're telling me the truth, but your clients are lying to you about that 'accident' and they're lying to you about the polymeth."

Wendy put her hands on her hips. "Okay, smart guy, I'll prove it to you. Would you recognize a polymeth fabrication lab if you saw one? I'll give you a tour of Charlie. I'll open every lab, every office, every conference room. We'll go crawling through the basement. And if we find a polymeth lab, *I* will go to the marshals and swear out a complaint against the Company. Okay?"

Michael stared at the lawyer. Chadwick was a corporate attorney, not a trial lawyer. He didn't know if she had a flair for theatrics. He decided to call her bluff. "Okay."

The pair stopped at Flynn's apartment for a flashlight, then rode the shuttle back to Satellite Charlie. This time, the airlock hatch responded to Chadwick's executive authority. That should have made Flynn realize that he wasn't going to find anything, but he was too excited by the prospect of the discovery that he hoped to make to think clearly.

Satellite Charlie was much smaller than Jupiter Station. It had only two occupied levels instead of twelve and the curvature of the decks was much more apparent. Chadwick needed less than two hours to open every lab and office for Flynn's quick perusal. Flynn took more time in the room containing the squat, gleaming stainless-steel sphere that was the ultrabaric chamber, supposedly used by Dr. Vasquez, but the chamber took up half of the tiny room and Flynn could detect no sign of a concealed doorway to a hidden laboratory.

The basement was much harder to explore. It was less than two meters high, and in many places that space was reduced by plumbing and air pipes. It was more poorly lit than the basement on the Station, but Flynn's probing flashlight beam found nothing that shouldn't have been there.

The shuttle back to the Station was a workboat with seats for only eight people. Six of the seats were still empty after Flynn and Chadwick boarded. Flynn stared glumly straight ahead. His companion, her splendid yellow suit soiled from prowling through the basement, said, "Satisfied?"

Flynn didn't look at her. "No."

Chadwick shut her eyes in frustration. "Why not?"

"We didn't see all of Satellite Charlie," Flynn explained wearily. "There are utility ducts, the support arms from the hub to the rim, spaces around the reactor . . . We'd need a complete set of the engineering drawings for that satellite, and measuring tools to make sure there aren't any hidden compartments . . ."

Chadwick stared at the investigator. "Okay," she agreed. "Okay! Those drawings must be in the computer system someplace. I'll find out where. We'll go back to Charlie and take the damn satellite apart, if that's what you want."

"Don't you see?" Flynn insisted. "It has to be there! Vasquez wouldn't have come here if he hadn't been able to get polymeth at Jupiter! He wasn't going to Charlie to use the ultrabaric chamber—it's not mentioned in his research papers. And what the hell else is the Company doing with a biochemist like Harry Yamaguchi?"

Chadwick was silent for a moment. "Why didn't you ask me that before?"

Flynn was taken aback by the thoughtful expression on the lawyer's face. "Because I thought I had a good enough argument without it. Why?"

Chadwick raised her head. "Because you've agreed not to publicize what you learn on this case, and I have not been instructed *not* to tell you what Yamaguchi's doing here." Flynn looked at the lawyer, eyes narrowed. She continued, "You've seen the pressure suits that people have to wear out here: cumbersome garments, thick and bulky to cut down the radiation. But if Yamaguchi could develop a drug that would enable living cells to repair radiation damage as it occurs . . ."

Flynn leaned back in his couch, thinking. The Company might well have instituted a research project along those lines. Conglomerated could have a legitimate need for a biochemist at Jupiter. "A polymeth lab facility would probably be highly automated. It wouldn't take much of Yamaguchi's time. Give him time to do other things."

Chadwick sighed in exasperation. "I give up. You're hopeless. Why don't you do something useful, like finding out who killed Kemper and Santino?"

Flynn shook his head. "Aside from the fact that I wasn't hired to solve that case? I suppose there's a small chance that they were rubbed out on Drake's orders—they might have been able to testify about some of the not-so-legal things that Drake is wont to do, and would have traded that testimony in exchange for having the charges against them dropped—but Drake's smart enough to have arranged an 'accident' to silence them instead of a headline-making murder. No, it's more likely that they were killed by their silent partner in the attempted theft of polymethyl two four that, according to Silvanus Drake and Marshal Wofford, wasn't there in the first place. Drake will ferret out who did it soon enough."

"Drake? Not the marshal?" Chadwick asked curiously.

"Drake is smarter than Wofford and has more resources," Flynn explained. "Besides, the killer had a laser pistol. That narrows it down to one of Drake's security guards, and Drake knows his people better than anyone else."

The shuttle docked at the Station. Flynn and Chadwick disembarked and boarded the elevator for the ride to the rim and usable gravity.

"So what are you going to do now?" Chadwick asked.

Flynn glanced at his watch. The tour of Satellite Charlie had wasted the entire afternoon. "I'm going to have dinner. Would you care to join me?"

The invitation took Chadwick by surprise. "Our professional relationship is still adversarial, Mr. Flynn. It would have to be a business dinner."

"Fine. We'll spend thirty seconds discussing the case."

Chadwick suppressed a smile. "What did you have in mind?"

"There's a little Italian place on this end of the Station, up on level nine, that serves terrific pizza."

"*Pizza?* Do you have any idea how much fat there is in a typical pizza?"

"If you don't want pizza," Flynn said, "you can order veal, chicken—raised right here on Satellite Bravo now—pasta—"

"Chicken's good," Chadwick said. "Pasta's overloaded with simple carbohydrates." She suddenly remembered what the tour of Satellite Charlie had done to her attire. "You said this was a small place?"

"Six or seven tables. If it weren't for the airball tournament, we wouldn't be able to get in without reservations. But the first evening game starts in an hour, so the place will be clearing out."

"Lead on, Mr. Flynn. We'll eat Italian."

Flynn led. Chadwick became concerned when she recognized the neighborhood that they entered. Her fears were confirmed when they reached the restaurant and she saw the name glowing above the door. "This is Greasy Gus's!" she protested.

"I've heard it called that," Flynn admitted.

"But there's more grease in the food here than there is in

the oil shale of the Rocky Mountains!"

"But it's very good-tasting grease," Flynn said, unconcerned. "And I don't think there's any in the chicken."

Wendy stared through the front window of the restaurant. Four of the seven tables were occupied, but as she
watched a couple at one table stood up to leave. She didn't
recognize any of the patrons. "If there isn't something
healthy on the menu, we go someplace else."

"Fair enough."

Gus was not only the chef in his restaurant, he was also
the waiter. He was of average height with dark hair, a large
black mustache, and a noticeable potbelly. He was delighted to see Flynn. "Mike Flynn! Just the man I need to
help me settle a bet! Were you, or were you not, arrested for
terminating those two goons?"

"Hello, Gus. I was, but I had an ironclad alibi. I was
back on the street in an hour or so."

Gus pounded his right fist into the palm of his left hand.
"Dammit, I just lost fifty bucks! I never thought they would
have suspected you. I didn't even know that you owned a
laser pistol."

"I don't," Flynn said, "but that didn't stop Wofford
from tearing my apartment apart looking for one. How's
business?"

"It was great until this airball tournament started," Gus
said mournfully. He was a football fan and had little use for
airball, which he considered to be more sissified than soccer
and beneath the dignity of real men—or even real women.
"I got to get me one of those large video displays to keep
the fans happy."

Flynn winced. "And spoil the atmosphere of this place?"

"The Company provides the atmosphere free of charge,"
Gus said. "They don't provide customers, without which I

don't need the atmosphere. Will this table be suitable?"

The tables were identical and in a restaurant as small as Gus's there was no preferred location. Flynn glanced politely at Chadwick before saying, "This will be fine."

Gus lit the candle that stood in the middle of the table. "You'll be having the usual?"

"Ah, I think we'll check the menu."

Flynn remembered not to help Ms. Chadwick with her chair. She selected one facing the back wall, so that if any of her acquaintances passed by she might go unnoticed. Flynn switched on the menu projector and the meal choices were displayed on the tabletop.

"How's the linguini?" Chadwick asked.

"I've heard it's outstanding."

Chadwick looked up from the table. "Heard from whom?"

"Gus."

Chadwick pursed her lips and changed the subject. "I didn't know that your apartment had been searched."

"Yeah, probably on Drake's suggestion." Flynn read the menu as he spoke. "With me in jail, I couldn't find out what happened to Asterbrook and Mondragon. He was so damned certain that Wofford could pin it on me that he'd already removed the microcams he'd planted in my place before Wofford searched it—at least, Wofford didn't mention them when he was questioning me." Flynn looked up from the menu. "I'm surprised that Drake didn't plant a laser in my apartment for Wofford to find."

Gus reappeared from the kitchen. "You'll have a pitcher?" he asked Flynn.

Mike looked at Chadwick. From her scowl he deduced that she wasn't a beer drinker. "Ah, I think we might go for . . . a bottle of wine?"

Surprise flashed in Chadwick's eyes. A brewery and a distillery had been included in the original plans for the Station—the Company knew how to keep miners happy—but wine was imported from Earth and hence was expensive. "I could go for a glass of wine with dinner," Wendy said.

"A carafe of the house red," Flynn said to Gus. "The lady will have the chicken picatta. I'll have a medium-sized pizza with sausage, green peppers, and extra cheese."

"Only a medium?" Gus said, squinting.

Flynn avoided Chadwick's stare. "I had a big breakfast," he lied.

Gus headed for the kitchen. The thought of wine made Chadwick realize that she hadn't seen Flynn take a drink all day. "How did you manage to withstand an entire day of sobriety?" she asked.

"I came out on the *Sagittarius*, a dry ship. Three and a half months from Mars without a drop of alcohol and I survived just fine."

"Then why can't you cut back to a drink or two a day?" It sounded more like a plea than a suggestion.

"Don't worry, Ms. Chadwick. I have a high tolerance for alcohol, bred into me by my Irish ancestry. We invented whiskey, you know."

Chadwick nodded. "I know. And have you heard the joke about the drunken Irishman? Oh, excuse me: I just repeated myself."

"My uncle used to tell that one all the time."

"Your alcoholic uncle?"

Flynn smiled. "That's the guy."

Chadwick studied the other customers in Greasy Gus's. Two were watching the evening news on a portable computer display. None were fashionably dressed. All of them were washing down their dinners with pitchers of beer.

Gus's Restaurant was Flynn's kind of place, where Flynn's kind of people ate Flynn's kind of food. It was a culture that she had avoided. "We could have gone to the Martian Nugget," she said.

"I'm surprised you're allowed to patronize the Martian Nugget."

Chadwick leaned back from the table. "Why shouldn't I be allowed to eat at the Martian Nugget?"

When the first astronaut to set foot on Mars tripped over a gold nugget as big as a football, he sent gold prices plummeting, leading pundits to suggest that the streets would soon be paved with gold because it would be cheaper than asphalt. When people realized that if there was a lot of gold on Mars, there could be a lot of other precious metals, too, all the precious metal prices fell, putting the Company in a precarious financial position. Prices didn't go back up until it was learned that there was very little gold on Mars. But if that nugget hadn't originated on Mars, it must have come from someplace else, so prospectors headed to the asteroid belt and, eventually, to the Jupiter system. Precious metal prices had dropped again, until the low concentration of heavy metals in the outer solar system became apparent.

"The Martian nugget incident nearly bankrupted the Company," Flynn pointed out.

"So did the construction of this station," Wendy replied. "But now we know that heavy-metal concentrations decrease as you go farther from the sun, much to the chagrin of the people who built this place. In fact, if there had been no Martian nugget, there probably would be no Jupiter Station. Ironic, isn't it?" She grinned. "Mercury and Venus are too hot to mine with existing technology, so precious metals are still precious and we still make a lot of money mining them. We're not upset when someone names a restaurant after an historical event that can't hurt us now."

Gus proudly brought the dinners. Chadwick saw the pools of grease on Flynn's pizza and felt sick. "Your arteries must be no more than half their original diameter."

Flynn shook his head. "Not according to my doctor. Exercise and youth drugs do wonderful things for the human body." He licked his lips and pointed at his dinner. "Real cheese. Imported from Earth. Real sausage, too."

"And real grease," Chadwick replied. "If this candle were to fall onto your pizza, the resulting conflagration could burn out the entire Station."

"Well, eat carefully, then," Flynn said. "We wouldn't want to be responsible for a disaster."

Chadwick sampled the chicken picatta and was surprised to find it delicious. Flynn poured a glass of wine and passed it to her. "I should really try to dissuade you from drinking that," he said. "Do you have any idea what alcohol can do to the neurons in your brain and the cells in your liver?"

Wendy suppressed a smile. "Touché, Mr. Flynn, but a glass of red wine with dinner is actually good for you."

"Wait a minute," Flynn said. He took his computer out of his pocket and made a show of opening it. "I think that's my line. Where the hell's the script . . . Ah-hah! I knew it! That's my line! You're saying my lines!"

"Eat your pizza, Mr. Flynn, before the grease congeals."

Chadwick couldn't get over how good the picatta was. She had to force herself not to wolf it down. "You never told me, the other night in your apartment, how you came to be here, on Jupiter Station."

"I came—" Flynn stopped when he noticed the look in Chadwick's eyes. "I was going to say that I came by spaceship, but you've probably heard that one before."

Chadwick nodded. "Dozens of times."

Flynn reached for another slice of pizza. "I was trying to locate a miner who'd been all around the system—the Moon, two continents on Earth, and Mars. I finally tracked him here. That was five years ago, just before Congress made this U.S. territory. There weren't any other private investigators here at the time. The thought of having no competition was attractive. I stayed."

Chadwick took a sip of wine. "Going to stay until retirement?"

Flynn pondered his answer. "I doubt it. Oh, I don't get claustrophobic or anything like that, and this place is cleaner and quieter than the other cities in which I've lived, but I can't get out of here on weekends. I haven't fished for striped bass or hunted ducks in five years. And the duck population is really high right now; the flight last fall set the record for this century."

"Have you tried one of those VR hunting games?"

Flynn made a face. "Ever try to eat a virtual duck?" He shook his head. "I can't get excited watching a virtual dog jump into a virtual pond to retrieve a computer-generated image of a duck." He took a deep breath. "I knew I was going to miss it when I came out here. I figured originally that some big PI firm would want a representative at Jupiter, and I'd get the job because I was already in place, and after I'd impressed them enough they'd move me back to planet three." He shook his head. "Hasn't happened. But what brought you out here?"

Chadwick flashed a smile. "Besides a spaceship, you mean?" She cradled her wine glass in her hands and stared at the contents. The wine blurred her view of the bottom of the glass. She wished she could blur her memories that easily. "I knew before I started law school that I wanted to specialize in corporate law," she said. "But big law firms pay junior associates with no experience very low salaries. Corporations pay their staff attorneys better. I took the offer that Conglomerated made to me." She was still looking at her glass. "The most rapid promotions in the Company come on Jupiter Station, so I jumped at the first opening in the Legal Department here. That was a bit over two years ago. Last year Ed Warshovsky made me department head. And if I do a good job here, next stop is a position—a high-level position—in the corporate headquarters legal office."

"And from there?"

Chadwick hesitated. She glanced around: the other patrons were engrossed in their own conversations, but the security camera above the door was activated. She lowered her voice. "Probably a law firm, eventually. Corporate HQ pays very well, but it's just a fraction of what a partner in a good firm can make. And with the experience I'm getting, I'll be able to get a partnership in a good firm."

"What prompted you to go to law school?" Flynn asked.

The answer to that question required the story of Chadwick's life. Wendy was the only child of a pair of lawyers who had worked for different firms and had faced each other in court several times. She had been seven years old before she had realized that not everybody grew up to be an attorney. She had graduated sixth in her class from Yale Law School. Five prestigious legal firms had recruited her; Conglomerated had offered her twice as much as any of them. Since moving to the Station she rarely socialized, preferring to spend her free time playing her electronic piano and reading the novels of classic adventure writers like Stevenson and MacLean.

The tables in Gus's were small and Flynn couldn't help bumping his knees into Wendy's, which only reminded him of the beautiful legs inside her glossy yellow tights. If she hadn't been a lawyer and a slave to fashion, Flynn would have considered her to be an interesting and attractive woman.

The first airball game of the evening began. The electronics technicians were taking on the team from the Gymnasium Club. The outcome was a foregone conclusion—the techs were going to get stomped—but the shouts and cheers from the other restaurant patrons, watching the video coverage on their computers, made conversation difficult. Flynn paid Gus and he and Wendy left the restaurant.

Chadwick's apartment was on Flynn's way home, so Michael walked with Wendy. The lights had been dimmed for Jupiter Station's artificial night. The streets were unusually deserted for a Saturday evening; the airball tournament had drawn a large fraction of Jupiter Station's population to video displays.

Chadwick turned off the main street onto a side corridor. "I thought you lived on the next street," Flynn said.

"My apartment faces the next street," Chadwick explained, "but this is all one big apartment block. It's a bit shorter if I cut through the patio instead of going around the block."

Chadwick led Flynn through a hallway from the street to the patio behind her apartment. The air was humid and smelled like a swimming pool. The trees in the middle of the patio were real. Diffused blue light from the underwater lamp in the pool danced off the walls and windows of the surrounding apartments. On the door through the safety fence around the pool was a white sign with large red letters that proclaimed:

NO CHILDREN 20:00—08:00
SWIMSUITS OPTIONAL 22:00—06:00

They went through another hallway and exited onto the street that fronted Chadwick's apartment, then climbed the ramp to the balcony. Chadwick's balcony was fancier than Flynn's, with more potted plants and an ornate, rather than utilitarian, railing. Chadwick stopped in front of her door and turned to Flynn. "Well, Mr. Flynn, this has been another day that I won't soon forget."

"The picatta was that good?"

Chadwick didn't know if she should sigh or laugh. Cheese and sausage shipped all the way from Earth were not cheap. Wendy had seen the prices on the menu and knew that Flynn had paid a lot for dinner, more than a private detective could afford. "The picatta *was* good. Thank you for dinner."

Flynn looked into her eyes. They didn't say anything. He leaned slowly toward her; the eyes remained expressionless. Just before their lips met, the eyes closed. Flynn kissed her gently, savoring the softness of her lips against his. He leaned back and her eyes opened. They still didn't say anything.

"I'm sorry," he said. "I shouldn't have done that."

The blue eyes seemed to sparkle. Wendy shook her head once. "No. You should have done that a long time ago." She took a deep breath and abruptly turned away. "Forget I said that." She opened the door to her apartment and stepped through it quickly. "Good night, Mr. Flynn." The door closed.

Flynn turned and walked down the balcony toward the ramp to the street, wondering how, for a man who dated as many women as he did, he could do such stupid things with them. A lawyer, of all people! And the Company's top lawyer on the Station. Flynn might have made himself a very powerful enemy.

Inside her apartment Chadwick stood in front of the wall and slowly and repeatedly banged her head into it. She could *not* be falling for Mike Flynn. He poisoned his body with fat and alcohol and changed girlfriends more often than other men changed their socks. She had almost nothing in common with him, either—upbringing, interests, friends—nothing. She was a lawyer, trained to control her emotions, to think logically. She *would not* fall for Mike Flynn. She didn't need the emotional agony that would inevitably follow.

Furrball greeted Flynn when he reached his apartment. Flynn had been neglecting the cat, so he carried his pet up to the bedroom. He put the cat on the bed and removed his telephone, computer, and stun pistol from the pockets of his sport coat. The gun went into the drawer of the bedside table; the coat was hung in the closet. He took the computer and the phone downstairs to his desk. He had no voice messages, but two requests for background checks had come from Earth.

The door alarm chimed. Flynn checked the security camera feed. Missy Adamly, attired in tee shirt and shorts, was at the door. She looked nervous. Flynn wondered what had prompted her to risk seeing him in person. It had to be something important. He walked to the door and opened it. "Hi, Missy," he said cheerfully.

Missy was eclipsed from view as a very large, very male figure stepped in front of her. It was wearing blue jeans and a tee shirt advertising Coors™ beer, and was half a head taller and a good deal wider than Flynn. "I'm going to teach you to stay away from my wife!" the figure said. It drew back its right fist.

Chapter 11

Jack Adamly was ten centimeters taller and thirty kilos more massive that Mike Flynn, and none of that extra mass consisted of fat cells. Adamly's shoulders were broad, his upper arms looked like telephone poles, and his fist, drawn back behind his ear in preparation for caving in Flynn's face, was huge. Flynn had either to talk fast or start praying.

But the odor of beer was strong on Adamly's breath and intoxication reduced speed and coordination. That gave Flynn hope. As Adamly's fist started forward with all of the man's considerable weight behind it, Flynn stepped back and leaned to the side. He threw up his arm to deflect the blow and the approaching fist just missed Flynn's ear. Adamly's momentum carried him into Flynn's apartment and Flynn turned with the blow, grabbed the arm, and helped Adamly along. Flynn extended his leg across Adamly's path and sent his attacker sprawling along the hall next to the staircase. Adamly skidded to a halt on his face in the living room, which was small for normal people but looked tiny with Jack in it.

Adamly started to push himself up, but Flynn dove on top of him, grabbed his left arm, and twisted it cruelly behind Adamly's back. Jack grunted in pain as Flynn drove the arm as far toward the man's head as he could.

"Don't hurt him, Jack!" Missy pleaded.

Adamly was still trying to get up, so Flynn twisted the arm again. "Sorry, Jack," he said, "but I can't fight you fair. You're much too strong for me. If you insist on fighting, I'll have no choice but to break your arm off and beat you with it." He gave the arm another twist to make the idea seem plausible. "What's all this about, anyway?"

"You've been—Ah! You've been . . . messing with my wife!"

"Messing with Missy? Don't be daft, Jack. I've seen her . . . what? Once? Twice, since you've been married?" Flynn looked back at Missy for confirmation. Furrball was rubbing against her ankles. "The Station isn't all that big. I can't keep from bumping into her on occasion. You can't blame me for saying hello when I see her, can you?"

"I heard you were doing a lot more than saying hello! Ouch!"

"Sorry, Jack," Flynn said, "but you've been misinformed. Hell, we didn't do a whole lot more than say hello when we were dating."

Adamly managed to twist his head enough to see Flynn out of the corner of his eye. Jack had brown hair, thick eyebrows, and a bushy brown mustache. Lines of puzzlement creased his forehead. "You mean, you didn't—"

"I could scarcely get to first base. Why do you think I dumped her?"

"But . . . you dated her for months!"

"Yeah, the longest months of my life."

"You really never—"

"Never. Hell, don't take my word for it. Ask Missy."

"Please don't hurt him, Jack!" Missy said again.

"I . . . how do I know I can believe her in a case like this?" Jack said.

"You don't," Flynn admitted. "But how do you know you can believe the people who've been telling you these stories? Who are you going to trust, them, or your wife?"

Adamly sighed. Pain had a sobering effect. "Yeah, I

guess you're right. Let me up, will ya?"

"You're not going to hurt him, are you, Jack?" Missy said.

Flynn released Adamly's arm and got off of his back. Jack grunted in pain as he straightened his arm. Flynn extended his hand to help Adamly to his feet. "Actually, I've been looking forward to meeting you," Flynn said.

"You have?"

"Yeah. I'd like to find out how you did it. Succeeded where I failed so miserably, I mean. Tell you what: come on down to Betty's with me and I'll buy you a beer. Just a second while I get my coat."

Flynn trotted up the stairs to the bedroom. He slipped his stun pistol into his coat pocket just in case Jack decided to have another jealousy attack.

When Flynn came back downstairs Adamly was holding Furrball and scratching his ears. "Nice cat," Jack said.

"He likes you," Flynn observed. "And he's a good judge of character, too. He liked Missy." Flynn scooped his telephone from the desk and put it into the pocket of his coat.

Adamly put the cat gently on the floor. "Where did you learn that move you put on me?"

Flynn led the way out to the balcony. He made sure the door locked. "Marine Force Recon."

Adamly's eyes opened and his moustache quivered. "Pendleton?"

Flynn shook his head. "Parris Island."

"I was in Force Recon at Pendleton!"

"Really? When?"

"Got out . . . eight years ago. I made sergeant." Adamly smiled with pride. "We were the first unit to get the M-38 laser rifles."

"First Marine unit," Flynn corrected. "Army got 'em first."

"Yeah," Adamly said dejectedly. "Army always got everything first."

Betty's Bar was more crowded than usual for a Saturday evening. The night's first airball game was on the video display and Betty's patrons were cheering loudly. Jack looked sadly at the display and said, "We could have beat either of those teams."

"We?"

"Our team from the aluminum smelter," Adamly explained. "But Gunny had to choose this weekend to get married. O' course, he didn't know the tournament would start this weekend when he and his fiancée set the wedding date. And what are the odds that we'd get drawn to play on his wedding day, eh?"

"According to a guy named Murphy, about one to one."

Flynn led his companions to the far end of the bar, away from the crowd in front of the video display. Betty saw him come in, then did a double take when she saw his companions. She ignored a couple of patrons pounding empty glasses on the bar and went over to where Flynn was standing.

"Beers for me and my friends," Flynn said. Adamly had taken a strategic position between Flynn and Missy. Flynn leaned forward to look around him and asked Missy, "Still drink light?" She nodded. "Light beer for Mrs. Adamly. You remember Missy, don't you?"

Betty took the hint. "Yeah. It's been awhile, though. Nice seeing you again, Missy." She pointed to Jack. "Is this the guy you married?"

Missy hugged Jack's arm. "Yep. This is my husband, Jack. Jack, this is Betty O'Brien."

Jack took Betty's hand and gave it a brisk shake. "Nice to meet you, ma'am."

Betty took her hand back and flexed the fingers to make sure they were all still working. She had detected the odor of alcohol on Adamly's breath. "You sure you need more beer?"

"I'll see to it that he doesn't cause any trouble," Missy said, giving Jack's arm another hug.

"Don't worry, Betty," Flynn added. "We'll take care of him."

"You?" she said, squinting. "Take care of *him?*" She shook her head. "Maybe with three big guys to help you. No, I'll trust Missy to take care of him. I'll get those beers."

A roar from the crowd at the other end of the bar drew Jack's attention to the video display. "Blocking foul!" he shouted. "Blocking foul! Damned refs couldn't see a brick wall if you pounded their faces into it!"

Flynn looked at Missy and she silently mouthed the words, "Thank you."

"Jack Adamly, is that you?" someone said from the crowd in front of the video display.

Adamly recognized the speaker and his face broadened into a smile. "Juan Espinosa! I didn't know you did your drinking in here!" He headed to the far end of the bar and was quickly out of earshot.

" 'Don't hurt him, Jack,' " Flynn mocked, looking at Missy from the corner of his eye. "Who had whom on the floor? Who was twisting whose arm?"

"Jack's kind of . . . vain about his physical ability," Missy explained. "I didn't want him getting mad."

"Oh, he seemed real calm when he tried to flatten my face."

"He could still have hurt you," Missy insisted. "I've seen him fight."

"Hey, Flynn!" Adamly bellowed from the far end of the bar. "Come on down here and meet my friend, Juan!"

Flynn walked down to the end of the bar where the video display was located. Betty handed him and Adamly their glasses, then walked down the bar to where Missy had been left standing alone. She placed a glass of beer on the bar in front of Missy, then leaned across the bar so that she wouldn't be overheard and said, "Did you raise the subject of marriage with Michael?"

Missy frowned. "So what if I did? We'd been dating for over six months! He said he loved me!"

Betty sighed. "I suppose you were suggesting names for the children, too."

Missy glared in reply. "He adores his father! I thought he'd be delighted to name a son Billy! Then along comes Barbara and her long legs—"

Betty shook her head. "Oh, Missy, Missy . . . Barbara had nothing to do with it. She just passed through Mike's field of view at a critical moment. Mike's father didn't get married till he was forty-four. And his grandfather got married at forty-two."

Missy inhaled sharply. "So I was supposed to wait another five years for Mike to decide he was old enough to get married?"

Betty tried to adopt a motherly appearance, but due to the youth drugs she was taking she didn't look old enough to be Missy's mother. "You should have let me handle it. I could have hinted to him that it was time to settle down, without scaring him off. Then you wouldn't be married to King Kong now."

"I love Jack!"

"You dated him—what, two months—before you got married?"

"At least he proposed!" Missy answered, staring Betty right in the eye. "And he really loves me! He brings me flowers every week!"

Betty cocked an eyebrow. "And if he ever gets mad at you?"

Missy looked down at her beer. "He doesn't get mad at me. His feelings just get hurt. He gets an expression like a big St. Bernard that's been mistreated and can't figure out why. He'd never lay a hand on me. No matter how badly I hurt him."

"Too bad he doesn't feel the same way about other people," Betty replied. "Better keep bail money on hand."

Missy stared toward Mike Flynn at the other end of the bar. "I knew he could wrap women around his finger, but look at him: Jack wanted to beat him to a bloody pulp fifteen minutes ago, and now Mike has him eating out of his hand."

"From what I've heard of your husband," Betty said, "he gets mad quickly and gets over it just as fast."

"Not where I'm concerned." Missy took a sip of her beer.

Flynn, at the other end of the bar, wasn't interested in the airball tournament. "Muscles," he said.

"Huh?" Jack said, turning from the video.

"That's what you have that I don't," Flynn said. "That's why I couldn't get anywhere with Missy. I should have figured it out as soon as I heard the two of you had gotten married. Compared to you, I'm wimpy."

"Wimpy you're not," Jack said, rubbing his still sore left arm. He looked toward the other end of the bar to make sure that no one was getting close to his wife. "They don't allow wimps in Force Recon."

"Who was the turkey that told you that I was hitting on your wife?"

"Ah, I don't think I ever got his name . . ." Jack searched his memory without success. "He was at the bachelor party Thursday night, then I saw him again this afternoon—"

"This afternoon! Took you long enough to get mad."

"Like hell it did! Aren't you ever at home?"

"I've been busy lately," Flynn said.

"He was one of Gunny's neighbors, I think," Jack continued.

"Gunny?"

"My friend Bob Gunther," Adamly explained. "The one that got married."

Flynn shook his head. "Don't know him. What did this big-mouthed turkey look like?"

"Short—er, about your height," Jack said. "Black hair. Broad shoulders."

Flynn pursed his lips, thinking. "Doesn't ring a bell. Company man?"

Adamly shrugged. "Probably. Most everybody on the Station is."

"Well, Missy would never step down from you to anyone else. Don't listen to clowns like that in the future."

"Yeah. Hell, if I'd known you'd been in Force Recon, I wouldn't have listened to this one. No Recon man would ever mess around with another's woman!" Jack grinned and he gave Flynn a friendly slap on the back. Mike felt like several vertebrae had been dislocated. "But the next time I see that guy, I'm going to teach him not to tell lies about my wife!"

"I got to get back to this case I'm working on," Flynn said. "I'll see you around."

"I owe you a beer," Adamly replied. "Stop into Joey's Joint after the end of the day shift sometime and I'll buy you one."

Flynn nodded. "I'll do that." He waved goodbye to Missy and left the bar.

The street in front of Betty's was quiet. Flynn took his phone from his pocket. "I want the address for Bob Gunther."

"Four five zero Eighth Street, level three," the computer replied.

Eighth Street ran circumferentially around the Station on the far side of the park. Number four fifty on level three was in the low-rent district. The apartments all opened directly onto the street—no balconies—and the street itself was less than three meters from deck to overhead. It was, however, a public street, and the security cameras didn't need to show a red light when they were active. Fortunately, just five doors down from number four fifty, Eighth Street intersected an axial boulevard, and on the other side of the boulevard the street opened up horizontally and vertically into a playground. The playground was nearly deserted. Flynn took a seat on a bench from where he could see across the boulevard and along Eighth Street almost to Gunther's apartment. His watch showed twenty forty-five.

The handful of children using the playground went home at twenty-one o'clock. A few pedestrians and the occasional electric taxi went past on the boulevard. Eighth Street was deserted. Traffic picked up when the airball tournament ended for the night at twenty-two thirty, and a man and a woman turned from the boulevard onto Eighth Street. Flynn got up from the bench and watched them until they disappeared around the curvature of the Station. Traffic died down again.

Flynn was getting sleepy. He started taking short walks along the boulevard to keep himself alert. A Company security car rolled past but its occupants paid Flynn no attention. Michael saw no marshals on patrol; those on duty were either watching the taverns where rowdy Company employees were likely to make trouble or they were investigating the murders of Santino and Kemper.

Midnight finally came. If Flynn was right he wouldn't have to wait much longer. Twenty minutes later a man approximately as tall as Flynn with a stocky build and black hair turned from the boulevard onto Eighth Street. He entered the apartment two doors down and across the street from Gunther's. That qualified him as Gunther's neighbor. His orange coveralls qualified him as a Company security guard.

Flynn walked toward his apartment. Silvanus Drake had tried to get him off the Asterbrook case by provoking Jack Adamly into putting him in the hospital. Or maybe Drake had hoped that Adamly would shut Flynn's mouth permanently, before the investigator could tell anyone that he knew that the Company was producing polymethyl two four on Satellite Charlie.

Flynn doubted that the Company was involved in too many illegal activities; the polymeth and the deaths of Asterbrook and Mondragon had to be connected. Maybe . . . Warehouse twelve, where the bodies had been discovered, had a hatch to the outside. Asterbrook and Mondragon could have died on one of the satellites and their bodies moved to warehouse twelve by space shuttle. They had been hired because the construction of Satellite Juliet was behind schedule; they had been charging their time to that project. Maybe they had been involved in the construction of a new, improved polymeth factory on Juliet.

Missy had said that the computer system on Juliet still wasn't working. Maybe the new polymeth factory wasn't working yet, either. Maybe Yamaguchi and Dornhoeffer had been working to increase the production of the polymeth lab on Satellite Charlie, to make up for the lack of production from Juliet. Maybe.

Flynn had too many suppositions. He needed *evidence*. His pace quickened and he strode back to his apartment with renewed purpose.

That Sunday should have been the end of the Red Sox losing streak. Carver was pitching, and Carver had already won thirteen games that year. But Gutierrez, the all-star catcher, was out for two weeks with a broken finger, and Libinowicz, his rookie replacement, couldn't handle Carver's wicked knuckle ball. Belson was batting for Havana, waving his huge bat over the plate and looking menacing. Carver stared at the pinch runner on third and pitched from the stretch. The ball headed for the middle of the strike zone, then dived abruptly toward the dirt. Libinowicz was slow to get his glove down and the ball bounced through his legs.

"Dammit to hell!" Flynn said, slamming his beer bottle onto the side table and scaring Furrball, who sunk his claws deeply into Flynn's legs as he launched himself from Flynn's lap. Flynn threw a handful of popcorn at the video display as the runner trotted home from third.

The door chime sounded. Flynn switched the video display to the security camera and saw Jack and Missy Adamly at his door. Jack was standing in full view of the security camera and not using his wife as a decoy, so Flynn guessed that Jack was paying a social call. Michael toggled the game back on. As a precaution, he took his sport coat from the chair by the kitchen table and made sure his stun pistol was in the pocket.

Flynn feigned surprise when he opened the door. "Well, if it isn't the Adamlys! To what do I owe the honor of this visit?"

"I owe you a beer, remember?" Jack said. "Come on, I'll buy you one."

Flynn hesitated. He glanced over his shoulder at the Red Sox game. Every other display on Jupiter Station was probably showing the airball tournament. Flynn wanted to see if the Sox could come back from three runs down with two innings to play. "I was watching the Red Sox—"

"The *Red Sox?*" Adamly made a face. He was wearing a different tee shirt, advertising a different brand of beer, than the one he had worn the night before. It was a size too small and it stretched tightly across his shoulders, making his muscles look even more imposing. "Bunch of wimps! What's the highest batting average on the team, two eighty? With twelve lousy homers. San Diego: now there's a team with firepower!"

"Wrong league," Flynn said. He instructed his computer to record the end of the baseball game. Furrball had reappeared and was rubbing against Missy's ankles again. Missy was wearing a plain white tee shirt that was almost long enough to conceal the fact that she was wearing bright blue shorts. Flynn didn't need his cat to draw his attention to Missy's legs. Although she had always been self-conscious about her stature, Missy had great looking—albeit short—legs. Flynn didn't want Jack to catch him gazing at his wife's limbs. Mike grabbed the cat and tossed him gently into the apartment. "Let's go." He closed the apartment door.

"I didn't know if you'd be home in the middle of the afternoon," Jack said, "but Missy won't let me go out at night if I have to work the next day." He gave his wife a brief hug. Jack was more than twice as big as Missy.

Flynn wondered for the thousandth time why the biggest men always wound up with the smallest women. "Where are we going?"

"How about that little place you took us to last night?" Adamly suggested. "I liked it there."

"You like anyplace that serves beer," Missy said dryly.

"You're a San Diego fan?" Flynn said.

"I was born in San Diego," Jack explained. "Grew up there. Used to go to Padres games whenever I had enough money."

Flynn made a show of looking over Adamly. "I bet you can hit the ball into orbit from the bottom of Death Valley. Did you ever consider a career in pro ball?"

"I had a baseball scholarship," Adamly replied. "Arizona State."

"Ooh! Powerhouse!"

Adamly was looking where he was going. "Yeah. I played hard and I partied hard. I did everything but study hard." He looked at Flynn and smiled. "Flunked every subject. Lost my eligibility and my scholarship. Said the hell with it and joined the Marines."

Flynn shrugged. "The Corps certainly needs people like you, but some ballplayers still come through the minors. Didn't you try out for any teams?"

Adamly shrugged. "To be honest, I couldn't hit a curve ball worth a damn."

They reached Betty's just as an electric car with two orange-suited Company guards drove past. Jack watched them through narrowed eyes. "I wonder if one of them did it," he said. He turned to Flynn. "Don't you find yourself wondering which one of them killed those two guys?"

"All the time."

"That stupid marshal will never catch the killer," Adamly continued. "He's been trying to trace the victims' recent movements. I don't think the motive for murder was recent. I think it was years ago, maybe not even on the Station."

"So Marshal Wofford should be looking for a killer with a lot of patience?"

"Umm, no, not necessarily," Adamly said. "The victims were goons. They carried guns all the time. But last Thursday they got arrested . . . for shooting at you!" Adamly said it as though he had just realized Flynn's role in the affair. "And the marshals made Drake take their guns away. For the first time since those two set foot on Jupiter Station, they were unarmed." Adamly pointed his finger down the street. "Zap! Zap! Easy victims, both of 'em."

Adamly's theory about the murders was being voiced by more and more people as Wofford's frantic investigation of the movements of the victims shortly before their deaths continued to go nowhere. It was more obvious than the third possibility, and hence more likely to have occurred to Jack, who had the reputation of being big, strong, and not very bright.

Most of Betty's patrons were clustered around the end of the bar nearest the door, in front of the video display. Flynn glanced at the display only long enough to read the score displayed at the bottom: Electronics Maintenance was holding a one-goal lead over Steel Converter Number Four. Two of the tables at the other end of the bar were vacant. Flynn led the way to one of them.

"Hi, there, Betty my dear!" Jack boomed above chatter of the airball fans. He held up three fingers and pointed to

Flynn and Missy. Betty smiled and nodded.

Flynn slid onto a stool on one side of the table. Jack had his wife take the stool closest to the wall on the other side of the table, then took the seat next to her. Betty brought three glasses of beer to the table.

"Betty, 'my dear'?" Flynn said.

"Oh, we got to be good friends after you left last night," Betty explained. She took the two twenty-dollar bills that Jack waved in her face. "I'll get your change in a sec."

"You could have learned to hit a curve ball," Flynn said.

Adamly shrugged. "I dunno. I could hit 'em all right in high school, but the first day of practice in college, I'm in the batting cage and pounding fastballs over the fence. The coach watches that for about a minute, then signals the guy working the pitching machine and up comes a curve ball. A major-college curve ball. It floated up to the plate and then dropped half a meter, just like that." Jack slammed the palm of his hand on the table to illustrate the break of the pitch. "I missed it by about that much, too. And I kept on missing 'em. The coach shook his head and walked away." Adamly contemplated the foam on his glass of beer. "Just as well I flunked out. Saved me the embarrassment of being cut."

"Why did you leave the Corps?" Flynn asked.

The look in Missy's eyes told Flynn that he was trespassing into forbidden territory, but Adamly said, "I was in South America. Mortar round landed about a meter from my left arm. Riddled that side of my body with shrapnel. Broke my arm and my leg and collapsed my left lung." He took a drink of beer. It had been an American-made mortar round, sold to a South American government and resold to the drug lords. "The docs put the bones back together okay, but a lot of the alveoli in my lung were blown to hell and had to be removed. After a year of recuperation I still didn't have enough endurance to pass the Force Recon physical."

Flynn nodded in understanding. Adamly would have considered a transfer to a regular Marine unit to be a demotion. "I missed South America," he said. "We were in Africa at the time, rescuing those Red Cross workers."

Missy looked surprised. "You never told me you were involved in that! I saw video coverage: you guys were heroes!"

Flynn made a face. "Slow news day. The Red Cross workers were in no danger—Africa's much more civilized than it was last century. We were really distracting attention from the operation in South America, which was still secret at that time. The networks had nothing better to put on the air and tried to make our operation look dangerous to get viewer interest. I didn't hear a shot fired in anger."

Missy was looking at her husband as though she was seeing him for the first time. He had never told her the details behind the scars on his body. Wives, apparently, didn't rate the same as fellow Marines.

Betty brought Jack's change and a bowl of popcorn. "Just wave if you want anything else."

"Say, you couldn't put the Red Sox game on, could you?" Adamly asked.

Betty looked at the mob in front of the video display, then back at Jack, an expression of disbelief on her face. "Do you think you could quell the resulting riot all by yourself?"

Jack started to rise from his chair. "I'd like to see the man in that crowd that could stand up to me!" He looked across the table at Flynn. "Mike and I could handle 'em!"

"Yeah, well, maybe you could," Betty agreed, "but then they'd go elsewhere, and I need their business. I'll get my computer. You can watch the Red Sox on that."

"Don't bother, Betty," Flynn said. "Jack's not a Red Sox fan, anyway."

Betty left the table before Adamly could object to Flynn's statement. He really wasn't a Red Sox fan, and he quickly forgot about the game. "What made you leave the Marines?" Jack asked.

"Downsized," Flynn said, "when the Recon battalion at Parris Island was deactivated."

Adamly squinted. "I thought all those guys were transferred to other units."

"It was a big deficit year."

Missy was looking at the door. "You have company," she said to Flynn. She had the disapproving look on her face that she had always worn whenever Flynn had eyed other women.

Flynn scowled. "Damn it! I thought I'd gotten rid of Barbara! Don't look at her. Maybe she won't notice us."

Missy's expression didn't change. "It's not Barbara."

Flynn looked over his shoulder. Wendy Chadwick was standing at the bar. She was wearing a stylish, metallic blue outfit—tights, decorative skirt, and blouse—with a casual shiny blue coat that had naturally rounded lines instead of the boxy shoulders of a business suit. She was talking with Betty, who was pointing in the direction of Flynn's table.

Flynn could feel Missy's eyes glaring at the back of his head. "You told me you *didn't* dump Barbara for her," she said.

"I didn't," Flynn replied, knowing that he was wasting his breath.

Chadwick made her way cautiously through the crowd to Flynn's table. "Mr. Flynn," she said hesitantly, "I hate to disturb you on a weekend, but we have business to discuss."

Jack poked his wife with his elbow. "Let's go watch the airball game."

"We can see it fine from here," Missy replied.

"They have business to discuss!" Jack insisted. "It's probably confidential! Come on, let's go." He took Missy's elbow and pulled her to get her moving.

Flynn pointed to the stool that Jack had vacated. "Have a seat," he offered.

"Thank you." Chadwick had a small blue handbag that she held on the table in front of her.

"What's come up?" the investigator asked. He hadn't heard of any new developments.

"Actually, it's about last night." Chadwick was looking at her handbag instead of at Flynn.

Michael squinted. "Nothing happened last night."

Chadwick looked up from her handbag. She seemed relieved. "Thank . . . that's right."

Flynn suddenly understood. "Nothing worth discussing, anyway. We went to dinner. I walked you home. Then I went home."

"I'm glad you remember it the same way that I do."

Their eyes met. Flynn couldn't help but notice how large Wendy's were, and how perfectly her red hair framed her face.

Betty appeared at Flynn's elbow. "Oh, ah, Ms. Chadwick will have a . . . club soda?"

Betty looked at Flynn to make sure that she had heard him correctly.

"That won't be necessary," Wendy protested. "Since we've concluded our business, I should be going."

"You can have a club soda," Flynn said.

Wendy didn't contradict him, so Betty said, "One club soda coming up," and went to get it.

"How did you find me here?" Flynn asked.

"Drake's file on you said that this was your favorite saloon."

Betty returned with the club soda. "I added a shot of reconstituted lime juice," she said to Chadwick. She looked at Flynn and asked, "On your tab?"

Michael nodded. He didn't watch Betty walk away and didn't see her pick up her telephone.

Wendy was looking at her handbag again. "It wouldn't have worked."

"What wouldn't have worked?"

"What didn't happen last night."

"Oh, that." Flynn nodded. "Of course not."

"We have nothing in common."

"Obviously."

"I'm a Company employee. I could be transferred someplace else tomorrow."

"That's true."

She laughed nervously. "And I don't drink."

"You hardly even eat," Flynn added.

Wendy looked around the tavern. "Is there a restroom in here?"

Flynn looked over her shoulder. "Right behind you. Lock the door; it's unisex."

Chadwick took her handbag with her to the restroom. Betty appeared at the table. Flynn's glass was nearly empty. "You want another one?" she asked.

"Ah, yeah. And get Jack and Missy one, too."

Betty nodded. She leaned close to Mike and said, "Don't let this one get away."

"Hmm?" Betty glanced toward the restroom. Flynn pursed his lips. "I'm not seeing her, Betty. This is a business meeting."

Betty snorted. "The way you two were looking at each other? Monkey business, maybe. Don't blow it this time. Oh, you take youth drugs and you'll look young and handsome until you're sixty, but that doesn't mean you can keep on changing girlfriends. The good ones get claimed and you're left with people like Barbara."

"There are always new ones coming along, Betty."

"Just because you don't look old doesn't mean you aren't old. You can't relate to twenty-year-olds anymore, Michael. They're a different generation. They listen to music groups that you never heard of."

Flynn shook his head. He pointed at the restroom. "I can't date her! She's a lawyer, for crying out loud! Lawyers are the scum of the earth!"

Betty smiled sweetly. "We're not on the Earth."

"Okay, then they're the thick green scum on the recycling bins that the maintenance crews have to remove with high-pressure steam!"

Betty smiled again and patted Flynn's hand. "You're not going to get many more chances at women like her."

"How do you know what she's like?"

"I called around." She waved her finger at Flynn. "Don't blow it!"

The door to the restroom opened and Betty returned to the bar. Wendy came back to her seat. This time she held her handbag in her lap. "This is a surprisingly nice place," she said.

A thunderous cheer from the crowd in front of the video display got their attention. The Steel Converter team had scored a goal as time ran out—their second goal in the last three minutes—to beat Electronic Maintenance. Jack and Missy returned to the table. Flynn and Wendy slid over to the stools next to the wall and Jack and Missy took the seats thus vacated. Jack was grinning broadly.

"I won fifty bucks on those guys!" he beamed. He signaled to Betty. "Hey, sweetness! Another round."

"I really can't stay," Wendy said.

"Aw, sure you can," Jack insisted. "Don't be a party pooper, Ms. . . ."

"Oh, excuse me," Flynn said. "Wendy Chadwick, Jack and Missy Adamly."

Jack cocked his head. "Aren't you the head of the legal department?"

Chadwick nodded. "That's right."

Adamly feigned an expression of horror. "A lawyer!" He looked quickly around the tavern. "I hope nobody I know sees me talking with a lawyer. My reputation will be ruined."

"Jack," Missy said, "no lawyer jokes today."

"Oh, that's all right," Wendy said with a sigh. "I've heard them all, anyway."

"Oh?" Jack said, taking that as an invitation. "What do you have when five lawyers are trapped in an airlock with only enough air for one of them?"

Chadwick started to respond, hesitated, squinted, and finally said, "That's a new one."

"Too much air!" Adamly said, roaring with laughter.

"No more, Jack, please," Missy said. "It's not against the law to be polite to a lawyer."

Jack looked surprised. "It's not?" He laughed again.

"You look familiar," Chadwick said to Missy. "Have we met?"

Missy avoided making eye contact. "We use the same gym."

"Ah!" Chadwick nodded. "You're a . . . computer programmer, aren't you?" She knew exactly who Missy was;

Drake's file on Flynn included complete descriptions of all of his girlfriends.

"System analyst," Missy corrected.

"She's the one that keeps the computers on the Station talking to each other," Jack said. His wife was better educated than most of his friends and he enjoyed bragging about her capabilities. "Say, can we get food in this place?"

"Not directly," Flynn said. "Betty has a deal with Wan's Chinese around the corner: he doesn't sell drinks and she doesn't sell food. But Wan delivers, and you can order from here." He flipped the switch and the menu was projected onto the tabletop.

Adamly jabbed his finger at an item that immediately caught his interest. "They have egg foo yung! I'll have a double order!"

"I can't stay for dinner," Chadwick said, but she didn't stand up.

"Aw, you can stay," Jack said. "Hell, telling lawyer jokes is no fun if there's no lawyer around to hear 'em."

Wendy looked across the table at Flynn. "Is the food from Wan's restaurant any good?"

"Umm, not really. Not enough grease."

"I like Chinese food," she replied. "I'll try the egg-fried rice with chicken."

Wan's Restaurant had been deluged with orders at the end of the airball game so the food was slow in coming, but it proved to be worth waiting for. Jack pronounced the egg foo yung delicious and ordered another helping. Betty found a bottle of plum wine and brought it to the table. The tavern filled with people as the day shift ended and the weekend workers dropped in to celebrate the four days away from work that they would enjoy.

Wendy tried to pay for the meal. "You bought me dinner

last night," she pointed out.

Flynn shook his head. "My father taught me that a gentleman always pays for a lady's meal."

Adamly poked him playfully in the ribs with his elbow. "Aw, come on, Mike. You're among friends. You don't have to pretend to be something you're not."

"Ah," Flynn said, holding up a finger, "but I am a gentleman. By act of Congress, no less—an officer and a gentleman."

The grin that had creased Adamly's face wavered. "You were an *officer?*" He pursed his lips. "Hell, I can't be friends with you! I hate officers!" His forehead wrinkled. "You were an officer and they *still* downsized you?"

Flynn answered, "If I'd been an Academy grad they'd have kept me, but I was ROTC—cheap and expendable. Excuse me for a second."

Flynn ducked into the restroom and Wendy took the opportunity to step to the bar. Betty came over to her immediately.

"Mr. Flynn has an account here, correct?" Chadwick asked.

Betty nodded. "He pays it off whenever it gets around a thousand dollars."

Chadwick blinked. She didn't want to think about a thousand-dollar bar tab. She opened her purse and took out her money card. The dinners had cost thirty dollars each. "I'd like to pay sixty dollars against his tab."

Betty raised her eyebrows. "First time I've ever seen a woman buy dinner for Mike Flynn." She slipped the money card into the card reader and smiled. "You got yourself a good one. Oh, he has a reputation as a womanizer, but I've known him since he first arrived on the Station—that's five years, now—and he's never had more than one girlfriend at a time. He's getting ready to settle down, too."

Chadwick stared at the tavern owner. "Mr. Flynn and I are not . . . involved. We had business to discuss today, that's all."

Betty suppressed a smile. "You make eyes like that at all your business meetings?" She returned Chadwick's money card just as Flynn came out of the restroom.

"We have to be going," Jack said to him. "I'm working tomorrow."

"It's about time I was going, too," Wendy said. "I had never intended to stay this long."

"Betty," Flynn called, "everything paid for?" She nodded. "Let's go."

Flynn walked out of the bar with Chadwick. "Did you have a good time?"

"Yes, I did," she admitted. "The pulleys on those cranes had been switched," she said. "That makes us liable for damages. I'm going to offer your clients a six-million-dollar settlement. I'll offer Jonny Mondragon's family the same."

Flynn shook his head. "My clients won't accept it. They don't want money. They want to know what really happened to their son."

"You found out what really happened," Chadwick said. "The pulleys were switched. The one in warehouse twelve was too small for the cable in use."

"That's not what the Company's covering up," Flynn replied. "The Company made no attempt to conceal the fact that the pulley on the crane in warehouse seven was too small—the pulley diameter is mentioned in the Company report, the marshal's report, and the OSHA report. And the people who transferred from the Station were those who were least likely to notice the undersized pulley. The men that moved the machinery frame off the bodies might have noticed it and they're all still here. The pulley's a clue but it's not what prompted the transfers. Besides, you said the settlements would be only six million each. Satellite Juliet is twenty-eight million over budget and no one had to pay with his head. But those people couldn't have been transferred to other Company facilities without the connivance of the Board of Directors. So whatever it is, it's worth more than twenty-eight million. Much more. Like the systemwide monopoly on the production of polymethyl two four, for example."

Chadwick clenched her teeth. She tried to avoid revealing her disappointment. "The Company had—still has, I guess—security guards that shouldn't have been allowed to carry deadly weapons, but it's not covering up anything. And we are *not* producing polymethyl two four!" She hesitated. The lights in the Station had been dimmed to simulate evening. "I'll see you around."

Flynn nodded. "Have a nice evening."

He watched her walk away. She really did have terrific legs. Put her in regular clothes and she'd be irresistible.

Flynn walked back to his apartment. There were quite a few people on the street; it was the start of the "weekend" for the weekend shift. They had their own airball tournament, that would begin that evening. Flynn didn't know what to do next on the Asterbrook investigation. He had two background checks to do; he could start on them until he figured out what to do about Asterbrook, Mondragon, and the solar system's most abused drug.

The computer in Flynn's apartment recognized him as he approached and unlocked the door. Flynn stepped into the apartment and flipped on the light, then stopped dead in his tracks.

Silvanus Drake was sitting behind Flynn's desk.

Chapter 12

Flynn reached for the stun pistol in his pocket while he glanced up the stairs to make sure that Drake didn't have any friends hiding there. He saw no one, but goons might have been hiding out of sight in the bedroom.

"Don't get excited," Drake said calmly. Furrball was sitting in his lap and Drake was stroking the cat's ears. "I'm alone. Come in and close the door. If anybody sees me here, this visit will have been a waste of time."

The open door gave Flynn an avenue of escape, but Drake could have posted guards in the street to stop him. Flynn closed the door. "You're in my chair," he said.

Flynn thought he saw the flicker of a smile on Drake's lips. "Sorry," the security chief said. "Force of habit." He put Furrball on the floor and stood up. He stepped carefully across some popcorn on the carpet as he moved to the other side of the desk. He took a seat there without being asked. Furrball leaped lightly onto Drake and traitorously curled up on his lap. Drake resumed stroking his ears. "Friendly cat."

"Going senile in his old age," Flynn said. Furrball was four years old. "He used to be a good judge of character." Michael walked cautiously to his desk, hand still on the grip of his pistol. There was no one hiding in the kitchen. Flynn sat down. He stared across the desk at his visitor. "What prompted you to break into my apartment?"

"I have a mystery to solve," Drake replied.

"Kemper and Santino?"

Drake nodded, almost imperceptibly. "Wofford has been no help. He has not requested—nor even permitted—our help in the investigation. He has two official reasons for that: first, the murders occurred in a public area of the Station where the Marshals Service is responsible for law enforcement, and second, the only people on the Station—besides the marshals, of course—who have laser pistols are my security guards, so requesting the assistance of Company guards would be requesting the murderer—or murderers—to help in the investigation."

"And his unofficial reasons?"

Drake leaned back in his seat. "Unofficially, he has not requested our help because he wants to solve the case himself. He's desperate: his wife is leaving for Earth next week on the *Emperor*. Wofford doesn't want to lose her. He needs the publicity he would get by solving this case to leverage a transfer back home."

Flynn had never met the marshal's wife but he had seen her on various occasions. She was a lissome brunette with the kind of figure that got bad actresses movie contracts. Unless she had a terribly obnoxious personality, Flynn wouldn't have wanted to lose her, either.

Drake continued, "Wofford's even keeping his own personnel in the dark, to reduce the chance that one of them will solve the case. That has reduced their efficiency considerably; it was two of my people who found the chemicals that Kemper and Santino stole from warehouse seven."

Flynn perked up. "Really? I hadn't heard. Where?"

"In one of the recycling bins. The shipping box and the containers within had been wiped clean of fingerprints and DNA residue."

Flynn shook his head. "Bummer."

"Wofford isn't smart enough to solve this case by himself," Drake said. "Nor does he have the resources. That puts the ball back in my court. I have to investigate my own people. And the guilty party knew I'd come looking for him before he committed the murders. He wouldn't have done it if he didn't think he could outsmart me."

Flynn smiled. "He has, so far."

"Yes," Drake admitted. "But he can't outsmart the two of us."

Flynn squinted. "What's this 'us' business?"

"I'm here to hire you to investigate the killings of Santino and Kemper," Drake replied. "You'll be paid twenty thousand in advance against your usual fee. That's almost seventeen days of your time. You solve the case in less than that, you keep the extra. You take more time than that, we pay you your twelve hundred a day. And if you solve the case, you get a fifty-thousand-dollar bonus."

Flynn's eyes narrowed. "Very generous of you, considering the twenty-eight-million-dollar overrun on Satellite Juliet."

"Your fee comes out of a different budget," Drake explained.

"The one you have for bribes?"

Drake's eyes remained expressionless.

Flynn had to suppress the urge to chuckle. Drake was getting desperate, though not about Kemper and Santino. "Why me?" Flynn asked.

"False modesty doesn't suit you, Flynn. We both know that the other four private investigators on the Station together don't add up to you in ability."

"I'm so great that I can investigate all hundred and forty goons by myself?" Flynn said wryly.

Drake replied, "They're not all suspects. Kemper and Santino were each shot twice through the head. The double

tap—two quick shots to the head—as taught by anti-terrorist forces throughout the system." He made a circle with
the thumb and forefinger of his right-hand and held it between his eyes. "The laser burns on each body were that
close together. Admittedly, the shooter was probably less
than four meters away, but he fired four accurate shots so
quickly that neither victim was able to utter a sound that
would have activated the security camera."

"Perhaps the security camera had been . . . temporarily
disabled?"

"It wasn't," Drake said. "You've had occasion to ob-
serve the shooting skill of my guards—"

"Couldn't hit a shower stall from the inside."

"And although I wish they could all shoot well enough to
have committed the murders, my budget precludes training
most of them to that level."

Flynn cocked his head. "Most of them?"

Drake explained, "If this station were attacked by terror-
ists, we would need a defense force that could use a pistol
for something other than a badge of office and a club. I
have twenty people—two squads of ten each—that can
shoot well enough to have done in Kemper and Santino. All
were trained in my version of the FBI's anti-terrorist pro-
cedures, including the double tap. Thirteen of those people
have alibis for the time of the killings."

"That leaves only seven," Flynn said. "You can't investigate seven people by yourself?"

"I grilled them with a lie detector. Came up with
nothing. I can't proceed in a more . . . heavy-handed
fashion without destroying the morale of my security force."

Flynn's eyes narrowed. Drake had a big advantage over
Marshal Wofford: as the guards' employer, Drake could legally require them to take lie detector tests. But even

electroencephalographic lie detectors could be beaten by people who could control their alpha and beta brain waves with biofeedback. "What about that new thought-pattern analysis technique I've read about?" Flynn asked.

"We've no one here trained to administer it."

Flynn relaxed in his chair and took his hand off the grip of his gun. "What if the killer wasn't one of your guards? What if he smuggled a gun onto the Station?"

Drake shook his head once. "Because of the Vasquez investigation, we know that *nothing's* being smuggled onto the Station. There are only the pistols issued to my guards and the extras in my arms locker. The arms locker is monitored by the computer and it was not opened between the time of the murders and the time we checked it to confirm that no lasers were missing."

"One of your guards—someone with an airtight alibi, because he knew a murder was about to be committed—could have loaned his gun to the killer," Flynn suggested.

"A definite possibility," Drake agreed. "He would have had to loan at least one activation ring, too."

"And the shooter wouldn't be suspected because he doesn't have access to a laser pistol," Flynn added. "I suppose we can rule out the children, but that still leaves eighteen thousand people who could have done it."

"We've already cleared many of them," Drake said. "They're in security camera shots taken in other locations around the time of the murders. Most of the rest can't shoot well enough to have done it, either, but I'm having the backgrounds of *everyone* without an alibi checked, looking for military or police training, shooting club membership . . . anything that would suggest the kind of marksmanship required."

Flynn didn't envy Drake's task. "That's a big job."

"Yes. It's also the less likely of the two possibilities. It's more likely that the killer is one of the seven people you'll be investigating."

Flynn shook his head slowly. "No."

Drake's eyebrows lowered. "No?"

"Drake, you are a devious, underhanded, amoral individual. You don't fool me for minute. This visit has nothing to do with the deaths of Kemper and Santino. For all I know, you knocked them off yourself—"

"I was with witnesses—"

"Okay, so maybe it was your gun that was loaned to the killer. But you don't care whether or not I find that killer. You just don't want me to discover what actually happened to Philip Asterbrook and Jonny Mondragon."

Drake gently lifted Furrball from his lap, placed the cat on the couch next to him, and got to his feet. "Sorry to have bothered you."

Flynn felt like grinning. "Thought I'd be salivating over the bribe you just offered me so that I wouldn't see through it, eh? As soon as you learned that I was investigating that so-called 'accident,' you've been trying to get me off the case. Oh, the Company tried lawyers first, but you knew that wouldn't work. You bugged my apartment. Probably programmed the security cameras to watch me, too." Flynn couldn't tell Drake that he *knew* that the cameras had been watching him without giving Drake reason to suspect Missy. "While you were bugging my apartment, you sabotaged my stun pistol, so I wouldn't be able to defend myself. Then Ms. Chadwick and I visited warehouse seven. Kemper and Santino wouldn't have gone in there after us if *you* hadn't sent them. They didn't open fire on your orders—they'd learned about the shipment that Vasquez had ordered, and, unaware that Vasquez was getting his dope right here from a secret Company lab, assumed it contained Vasquez's re-supply of polymeth—but you wouldn't have been unhappy if they had put me permanently out of action. Then, after Chadwick and I escaped, you tried to protect your trigger-happy guards so that I would be arrested for the fracas. And when Kemper and Santino were murdered, you let Wofford think that I had kept one of the lasers I'd taken from your goons the night before so that I would be arrested for the crime. That didn't work, either, so when I come this close—" Flynn held his thumb and forefinger a millimeter apart, "to finding your polymeth lab, you had one of your goons inform the very big, very jealous husband of an ex-girlfriend of mine that I've been seeing his wife, figuring that he'd put me in a body cast for several months. And since that plan didn't work, you're trying to buy me off."

Drake had started walking toward the door, but he stopped at the entrance to the hall and turned to face Flynn. "I didn't have to arrange to have you beat up, Flynn. You've managed to upset most of my guards during the last week; some of them probably tried to exact vengeance. And after Wofford and all of his deputies had been investigating the murders from twenty-three o'clock until six the next morning—scouring the crime scene, questioning everyone with tickets to the airball tournament that night, interrogating Kemper and Santino's significant others, checking out the deceaseds' apartments for clues, doing all the things they were supposed to do in a murder investigation—but coming up with nothing, then, when Wofford thought of you and came to me for confirmation that you might have a laser pistol, I told him that we weren't missing any, and that you couldn't have done it."

Flynn stared at his uninvited guest. Without taking his

eyes off of Drake, he opened the top drawer of his desk and took out the copy of the search warrant. He scanned it quickly.

. . . The suspect admitted to having in his possession on the night before the murders a laser pistol that could have been used in the killings, and although he claimed to have thrown away said pistol he had been unable to lead Deputy Marshal Feldstein to the gun . . .

Flynn chewed his lower lip. "Okay, so he doesn't name you in the warrant. But you couldn't have tried very hard to convince him."

Drake's eyes narrowed. "He nearly pleaded with me to confirm that we were short a laser. I told him explicitly *three times* that we weren't missing any."

Flynn indicated his apartment with a wave of his hands. "Hell, Drake, he tore this place apart! He wouldn't have wasted his time doing that unless he believed that something was hidden here—"

Flynn had a sudden, frightening thought. It must have showed on his face, for Drake stared at him curiously. Flynn said, "Wofford hasn't figured out that Vasquez was getting his polymeth locally. You told me once that Wofford had had Vasquez's shipment checked out. Did you actually see the report from planet three or did he just tell you about it?"

Drake's eyes narrowed slightly. "I didn't see it. He told me what it contained."

Flynn slammed his fist into his desktop. "Sonuvabitch!" He scanned the top of his desk for his telephone before remembering that it was in his coat pocket. He pulled it out and opened it. "Connect me with Wendy Chadwick!" He tapped his foot impatiently as the switching computer tried to track Chadwick down. "Damn answering machine! Come on, Wendy, pick up the phone! This is Mike Flynn. This is business and it's important!" But there was only the patient silence of the recorder. "Wendy, when you get this, call me *immediately!* And lock your door and don't let *anyone* in!"

Flynn broke the connection. "Marshals Office," he barked into the phone. The watch commander answered. "This is Mike Flynn. Let me speak to Wofford."

"Marshal Wofford's not in," the deputy replied.

"Then transfer this call to his phone!"

"He left instructions that he didn't want to be disturbed," the deputy said. "He's investigating a murder."

"And I know who did it! So connect me with Wofford!"

The deputy was slow to respond. "Mr. Flynn, if you have information about the murders, you can tell me—"

"Do you think your boss will be happy when he finds out that you tried to keep me from giving this information directly to him?"

The deputy hesitated. "I'm trying to connect you . . . He's not answering his phone."

Flynn clenched his teeth. "He has a locator, doesn't he? Where the hell is he?"

"He . . . he must have turned off his locator."

"Dammit to hell!" Flynn shut off his phone and jumped to his feet. He brushed past Drake on his way to the door. "The laser was just an excuse to search this apartment," he said. "He was really looking for that stolen shipment, believing that it contained polymeth."

Flynn was nearly through the door before Drake said, "Whoa! Not so fast! You got your times mixed up!"

Flynn stopped in the doorway and looked back at Drake.

"Wofford got the warrant to arrest you and search this place after you wouldn't come in voluntarily for questioning," Drake pointed out. "He searched this apartment when he came here to arrest you and found you gone. You didn't discover that the shipment had been stolen until *after* you were released from custody later that morning. Wofford didn't learn about it until I reported the theft to the Marshal's Office."

Flynn scowled. "He would have known earlier if he'd killed Kemper and Santino for it."

Michael saw something that few other people had ever seen—a flicker of emotion on Drake's face. For just a second Drake's brown eyes seemed to go completely black.

Drake took his computer from his coat pocket and scanned the display. He took out his telephone and touched only one button. He didn't need to identify himself. "Put me through to Laska and Chong . . . Laska? Drake. Get to the apartment of Wendy Chadwick, two twenty-four Ninth Street, level six. Silent approach. Confirm that Ms. Chadwick is safe, then don't let anyone into her apartment until I get there." He broke the connection as soon as his orders were acknowledged and started abruptly for the door. "I have a car," he said.

Flynn had to hurry to keep up with Drake. The U.S. Marshal had figured out—or maybe some friend in Washington told him—that the Marshals Service was going to leave him at Jupiter until he quit or retired. Wofford had decided to feather his own nest. The report from Earth about Vasquez's shipment had contained something suspicious, something that Wofford hadn't told Drake, and the marshal had had no other leads. Wofford had figured that the polymeth had to be in the shipment.

But Wofford had outsmarted himself. He had kept Vasquez's laboratory sealed so that he would have access to it, thinking that when the shipment arrived Meditech would ask him to open the lab so they could put it in there. Then he could go back the lab "to conduct further investigations" and help himself to the dope. But because of the police seal, Meditech left the shipment in warehouse seven, where Wofford couldn't get at it without a search warrant. An attempt to get a warrant would have aroused Drake's suspicion, since the marshal had told Drake that the shipment had been cleared by the authorities on Earth. Wofford had needed an accomplice, someone who had legal access to the warehouse.

Flynn said, "Heaven knows how he got involved with Kemper and Santino. They might have been sniffing around the Vasquez case on their own, trying to break it themselves and impress you, and Wofford caught 'em and threatened to charge them with interfering with an official investigation if they didn't help him get the shipment."

"More likely, they were just greedy," Drake said. "Vasquez was a *very* heavy user. A two-year supply of polymeth for him would have had a street value of six hundred thousand, maybe three-quarters of a million. Not enough to retire, but enough for Wofford to start his own security firm after leaving the Marshals Service."

"Especially if he didn't have to split it with anyone."

They reached the bottom of the ramp at the street below Flynn's apartment. Flynn looked both ways along the empty street and said, "Where the hell's your car?"

"I parked it three blocks from here—no one could know that I'd hired you," Drake said. "I've summoned it electronically. It'll be here in a minute."

Flynn stared impatiently up the street. Wofford had tried

to blame him for the shoot-out in warehouse seven because Kemper and Santino wouldn't turn the stolen polymeth over to the marshal, nor could he easily dispose of them, while they were locked up. While they were in custody, he had arranged to meet them in the restroom near the weightless recreation facility. The conspirators had scheduled their meeting for right after the start of the airball game, when they would have the restroom to themselves. As soon as Wofford had seen the shipping box, he had made sure that the security camera wasn't activated, and then he had shot his luckless companions—the shooting training he got in the FBI's Hostage Rescue and Anti-Terrorist Courses, put to unintended use. When the second game ended, he had joined the throng leaving the rec center, picked up the box from where he had stashed it, and gone home.

"When he sorted through that shipping container and found no polymeth," Flynn said, "he figured that Kemper and Santino had held out on him. He checked their apartments under the guise of investigating the murder, but he was really looking for the polymeth. When it wasn't there, he remembered that I had been standing next to the shipping container when Kemper and Santino shot at me. He guessed that I had gotten to the shipment first and had removed the dope. He only wanted to arrest me so that he'd have an excuse to search my apartment. And he got mad when he discovered that Feldstein had put a security camera watch on me because that video record showed that I *hadn't* gone anywhere and retrieved any polymeth after leaving Feldstein that night. Where the hell is that car?"

Drake pointed up the street. "Here it comes. So Wofford went back to investigating everywhere that Kemper and Santino had gone, ostensibly looking for a third conspirator, but actually looking for the missing polymeth in every compartment they'd entered."

Flynn clenched his teeth. "And now it's dawned on him that there was another person in the warehouse the night he thinks the polymeth was stolen."

The car braked quietly to a stop at the curb and the two men jumped in. "Fasten your safety harness," Drake warned. He activated the flashing red lights and siren and left rubber on the metal deck plates as he blasted away from the curb. He skidded professionally into a hard left turn at the intersection next to Betty's Bar and headed along Denver Boulevard. Flynn braced himself against the car's dashboard.

"He has no legal excuse to search her apartment," Flynn said, "so he can't leave any witnesses." He took a deep breath. "I had thought that the killer was somebody stupid or overconfident. I overlooked the possibility that it could have been somebody desperate."

There were no other electric vehicles on the street at that time on a Sunday evening, just pedestrians and a scattering of bicycles. Drake swerved around the bicycles and let the pedestrians hurry out of his way. Ninth Street had no interlevel ramps, so Drake turned onto Eighth Street and took the first up-ramp. Chadwick's apartment was almost directly across the circumference of the Station from the ramp, but Drake shut off his siren as soon as he reached level six. He drove like a person who didn't have to fear the repercussions of running over a pedestrian. He slowed down as he approached Chadwick's apartment building only so that he could stop without squealing his tires.

Another Company vehicle was already parked in front of Chadwick's building. Two orange-suited security guards were standing on the sidewalk. They stepped over to Drake's car as it pulled up to the curb. One of them leaned forward and said, "There's more than one person in the apartment. We can hear them talking through the door."

Drake and Flynn got out of the car. Drake turned to the investigator and said, "He's probably here already."

Flynn nodded. "The deputy who answered the phone in the Marshals Office said he'd turned off his locator, so he doesn't want anyone to know where he is."

"We'll have to move fast," Drake said. "No time for re-inforcements." He opened his computer and studied the display. "There's no back door to her apartment, but she has a window—a real one—in the back wall."

Flynn nodded. "It looks out on the swimming pool."

Drake said, "All real windows on the Station can be opened for use as fire exits. We'll have to cover it. Chong and I will go in through the front door. You take Laska and cover the rear."

Flynn shook his head. "No. I'm going in with you."

Once again Flynn was treated to a rare show of emotion on Drake's face. "No, you're not. He killed two of *my* people. *I'm* going to take him down." He turned to Laska. "Follow him and do whatever he tells you." He nodded at Chong. "Let's go."

Drake started for the ramp to the balcony in front of Chadwick's apartment. Chong was right at his heels. Flynn sighed. He turned to Laska. The goon was no taller than Flynn, but had broader shoulders, dark brown eyes and hair, and a small beard. "Follow me," Flynn said.

He led the way through the hall on the first level of the apartment building to the patio at the rear. He could hear children splashing behind the safety gate to the swimming pool. He looked up at the building. Light streamed through two windows. Flynn guessed that the one on the left was Wendy's. He eyed the palm trees. A plan formed in his mind, but it wouldn't work—all the interior windows on the Station were made of impact-resistant glass, and a pulse from his stun gun wouldn't penetrate them.

Flynn turned abruptly to Laska. "Gimme your pistol," he ordered.

Laska stepped back, shaking his head. "No way. It's against regulations. Besides, you're not authorized—"

"What the hell did Drake tell you? You're supposed to do whatever I say! Give me the gun!" Laska still hesitated. "You want to shoot a U.S. marshal?" Flynn asked.

Laska's face blanched. "There's a . . ." He swallowed. "There's a marshal in there?"

"If there isn't, this isn't an emergency! Now give me the damn gun!"

Laska unlatched his holster and extracted his laser pistol. He disengaged the power supply and handed the gun butt-first to Flynn. He twisted the activation ring off of his left hand and handed it over. "You'll need this, too."

The ring was too large for Flynn's ring finger. The investigator put it on his middle finger, where it still threatened to slide off.

Laska pointed at the laser. "The selector switch—"

"I know how to use it." Flynn snapped the power supply into place. He took his stun pistol from his pocket and handed it to the guard. "Here. So that you won't be defenseless. And make sure those kids stay in that pool."

Flynn selected the palm tree that angled the most toward the horizontal. He put Laska's pistol in his coat pocket, wrapped his arms and his legs around the trunk, and shinnied up the tree. The bark was rough and snagged his coat. Looking down, Flynn guessed that he had climbed nearly to the overhead, but the glowing windows were still above him. Flynn could see over the safety fence and into the pool; the splashing children were oblivious of his presence. The tree trunk curved, becoming more vertical. Flynn began to think that his plan wasn't going to work. He pressed the edges of the soles of his shoes against the rough bark of the tree and pushed himself upward. Slowly he gained a better view through the unpolarized windows. The window on Flynn's left was definitely in Wendy's apartment: Flynn could see Wofford's head as the marshal paced back and forth. He climbed higher. Wofford was not wearing his marshal's uniform. Wendy was seated on her exercise machine, her hands cuffed behind her. The marshal suddenly slapped her across the face, twisting her head around.

Flynn looked down. "Tell your boss that it's Wofford, all right."

Laska nodded and spoke into his phone. "Hey, Flynn!" he called in a loud whisper. "The boss says he's going in now!"

"Tell him to wait. I'm not ready."

But Drake didn't wait. Flynn couldn't see the apartment door from his perch on the tree, but he saw Wofford snatch Wendy from her seat and hold her between him and the door. The marshal was trained in hostage rescue; he knew that his hostage would not deter stun pulses. Wofford reached under his coat, pulled out his laser, and pressed the muzzle against the back of Wendy's head. If shot or stunned, he might still kill Wendy. He kept his arm behind Wendy's body where a stun pulse couldn't reach it. Flynn could see Wofford's mouth moving. He couldn't hear what the marshal was saying, but he could guess.

Wofford's secret was exposed. He couldn't get off of the Station. His only options were to surrender peacefully or to take as many people with him as he could—the more likely possibility, since he hadn't been acting rationally. Drake wanted to avenge his two security guards, and only Wendy's body was keeping him from doing that. Drake didn't like lawyers; he might consider Wendy's death to be a small price to pay. Flynn couldn't allow either Drake or Wofford to decide the outcome.

Michael took Laska's laser from his pocket. He flipped the selector switch from stun to kill. All of the lasers on the Station, Flynn knew, had had their power levels adjusted so that they could not shoot through the steel plates that kept the air in and the vacuum out. The window wasn't transparent enough to let a laser beam through unhindered, and Flynn could only hope that enough energy would get through.

Flynn rested the gun against the tree trunk and put the red dot of the optical sight on the back of Wofford's head. His Marine Corps training came to his aid: although he was clinging to a tree five meters above the ground, his heart wasn't pounding and his hand wasn't shaking. But Wofford's gun was still pressed against the back of Wendy's skull. Even if the laser pulse got through the window, it wouldn't put the marshal down instantly. If Wofford reflexively jerked the trigger of his gun, fried pieces of Wendy's brain would be blown all over the dining room.

Wofford was unaware that the window behind him wasn't a holographic display. He suddenly pointed his gun at the door and fired. Wendy was temporarily safe. Flynn pressed the trigger.

A bright, orange flash punctuated the darkness of the patio. The laser pulse vaporized a narrow hole in the window. It had enough energy left to make a hole the size of a dime in the back of Wofford's head.

For an eternity nothing happened. Then Wofford turned

slowly, his arms dropping, his feet tangling together. He was nearly facing the window when he pitched forward and disappeared below the sill.

Chapter 13

Deputy United States Marshal Herb Rustin had a round, pudgy face that looked out of place on a law enforcement officer. He had lived on Jupiter Station less than one year since being sent from Earth to replace the chief deputy whose tour of duty had expired. He was a professional policeman who had argued repeatedly and unsuccessfully with his boss about the latter's handling of the Vasquez and Kemper-Santino investigations. Now Rustin knew why Wofford had resisted his arguments so obstinately.

When Rustin was agitated his pudgy face took on a tint of red. At that moment his face was florid. The two people across the table from him in the interrogation room were irritatingly relaxed for having just killed the U.S. Marshal. Rustin was sorely tempted to take Mike Flynn's computer and use it to slap the confident expression off of Flynn's face. Rustin took a deep breath to resume his interrogation. "You killed the United States Marshal—"

"I killed a murderer," Flynn corrected, "who was threatening to kill again and who shot and seriously wounded Company security guard Ray Chong—"

Rustin winced. "Seriously wounded? He was hit in the shoulder!"

"Upper chest would be a more accurate description," Silvanus Drake said calmly. "Ten centimeters lower and it would have taken out his right lung."

"But it wasn't ten centimeters lower," Rustin said, "and Chong will be out of the hospital tomorrow."

"Irrelevant," Flynn protested. "Wofford had no justification to shoot him at all, even with a stun pulse." He tapped his finger on the table to emphasize his point. "Wofford's the bad guy in this case, not us. Chong and Chadwick are the victims, not Wofford."

Rustin pointed at Flynn. "You think that's going to get you out of this?"

"*Something's* going to get me out of this," Flynn answered. "It's obviously justifiable homicide." He tapped his computer. "So says my lawyer."

Rustin gritted his teeth.

Drake gestured at the man seated to Rustin's right with a nod of his head and said, "If you won't take our legal advice, why don't you ask the U.S. attorney?"

Rustin avoided looking at Kyle Pierce. He knew what Pierce thought of Wendy Chadwick. The attorney was not going to take the lead in prosecuting the men who had saved her life.

Pierce knew that he was being ignored. "They're right," he said. Rustin still didn't look at him. "Their statements agree. The statements of all the witnesses agree. If it will make you feel better I'll convene a grand jury, but we'd be wasting everybody's time. It went down just like they said and the government's own hostage-rescue rules permit lethal force under the circumstances."

"Lethal force by law enforcement authorities!" Rustin said, pounding his fist on the table. "They should have called us in!"

Flynn leaned across the table and stared the chief deputy—acting marshal, now—right in the face. "There wasn't time! Or would you be happier with a live Wofford under arrest and a third murder with which to charge him?"

Rustin glared at him. "You had time to call the Marshals

Office, looking for Wofford! You could have told the deputy what you suspected!"

Flynn's frustration showed on his face. "Oh, and he would have believed me when I said his boss was a murderer? He might have put it down as a crank call, he might have called you, he might have called Mr. Pierce there, but he wouldn't have sent the hostage rescue team to Chadwick's apartment."

"That apartment block is exclusively for Company employees," Drake pointed out. "It is not open to the public and hence falls under the jurisdiction of my security force, not your marshals. Company Security *was* the appropriate law enforcement authority."

Rustin pursed his lips. "Maybe I can't get you for killing the marshal," he said to Flynn, "but I can still nail you for possessing a deadly weapon without a license!"

Silvanus Drake interjected, "Company security personnel are allowed to possess deadly weapons."

Rustin looked at him, his mouth open. "Since when has Flynn been a Company goon?"

Drake replied, "The reason I went to Flynn's apartment this evening was to hire him to investigate the Kemper and Santino murders."

Rustin glanced from Drake to Flynn and back to Drake. He slumped in his chair. "Two civilians kill the U.S. marshal, and there's not a damn thing I can charge them with. The solar system's going to hell in a handbasket. No wonder Wofford went ballistic."

"I had expected you to be pleased that we'd got the bastard for you," Flynn said innocently.

Rustin jumped to his feet, knocking over his chair. "We should have got him ourselves!" he shouted, confirming what the other people in the room had suspected. Wofford had become an acute embarrassment to the Marshals Service, but the marshals hadn't discovered it and remedied the situation. Outsiders had done it for them.

Rustin closed his eyes and shook his head. "How the hell am I going to explain this to Washington?"

"You want me to write the report?" Pierce offered.

"No!" Rustin thought for a moment, then said, "Yes. No. Oh, hell, I don't know. Ask me tomorrow." He turned and walked out of the room.

"Are we free to go?" Drake asked.

"We have your written statements," Pierce said. "Unless there are some surprising facts in this case that you haven't told me about, I'll be issuing a finding of justifiable homicide in a day or two. Until then, I'm afraid the marshals will have to keep your weapons." He got to his feet, took his computer from the table, said, "Let me make sure the *i*'s are dotted and the *t*'s are crossed," and left the room.

Flynn waited for the door to close behind Pierce. He looked at Drake. "Did you notice what he *didn't* ask us?"

Drake was looking at the tabletop. "He didn't ask if Wofford had any more accomplices. They're too stunned by his death and the revelation of his crimes to think. They're acting on instinct at the moment. Tomorrow, Tuesday at the latest, they'll be asking us about what else we know or suspect."

"I think his only two accomplices are already dead."

"Of course. Wofford was a lone wolf." Drake was silent for a moment. "I told you that I was going to take him down." Flynn gave him a warning stare, but Drake said, "Don't worry. They're not allowed to monitor us when we're alone with our 'lawyer.' " He nodded toward Flynn's computer. His tone revealed his disdain for such a piddling rule.

"You didn't have a clear shot," Flynn explained.

"He killed two of my men."

"He almost got a third."

"Chong shouldn't have cut across the doorway like he did," Drake said. "He's not trained for tactical situations."

"And he has the IQ of a salad fork," Flynn added.

"Wofford would have given me an opening," Drake continued.

"Before or after he killed Wendy?"

Drake elected to change the subject. "How did you discover that I'd put a microcam in your apartment?"

"Microcams," Flynn said, holding up two fingers. "I found the one in my bedroom, too."

"Okay, how did you find the microcams?"

Flynn considered his answer carefully. He could do no harm by telling the truth; Drake's goons were unlikely to make the same mistake a second time. "I'll make a deal with you, Drake: I'll tell you how I found the microcams—and I'll even forget about the polymeth that you're cooking up on Charlie, and probably Juliet, too—if you'll tell me what really happened to Asterbrook and Mondragon."

The room was suddenly still, as though the walls and the furniture were straining to hear Drake's reply. Flynn couldn't even hear the ventilation system.

Drake's face remained impassive while he considered the proposal. He nodded his head once. "Deal. But I asked you first."

Flynn tingled with excitement. He took a slow breath to calm himself. "The people who planted the microcams searched my apartment. They looked everywhere, even inside the automatic cat-food dispenser."

"So?"

"So, they cross-threaded the lid when they put it back

on," Flynn continued, "the safety switch didn't close, the dispenser wouldn't work, and Furrball ran out of food. When I discovered the problem, I realized that my place had been gone over, so I started looking for anything your goons had left behind."

Drake's face remained impassive. He didn't reply.

"Your turn," Flynn prompted.

Drake glanced quickly around the interrogation room, although there was no one else present. He leaned toward Flynn and lowered his voice, so that the walls wouldn't overhear his words. "They were attempting to lift a heavy object with an overhead crane," he said. "The pulley on the crane was too small for the ceramic-filament line they were using. The line kinked and broke, dropping the heavy object on them and crushing them."

Flynn stared at him. Drake's eyes were expressionless. Flynn couldn't even tell if they were focused on him. Michael was as angry with himself as he was with the security chief—he never should have expected, or even hoped, that Drake would tell the truth. "Do you have any friends, Drake? Does your wife like you? Does your *mother* like you?"

Wendy Chadwick was pacing back and forth in the marshals' outer office. Her face was sore but that wasn't why she was struggling to control the temper that had prompted her mentor in law school to advise her to stay out of courtrooms. Kyle Pierce was always bothering her when she wanted to avoid him; now, when she wanted to see him, he was avoiding her.

Ed Warshovsky and his wife Mary came through the door from the Government Plaza. "Wendy!" he said. "Are you all right?"

Chadwick turned reluctantly in his direction. She was not in the mood to deal with her boss if he was calling her by her first name; she didn't need a father figure at that moment. "I'm fine."

"Your face . . ."

"He slapped me a couple of times. Three times. That's all."

Warshovsky looked at her closely. The left side of her face appeared swollen. "Have you seen a doctor?"

"I don't need a doctor," Chadwick said testily. "I just need the imbeciles who enforce the law on this station to realize that they're persecuting the good guys again." She paused. "I need somebody to tell me what the hell is going on! Drake won't ask for an attorney and Flynn's being represented by that damned software of his, so they won't let me in there!" She stabbed her finger at the closed door to the interrogation room. "The U.S. attorney is treating me like a victim and a witness instead of an attorney—"

"You *are* a victim," Warshovsky pointed out. "Where's Mitch Habruch? He handles criminal cases for the Company."

"It's his wedding anniversary," Chadwick explained. "He's taking a couple of days off. I said I'd cover for him."

Warshovsky hesitated. "Well, the usual fights and such . . . But this is a serious matter. Habruch should be here."

Chadwick transfixed Warshovsky with her eyes. "I took criminal procedure! And I know justifiable homicide when I see it! *I* reviewed and signed off the Company's guidelines on the use of deadly force!"

"Of course it's justifiable homicide," Warshovsky agreed, "but they still have to investigate. Even if one of the marshals had killed Wofford, there'd be an investigation."

The door to the marshal's personal office, now taken over by Rustin, opened and Kyle Pierce walked through it. He nodded a greeting to the Warshovskys and walked up to Wendy. "You need to see a doctor," he said.

Chadwick clenched her teeth. "I do *not* need to see a doctor! I'm not badly hurt!"

Pierce shook his head. "It's for legal reasons, Wendy, not medical ones. I need a professional medical opinion of your injuries for my report."

Chadwick closed her eyes. She sighed. "Okay, I'll see a doctor."

Mary Warshovsky turned to her husband. "You once told me that Wofford had a reputation for honesty and incorruptibility. What turned him into a murderer?"

"His superiors," her husband said simply. But he could tell from his wife's expression that she wanted to know the details. "He was in charge of the Miami office of the Marshals Service before he was sent here," Warshovsky explained. "Did everything by the book. Wouldn't do favors for anybody, no matter how powerful and important they were. That did not endear him to the movers and shakers of south Florida, who pulled every political string they could reach to get rid of him. The final straw was the Hernandez case."

"The same Hernandez that was involved in the Nash scandals?" Mary asked.

"That was Roberto Hernandez," Warshovsky replied, "one of the richest people in Florida and the principal financial backer of former President Nash. The case that got Wofford transferred here involved Roberto's son."

"Ah!" Mary said, smiling as she remembered the news headlines. "It was drugs, wasn't it?"

"Apparently his son thought that the forty thousand a

month allowance that his father gave him wasn't enough," Warshovsky continued, "so he started dealing drugs. Killed an important member of the Miami mob when a drug deal went sour. The Mob put a half-million-dollar contract on the son's life. The Hernandez money couldn't get him out of that, so he agreed to testify against the Mob in exchange for a slap-on-the-wrist sentence, to be served in one of those luxury prisons that our government maintains for rich people who get caught committing no-nos. His pretrial protection was entrusted to the U.S. Marshals Service."

"Wofford," Mary said.

Her husband nodded. "Wofford put young Hernandez in a secret safe house surrounded by marshals. Roberto Hernandez wanted to supplement the marshals with a large force of private security guards. Wofford, per regulations, refused to tell Hernandez where the safe house was. Hernandez went over Wofford's head, all the way to President Nash herself. Wofford hadn't made himself any friends, and Nash needed Hernandez's money to get reelected, so what Hernandez wanted, Hernandez got. Wofford was reassigned to Jupiter Station."

Pierce interrupted, "His replacement welcomed Hernandez's private guards with open arms, and just before the trial the safe house was blown up by a precision-guided glide bomb, which had mysteriously disappeared from a military arsenal in South America."

"That's what I was remembering," Mary said. "That's what got the media attention and prompted the Congressional investigations."

"Which in turn made the Nash administration look so bad that the president decided not to run for a second term," Pierce remarked, "so she didn't need the Hernandez money anyway." Pierce did not dwell on the irony; he had voted for Nash.

"No wonder Wofford went bad," Mrs. Warshovsky said thoughtfully. "He does everything right and still gets treated like . . . Well, he must have been very bitter."

"And we paid the price," Pierce concluded.

Chadwick stared at the attorney. "What's this 'we' business, white eyes?"

"Are you done with Mr. Drake?" Warshovsky asked Pierce.

The U.S. attorney nodded. "For the time being. I was about to tell him that he and Flynn can leave."

Chadwick planted her hands on her hips. "Are you through with my apartment?"

Pierce nodded. "Wofford's body has been removed—"

"Damn. I was going to have it stuffed and mounted."

"And all forensic evidence gathered. You can go there if you want." He said it as though he didn't think anybody would want to go there. "Or, if you'd rather stay elsewhere for a few days, I have space in my apartment."

Chadwick hesitated before replying. "Thanks, Kyle, but no thanks."

Pierce nodded. "As you wish." He headed for the interrogation room.

Warshovsky said to Wendy, "I brought my car. We'll escort you past the press."

"The press?" Chadwick turned and looked through the glass front wall of the Marshals Office. She rubbed her hands in anticipation. "Goody! I'd love to give them an earful about the way this case has been handled!" Then she remembered that she was the Company's legal director. She sighed. "Could you tell them to wait until tomorrow?"

Warshovsky shook his head. "They're not our people.

We're keeping the story off of the local newscasts tonight. It's that woman from SSN. She won't wait until tomorrow. A U.S. marshal going bad and getting shot dead is big news."

The door to the interrogation room opened and Flynn and Drake walked out, followed by Pierce. Only Warshovsky noticed the slight wave of Drake's hand that meant that everything was under control.

"Michael knows that reporter," Wendy said. "Maybe he can charm her into letting us through without an interview."

"What reporter?" Flynn said. He looked through the glass, spotted a woman with tinted hair and dressed in fashionable metallic green, and waved to her. She waved back. He looked at Wendy. "You trying to avoid her? Why don't you just say, 'No comment,' like lawyers always do?"

"Because we always sound like idiots or criminals when we say it," Chadwick replied.

Rustin came out of his office just in time to hear Flynn say, "I don't feel like talking to her, either. Come on. I'll take you out the back way."

Rustin looked peeved. "How the hell did you find out about that?"

"Feldstein showed me," Flynn explained.

Rustin looked around the office for the deputy. "Sid?" he called. "Where the hell is Feldstein?"

"Off duty," the deputy behind the counter said.

Rustin headed back into his office. "Then I'll chew him out over the phone."

Flynn took Wendy by the arm. "Come on. I'll give you another behind-the-scenes tour of Jupiter Station." He led her to the counter and asked the duty deputy, "You don't mind if we go out the back way, do you?"

The deputy considered his answer carefully. He chewed his lower lip. "Well, Rustin didn't say you *couldn't* leave by the back door." He nodded at Chadwick, and Flynn inferred that the deputy was granting the favor to her and not to him. "I don't think anyone's in the locker room, but you'd better check before you take the lady in there."

Flynn led Wendy behind the counter and through the door into the inner reaches of the Marshals Office. The men's locker room was empty. Flynn walked to a utility access hatch in the wall next to the shower room and opened it. He gestured with his arm for Wendy to step through.

Wendy poked her head through the hatch into a narrow, dimly lit space lined with pipes and conduits. "What is this place?"

"Utility corridor," Flynn replied. "Got to get the water and air and electricity around the Station some way."

Chadwick stepped gingerly through the hatch. Flynn followed, closing the hatch behind him. He pointed to the electronic lock. "Anybody can get out this way, but only the marshals can get in."

Wendy looked left and right along the duct. "Which way do we go?"

"Either. But going to the left takes you to a street more quickly."

Wendy started in that direction. The deck and bulkheads were dirty. "The marshals actually use this?"

Flynn shrugged. "Rarely, I think. When they were sent here, they thought they should have a back way to their office, just in case they had to get an unpopular suspect in and out while an angry mob waited at the main entrance. That hatch we went through used to be in a janitorial closet that was located where the marshals' locker room is now. When the Government Plaza was built and the Marshals

Office was put here, they kept the access hatch to the utility corridor so they'd have more than one entrance. Sid Feldstein showed it to me last year."

Shadows shifted as the pair walked along. Chadwick was reminded of her flight through the basement, with trigger-happy security guards in pursuit. "I lived a pretty routine life until I met you," Wendy said. "I've known you one week and I've almost been killed twice." She shook her head. "And the second time was because we didn't . . . Well, Wofford was even more desperate than we thought."

Flynn had been walking behind Chadwick in the narrow utility duct, but he stepped forward and walked as close to her as he could.

"When he started slapping me around," Wendy continued, "demanding to know where the polymeth was, saying that I had to have it because Kemper and Santino and you didn't have it . . . That's when I knew that he'd killed Kemper and Santino. And that he was going to kill me. He'd have to: I knew his secret and there was no place he could run. Then Drake overrode the door lock and pointed his gun at us, and I looked at him, and . . . You know how you can never tell what Drake is thinking by looking at his face? Well, I could tell this time. I could see that he wasn't there to rescue me. He was there to get the man who'd killed two of his goons, and if I got caught in the crossfire, that would have been okay. But I wasn't frightened. I wasn't trying to think of a way to escape. I was thinking that, pretty soon, I was going to know what it was like to be dead."

Flynn put his arm around Wendy's waist. She didn't resist. They stopped walking. He looked at her; her head was down.

"I thought we agreed this afternoon that this would be

a really bad idea," she said.

"We did. It is."

She looked up at him and he kissed her. She threw her arms around his neck. "Michael Flynn, if you break my heart . . . If you break my heart, I'll kill you. Or I'll kill myself. Or maybe I'll kill both of us, but I cannot go through another . . . rejection."

Flynn stepped back, bumping into a shutoff valve in a water line. "Is there some history here that I should know about?"

Wendy looked down again. She swallowed. "I . . . I lied to you yesterday. In Gus's. I didn't come out here because I thought it would be good for my career." She looked along the corridor in the direction they had been walking. "I used to live with a man. When I was in Denver. Another lawyer—not for the Company; I met him at a Bar Association dinner. We fell in love. At least, I loved him. He *said* he loved me." A tear escaped from the corner of her eye. "We bought a condo together, moved in together. He took me to meet his family. I took him to my parents' place for Christmas. I thought we were going to get married, have a baby . . . We'd be just like my parents."

Wendy had to blink back tears before she could continue. "Then one day I came home from work and found him packing. He'd been offered a partnership in a big Washington law firm. Two million a year, minimum. He said he hadn't discussed it with me because he knew I wouldn't give up my career." She sniffled.

"Would you have given up your career?"

She turned her head toward Flynn. "I wouldn't have had to! Half the people in Washington are lawyers! I could have gotten a job there easily! As a partner in a big firm he was suddenly too good for me." She looked down at Mike's chest. "I walked around in a daze for a week. I didn't know what to tell my friends or my parents . . . I came out here so that I wouldn't have to explain to them, so that I wouldn't have to see things that reminded me of him. He sent me an offer to sell me his half of the condo. That's the last I heard from him. But he'd said he loved me. He said it a lot. And he lied each time he said it."

Flynn took her in his arms. She must have been reacting to her brush with death. Memories of a failed love affair could not be more traumatic than staring down the focus tube of Silvanus Drake's laser pistol. Somebody said, "I will not break your heart." A moment later Flynn realized that he had said it.

Flynn guessed that he was reacting to shooting Wofford. According to everything that Michael had ever read about gunfights and post-traumatic stress, he should have been dazed, almost in shock, but it had all seemed so much like a Marine Corps training exercise that it hadn't affected him. Until now. It had to be affecting him now. He couldn't be thinking about settling down with a lawyer. How could he explain that to his friends and family? And he had known Wendy less than a week. He had known Missy Russell for months before he had realized that his feelings for her were different from those he'd had for the other women he had dated. Tomorrow, when he had begun to recover from post-traumatic stress, he would feel differently.

He held Wendy closer. "I will not break your heart," he repeated.

She looked up at him. "We're being very stupid, you know."

"I know." He kissed her again.

"Tomorrow, we'll be more rational."

Flynn nodded. Wendy pulled his head down to hers and kissed him.

"I'd better get you to that hospital or by the time tomorrow gets here it will be too late," Flynn said.

They tried walking with their arms around each other, but the utility corridor was too narrow. When they reached the street they found it deserted.

"What time is it, anyway?" Wendy asked.

Flynn glanced at his watch. "Twenty-three thirty."

"Damn it," Chadwick said. "I was going to take a taxi but I don't have my debit card."

"You don't have a phone to order one, either." Flynn took his phone from his pocket.

They waited in silence until the taxi arrived. Flynn activated it with his debit card. He didn't get into the cab with Chadwick. "We'd be wise if we didn't spend too much time together for awhile," he said. "No sense giving Drake a chance to knock off both of us at the same time."

Chadwick squinted. "And why would he want to knock us off?"

"We're the only two innocent people who know about the polymeth."

Wendy closed her eyes and took a deep breath. "The Company is not making polymeth! And if Drake wanted us dead, he just missed a real good chance to get rid of me!"

"I just had a nice talk with Drake," Flynn said. "He was real unhappy that I shot Wofford when I did. He might have been waiting for the marshal to kill you, or maybe he was going to shoot you himself while 'trying to shoot Wofford.' And he conveniently put me on the far side of the apartment, where there was a chance that a stray laser pulse would have hit me."

"We were all alone on Satellite Charlie yesterday afternoon," Chadwick argued. "Why didn't he arrange a pressure leak or something?"

Flynn shook his head. "There are so many airtight compartments on Charlie that the chance of disposing of us in a lopa are too small. Besides, he doesn't want the authorities prowling all over Charlie investigating an 'accident.' They might find the polymeth lab."

Chadwick gritted her teeth. "Michael . . ." She grabbed the front of Flynn's shirt with her hands and looked him right in the eyes. "Michael, there *is no polymeth lab!* Trust me on this! *Please!*"

Flynn put his arms around Wendy. "Wendy, I trust you implicitly." He was surprised to realize that he really believed that. "I don't trust your employers."

Chadwick gave up. "One of these days, very soon, I'll be able to tell you the whole story. Then will you come to my place for dinner? You have a right to see what you're getting into."

"Is that a description of your cooking ability?"

Wendy sighed. "I'm afraid so."

"It's hard to cook without fat, salt, and other good-tasting ingredients."

She made a face. "I'll cook what I want and you'll like it!"

"Say good night, Wendy."

"Good night . . . Michael." She reached around his neck and kissed him again.

Flynn couldn't resist watching the taxi drive away. He walked back to his apartment, watching the traffic with more than his usual care, and wondering why he felt no sense of doom over the mess he was about to make of his life.

The popcorn that Flynn had thrown at the video display

was still scattered on the floor. Michael sat wearily behind his desk. Furrball jumped onto the desk and purred in his face. Flynn stroked the cat's ears. "Fat lot of help you are. Why didn't you clean up the popcorn?" The cat purred louder. A janitorial robot would come in the morning; Flynn left the popcorn on the floor.

The door alarmed sounded, startling Flynn. He glanced at his watch: it was after midnight. The monitor showed Brenda Stahl, SSN correspondent on Jupiter Station, and her camera operator. Flynn was suddenly much wearier. Maybe if he waited, she would go away. But Flynn had already angered the marshals; he couldn't afford to lose another potential ally. He went to the door slowly.

Flynn didn't even get a chance to say hello. Stahl's companion raised his camera and Stahl said, "Mr. Flynn, exactly what happened at Wendy Chadwick's apartment this evening?" She thrust her microphone into Flynn's face.

The investigator made a show of looking at his wristwatch. "Yesterday evening, actually."

"Yesterday evening, then. What happened?"

Flynn shook his head. "Sorry, Bren, but my lawyer has advised me not to make any statements until the U.S. attorney has issued his finding."

A look of irritation passed across Brenda's face. "Is that your way of saying, 'No comment'?"

Flynn sighed. "I'm afraid so."

"Are you facing charges?"

"I said that I'm not making any statements. Look, Brenda, I'm really sorry, but—"

"Sorry? Is that all you have to say?" She gestured with her free hand at the camera operator and he lowered the camera. "Michael, I was given the choice of Ceres or here. I chose the Station because I thought it had better long-term potential. Then that mineshaft blows out and Ceres is the biggest story in the solar system. I nearly gave myself a brain injury, pounding my head into a bulkhead. Now this happens. The biggest story of my career, and I can't get into the shooting scene. I get some shots of a body bag being wheeled away and that's it. The authorities say they can't comment on an ongoing investigation, Wendy Chadwick is either not answering her door or has disappeared, and now my friend Michael Flynn, the central character in the drama, says he can't talk about it, either. The only people who will talk to me are some children who were swimming in the pool behind Chadwick's apartment, and they all tell different stories which I think they made up. Can't you confirm that you saved Wendy Chadwick's life by killing Marshal Wofford when he was trying to murder her?"

"Brenda, the authorities will be making an official statement tomorrow—er, later today. Tuesday at the latest. Then I'll be able to tell you the whole story. I'll give you an exclusive."

Brenda made a face. "Oh, that's mighty generous of you, Mike! Who the hell else could you give the story to?"

Ms. Stahl had tinted the ends of her blond hair to match her metallic green outfit. Furrball crept out of the apartment and sniffed suspiciously at her shiny tights. "Brenda, I really am sorry, but until I know that I'm not going to be charged with a crime and that my investigator's license is safe, I can't say anything. Have you talked to the security guards?"

Brenda took a deep breath, then her expression changed. "Guards? Plural?" Flynn nodded. "There was another goon there besides Ray Chong?"

Flynn nodded again. "Maury Laska."

Brenda turned and head down the balcony, motioning for the camera operator to follow her. "Thanks, Mike."

"Don't mention it." Flynn doubted that Laska would say anything; Silvanus Drake would have told him to keep his mouth shut. He hoped that Laska wouldn't realize who had given his name to the press.

Flynn returned to his desk. He took the photographs of the accident scene in warehouse twelve out of the drawer. He still couldn't see what had prompted the Company to transfer the deputy marshal and the two medical technicians and retire the foreman.

Maybe there was nothing to see. Maybe it was something that somebody had said.

Deputy Marshal Kytel, the investigating officer, might have made an audio recording with his computer. That would have been an official government computer. It would not have gone with Kytel when he had taken the Company job on planet three. Flynn wondered what had happened to it.

Chapter 14

On Monday morning Michael Flynn got up before 06:00, jogged, and showered. He had eggs for breakfast, fresh eggs from the chickens that were raised on Satellite Bravo. He wanted to track down Deputy Marshal Kytel's computer, to see if it had an audio recording made at the accident scene in warehouse twelve, but he was not in the good graces of the U.S. Marshals Service and knew that no marshal—not even his friend Sid Feldstein—would cooperate with him. Not that Monday, anyway. So Flynn would start on two background investigations—one premarital and one pre-employment—that had been subcontracted to him from a detective agency in New York. He stroked Furrball's ears, told the cat to guard the apartment, and set forth to earn a living.

And discovered that he had become a celebrity.

Ed Warshovsky had kept the story of Wofford's death out of the Company's evening newscasts in order to give his favorite executive time to recover from her ordeal, but in a community as small as Jupiter Station that information could not be suppressed for long. Neighbor had told neighbor, word had reached the crowd watching the airball tournament, and Brenda Stahl had filed a story with SSN. Before Flynn had gone to bed most of the people on the Station had heard the story in one form or another. On Monday morning the Company news service ran the story and the Station inhabitants got the Company version of Sunday night's events.

A chronic concern had been lifted from the shoulders of the residents of Jupiter Station. The murderer among them had been identified and killed and they were safe again. Better still, the murderer had not been a Company employee. The reputation of the Conglomerated Mining and Manufacturing Company had been restored. Everyone felt guilty for having assumed that a security guard had done in Kemper and Santino. They expiated their guilt by going out of their way to treat the normally detested guards nicely. People were smiling at goons, patting them on the back, and buying them drinks.

And the royal treatment being given the security guards was nothing compared to what was bestowed on Michael Flynn. Flynn had solved the case. Flynn had slain the murderer when the fiend was about to kill yet another Company employee. Flynn had saved them all. Flynn was the Station's new hero, more popular than any airball player. People he didn't know greeted him on the street by his first name. Children ran up to him and asked for his autograph. Bartenders vowed that Michael Flynn would never have to pay to drink in their establishments. And the Company guards who had been giving Flynn a hard time since the shoot-out in the basement were now doing everything they could to help Flynn. No Company door was closed to him. Goons offered to track down people Flynn wanted to interview. Flynn felt like the king of Jupiter Station. He was more than a king, he was bulletproof—Silvanus Drake couldn't do anything to him without creating an uproar that would produce a thorough federal investigation.

By the middle of the afternoon, Flynn had completed both background investigations without having had to bribe anyone for information. His new efficiency was a mixed blessing for a self-employed professional who got paid by the day: he could bill each investigation for at most one-half day's labor. If he was going to be a far more efficient detective he was going to need far more work to maintain his income. He regretted not having been more cooperative with Brenda Stahl; he could have used the system-wide publicity that an interview on SSN would bring.

Early in the afternoon, Flynn's computer relayed the news that Kyle Pierce had ruled the shooting of Marshal Wofford to be justifiable homicide. Later, after Flynn wrapped up his second investigation of the day, his computer reported that his bank was holding in escrow an unauthorized deposit of fifty-three thousand, two hundred and twenty-eight dollars to his account. The payer was the Conglomerated Mining and Manufacturing Company.

Flynn stared at his computer display, his lips pressed together. Silvanus Drake, afraid that Flynn's sudden popularity might cause someone to answer questions about the deaths of Asterbrook and Mondragon or talk about mysterious goings-on in Satellite Charlie, had taken preemptive action. Flynn would need three months of steady employment to earn fifty-three thousand after-tax dollars. He sighed, and pressed the key on his computer to refuse the payment. Honesty was an expensive virtue.

Flynn folded his computer and put it into his coat pocket. He would stop at the Marshals Office and collect his stun pistol. Then he would find Brenda Stahl and keep his promise of an exclusive interview as soon as the U.S. attorney had cleared him. He needed the publicity.

The computer on the desk of Fred Zoldas beeped. Zoldas scowled. He hated to be bothered less than two hours before quitting time. He activated the video link and the thin face and hawkish nose of Stuart Lavochkin appeared on the display. Lavochkin was in charge of Company Payroll on Jupiter Station.

"Yes?" Zoldas said, letting his irritation show in his voice. He wanted Lavochkin to know that this had better be important.

"Sorry to bother you," Lavochkin said, "but a temporary employee has rejected his compensation."

Zoldas took a deep breath to calm himself. Someone had miscalculated what the Company owed him and was trying to make sure he had the best possible legal grounds to collect what he thought he had coming. Payments to temporary employees seldom exceeded two thousand dollars. Zoldas's quiet afternoon had been ruined by a few thousand lousy bucks. "How much does he claim we underpaid him?"

"He doesn't," Lavochkin replied. "Just refused the electronic deposit."

"And how much do we owe him?"

Lavochkin squirmed. "That's the problem. I can't find his employment record, and the payment he bounced was for seventy thousand dollars. Less taxes, of course."

Zoldas sat bolt upright in his chair. "Did you say seventy *thousand?*" The face on the monitor nodded. Zoldas grunted. "How about that. An honest person. Somebody hit the wrong key on a computer and overpaid him." Grossly overpaid him. No temporary employee could have earned seventy thousand dollars, especially if he had left no employment record. "Okay, show me the file."

What little information Lavochkin had appeared on Zoldas's display. The payment had been authorized by Silvanus Drake. Zoldas started to snicker—Drake always acted like he never made mistakes. "Wait a minute! Michael Flynn? The guy that shot that murdering marshal?"

Lavochkin shrugged. "I can't be sure, but there's only one Michael Flynn in the directory."

"Seventy thousand . . . How long would a private investigator have to work for us to earn seventy thousand dollars?"

Lavochkin shrugged again. "Beats me. You're looking at everything I've been able to find, which is almost nothing."

"Hold everything," Zoldas said, relieved. The problem wasn't his to solve. "A private investigator—that would be hiring a professional, like a lawyer or a consultant. That should have been handled by Purchasing, not Human Resources."

"I checked," Lavochkin said, dashing Zoldas's hopes. "Purchasing can't find a professional-services contract for anyone named Michael Flynn. Besides, we wouldn't have withheld taxes in that case."

"Well, there has to be a contract!" Zoldas said, exasperated. "No way Silvanus Drake would authorize a seventy-thousand-dollar debit against one of his Security accounts unless Flynn had an ironclad contract!" A thought occurred to him: contract! "Check with the Legal Department," he ordered. "Any contract would have been approved by them, and they never delete *anything*."

"Okay, boss. I'll give it a try."

Zoldas broke the video link. The key to running an efficient organization was to avoid doing other people's jobs for them. Lavochkin had overlooked the fact that Legal would have to know about the contract. Zoldas shook his head. Nothing got done in Human Resources unless he did it.

A contract for the delivery of thirty thousand tons of stainless steel from Jupiter Station to planet three glared at Wendy Chadwick from her holographic display. It was a standard contract, and the computer had found no loop-holes or fine-print clauses that would discomfit the Company. Chadwick approved a dozen such contracts every week. She was reading the last paragraph when her computer signaled her.

She switched the display to her video link and the face of her office manager appeared. "Yes, Susan?"

Susan hesitated. "Do you remember a contract between Security and Michael Flynn?"

Chadwick couldn't help reacting to Flynn's name. "The investigator?"

"I don't know," Susan replied. "All I know is that Silvanus Drake authorized a payment from a Security account through Payroll to a Michael Flynn, and that Flynn rejected it. Payroll couldn't find an employment record and wondered if the Company had contracted with him for professional services."

Wendy moistened her lips. Drake had hired Flynn verbally. "There's no written contract," she said, "but I know what this is about. I'll take care of it." She broke the connection and ordered her computer to connect her with the detective.

Flynn's computer wasn't activated; Wendy had to settle for an audio link to Michael's telephone. "Mike? It's Wendy."

"Hi, beautiful. I've been meaning to call you. Looks like Drake can't do anything violent to me for the moment, so you're probably safer with me than you are anyplace else. How about dinner?"

Chadwick inadvertently glanced at the clock in the corner of the video display before she remembered what had prompted her call. "Ah, Mike, this isn't about dinner. Did you reject the compensation that Drake offered you when he hired you?"

"Yes, I rejected the payment, but no, he didn't hire me."

Chadwick stared at her display without seeing the contract shown therein. "What do you mean, he didn't hire you?"

"I turned him down," Flynn explained. "He was walking out of my apartment when I figured out whodunit."

"That's not what you told Rustin and Pierce in a sworn statement last night!"

"I did not claim that I had been hired by the Company," Flynn averred. "I wrote in my statement that Drake had come to my apartment with an *offer* of employment. Maybe Drake claimed to have hired me."

"Just a minute," Wendy said. The Company had been provided with official copies of the sworn statements of everyone involved in the incident. Chadwick skimmed the statements as well as the transcript of the interrogation. Flynn was right: he hadn't stated that he had been hired by the Company. Drake hadn't claimed to have hired Flynn, either. The security chief had carefully chosen his words to imply that Flynn had been working for the Company, and Rustin and Pierce had been in such a perturbed state that neither had noticed it. She swallowed. "Mike, you can't reject that payment."

"Are you telling me that there's some law that *requires* me to accept money that I didn't earn?"

"No! But if you weren't working for us you had no right to possess the laser you used to shoot Wofford!"

"Wendy, it was justifiable for *anybody* to pick up that pistol and shoot Wofford! He was hitting you—causing physical injury—and holding a gun to your head and threatening to kill you, and the window pane would have stopped a stun pulse!"

"You didn't 'pick up that pistol'!" Wendy responded.

"You *told* Laska to give it to you! And you could not see Wofford beating me from where you were when you directed Laska to give you the gun!"

"Wendy, my logical deductions that led me to conclude that Wofford was the killer are in my statement. I could reasonably assume that you were in mortal danger."

Wendy bit her lip. "Mike, you could be in big trouble. We have to discuss this. Can you come to my office?"

There was a pause. "I'm being interviewed by SSN, but I can be there in fifteen minutes."

"I'll be waiting."

At the end of the hall outside of Chadwick's office, Susan DuJong, the Legal Department's office manager, sat at her workstation, smugly admiring her glaring white nail polish. She organized the legal paperwork so that the Company's lawyers could give the documents their blessings. She had known that there had been no contract with Michael Flynn because she had no file for contracts with private investigators, but that brain donor Lavochkin hadn't believed her and had made her bother the boss. On this, of all days, when Susan hadn't even expected Chadwick to come to work—Susan would never have come in the morning after a murderer had held a pistol to her head and used her as a shield. But Mitch Habruch was taking a few days off, the Department was short-handed, and Chadwick was the boss, so Chadwick had come in.

DuJong could tell that Chadwick was much the worse for her harrowing experience. The other attorneys in the Legal Department were stuffy, self-important snobs who dressed in staid business suits and treated Susan like a secretary. Wendy Chadwick, on the other hand, was open-minded, friendly, wore the latest fashions, and treated her like a professional. But that morning her boss had shown up in a conservative suit that had been out of style for five years and that made her look like . . . like a *lawyer*. And for most of the day Chadwick had had to endure visits from other Company employees who ostensibly came to wish her well but who actually wanted to hear the details of the biggest news story on Jupiter Station directly from the only eyewitness who had been there from start to finish, so as the day progressed DuJong had heard her boss grow short-tempered and caustic. Chadwick didn't need any more harassment that afternoon, and then that idiot Lavochkin had called. At least Susan had managed to deflect Lavochkin's demand to speak to Chadwick personally.

The door to the outer corridor opened and Michael Flynn walked in. *The* Michael Flynn. DuJong could not be mistaken. He had been in the office the previous week and his picture had been on news telecasts all day. Now the hero of the moment was walking up to Susan's desk.

"Michael Flynn to see Wendy Chadwick," he said, with a trace of a smile. "I'm expected."

"Ah . . ." DuJong swallowed. "I'll, ah . . . Let me check." She keyed her computer but kept her eye on Flynn. "Ms. Chadwick? Michael Flynn is here to see you."

"Send him in, Susan."

DuJong swallowed again. "You can go in, Mr. Flynn."

"Thank you."

Susan watched Flynn walk the length of the corridor to Chadwick's office, open the door, step through it, and close it behind him. DuJong turned quickly to her display. "Get me Phyllis!" she ordered. The face of an olive-skinned brunette appeared on the display. "Phyllis! You won't *believe* who just came in to see the boss!"

★ ★ ★ ★ ★

Inside her office Wendy Chadwick stared at Flynn incredulously. "You turned down *seventy thousand dollars?*"

Chadwick was wearing a cream-colored blouse and a conservative suit with a brown and gray weave. Flynn thought she looked fantastic. "Well, fifty-three thousand, after taxes," he said casually.

"Drake offered you *seventy thousand dollars?*"

"A twenty-thousand-dollar retainer and a bonus of fifty thousand when and if I solved the case—which was about five minutes after Drake made the offer."

The look of stunned disbelief on Wendy's face made Flynn pause. Chadwick said, "I've never heard of anyone paying *seventy thousand dollars* for the privilege of being in legal trouble."

Flynn didn't understand her concern. "I'm not in legal trouble, Wendy. Pierce ruled the shooting justifiable homicide." He lifted his stun pistol out of his coat pocket, holding the gun daintily with thumb and forefinger, and showed it to Chadwick. "He even gave me my gun back."

"He is under the impression that you were acting as a Company security guard!" Wendy shot back. "Drake had Payroll withhold taxes on the payment as proof that you were our employee! When Pierce learns that you weren't, he might reverse his finding and charge you with second-degree murder!"

"He can reverse his finding all he wants," Flynn said casually. "He needs a grand jury to indict me, and no grand jury on this station is going to indict anyone for shooting Wofford. And if one of Wofford's relatives files a wrongful death suit, I'll countersue for harassment and collect enough to retire—even if the plaintiff is on Earth, the incident occurred here and the court here has jurisdiction."

"Ever hear of 'change of venue?'"

"Who's going to pay to transport all the witnesses from Jupiter Station to another court?"

Chadwick didn't want to lose a legal argument to a private investigator. "That still leaves the possibility of illegal possession of a deadly weapon."

Flynn gritted his teeth. The legal mind was such a labyrinth of convoluted reasoning. "Wendy, if I could legally shoot Wofford, I obviously could legally possess the pistol I used to shoot him."

Chadwick shook her head vigorously. "No, Michael. There are plenty of legal precedents in which juries found people not guilty of murder because they acted in self-defense, and at the same time found them guilty on weapons charges."

"They won't in this case. Not on Jupiter Station."

Wendy had heard what the Station residents were saying about Flynn. She changed her tactics. "The government doesn't need a grand jury indictment to get your investigator's license suspended," she argued.

"Pierce would try something like that?"

Chadwick shook her head. "Not Pierce—the government. Washington might want to make an example of you to discourage citizens from taking lethal weapons they are not licensed to possess and killing federal officers with them."

Flynn considered Chadwick's words. He didn't think that Pierce would have ruled the shooting justifiable without having checked with Washington, but Pierce was fond of Wendy. He might want to protect the person who had protected her.

"If you were working for Company Security you had a legal right to possess that pistol," Wendy went on, "and the shooting was completely within our policy for the use of deadly force. There's nothing the government could do."

"But, Wendy, I *wasn't* working for the Company! I'd turned Drake down!"

"The authorities don't know that! They think exactly the opposite!"

Flynn's brow furrowed. "Are you advising me—giving me legal advice—to falsify the record?"

Chadwick gritted her teeth. "No! I'm saying that although you had turned Drake down in his apartment, Drake had renewed his offer by taking you with him to my place and that you had accepted the offer by your actions."

Flynn shook his head. "Oh, you lawyers! I didn't accept the offer! I wasn't working for Drake! I was merely trying to save your life!"

Chadwick closed her eyes. She didn't want to argue with Flynn. "I know that! But I don't know what the government might do! I only know what they *could* do, and if you were a Company employee during the incident they couldn't do *anything!* Collecting seventy thousand dollars for half an hour's work can't be that painful. Why don't you just accept the damned money?"

Flynn sighed. "Something a lawyer would never understand—ethics."

Wendy's eyes narrowed and her expression turned cold. "I can quote the entire lawyer's code of ethics by heart!"

Flynn considered the term "legal ethics" to be an oxymoron. "I'm talking about private investigator's ethics," he said. "I am being paid by the Asterbrooks to find out what the Company is covering up about their son's death. I have not succeeded in that task. I might *never* succeed in that task. If I accept Drake's money although I wasn't actually working for the Company, it will look like I was bribed to fail. If the government wants to revoke my license, they'd get it easily that way."

"But you've solved the Asterbrook case!" Wendy replied. "You proved that someone switched the pulleys without logging that fact. That makes us liable. I sent a settlement offer to the Asterbrooks this morning."

"Wendy, if the Company isn't producing polymethyl two four out here, and if Philip Asterbrook and Jonny Mondragon died accidentally as claimed, why did Silvanus Drake pay me seventy thousand dollars that I didn't earn?" Flynn could see that his argument had scored points, so he continued. "I'll tell you why. Today people on this station are treating me like a king. Drake was way ahead of me on this one. He realized before we got to your apartment last night that whoever got Wofford was going to be a hero. That's why he took Ray Chong with him to your door and sent me around the back, where he thought I couldn't do anything except get conveniently shot by a stray laser pulse. He didn't want me to be the hero.

"Now Drake can't do me physical harm, even in a carefully staged 'accident,' without causing an uproar that would trigger an official investigation," Flynn went on. "And if I ask questions about the accident or polymethyl two four, somebody might tell me something the Company doesn't want me to know. But if I accept those seventy thousand dollars under false pretenses, Drake doesn't have to worry about that because he *owns* me. He knows damn well I rejected the offer, he knows it will look like a bribe, and I'll have to do what he says or he'll have one of his flunkies make an anonymous call to the Licensing Board and my license will be revoked!"

Wendy stared at Flynn. "If Drake wants you out of the way, all he has to do is tell Marshal Rustin that you weren't working for the Company, and you'll be arrested!"

Flynn shook his head. "I told you, Wendy: no grand jury on this station is going to indict me for anything connected with Wofford's death. Not for the next several months, anyway. And Drake knows that. He realized that last night."

Wendy put her elbows on the desktop and rested her head in her hands. Drake might have paid Flynn for exactly the reason that Flynn suspected—Drake knew that the Company didn't owe Flynn the money. But that implied that the Company really was hiding something about the deaths of Asterbrook and Mondragon, and Chadwick had convinced herself that the deaths had been accidental. Unless . . . "If you weren't working for the Company, Maury Laska committed a felony just by giving you his laser," Wendy said. "Drake might be trying to protect him."

Flynn made a face. "Drake *ordered* Laska to do anything I told him to do!"

Chadwick's eyes slowly opened wide. She held up her hand to quiet Flynn while she scanned the sworn statements glowing in her holographic display. She stabbed at the display with her finger. "You're right! All the statements agree on that point!" She sat back, satisfied. "That's *it!* By putting you in charge, Drake was making you a *de facto* offer of employment! You accepted it by taking charge of Laska!"

Flynn shook his head and sighed. "Lawyers! Aagh! Okay, Wendy, you win. I was working for the Company. But I'm *not* accepting the seventy thousand!"

"Oh, we don't owe you seventy thousand," Chadwick replied, cheerful now that she had won the argument. "The employment you accepted was manifestly different from the offer that you rejected in your apartment. We owe you for, oh, about half an hour, maybe an hour, of a goon's wages.

Would the Licensing Board think that's a bribe?"

The computer beeped. Susan DuJong's face appeared on the display.

Chadwick's day had been a series of interruptions. She didn't need another one. Her good mood vanished. "Yes, Susan?"

"A couple of Company employees just had a fight in a bar. One of them got beaten up pretty badly. The marshals are holding the other one. He's asking for an attorney. Do you want me to call Mr. Habruch?"

Wendy started to close her eyes but resisted the urge to do so. She forced herself to be calm. "No, I'll handle it. What's the employee's name?"

"Delbert Carlton." Susan had anticipated the question and had Carlton's personnel file already accessed and in Wendy's display.

"Where are they holding him?" Chadwick asked while scanning the file. "Marshals Office?"

DuJong shook her head. "He's still at the scene of the altercation, a bar called the High Vacuum."

"Inform the marshals that I'll be right there. Ask them to keep Mr. Carlton at that location until I arrive—I don't want to have to chase him all over the Station."

"Will do, Ms. Chadwick."

Wendy broke the video link. Her shoulders slumped. "I didn't need that."

"I'll go with you," Flynn offered. "We can stop someplace for dinner afterward."

Chadwick shook her head. "No, I offered to make dinner for you, remember? Besides, I can't accept your help. This is legal business for the Company, involving lawyer-client confidentiality. I couldn't let you help unless I hired you, and we know you don't work for the Company." She smiled. "But you can tag along if you want. You're the only person that I actually wanted to see today. Just stay out of earshot when I'm talking to Carlton."

Wendy stood up. She took her portable computer and telephone from the top drawer of her desk and dropped them into the pouch on her belt. She switched off her computer display and looked around her office to make sure she wasn't forgetting anything. She gestured at the door. "Shall we go?"

At the end of the corridor Susan was sitting at her workstation, talking to her friend Phyllis who was standing beside the desk. The outfit Phyllis was wearing was metallic red except for black vertical stripes on the shorts. She had tinted her hair and fingernails to match the clothes. Phyllis's red, combined with her dark complexion, contrasted sharply with Susan's bright white and pale skin.

"I don't expect to be back today," Chadwick said to her office manager. "If any more emergencies pop up, beep me."

"Yes, Ms. Chadwick."

Susan was facing the attorney but Chadwick noticed that her eyes were ogling Flynn. "Is that a new outfit?" Wendy asked.

DuJong was surprised. Chadwick had seen her in that suit before, and Chadwick knew clothes. "Not brand new," Susan said. "I've worn it to the office before." The usual glint of approval was missing from Chadwick's eyes. "Is there something wrong with it?"

"Oh, no. It . . . it just makes you look like something that belongs on top of a Christmas tree. Have a car meet me out front."

Chadwick headed out the door, Flynn at her heels. Susan and Phyllis watched them go, then turned and looked at each other. "Who put cracker crumbs in her undies?" Phyllis said.

Flynn had to hurry to keep up with Wendy. "I was counting myself lucky that there weren't any fights after the airball game last night," she said. "This might have something to do with this afternoon's game. It might also be due to a pressure suit that Carlton managed to lose."

Flynn raised an eyebrow. "Pressure suit?"

The Company car pulled up just as the pair left Company headquarters. The car differed from a taxi only in that it didn't need to be activated by a debit card. Flynn caught himself before he offered to help Wendy into the car. She took the left seat. "The High Vacuum," Chadwick ordered, and the car accelerated smoothly across the Company plaza. "Do you know where this bar is?" Chadwick was making conversation; she assumed that Flynn knew every bar on the Station intimately.

"Other end of the Station, close to the cargo docks."

"What kind of place is it?"

"Working class. A lot bigger than Betty's."

"Are there fights in there often?"

"Fights that require the intervention of law enforcement personnel?" Flynn squinted while he pondered the question. "Not more than two or three a month."

Chadwick concluded that the tavern was a dump. "Terrific." She glanced at Flynn, who was looking straight ahead. "I'm sorry, Mike. I'm not being very good company at the moment. Today's been one exasperating interruption after another and then this comes up . . . And I was just very rude to my office manager, and if she gets mad and transfers . . . I don't want to lose her. I might get stuck with someone like that cretin Zoldas in Human Resources."

"She did look like an angel on the top of a Christmas

tree," Flynn said, trying to make Wendy feel better.

"That doesn't mean I should have said it! Susan takes pride in her wardrobe."

Flynn knew how Chadwick felt about clothes. "May I say that you look very fetching in that outfit?"

Chadwick suddenly felt self-conscious and almost blushed. "I've had this old thing forever. I bought it for my interview with the Company."

"That kind of suit never goes out of style," Flynn said. He liked the suit's soft material and its classic lines. It made Wendy look professionally powerful and feminine at the same time. "Of course, you even look good in those skin-tight, metallic-sheened abominations."

"My new clothes are all in the wash," Chadwick said. It wasn't true. She took her computer from her pocket, opened it, and contacted her office manager. "Susan: I want to apologize. I was very rude to you."

Ms. DuJong seemed surprised. "Oh, ah, I . . . hadn't really noticed."

Of course Susan had noticed. She was too good a manager not to notice when someone was being rude. "Well, I'll still approve three hours of overtime for you tonight," Chadwick said.

"You really don't have to—"

"I'll see you in the morning." Wendy broke the connection.

Chadwick was distracted by a group of pedestrians pointing at the car as it passed them. Flynn pretended not to see them.

"They were waving at you," Chadwick said. "You're their new hero."

"The public is easily impressed," Flynn replied. "I didn't do anything heroic."

"You saved my life!"

"By shooting a man in the back," Flynn explained, "an act that required no courage on my part."

"You don't have to be courageous to be heroic," Wendy pointed out.

The car came to a smooth stop in front of the High Vacuum just as two emergency medical technicians in white coveralls wheeled a gurney out of the bar and up to the back of an ambulance. The face of the man on the gurney looked like raw steak.

Wendy hopped out of the car and hurried to the gurney. "Will he be all right?"

One of the EMT's nodded. "He's got three broken ribs, a broken nose, and a broken jaw, and he's missing quite a few teeth, but I think his spleen's okay. He's stabilized now." The EMT turned to Flynn. "Good job yesterday, Mr. Flynn. Let me buy you a drink sometime."

Flynn forced a smile. "Thanks, but I'll probably be dead of cirrhosis by then. You're the two hundred and sixteenth person to offer to buy me a drink today."

Chadwick watched the ambulance drive away, then turned toward the bar. She watched the glowing name of the tavern cascade through the color spectrum and asked, "Did two hundred and sixteen people really offer to buy you drinks today?"

"I haven't been keeping count," Flynn admitted, "but it seems like that many."

The interior of the bar looked like the scene of a tornado's temper tantrum. Tables and chairs were overturned. Bottles and glasses were strewn on the floor. In the far corner a burly man with dark skin, his hands handcuffed behind him, stood between two marshals. Flynn looked at him. "So his name is Delbert Carlton," he said softly.

"Hmmm?" Wendy was surprised by how bright and clean the tavern was. It wasn't the dump she had been expecting.

"Nothing."

"I'll have to talk to my client alone," Wendy said. Flynn nodded and headed to the bar. Wendy assumed he was going to get a drink. She sighed, then walked over to her client and the marshals.

"He wanted to talk to Edwin Warshovsky," one of the deputies said. "We persuaded him he needed a lawyer more than his head honcho."

"What are you charging him with?" Chadwick asked.

"If the victim—a man by the name of Simmons—recovers, probably aggravated assault. The U.S. attorney will decide on the exact charges."

"Witnesses?"

The deputy glanced toward the bar. "The bartender. Those people along the back wall there. That group near the door came in after we did."

Wendy nodded. She pointed her thumb over her shoulder at the door. "Leave me alone with my client, please."

The marshals knew the drill and walked to the doorway, far enough away so that they couldn't overhear. Wendy looked at Carlton. She took out her computer to record the conversation. "I'm Wendy Chadwick. I'm the head of the Legal Department. I'll be your attorney for the time being. What have you told them?"

Anger showed on Carlton's face. "Nothing! I didn't want to talk to *them!* I want to talk to Mr. Warshovsky!"

"Why?"

"Because no one in Security would do a damn thing about my case!" Delbert explained. "I told Security when my suit disappeared that I had secured it properly, and that Simmons' suit had been in the rack after mine. But do they believe me? No! The Company docks my earnings to pay for my suit, just 'cause they're looking to make an example of somebody since they've already written off two suits on Juliet! So I take your friend's advice," he said as he nodded toward Flynn at the bar, "and I ask questions where Simmons does his drinking, and I spread a little money around, and *I* find evidence that it was Simmons that set my suit loose! And when I go to Security with that info this morning, they don't do a damn thing! They tell me that *they'll* do the investigating around here! They tell me to get to work! So I had take things into my own hands! *That's* what I wanted to tell Mr. Warshovsky!"

"Did you throw the first punch?"

Carlton flashed a smile. "The first, the second, the third. He couldn't fight worth crap."

Chadwick indicated the deputies with a flick of her head. "They're going to take you to the Marshals Office for processing—fingerprints, retinals, and so forth. I'll be along after I've talked to the witnesses. Don't talk to them unless I'm present! Understand?"

Carlton nodded. "I've been in bar fights before. Been arrested before, too."

"Ever beat up anyone this badly?" Delbert didn't answer. Wendy continued, "If Simmons doesn't take a turn for the worse you'll probably be released on bail in a couple of hours. The Company will post it for you."

" 'Bout time the damn Company does something for me!"

Dinky the bartender couldn't help smiling as Flynn walked up to the bar. "Michael Flynn, of the *infamous* Boston Flynns! Glad to see you! Take a seat—I think that stool's clean. The whiskey's on me!" He reached for a glass and bottle.

Flynn's mouth started watering, but he said, "Ah, hold it, Dinky. Could I take a rain check on that?"

Dinky turned to look at him, surprised. "Are you trying to make SSN two days in a row? I've never heard of Michael Flynn turning down a free drink!"

"I'm not turning it down, Dinky. I'm postponing it. I've had so many offers of free drinks today that I can't appreciate any more." He pointed over his shoulder at the man in handcuffs. "What happened?"

Dinky glanced at Delbert. "He was in here yesterday. Walks up to the bar, puts down one hundred green, and asks me if I've overheard Thag Simmons saying anything about getting someone in trouble by losing his pressure suit. I'd never seen him before," Dinky said as he looked again at Delbert, "but Simmons comes in here all the time. He's a jerk: lets other people buy him drinks but hardly ever buys a round himself, and he's always bragging about how he's sabotaged people who've offended him. Yeah, I'd heard him say he'd set someone's pressure suit loose in an airlock on Juliet." Dinky nodded at Carlton. "I told him, but he doesn't say anything. Just turns and walks out. End of shift today, Simmons comes in, sits at that stool right next to the one you're on. Fifteen minutes later *he* walks in, steps up to Simmons, and *pow!*" Dinky slammed his right fist into the palm of his left hand. "Belts Simmons hard, right in the nose. I heard it break. Simmons goes down on the floor. He picks him up and belts him in the face again. Simmons' broken nose has started bleeding, and blood splatters everywhere—watch where you put your elbows; there's some on the bar here. He starts punching Simmons around the room."

Flynn surveyed the devastation. "Must have been a hell of a fight."

Dinky shook his head. "It wasn't a fight. It was a beating. He's a head taller and has twenty kilos on Simmons. Simmons managed to throw a few punches of his own, but he just shrugged 'em off. He opened cuts on Simmons's forehead and cheek—big ones; splattered more blood around. I started getting worried—hit somebody in the head that often and that hard, and you can cause brain damage. I tried to break it up, but he pushed me away and I slammed into the bar and probably screwed up my back. So I yelled 'emergency' to get the attention of the security camera. If those marshals hadn't been right down the block, Simmons would have left here in a bag."

"Anybody else try to help Simmons?"

Dinky nodded at a man in blue Company work coveralls standing along the back wall. "He tried. Hit whatsisname—Carlton?—over the head with a beer bottle. Didn't even slow him down."

Wendy came walking up to the bar. She was pleasantly surprised to see that Flynn wasn't drinking. "Are you working for him?" She indicated Carlton by glancing at the man over her shoulder, just as the marshals took him by the arms and led him toward the door.

Flynn shook his head. "I turned down the privilege. He couldn't afford me."

"But you did suggest that he spread some money around to try to find if someone had heard Simmons talk about losing his pressure suit?"

Flynn nodded. "That's all I would have done. Seemed a waste to charge him twelve hundred a day for something he could do himself. Why do you ask?"

"I'm just confirming what he told me," Wendy explained. "I don't want any surprises in court. This was not what is euphemistically referred to as a friendly fight. Simmons will press charges." She moved closer to the bar.

"Watch where you're walking," Dinky said. "You'll track blood all over the place."

Wendy looked down. The floor was light-colored tile, and clean except for drops of blood scattered everywhere.

The marshals were leading Carlton through the door. "Do you think I could get a permit for a stun pistol *now?*" Dinky called to them.

The deputy closest to the bar replied, "We got a new marshal, thanks to Flynn there. Go ahead and apply. What do you got to lose?"

"Can I mop up?" Dinky continued.

"Fine by us," the deputy said, as he and Carlton and the other marshal stepped through the doorway. "We're done in here."

Dinky reached for the mop that lived in a corner behind the bar. "Three times I applied for a permit to keep a stun gun! Three times that bastard Wofford rejected it! Some day somebody's going to kill someone in here and I won't be able to stop it. Is that what the hell they're waiting for?"

Flynn shrugged. Wendy was scowling at the floor. "There's blood everywhere!" she said, amazed. "There wasn't this much blood in warehouse twelve after the fatal accident! Better let me get some photos of it with my computer before you start cleaning." Wendy hesitated, wondering where she should begin. "Mike, would you please make sure that none of those witnesses . . . Mike?" She looked over one shoulder, then the other, then turned all the way around. "Where did Flynn go?"

Flynn headed for his apartment as fast as his legs would

carry him, cursing himself for not having scanned the photographs of the accident scene into his computer. Two occupied taxis passed him before he spotted an empty one and got its attention. The streets were full of pedestrians, homeward bound at the end of the day shift, and the taxi had to go slowly to avoid them. Flynn remembered the dash to Wendy's place in Drake's car and wished he had an emergency vehicle of his own. He told the cab to wait in front of his building and ran up the steps to his apartment. The photos of the accident scene in warehouse twelve were in the top drawer of his desk. The first photo showed the scene as it had been discovered, with only one undamaged hand from each victim and a few small trickles of blood extending from beneath the machinery frame that covered the bodies. He looked at each photo and confirmed why he had not been able to see why the Company had transferred the people who had responded to the scene. The evidence for which he had been looking was what *wasn't* in the photos.

Flynn took his telephone from his pocket and flipped it open. "Connect me with Wendy Chadwick!" he ordered.

The call was answered with an irritated, "Yes?"

"Wendy? It's Michael. Are you still at the High Vacuum?"

"Michael? No, I just reached the Marshals Office. Where the hell are you?"

"On my way to the Marshals Office," Flynn replied. It was true; he was walking through his apartment door, putting the accident photos in his pocket, as he said it. "Don't leave till I get there." He broke the connection, cutting off Wendy as she as about to respond.

The taxi ride to the Marshals Office was almost as slow as the trip home had been. Flynn wanted to scream at pedestrians to get them out of the way. Most of the government employees had already left for their homes and the Government Plaza was almost empty. Flynn jumped out of the taxi in front of the Marshals Office and dashed through the door.

Wendy was standing at the opposite side of the ante-room, talking with Acting Marshal Rustin. Flynn dashed to the pair, grabbed Wendy by the arm, and dragged her to the other side of the room.

"I was talking with—" Chadwick protested.

"Wendy," Flynn said as he took the photos from his pocket, "look at these! Asterbrook and Mondragon were crushed against a steel deck by a two-hundred-ton machinery frame. They were smashed flatter than pancakes, bones splintered and forced through the skin, internal organs ruptured." He held the photo of the bodies, taken after the frame had been lifted from them, in front of Wendy's face. Only the blood-soaked Company coveralls and the two undamaged hands hinted that the distorted figures had once been human. "There are *four liters* of blood in the average adult male. Eight liters between the two of them. It should have been pressed out of them like grape juice in a wine press. It should have run all over the place. Where is it, Wendy?" Flynn demanded. "Where the hell's the blood?"

Chapter 15

The Jupiter Station Morgue was located on level one directly beneath the Company hospital. Michael Flynn and Wendy Chadwick were in the Company Plaza on level three, heading for the elevators that serviced the hospital, when Flynn suddenly took Wendy by the arm and countermarched her around the plaza's waterfall.

"Change in plan?" Wendy asked.

Flynn, ignoring the spray, peeked around the edge of the waterfall. "See that guy over there in the maroon turtleneck? He might be looking for me and I'd rather not deal with him now."

Wendy took a cautious step from behind the waterfall. The man that Flynn had spotted was slender and not very tall. He didn't look threatening. "Another violent boyfriend of an ex-girlfriend?"

"Another private investigator," Flynn explained, "by the name of Peter Chow."

Chadwick watched Chow stride purposefully along the plaza. She wondered if private detectives were prevented by law from wearing fashionable clothes. "And why would a private investigator be looking for you?"

"Because I had eight subcontracted background investigations in my message file this morning," Flynn said. "That's probably every one that came into the Station overnight. Normally, I'd be lucky to get two of them, but I gave SSN an interview yesterday and they ran it several times last night. My new fame is costing the other investigators here their usual business."

Flynn and Chadwick kept the waterfall between themselves and Chow while the other investigator walked past, then they made a beeline for a door next to the hospital elevators. The door led to a stairwell, and Flynn headed down the stairs toward the lower reaches.

"You've been to the morgue before," Chadwick surmised.

"Yeah, a couple of times. On business." Flynn stepped through the door at the bottom of the stairwell and held it open, as unobtrusively as possible, for Wendy.

"Well, I didn't think you'd been a customer," Chadwick said. She started down the corridor, hoping that the man they had come to see could erase the new doubts that Flynn had sired in her mind. "We should have tried his office upstairs first. He's much more likely to be there than here."

"There are fewer Company personnel down here," Flynn explained.

But Dr. Reuben Luk, the Company's medical director on Jupiter Station, was in the office next to the morgue. Dr. Luk was also the Station's chief medical examiner, and that morning he was functioning in that capacity, finishing the paperwork on an autopsy.

"Wendy Chadwick!" Luk exclaimed when Chadwick and Flynn walked through his door. He stood up behind his desk. He was wearing a white shirt and white lab coat over brown slacks. Youth drugs had been invented in time to save his thick black hair. He had broad shoulders and a head to match. His eyes darted to Wendy's companion and he did a double take. "And Michael Flynn!" Luk reached across the desk to shake hands with the investigator. "Pleased to meet you! That was a hell of shot you made the other night!" The doctor had hunted big-game back on

Earth, and he appreciated good marksmanship. "Right through Wofford's medulla! Put out his autonomic nervous system like that!" He snapped his fingers. "You couldn't have killed the bastard any faster if you'd decapitated him. Want to see the corpse?" Luk pointed at the wall between his office and the morgue. "It's right next door."

"No, that's okay," Flynn said. "I saw enough of it in Ms. Chadwick's apartment."

Luk seemed disappointed. "Oh. Well, what can I do for you?"

Flynn took his photos of the fatal accident from his coat pocket and placed them on Luk's desk. "Remember this accident?" he asked.

Luk's eyebrows rose. "Yeah. Mondragon and . . . Asterbrook? Yeah, Asterbrook." He picked up the photographs and leafed through them.

"They were crushed beneath a two-hundred-ton machinery frame," Flynn said. "Crushed flat. Their blood was pressed out of them, according to the autopsy report."

"Two hundred tons above and a steel deck below will do that to you," Luk said.

Flynn took the photos from the doctor, found the one that showed the machinery frame with the two human hands protruding from the edges, and handed it back to Luk. "Then where is it?" he asked. "The blood—where is it?"

The doctor stared at the picture, his brow furrowed. He shrugged. "Under the frame, I guess."

Flynn handed him the photo taken after the frame had been lifted from the remains. "Guess again."

The furrows in Luk's brow deepened. He tapped the photo with his finger. "Their clothes are saturated with blood," he pointed out.

"Those Company coveralls are almost stain-proof," Flynn replied. "They don't soak up much of anything. Certainly not the four liters of blood that each of the bodies contained."

Luk took a deep breath. "Maybe it's under the bodies."

Flynn took back the photo and handed the doctor another one, showing the deck after the bodies had been removed. There were only the discolored stains in the shapes of the crushed bodies, certainly nowhere near eight liters worth of blood. Luk shrugged. "That frame would have hit them pretty hard," he suggested. "The blood could have been splashed all over the warehouse. Onto the walls, even."

Wendy shook her head. "We went over that warehouse last night with a crew of technicians from a chemical-testing laboratory, doing radiometric resonance tests for hemoglobin. What you see on those photos corresponds to everywhere we found evidence of blood."

Luk pursed his lips, then turned and sat at his computer. "Dr. Vasquez did that one, as I recall." The file on the autopsy of Asterbrook and Mondragon included a video recording of the entire procedure. Luk skimmed it at high speed, stopping it only at the most important times. "Looks like the written report," he said. "Bones shattered. Internal organs crushed. There's some blood trapped in the thoracic and gastrointestinal cavities, but it doesn't look like very much. I'd have to agree with Vasquez: the bodies were exsanguinated." He turned back toward Flynn and Chadwick. "I guess I would have expected to find more blood on the deck."

Flynn could not suppress a triumphant smile. "So what happened to it?"

Luk shrugged. "I've seen patients bleed to death on operating tables without a drop being spilled. And just because it didn't look like there was a lot of blood in the warehouse doesn't mean it wasn't there. Some of it might have adhered to the underside of that two-hundred-ton frame. I rolled on police cases when I was in emergency medicine, back in Seattle, and I was surprised to see that a person could bleed to death and leave such a small bloodstain on the sidewalk. Dr. Vasquez didn't make a quantitative measurement of blood loss—nor would one be expected when the injuries were so obviously compatible with the accident scene—so maybe there was more left in the bodies than was apparent in the autopsy."

Flynn said, "According to Vasquez's report, the victims had been dead for several hours before the bodies were discovered."

Luk nodded. "They had probably died shortly before noon. There was no lunch in their stomachs."

"If that machinery frame had been dropped onto Asterbrook and Mondragon hours after they died, their blood would have started to coagulate. It might not have flowed all over the place."

Luk shook his head. "In that case, the damaged tissue would look different under a microscope than if they had been alive when crushed."

"Did Vasquez do any such tests?"

Luk looked at the computer display. He scanned through the record. "Hmmph. He took tissue samples only for toxicology screening, which turned out negative, by the way."

"Do you still have those samples?" Flynn asked.

Luk hesitated. "Let me check. They'd be in the freezer." He went through the door that led to the interior of the morgue. Flynn followed. Wendy reluctantly joined the parade.

Luk opened the freezer used to store tissue samples. He pulled out one storage shelf after another. "Nope," he said. "Nothing here. Probably destroyed." He closed the freezer and turned to Flynn. "In an open-and-shut case like this, once the marshals and OSHA closed their investigations there would have been no reason for us to keep tissue samples. Dr. Vasquez probably disposed of them. You think they died long before that frame fell on them just because there was so little blood?"

"That's only one of the reasons, Doctor." Flynn shook Luk's hand again. "Thank you. You've been very helpful." He turned to Wendy. "Let's go."

In the corridor, Chadwick said, "He didn't seem to think that the lack of blood in warehouse twelve was significant."

Flynn was upbeat. "Oh, but he did. You weren't watching his eyes when he first saw the photos. Luk didn't think there was enough blood there. That's why those people were transferred off the Station: they had jobs where they would see other accidents, accidents with more blood. They might have started talking, started wondering out loud how two people could get crushed flat and leave so little blood. They might have begun to suspect that the accident scene wasn't kosher. The Company couldn't afford that, and spread them all over the solar system. But the security camera in warehouse twelve was watching us last night; Silvanus Drake knew what we were doing. Asking Luk to review the autopsy results was our obvious next step, so Drake was probably in here last night, disposing of those tissue samples." Flynn was looking at the security camera mounted on the corridor wall. The camera was looking back at him. "Without those tissue samples, Luk doesn't have enough evidence to reopen the investigation. But now he knows that there wasn't enough blood in warehouse twelve, and Silvanus Drake knows that he knows. So one of these days Luk will find himself promoted into a higher-paying Company job someplace else, before he starts sharing his suspicions with others."

Wendy looked at Flynn out of the corner of her eye. "I know about the blood, too. Do you foresee rapid promotion to Company HQ legal staff in my future?"

"They don't have to worry about you. You're their attorney. You can't tell anybody anything that would be detrimental to your clients' interests."

Wendy stared straight ahead as they walked past the security camera. She wanted Flynn to be wrong about the blood at the accident scene. She had hoped that Dr. Luk would have provided a convincing argument. She didn't know what to believe. "What do we do now?"

"What we normally do on Tuesdays," Flynn replied. "You have your Company job. I have eight background checks to do." And one more avenue to pursue in the Asterbrook investigation, one that Silvanus Drake didn't know that Flynn knew about. One that Drake couldn't close before Flynn could follow it.

Marvin Chalmisiak always got to the weekly executive meetings early enough to claim the seat at the opposite end of the table from Ed Warshovsky. It made it easier for Chalmisiak to keep an eye on him. Chalmisiak had volunteered for his assignment on Jupiter Station, but not because it was the Company's most profitable enterprise. Chalmisiak had come to Jupiter Station because it wasn't profitable enough. He didn't think that the general manager of Jupiter Station walked on water, expelled demons, raised the dead, or did any of the other things with which he was credited back at corporate headquarters. In Chalmisiak's eighteen months on the Station he had become convinced that Ed Warshovsky was an empire builder, constructing his own kingdom far from the supervision of the board of directors and government authority. And Warshovsky was building his empire with money that belonged to Company stockholders.

The door behind Chalmisiak opened and Wendy Chadwick entered the conference room. She was wearing a conservative business suit instead of the hideous fashion that had swept the solar system and she actually looked like a lawyer. Chalmisiak wondered if it was her brush with death or Warshovsky's memo on executive dress that had prompted Chadwick's change of attire. Chadwick opened her computer and placed it on the table as she took a seat across from Silvanus Drake. Drake always sat at Warshovsky's right hand. Warshovsky liked to have his security chief close by. To Chalmisiak, that said a lot about the general manager's mindset.

The door at the opposite end of the room opened and Ed Warshovsky walked in. He glanced around the table to make sure everyone was present. His eyes lingered on Ms. Chadwick: she was sensibly dressed for a change. Only Kevin McSheridan and Clarisse Jackson were wearing garish clothes. Warshovsky assumed that his memo was starting to have its intended effect. He was smiling as he took his seat. "Well," he said, "we've certainly had an exciting week, haven't we?"

Lisa Reisbach slammed her fist onto the table. "Yeah! We showed you guys how to play airball!"

Everyone but Drake and Chalmisiak chuckled. The accounting head waited for the noise level to drop and said, "Is it to prevent further excitement that the budget for training security guards has been increased by three million dollars?"

Drake and Warshovsky looked at each other. Drake said, "The excitement last Wednesday proved that the majority of our security guards will overreact in critical situations and can't hit what they're shooting at."

"So why exactly must their training be increased?" Chalmisiak persisted. "Because they overreacted to the guided tour of our facilities that Ms. Chadwick was giving that investigator, or because they failed to kill her?"

Only McSheridan, the Operations Manager, laughed.

"Both," Drake said.

Chadwick glared at him.

Chalmisiak continued, "So we'd be saving three million dollars a year if Ms. Chadwick had kept that investigator out of Company property like we had decided, instead of helping him investigate the Company."

Chadwick eyed Chalmisiak coldly. Since her brush with death everyone had been treating her with kid gloves; she hadn't been expecting the accountant's barbed comments. "Mr. Flynn managed to do in two days what three official investigations couldn't do in months," she replied. "He found out what caused the accident in warehouse twelve that killed Mondragon and Asterbrook."

McSheridan squinted at Wendy. "The official investigations all concluded that a line got pinched around a pulley that was too small for it, causing the line to fail while it was lifting a heavy machinery frame."

Chadwick nodded. "But Flynn discovered *why* a pulley that was too small was on that crane. Someone had moved it from the overhead crane in warehouse seven without logging the fact. After the investigations, it was moved back to where it had come from, again without being logged."

McSheridan seemed surprised. "How the hell did that happen?"

Wendy shrugged. "You're the Director of Operations. You tell me. Flynn was bringing his discovery to my attention when we stumbled into Kemper and Santino's plan to steal a shipment of polymethyl two four that wasn't there. That's what started the excitement."

"I hate to think how much all that excitement has reduced our productivity," Chalmisiak said. "People seem to be talking about it even more than they're discussing the airball tournament." Chalmisiak thought that the fun and games that the Company provided for its employees were a drain on profits.

"Actually," Reisbach, the Manufacturing Manager, said, "production was up almost half a percent last week."

"Those pulleys," McSheridan asked, "if they hadn't been switched, the accident wouldn't have happened?"

Wendy nodded. "Looks that way."

McSheridan hesitated. "Does that mean we're liable?"

Wendy nodded again. "I sent settlement offers to the families of Asterbrook and Mondragon yesterday."

"For how much?" Chalmisiak demanded.

"The going rate for such negligence: six million apiece."

Chalmisiak stared dourly at the Company attorney. "On whose authority?"

Chadwick glanced at the head of the table. "Mr. Warshovsky's."

"I didn't know that the investigations had been reopened," Chalmisiak said.

"They weren't," Wendy replied

"Then the official findings haven't changed," the accountant said. "Why are we paying twelve million dollars in damages if the official findings haven't changed?"

Warshovsky leaned across the table. "Because it was our fault," he said, staring at Chalmisiak with an expression that made it plain that he thought he was stating the obvious.

"Twelve million dollars," Chalmisiak muttered. "A hell of a lot to pay to be done with that investigator's interference."

"Well . . ." Chadwick hesitated. "Flynn's not done yet. He keeps poking around, discovering things that don't jibe with the official reports, the kind of things you'll find in any investigation but which give conspiracy theorists material for their books."

Chalmisiak frowned. "Such as?"

"Such as, there was surprisingly little blood at the accident scene."

McSheridan looked puzzled. "What do you mean, surprisingly little blood? Those bodies were crushed into pulps!"

"People," Warshovsky interrupted, "we have more important things to discuss. Satellite Juliet is becoming operational. We have eight hundred construction workers who no longer have anything to do. I trust that all of you have read my proposal. What do you think about it?"

"I think that spending two billion dollars on another satellite will not improve our profit-and-loss statement," Chalmisiak said, "especially when the proposed satellite will do nothing to increase our production."

"Ah! But it will increase our production!" Warshovsky said. "Of food! A satellite such as I propose, designed for food production, with the latest in aeroponics, will allow us to feed ourselves. We won't be dependent on food from Earth—shipped at high cost, by the way."

"Won't have to ship fertilizer back, either," McSheridan pointed out.

"But those ships have to come out here anyway to pick

up our products!" Chalmisiak said. "You're using old cost data, from before we were in full production and those ships went home empty!"

"We have become more than just another site of Company operations," Warshovsky stated. "We are a colony, the first colony at Jupiter. Historically, colonies that couldn't feed themselves ultimately failed."

"More fresh food would improve morale," Clarisse Jackson added, her mouth watering at the thought of fresh fruit and vegetables.

Chalmisiak wasn't interested in founding colonies or improving morale. "We can't afford it! Your financial analysis ignores the fact that we won't have a monopoly out here for very long. The Asian consortium starts construction later this year. Our market share drops the day they start shipping products."

"There's the Brazilians, too, now," Louis Cheng said, his eyes avoiding everyone else's while he traced random patterns on his computer keyboard with his finger.

"Just where the hell did Brazil get the money to get into this business?" Reisbach asked.

"Brazil has much greater financial resources than Conglomerated Mining and Manufacturing," Warshovsky said. "But you are making problems out of opportunities. The people that will build the Asian and Brazilian facilities, the people that will live there: what are they going to eat?"

Chalmisiak looked aghast. "You propose to feed our competition?"

"And all those ships that come out here," Warshovsky continued. "Eight- to ten-month round trips, depending on planet positions. Don't you think they'd like to restock with fresh food when they get here? More facilities out here, more ships, more demand for food—food that we'll be able to supply for, oh, about fifteen percent less than the cost of food shipped from planet three."

Chalmisiak took a deep breath to retort, caught himself, and punched some numbers into his computer. "Fifteen percent less . . ." He pursed his lips and ran the numbers again. His computer was trying to tell him that Warshovsky's addlebrained idea was going to make the Company a fortune.

"And we save the cost of shipping those eight hundred construction workers—plus their families—back to Earth," McSheridan added.

"We're in agreement, then?" Warshovsky asked.

Chalmisiak still didn't like the idea. Warshovsky was trying to make his empire more independent. "What does the Board think?" He was stalling—he knew the Board would go along with anything that Warshovsky proposed.

Drake's telephone beeped. The security director almost looked annoyed as he took the instrument from his pocket. "I'm in a meeting," he said into it. His face did not betray his thoughts as he listened to the reply. "No. I'll handle it." He closed the phone and slipped it into his pocket. "Excuse me, but something's come up that requires my immediate attention." He rose to leave.

Wendy almost jumped out of her chair. "Better let me handle it," she said as she closed her computer.

Drake's eyes narrowed as he looked across the table at her. "You don't even know what it is."

"It's Michael Flynn," Wendy said.

"What makes you say that?"

"Because everyone on the Station is treating him like a prince right now, so you can't trust your underlings to take care of him," Wendy explained. "He's the *only* person on the Station that you can't trust your underlings to handle.

That's why you're going yourself. But I can handle him better than you can."

The lawyer and the security chief stared at each other. "We'll both go," Drake stated.

"I can handle him better if you're not there," Chadwick replied. "For some reason, he doesn't trust you."

"What's Flynn up to now?" Warshovsky asked.

"He's trying to gain access to some of our computer files," Drake replied.

"Through his ex-girlfriend, who happens to be one of our computer system analysts?" Chadwick asked. Drake nodded. "Not an unexpected turn of events, I should think. I'll take care of it." She turned and headed for the door, as though the matter had been settled.

"Let me know how it turns out," Warshovsky called after her.

Missy Adamly hunched over her holographic display, running one fruitless search after another. "I'm a systems analyst, not a damned auditor!" she complained. She gestured at the listing that filled her display. "There are *thousands* of references to pressure suits, but not a word about those two after they were officially written off."

"Check the recycling records," Flynn suggested. "Quickly, Missy, before the records of those suits are deleted, just like the other records associated with this case."

There was a light rap on Missy's office door. Missy and Flynn both looked at the door latch, to confirm that the door was still locked.

"Could someone have discovered what you're doing?" Flynn said quietly.

Missy shook her head. "I'm using my trapdoor. The computer system doesn't even know what I'm doing. Wait a sec." She accessed the security system and the output of the security camera in the corridor outside Missy's office appeared on her display.

Flynn stared at the monitor. "What the hell is she doing here?" He stepped to the door and opened it.

Wendy Chadwick didn't bother to say hello. "You have set off major alarm bells in Company Security," she said. "Silvanus Drake was paged in our executive meeting to be informed of your actions. I barely managed to preempt him from coming here himself to put a stop to them."

"Very kind of you to intervene," Flynn replied dryly.

Chadwick glanced at Missy. "Excuse us for a moment, please." She pulled Flynn through the door and into the corridor, then closed the office door behind him. She glanced at the security camera at the end of the corridor. Its red light was off so it wasn't active at the moment. She opened her computer. "I made a video recording of our executive meeting this morning," she whispered. "I examined that video record as I walked down here from the conference room. I didn't watch Drake during the meeting, so he wouldn't be on guard, but look at his expression when I said that you thought there wasn't enough blood in warehouse twelve."

Wendy glanced again at the security camera. To be safe, she held the computer so that the display could not be seen by the camera while Flynn looked at the video recording. "He doesn't even blink," he said softly.

"As usual," Wendy replied. She replayed the scene. "Now watch Ed Warshovsky. I've never seen anyone's eyes bulge that far out of their sockets." Flynn watched the scene in silence. Wendy swallowed and said, "I guess I'm ready to admit that we're covering up something." Flynn looked at her. Her blue eyes lacked their usual sparkle.

"You're having Ms. Adamly use our computer system to do background checks for you?"

"Actually, she's doing something for you," Flynn said. "About your client from yesterday. Remember why Delbert Carlton's earnings got docked to pay for his lost pressure suit?"

Wendy nodded. "Because it was the third one written off on Juliet. Marvin Chalmisiak, head of Accounting and our resident Scrooge, had a conniption after the second one was lost. We wasted almost an entire executive meeting discussing the issue. Warshovsky had to promise to do something about careless destruction of expensive Company property to get Chalmisiak to lay off. So?"

"So, did you know that the first two pressure suits were signed out to the same person?"

Wendy's eyebrows shot up. "The same person had *two* pressure suits damaged beyond repair? Who?"

"Roger Ajanian."

Wendy was slow to reply. "Asterbrook and Mondragon's foreman?" Flynn nodded. "This has nothing to do with Delbert Carlton," Wendy said suspiciously.

"Sure it does. If he hadn't told me about his problem, I wouldn't have known about the other suits, both of which were reported as damaged beyond repair *after* Asterbrook and Mondragon were killed."

"Those suits couldn't have had anything to do with Asterbrook and Mondragon," Wendy said. "They were L3's—not trained to work in vacuum. Ajanian ramrodded Satellite Juliet. Spare suits—suits that people would wear while their own were being repaired—would have been signed out to him."

Flynn shook his head. "No, I was right last week: Asterbrook and Mondragon *were* killed in warehouse seven, not twelve. But we couldn't—er, you couldn't—find any blood there because the outer hatch to warehouse seven was open and they were wearing pressure suits when something heavy fell on them."

"But they were L3's!" Wendy protested. "They weren't trained for it!"

Flynn smiled. "And what does that do to Company liability? Enough to make a cover-up worthwhile?"

Wendy sighed. She closed her computer. "Come on," she said, "let's see what happened to those suits." She opened the office door.

Missy was still staring at her computer display. "You asked a favor of the wrong person," she said without looking up. "Why the hell didn't you go to someone who knows something about our property control system? You're a hero, Michael. You can get anybody to do favors for you."

"Marvin Chalmisiak made those pressure suits a personal crusade," Wendy said. "Can you access his files?"

"Piece of cake," Missy said. She pounded her keyboard furiously. "There. Chalmisiak's personal directory. Now where to?"

Wendy leaned over Missy's shoulder and studied the display. "I recognize all of these account numbers . . ." She pointed to the display. "That file name isn't suggestive of anything."

Missy squinted. "Hmm. Might be important. It's personally enciphered."

"Can you read it?"

"Not without his personal cipher," Missy replied, "but, if he's as foolish as most people, he probably stored it somewhere in his personal directory. With my system-analyst privileges, I should be able to find it easily enough."

"Is that legal?" Wendy asked.

"It is when done at the behest of the Station's legal director . . . There."

Chadwick began reading the file, her eyebrows slowly lowering. "What the . . . This is a file on Ed Warshovsky! That crumb Chalmisiak is keeping track of every dime that he thinks Warshovsky's wasted!" When she got over her anger, she said, "That's probably a good place to start."

Flynn was standing against the back wall. Opposite him, above Missy's desk, a computer-generated window was displaying a sun-drenched beach that looked like the Gulf Coast of Florida. On the wall next to Flynn was one of the inexpensive paintings with which the Company had decorated Jupiter Station. This one was abstract, with bright geometric patterns that reminded Flynn of a flag of one of the new African republics. He gingerly eased the painting away from the wall and looked behind it.

"Why don't you let me sit there?" Wendy said. "I think I can track down those suits faster myself than I can tell you how to do it."

"This is my computer!" Missy protested. "I'll run it, okay?"

"Missy," Flynn said, "let Wendy do it. I'll buy you a Coke."

"I don't want a Coke!"

"Sure you do. Come on."

Missy got up reluctantly. "I said you should get somebody else to do it," she said to Flynn. "I didn't mean that you should get somebody else to do it with my computer!"

Flynn opened the office door. "We'll be right back," he said to Wendy.

Out in the corridor, Flynn asked, "She can't screw up anything back there, can she?"

Missy glanced toward the security camera. "Nothing that anyone with system privileges couldn't do. I switched to regular access. She's not bypassing the supervisory level."

The soda machine was at the end of the row of offices. Flynn flashed his debit card at the machine and let Missy select the flavor she wanted. "That trapdoor of yours: will it work for you alone? Does it check your retinal patterns or require a password?"

Missy looked beyond Flynn to make sure no one could overhear them. They were out of sight of the security camera. She shook her head. "There's no security on it. It doesn't need any. I'm the only person who knows it's there and how to access it."

"So if someone had been watching when you installed it, that someone could use it?"

Missy looked exasperated. "Nobody was watching when I installed it!"

"Oh, yes, someone was. Wendy said that Security knew what we were up to. But the computer system couldn't have alerted them because you were using your trapdoor, so I looked behind that painting on your wall. There's a microcam back there."

Flynn thought that Missy was going to drop her soda. She tried to speak but no words came from her mouth. She managed to swallow. "Drake knows about . . . My job . . . I'm toast. Mike, there are legal reasons for using an operating system that will detect and log all file changes." She put her hand to her cheek. "People have gotten ten years for what I've done!"

"Oh, don't worry about going to jail," Flynn said cheerfully. "If Drake turns you in, he loses his ability to modify files surreptitiously. He'll never do that. But now we know who's behind those suspicious file system packings you discovered last week."

"Drake's been using *my* trapdoor to falsify our computer records?"

Flynn nodded. "He has the motive, he has access to your office whenever you're not there, he knows about file checksums, and he doesn't know enough about computers to falsify the file-packing logs."

Missy bit her upper lip. "Are you sure he won't turn me in?"

"Missy, if you hadn't built that trapdoor on your own, Drake would have dug up something he could have used to blackmail you into building it for him."

"And he's still watching . . . I've changed clothes in that office!"

"Well, you'd better use the restroom from now on."

"Like hell! I'm not going to have that creep looking over my shoulder all the time! I'm going to take that microcam and shove it down his throat!"

Flynn shook his head. "No, you're not. You know about that one, Missy. Destroy it, and Drake will replace it with one you don't know about. Come on. We'd better get back."

Wendy was waiting for them. "Got it," she announced. "Both suits were scrapped, but *not* on the same date."

Flynn made a face. "Of course they both weren't reported on the same date. That would look too suspicious. What does 'scrapped' mean?"

Wendy turned back to the display. "Ah, let's see . . . Here it is: the first one was sold as part of scrap lot fifty-four forty, the second went in lot fifty-four fifty-eight." She looked back at Flynn and smiled.

"Sold to whom?"

Wendy sighed and looked at the display again. "Ah . . . Oh! Joe Aguirre. He's a scrap merchant here on the Station. He has a workshop—"

"I know Joe Aguirre," Flynn said. He turned to Adamly. "Thanks, Missy. We'll be off."

"Yeah, and thanks for ruining my day," Missy said dryly.

Out in the corridor, Wendy said, "You ruined her day by getting her to steal Company secrets for you?"

Flynn wanted to trust Wendy, but he didn't know what her legal ethics would compel her to do with the truth. So he said, "Security discovered her search, so she thinks she'll get yelled at for trying to assist me."

Flynn set a rapid pace—Drake knew what he was doing, so he had to move fast before the last evidence disappeared. Wendy had to hurry to keep up.

"Where are we going?" she asked.

"To see Joe Aguirre, of course."

Chapter 16

Joe Aguirre, bathed in a pool of light from an overhead fixture, bent over a bin of broken machinery parts as he inventoried the contents. He looked up when he heard the airlock hatch open. "Well, how about that!" he said. "You don't come around for months, then I see you three times in a week!"

Flynn was climbing down the ladder. "Last time I was down here you said you were lonely."

"I could use a break," Joe said, putting down his computer. "How about we go up to the Moonshine and I'll buy you a drink?"

"Thanks, Joe, but I'm in a hurry at the moment. I'll let you buy me a drink some other time." Flynn glanced over his shoulder as Wendy stepped off of the ladder. "Oh, by the way, this is Wendy Chadwick."

Wendy stepped forward, extending her hand in greeting. "Pleased to meet you, Mr. Aguirre."

Aguirre recognized Chadwick from the news reports of Wofford's death. A look of suspicion flitted across his face. "I'm not in some sort of legal trouble, am I?"

"No, Joe," Flynn assured, "we're just checking on a couple of lots of scrap you bought."

Aguirre almost breathed a sigh of relief. He picked up his pocket computer. "Which ones?"

"Fifty-four forty and fifty-four fifty-eight."

Aguirre repeated the numbers to his computer. "Damaged and broken stuff, made of materials the Company doesn't recycle here," he said, reading his display. "What are you looking for?"

"Damaged pressure suits."

Aguirre didn't even glance at his computer. "I haven't seen a damaged pressure suit in, oh, four, maybe five years. Not since the Company switched to suits with the ceramic mesh outer layer. Nearly impossible to tear. It'll stop most micrometeorite impacts. You can't even burn it with a standard torch."

Flynn's heart sank. Those suits were his last lead. "There weren't even parts of a pressure suit in those lots? Air processors? Power supplies?"

Aguirre shook his head. "Even if a suit was damaged—and they aren't indestructible—the Company's suit-maintenance department would scavenge stuff like that for spare parts."

Flynn suppressed the urge to use foul language. "Thanks, Joe. Now I owe you a drink."

"No, no!" Aguirre protested, holding up his hands. "I'm not going to be the first person on the Station who lets Mike Flynn buy him a drink! It's on me! And soon!"

Flynn forced a smile. "Okay, soon." He turned to Wendy, but avoided looking her in the eye. "Let's go." They headed for the airlock ladder.

"So where are those damaged suits?" Wendy asked quietly.

"Probably the same place as the mortal remains of Philip Asterbrook and Jonny Mondragon," Flynn said disgustedly. "Burned up in Jupiter's atmosphere. They might have been right in the coffins."

"Then how are we going to prove what happened?"

They reached the ladder. Flynn let Wendy climb into the lock first. "We can't. Drake's disposed of the evidence." He gritted his teeth. "I thought I'd finally gotten a step up on Drake, but he beat me to the punch by four months. Those suits were my last avenue of investigation. Now all Drake has to do is wait for the Asterbrooks to get tired of paying me twelve hundred dollars a day with no results."

Flynn followed Wendy up the ladder. His eyes lit upon the gasket for the lower hatch. It was smooth, flexible, and in excellent condition. Flynn hesitated, running his fingers over the gasket, then backed down the ladder. "Hey, Joe?"

Aguirre looked up from his bin of broken parts. "Yeah?"

"When were these hatch gaskets replaced?"

Aguirre scratched his head. "They've never been replaced, at least, not since I've been here. They're made of a miracle material from Dupont. Flexible in conditions ranging from direct sunlight to almost absolute zero. Very long lasting."

"This hatch must get more traffic than just about any other basement hatch," Flynn said.

Aguirre nodded. "That one, and the ones used by the crews that clean out the recycling bins and maintain the air and water recycling equipment."

"What would cause one of these gaskets to wear out?"

Aguirre shrugged. "Drag a lot of heavy objects over one and you won't do it any good."

This time Flynn's smile wasn't forced. "Thanks, Joe."

"What for?"

Flynn looked up at Wendy in the airlock. "Have you ever seen the Station's liquid recirculation pumps?"

Chadwick's forehead wrinkled in puzzlement. "No. Why?"

"It's a very impressive facility. You really owe it to yourself to see it."

Wendy started to protest that she didn't have time to

waste on such things, but then she realized that Flynn's mood had suddenly improved. "What's going on?" she asked suspiciously.

"You have your computer with you, don't you? You said Saturday that the engineering drawings for Satellite Charlie were in there, so the Station drawings are probably there, too."

"Well, yeah," Wendy admitted, "but I don't know where in our file structure—"

"Hey, Joe," Flynn called over his shoulder, "where in the Company's computer records are the Station drawings located?"

"There's a set in the plant-engineering directory," Aguirre replied.

Chadwick reluctantly climbed down from the airlock. She took her computer from her pocket. "He said the plant-engineering directory, didn't he?" She opened the computer and stabbed the touch-sensitive display with her finger. "This is a big help! Where in plant engineering?"

Flynn pointed to a likely subdirectory. "Try engineering drawings. You have access, don't you?"

"Yeah, I have access to everything . . . There. Is that what you want?" A multicolored skeletal view of Jupiter Station filled the computer display. "Why do we need this, anyway?"

"So we don't get lost," Flynn explained. "Joe, do you have a flashlight we can borrow?"

Aguirre opened the top drawer of his desk and extracted a black flashlight. He tossed it to Flynn. "Here, you can use this one." He pointed to his left. "You go through the bulkhead hatch down there, and the recirculation pumps for this quadrant of the Station are about two hundred meters right in front of you."

"Thanks, Joe."

Flynn led Chadwick through the hatch that Aguirre had indicated. "If we have to see the damned pumps, why don't we just go up to level one and walk to their access airlock?" the lawyer asked.

"Because there are security cameras all over level one," Flynn replied, "but aside from the camera in Joe's workshop, and the cameras covering the work sites around the recycling chutes and places like that, there aren't any in the basement. Silvanus Drake can't see where we're going."

Chadwick looked askance. "Where *are* we going?"

"Warehouse seven."

Chadwick stopped walking. Flynn turned around to face her. "Come on. No one's going to shoot at us this time—they won't know we're there. Let's see that computer."

Even with the Station drawings, Flynn needed almost an hour to find his way to the airlock to warehouse seven. The hatch from the basement wasn't locked—a safety precaution, in case the basement lost pressure when someone was in it. Flynn opened the hatch and was nearly blinded by the bright light in the airlock. He extended his hand and helped Wendy into the lock, then closed the hatch so the lock could come up to Station pressure.

Flynn opened the overhead hatch that led to the warehouse. The warehouse lights were off, but Flynn could feel the emptiness around him. Most of the containers that had been in warehouse seven the week before had been moved to Satellite Juliet, and Flynn could see the glowing Exit sign above the main airlock hatch. The red lamp on the security camera on the bulkhead near the Exit sign was lit. He kept his head below the level of the hatch and ran his hand over the gasket. "Oh, yeah," he said. "Look at the way this gasket is worn. I noticed it when we used this airlock to get away from Kemper and Santino. I was afraid the hatch wouldn't seal behind us."

Wendy climbed up the ladder next to Flynn and pinched the gasket between her fingers. "Aguirre says these things last forever."

"But you can wear them out by dragging heavy objects over them." He hazarded a peek into the warehouse. "They were in pressure suits; the outer hatch was open . . . They must have been moving something through the warehouse and into the basement—if they were moving something the other way it would have been long gone before we got here last week and Drake wouldn't have gotten so excited when we came here from warehouse twelve and then went through this hatch. Drake thought we knew everything— that's why he didn't restrain his goons, who were under the false impression that we'd killed one of their number." Flynn stared downward at the hatch beneath him. "Whatever Asterbrook and Mondragon were moving is down there."

Wendy wasn't eager to return to the basement. "We were just down there," she pointed out. "We didn't see anything."

"We weren't looking for anything."

Flynn closed the warehouse hatch. He waited impatiently for the lock pressure to drop to that of the basement, then opened the lower hatch and climbed down the ladder to the deck. The lighting in the airlock was much brighter than the lighting in the basement, and, standing in the pool of light from the open airlock, Michael could see only black, overlapping shadows, punctuated with glowing patches from distant lamps. "Close that hatch behind you."

Wendy did so, and the area around the ladder was plunged into darkness. Wendy had to feel her way down the ladder. "Now what?" she asked.

Flynn took his flashlight and probed the nearby shadows. The beam revealed nothing but steel girders and bulkheads.

"They've had plenty of time since we were here last week to dispose of whatever it was," Wendy suggested.

Flynn directed the flashlight beam toward the deck at his feet. "Ah-hah! Look at these marks! Something scratched the deck here!" His beam followed the markings, which extended in an intermittent line for about five meters to another hatch set in the deck. "What the hell . . ."

Wendy squinted. "I thought you said that led to the outside."

"It does," Michael answered. "Well, it leads to the radiation shield, which is open to the vacuum . . . Hell, this isn't a simple pressure hatch! It's an *airlock* hatch! There's an airlock here for easy access to the radiation shield! Every other hatch to the radiation shield I've ever seen was a simple pressure hatch. Let me see your computer for a second." Flynn called up the Station drawing he had been using as a map and zoomed in on the area where he and Chadwick were standing. The airlock was shown on the drawing. "Look at the modification date on this drawing: this airlock was added six months ago, around the time Asterbrook and Mondragon started working for the Company." Flynn couldn't imagine anyone stashing polymeth fabrication equipment in the unpressurized radiation shield. He glanced back at the airlock to warehouse seven: its hatches, as well as the hatch to the radiation shield, were too small for a standard-sized packing case. The cases must have been opened, and their contents transferred piece by piece . . . Asterbrook and Mondragon might have seen what they were handling.

Chadwick interrupted his reverie. "What exactly is in the radiation shield?"

"Oh, ah, pieces of rock, mine refuse, stuff like that," Flynn replied. "Anything cheap and otherwise useless that will absorb radiation . . . When the Company moves production facilities from an old satellite into a new one, production is shut down for awhile, right? Does the Company suspend shipments during that period, or what?"

"We usually put on extra shifts and stockpile products ahead of time, so we can fill orders on schedule."

Flynn nodded. "So if the Company was going to move a polymeth fabrication lab from Satellite Charlie to the brand-new Satellite Juliet, they would have stockpiled polymeth ahead of time."

Chadwick clenched her teeth and stamped her heel on the metal deck. "For the millionth time, Michael, there is no illegal polymeth factory on Charlie!"

"Not anymore," Flynn agreed. "That's why Drake didn't impede our search of Charlie Saturday afternoon. It's been moved to Juliet, and probably expanded in the process."

Wendy wracked her brain for a good argument. "So you no longer believe that Yamaguchi and Dornhoeffer were illegally producing polymethyl two four on Charlie when we went there Saturday afternoon?"

"They didn't have very much," Flynn said. "They might have been testing a sample from the new factory on Juliet. I hear that the computer system on Juliet is way behind schedule; production from the new polymeth lab might be just beginning."

"Michael, you think Mondragon and Asterbrook were killed when a cable hoisting a heavy crate broke." She indicated the marks on the deck with the toe of her shoe. "Look at these marks: whatever scratched the deck here was *heavy!* Polymethyl two four has a street value of a two thousand dollars a gram! A ten-ton crate would be worth twenty billion dollars! The Company's not that rich, Michael!"

Flynn cocked his head. "You sure? Where in the Company books would profits from illegal drugs be recorded?"

Wendy tried a different argument. "The radiation shield isn't heated, right? It's cold down there. I know you can't freeze polymeth."

Flynn said thoughtfully, "The Station rotates a couple of times a minute. Direct sunlight could warm the radiation shield. And the Station is made of steel. Move steel in Jupiter's magnetic field and you generate eddy currents, which also warm the radiation shield. Want to bet that the average temperature down there is just about perfect for long-term storage of polymethyl two four?"

Chadwick took a deep breath and let it out slowly. "Okay, Michael. I don't know what's down there, but I'll prove to you it's not polymeth. As a member of the executive board of the Station, I'm sure I'm allowed to borrow pressure suits if necessary to inspect Company property."

Flynn nixed that idea. "Pressure *suit*, Wendy, not *suits*. You don't need one."

"Oh, yes I do!" Chadwick replied, nodding her head vigorously. "I want to see your face when you find no polymeth there."

"Wendy, I *hope* that Silvanus Drake thinks that we're scouring the basement for a polymeth lab, like we did on Charlie last Saturday, but I can't be sure of that. If he comes down here while we're in the radiation shield and jams that hatch shut, we'll be stuck down there until our air runs out—a tragic accident that solves Drake's problem."

Wendy put her hands on her hips. "I thought your new hero status had made you bulletproof."

Flynn hated having his own arguments used against him. "Wendy . . . It might be booby-trapped."

"Michael," she interrupted, "let me put it this way: if I don't go along, I'm not getting any pressure suits."

"Wendy—"

"Michael . . . I love you. If we die, we die together."

Flynn gave up with a sigh. "Can you have your office manager pick up the suits and deliver them to Aguirre's workshop? I don't want to go upstairs and get back on Drake's radar. As soon as he sees us with pressure suits, he'll know exactly where we're going."

"I suppose that makes sense," Wendy agreed.

The return journey took almost as long as the outbound one. Ms. DuJong was a very efficient office manager, and the pressure suits were waiting with a puzzled Joe Aguirre when Flynn and Chadwick returned to the warehouse. Flynn touched his finger to his lips to keep Aguirre from voicing the question that Flynn could read in his eyes. "I'll explain when we return," he promised, then he and Chadwick headed back to the space beneath warehouse seven. Flynn had learned the route on the first trip and they needed only half an hour the second time, even though they were carrying the bulky suits.

"Ever wear one of these things before?" Flynn asked, offering to help Wendy with the garment.

"Yeah," Wendy said as she started to don her suit. "I took the obligatory walk outside soon after I got here."

Flynn put his stun pistol on the deck while he donned his suit, but when he picked up the gun he discovered that it had not been designed for operation by someone with thick gloves. Flynn reluctantly opened the suit and put the pistol in his coat pocket, where it would be out of reach as long as he was in vacuum. Chadwick was fully enclosed and wearing a smile of superiority when Flynn finally locked his helmet into place. He left his faceplate partially open.

"The radios in these suits have hundreds of channels," Mike said. "Do you know which ones Company personnel usually use?"

Wendy searched her memory. "The lower-numbered ones, I think. Tourists use the higher numbers."

"Okay, let's pretend we're tourists and use channel three ninety-nine." Flynn twisted the selector switch until the channel number appeared on the display that was laser-beamed directly into his eyes. "I don't think a radio signal will penetrate these metal walls, but you'd better set the power to minimum—no sense taking chances. Besides, I don't know if the repeaters down here will relay these suit channels."

"They do," Wendy said. "A safety precaution for people working down here in pressure suits."

Flynn turned his power as low as it would go, then closed and locked his faceplate. "Are you receiving?"

Wendy nodded behind her faceplate. "Can you hear me?"

"Perfectly. Let's do it."

The hatch to the airlock beneath them had no locking device, but the airlock was depressurized. They had to wait for it to fill with air before they could open the hatch. The airlock from the basement to the radiation shield was larger than the airlock from the basement to warehouse seven and had larger hatches. There was enough room for two people in pressure suits. The exit hatch was in the side of the air-lock instead of the bottom, since the bottom of the airlock was the outermost skin of the Station. The radiation sensor inside Flynn's suit was showing a level that would be un-healthy if endured for long periods.

"Would you look at all those dusty footprints on the deck," Flynn said. "This lock's seen a lot of use."

"I figured that from the marks on the deck above," Wendy replied.

The airlock pressure reached zero and the status light on the exit hatch changed from red to green. Flynn spun the latch handle and swung the hatch inward. Light from the airlock illuminated a narrow swath in front of him. Flynn switched on the powerful lights built into the suit helmet to see more of the space in front of him.

Flynn had been wondering if he would discover disassembled polymeth fabrication equipment or crates containing a fortune in polymeth two four. He was completely unprepared for the sight his probing headlamp beams revealed.

Chapter 17

"Rocks!" Chadwick exclaimed, in disbelief as much as in surprise. She switched on her own headlamp and added its light to that of Flynn's. "Nothing but rocks!"

The radiation shield was just two meters high, and only next to the airlock was there that much headroom. The layer of mining debris that insulated the Station from Jupiter's radiation sloped upward from the deck until it was nearly to the overhead only ten meters from where Flynn and Chadwick stood.

Flynn was too stunned to reply. Chadwick, with lower expectations than her partner, recovered first. "But no polymeth," she pointed out. Flynn still didn't say anything, so the lawyer added, "Whatever the Company's covering up, it's not here."

Flynn wouldn't concede defeat. "Then why this new airlock?"

Wendy shrugged, but it didn't show through her pressure suit. "The Company must have been thickening the radiation shield here."

Flynn made a face, a gesture also lost behind the faceplate of his helmet and the glare of his headlamp. "While Satellite Juliet was so far behind schedule that the Company was hiring extra people to work on it? I don't think so. No, whatever Asterbrook and Mondragon were working on was more important than that. They were working right here and were killed right around here someplace."

"Killed doing what? Moving rocks? That's not worth a cover-up!"

Flynn stared at the dark gray rocks in front of him. He didn't *know* that the layer of rocks reached all the way to the overhead everywhere. He pointed at the debris. "It's right *behind* those rocks!"

Michael stepped out of the airlock, treading carelessly on the multitude of boot prints in the dust. Two steps brought him to where the rocks began. He clambered up the incline, dislodging rocks that rolled back toward the airlock. He had to bend over to keep his helmet from striking the overhead. Flynn began pulling rocks from the top of the pile. They ranged in size from smaller than his fist to larger than his helmeted head and were irregular in shape, the result of being run through rock crushers. Some had smooth surfaces, as though they had been cut from large blocks.

"Michael, you're wasting your time," Wendy said. "We've no idea how much debris was in here before the accident. Look around you! You'll run out of air long before you run out of rocks!"

"It has to be here!" Flynn insisted. He kept pulling rocks from the pile and pushing them backward. He grabbed another one but it didn't move. He focused his headlamp on it to see what was holding it in place, and discovered that nothing was holding it. It was simply heavier than the other rocks.

Much heavier.

Flynn picked up the rock. It was the size of his fist but as heavy as a bowling ball, and it wasn't the only one of its type. Flynn quickly found many more, of different sizes and shapes. He slowly backed down the incline.

"Did you find something?" Wendy asked.

Flynn picked up one of the rocks he had pushed back toward the airlock and handed it to Chadwick. "Here. Feel this." She took it in her left hand and hefted it. Flynn handed her the rock had aroused his suspicions. "Now feel this."

Wendy almost dropped it. "Whoa! That's heavy!" She looked from the rock in her hand to Flynn. Michael could see only the glare of her headlamp. "What is it?"

"I don't know," Flynn replied. "Something very heavy and very dense, and there's a bunch more under the lighter stuff." Flynn took the rock back. It wasn't as dark in color as the other rocks. "Reminds me of armor-piercing ammunition, made of depleted uranium, that we had in the Marines."

"There are only insignificant concentrations of uranium at Jupiter," Chadwick protested.

"This is the wrong color, anyway," Flynn said. "Besides, uranium wouldn't be worth a cover-up." He hefted the rock while he mulled over the possibilities. "This might be something worse: plutonium."

Wendy quickly checked the radiation sensor in her suit, then caught herself. "Concentrations of all heavy metals are very low at Jupiter. Besides, I thought plutonium was man-made."

"Only trace amounts exist in nature," Flynn agreed, "on Earth. Out here, who knows? And plutonium can be concentrated by simple chemical processes, so you don't need laser isotope separation to make an A-bomb." He let that point sink in. "Do you think that's worth a cover-up?"

Chadwick looked into the glare of Flynn's headlamp. "I hope we wouldn't advertise it. You think this is what Asterbrook and Mondragon were working on?"

Flynn nodded behind his faceplate. "Must be. But . . ." He held the rock next to his suit's radiation sensor. "Huh.

Doesn't seem to be radioactive. Plutonium's a pretty hot alpha emitter." He stared at the rock in his hand. "It can't be plutonium," he concluded. "It looks like nearly pure metal, not an ore, and this much pure plutonium would be a critical mass. Come on; let's get this analyzed."

The pair climbed back through the airlock into the basement. They had no sooner removed their suits than the hatch to the warehouse above opened and light flooded the area around the ladder. Flynn grabbed Wendy by the arm and pulled her behind a girder. Silvanus Drake climbed carefully down the ladder, his footsteps on the rungs ringing hollowly from the metal bulkheads. Flynn took his stun pistol from his pocket.

Drake had a flashlight. It took him less than a second to spot Flynn and Chadwick. He let the flashlight beam dwell on them, then swept it to Flynn's discarded pressure suit and the rock on the deck beside it. "I think the two of you should come with me."

Flynn brandished his pistol. "I'm the one with the gun. I'll do the thinking."

"Don't be melodramatic, Flynn," Drake said wearily. "If you want to know what you found, come with me."

"I don't want it to be the last thing I ever know," Flynn replied, "so I'm not going anywhere with you. If you want to tell me what that is, you can tell me right here."

"I don't have the authority to tell you what that is," Drake said. "Only Edwin Warshovsky can tell you, and he's not coming here. Now, do you want to accompany me to his office?"

Flynn hesitated. "What do you think?" he said quietly.

"I don't know what to think," Wendy replied, just as quietly. Her eyes were fixed on Drake.

"We don't have all day," Drake said.

Flynn made up his mind. "Let me have your gun. But first, take off those activation rings, both of them, and put them in your pocket."

Drake put the activation rings in his right coat pocket. He pulled back his coat so that Flynn could see his laser pistol in its holster on his hip. He extracted the gun, un-latched the power supply, and extended the gun butt first.

Flynn left the minimal security of his girder and walked quickly to Drake, keeping the security chief covered with his stun gun. He glanced upward into the airlock to make sure that Drake had come alone. He took Drake's laser and dropped it into the coat pocket where his stun pistol usually resided.

"You can leave the pressure suits here," Drake said. "I'll send someone for them. But bring *that,*" he pointed at the rock, "with you."

"Okay," Flynn replied, "take us to Mr. Warshovsky. But you're going through that airlock before us. If there are some unfriendly people up there, you're going to be the first person shot."

The axis of the Station was pointing at Jupiter, and through the window in his office Ed Warshovsky watched the giant planet somersault one and a half times every minute as the Station rotated. The Great Red Spot was approaching the evening terminator. Some astrophysicists believed that the Spot had been created when Jupiter had swallowed an object the size of Io. The Great Red Spot was fading, and from the rate of fade the time of the Spot's creation could be estimated to coincide with the end of Earth's last ice age. A bolt of lightning, hundreds of kilometers long and bright enough to be seen across the quarter-million-kilometer void, flashed through Jupiter's clouds. The planet was telling him to keep his distance and tread carefully. Jupiter, not man, ruled this part of the solar system.

"It was all my fault," Warshovsky said.

He turned around and faced the three other people in his office. The detective, Flynn, had his hand in his coat pocket. He had a gun there, no doubt. Warshovsky avoided looking at Wendy Chadwick. He had seen the pain in her eyes; he had disappointed her greatly. He had cared for her like he would have cared for the daughter he didn't have, and never again would she be able to look at him with respect.

"If I had been wiser, no one would have died," he said.

Flynn was impatient. "What, exactly, happened?"

Warshovsky glanced at Drake, but the security chief remained silent. Warshovsky would have to tell the story. "Last January, our detection network spotted a rock, the size of this office, on an eccentric orbit. It was passing close to the Station at that moment. It would be our best chance to capture it, but because of its eccentric orbit none of the cowboys had an intercept vector. Roger Ajanian was headed to Satellite Juliet in a shuttle, and traffic control asked him to corral the rock. Ajanian's magnetic grapple didn't hold, so it wasn't nickel or iron. The rock was rotating very slowly and Ajanian was able to bring the shuttle against it to give it a push. It hardly moved. It had to be very massive, much too massive to be aluminum. Ajanian reshaped its orbit to keep it close to the Station. He chipped off a sample, about as big as his finger, and brought it back for analysis. As soon as he got the sample into gravity he was certain that he had something very heavy and very valuable."

Flynn glanced at the fist-sized rock that he had carried all the way from the basement, and which was now resting on Warshovsky's desk. He said, "It can't be gold," the yellow metal that had inspired so many dreams of wealth, the stuff of which regents' crowns and pirates' doubloons were made, the product of the mines of Ophir which had enriched Solomon. It was the wrong color.

Warshovsky shook his head. "No, not gold. But something just as bad: platinum."

The room fell silent. Flynn imagined he could hear his heart beating, could hear everyone's hearts beating.

"The rock was over eighty percent pure," Warshovsky continued. "Almost fourteen thousand *tons* of platinum."

Flynn stared at his host. Conglomerated Mining and Manufacturing had gotten its start in precious-metal mining and still mined platinum, gold, and silver wherever it could do so profitably. The discovery of that much platinum should have caused exuberant celebration, but Warshovsky looked depressed. "That would be the largest precious-metal find in history, wouldn't it?" Flynn said. "At present prices it would be worth . . . a trillion dollars!"

Drake finally spoke. "And why is platinum worth so much?"

Flynn scowled at Drake. He didn't want to belabor the obvious, but he said, "Because it's so—" He caught himself before he said something foolish. If fourteen thousand tons of platinum were dumped on the market, it wouldn't be rare—or expensive—anymore.

Warshovsky's problem suddenly became crystal clear to Flynn. The discovery of a gold nugget the size of a football on Mars had knocked the bottom out of the precious metals market for over a year. Only after people learned that heavy-metal concentrations varied inversely with distance from the sun had the prices for Conglomerated's primary product recovered. The discovery of fourteen thousand tons of platinum would sink precious-metal prices permanently.

Thirty-five percent of the Company's assets were in precious-metal mines. Public knowledge that so much platinum had been found could bankrupt the Company.

"We borrowed against everything we owned in order to build this station," Warshovsky continued. "Those loans can be called at any time if the value of their surety decreases. Here and Ceres are the only places where the Company mines base metals. Most of our other facilities are involved in precious metals and gemstones. The precious-metal facilities would have become worthless overnight. The banks would have called in their loans. The only way we could have paid them would have been to mortgage or sell Jupiter Station. We probably would have had to sell. No one would have loaned us money if, by waiting until we declared bankruptcy, they could have bought this station for a song.

"But Ajanian realized all that and kept his mouth shut," Warshovsky said. "He brought the sample directly to me. I had it analyzed after normal working hours by a technician who could be trusted to keep quiet. And when the bad news was confirmed, I made my mistake."

Warshovsky turned back to the window. "Heavy atoms are supposed to be formed in supernovas. That damned rock might have been spewed out of a cataclysmic eruption on the other side of the galaxy, and drifted through space for a billion years before being caught in Jupiter's gravitational field." He stared at the giant planet. "I should have had that rock put on a trajectory for Jupiter's atmosphere. Should have gotten rid of it forever. The Company would have been saved and no one would have been hurt."

"Why didn't you?" Flynn asked.

Warshovsky turned around again. "Because platinum is more than a precious metal. It is a wonderful catalyst, used in the manufacture of all sorts of products. I could not deprive mankind of such a treasure. I just had to keep it a secret. In five years we'll have paid off our loans. In five years it won't matter if we develop the technology to mine the rich veins of Mercury. In five years it won't matter if precious-metal prices fall through the floor. I had to put that rock someplace where it wouldn't be found for five years, and with that Asian consortium announcing plans to build a facility out here, and with forty scientists on the Station studying the Jovian system, I couldn't leave it in orbit around Jupiter."

Warshovsky pursed his lips. "I thought of putting a transponder on it and boosting it out of orbit," he continued, "but it was too massive for our shuttles to move very far very fast. Our own detection system would have spotted the move—a highly suspicious move. More people would know; more people might talk."

Drake took over the storytelling. "No one has ever kept a precious-metal find secret for very long," he pointed out, "but Ajanian came up with a plan: the radiation shield under warehouse seven had never been completely filled—a warehouse doesn't need as much shielding as places where people live and work continuously. He offered to cut up that rock and pack it into the empty space below warehouse seven. He made it sound easy."

"And that's where Asterbrook and Mondragon came in?" Flynn asked. "Why them? They were completely untrained for what had to be done."

"That's exactly why they were chosen," Warshovsky explained. "Ajanian had known that he was dealing with a heavy metal as soon as he contacted that rock, and he could tell that it wasn't lead. Any other space-experienced employee would have realized the same thing. We needed people who were inexperienced, who wouldn't realize that they were dealing with something unusually dense, and who didn't have a lot of friends working for the Company who would wonder what they were doing with their time all of a sudden.

"They were hired with the proviso that they wouldn't tell anyone what they were doing," Warshovsky said. "We told them that the space beneath warehouse seven had been accidentally left empty when the Station had been constructed, and that we didn't want to panic the residents of the Station with the thought of excessive radiation exposure. We told them that they were going to get a three-year dose of radiation on this rush job, and that we couldn't spare any regular workers for it. Ajanian trained them to work in vacuum and zero gee, but when this job was done we were going to transfer them to a diamond mine on Earth or Mars, ostensibly because they would need time to recover from the radiation exposure, but actually because we couldn't let them work with heavy metals again. That way they'd never get a chance to realize that they'd been dealing with very dense material here."

"But, they were L3's," Chadwick protested. "If they'd been trained to work in vacuum or zero gee they'd have been at least L2's."

"Officially, they were L3's," Warshovsky replied. "We couldn't have people in Human Resources wondering why we'd hired two untrained people and immediately trained them to the L2 level when we had long-term employees applying for that training. We told them that their job classification was part of the project secrecy, and that we'd make up the wage differential with a bonus when the job was done.

"Ajanian's plan worked perfectly," Warshovsky went on.

405

"He cut up the rock himself, and packed it in shipping containers with aluminum ore to reduce the density. Every morning Asterbrook and Mondragon would report for work in a room with an airlock to the outside. They'd don the pressure suits that were stored there for them and Ajanian would pick them up in a shuttle. They'd collect the containers and take them to warehouse seven. Lots of equipment for Satellite Juliet was stored there; Ajanian was ramrodding Juliet; his shuttle visiting warehouse seven aroused no suspicion. Asterbrook and Mondragon would unload the containers of platinum from the shuttle, move them to the deck hatch with the overhead crane, and lower them into the basement. They set up a conveyor to move the rocks between the hatches in the basement. Kilo by kilo the platinum was moved into the radiation shield."

Warshovsky hesitated. "But one day, while they were moving a container out of the shuttle, the cable from the crane broke. The load had been swinging, and Mondragon and Asterbrook were both under the container, trying to stabilize it. Ajanian had told them to stay out from underneath suspended loads, but they were inexperienced. They made a mistake. There were ten tons of platinum and bauxite in that container. Mondragon and Asterbrook were crushed. Ajanian was in the shuttle when it happened. He got to them as quickly as he could, but they had been killed instantly. That's when he noticed how small the pulley was on that crane in seven. He knew immediately why the cable had broken."

Drake said, "There were thirty crates—smaller than usual so they would fit through the deck hatch into the basement; nonstandard crates that would certainly arouse the suspicions of investigators—containing platinum in warehouse seven. Three hundred tons of evidence. There was no way we could have moved it out of there before Mondragon and Asterbrook were missed. But Ajanian realized that the pulley assembly would fit the crane in warehouse twelve, which was where Asterbrook and Mondragon were supposed to be working that day. So we just moved the accident scene to twelve. I rigged the security camera so that it wouldn't show anything—easy to do, since all the cameras are linked directly to Security Control. We took the bodies out of the pressure suits—L3's shouldn't have been wearing pressure suits—pressed Mondragon's fingers against the crane controls to leave fingerprints, lifted the machinery frame that was being prepared for Satellite Juliet, put the bodies under the frame, and dropped it on them. We ran the broken cable through the pulley."

"And then you waited for Dr. Vasquez to become the on-call medical examiner," Flynn stated, "because a competent autopsy would reveal that many of the injuries had occurred long after death. But you could control Vasquez."

For a moment, Flynn thought he saw Drake's eyes narrow. "Vasquez had applied for a Company job," the security chief explained, "and our background check had revealed a pattern of behavior consistent with addiction to polymethyl two four, so we didn't hire him. When Vasquez got the Meditech job, I kept him under surveillance and noticed the same behavior pattern. When he responded to the scene, I took him aside and told him that I'd reveal his addiction if he didn't cooperate."

The security chief still wouldn't admit the Company had been supplying Vasquez with polymeth. Flynn decided not to press the point. "But when the machinery frame was lifted off of the bodies, you saw that there wasn't enough blood," he guessed.

Drake gave a brief nod. "It took several hours to stage

the fake accident, and the blood had coagulated in the suits. Eventually the emergency personnel might have realized that there wasn't enough blood at the scene, so we got them Company jobs elsewhere. We gave Ajanian a huge bonus so that he could retire, just in case he started babbling about the accident—which really upset him, by the way—when he was drunk some night. We took care of everything. And then the Asterbrooks ruined it by asking us to hold their son's body. We couldn't let them take it home—if they'd had it autopsied, the fact that many of the injuries had occurred long after death would have been revealed. So we transferred Egleiter, who had communicated with the Asterbrooks, to Ceres, and buried the body."

"And erased all of Egleiter's records," Flynn added.

"How did you manage that?" Wendy asked critically. "The computer system would never have recognized either of you as Egleiter."

"As general manager of the Station, I have access to all computer records," Warshovsky said. "You know that, Wendy."

"But Egleiter had stored Asterbrook's personal belongings right in Human Resources," Drake said, diverting Wendy from that line of inquiry, "and instead of recording that fact in the Human Resources record, where it belonged, he put it in the accounting file. I didn't think to look there. Asterbrook's form nine had instructed us to send home his books and all handwritten documents. After Human Resources had packed his belongings, I let myself into his apartment and paged through his last journal." Drake shook his head. "He'd written *everything* down. I thought it would look suspicious if only the last journal disappeared, so I got rid of all of them. We transferred the person who'd packed the belongings to planet three, just in case she remembered packing the journals. We even transferred Asterbrook's 'girlfriend' just in case he'd said something to her."

"The journals were disposed of with the pressure suits?" Flynn asked.

Drake nodded. "But the Asterbrooks knew about their son's journals. Their disappearance made them more suspicious, so suspicious that they hired you. You took surprisingly little time to find your way to warehouse seven."

"I'd noticed the previous day that the pulley on the crane in warehouse twelve was larger than the pulley the investigators had concluded had caused the line to fail," Flynn explained. "Warehouse seven contained the only other Manitowoc crane with a pulley assembly of the right size."

"Ajanian had switched the pulleys back after the investigation in order to facilitate moving the machinery frame in twelve to Satellite Juliet," Drake said. "I sent Kemper and Santino to evict you because they were the closest to the warehouse. They were close to it because they were looking for a chance to get in without unlocking the door themselves so that they could steal Vasquez's chemical shipment, mistakenly believing that it contained a fortune in polymethyl two four. They thought you were trying to get the shipment, so they tried to kill you. You got away through the basement hatch, through which we'd moved the platinum. I thought you'd figured out *everything*. There was nothing to do but to bring you to Mr. Warshovsky for an explanation, before you could tell the rest of the solar system what you'd discovered. I directed every guard on duty to get you—"

"*Get* us? They tried to kill us!" Wendy interrupted, her eyes glaring.

Drake barely glanced at Chadwick. "But later that night,

in the Marshals Office, I realized that you really had no idea what we were concealing, and that you'd only been trying to get away."

Flynn asked, "Is that when you took the microcam out of my apartment?"

Drake shook his head. "That was a day later, when Wofford started suspecting you of the murders of Kemper and Santino. I knew he'd get a warrant to toss your place. I couldn't let him find the microcams, so I was waiting outside your apartment when you went jogging that morning and retrieved my surveillance gear before Wofford got there. I didn't know at the time why he seemed so eager to pin the killings on you, but I expected him to keep you out of circulation for a week or so." For a moment, Flynn thought he saw a grudging trace of admiration in Drake's eyes. "Wofford hardly slowed you down at all."

"So you tried to bribe me."

"We weren't trying to bribe you!" Warshovsky said quickly. "Mr. Drake wasn't certain that he could ferret out the killer of Santino and Kemper. He said you were the only private investigator on the Station smart enough to solve the case, so I authorized him to hire you. We really wanted you to find the murderer, but you insist on putting a sinister connotation on everything we do. We didn't really do anything wrong."

Wendy's jaw dropped. "You didn't do anything *wrong?*" Her eyes were open wide. "You fabricated evidence in an industrial accident! You hindered two official investigations! You blackmailed a medical examiner into falsifying autopsy results! You attempted to defraud the families of Philip Asterbrook and Jonny Mondragon by concealing Company liability in their deaths! You've committed enough felonies to serve twenty years in prison!"

"How so?" Drake said. "Asterbrook and Mondragon really were killed when a heavy object they were attempting to move fell on them—which it wouldn't have done if they had stayed out from under it, like they had been instructed—just like the official investigations concluded. All we did was see to it that the investigations got a few insignificant details wrong."

Chadwick clenched her teeth. *"Insignificant details?"*

"Wendy," Warshovsky pleaded, "the survival of the Company was at stake! And the monetary fluctuations that news of this find would cause could plunge the solar system into an economic depression! Governments might fall!"

"That doesn't justify your crimes!"

"It doesn't matter whether or not it justifies what we've done," Drake said calmly. "You can't tell anyone about it—you're our lawyer."

"But I just sent settlement offers to the families of Asterbrook and Mondragon based on information I now know is incorrect," Chadwick pointed out. "Since neither of those offers has been accepted, I have to replace them with offers that do not misrepresent the facts."

"You don't have to tell them about the platinum," Warshovsky said. He looked at Flynn. "And you have agreed not to publicize anything you learned in your investigation."

Flynn shook his head. "Doesn't matter. As a licensed private investigator I am required to report what I learned to my clients. And since I'm not working for an officer of the court, I am required to report all felonies which I discover to the authorities."

"To be precise," Drake interrupted, "you have to turn over all *evidence* of felonies you discover to the authorities." Drake almost smiled. "You don't have any evidence. What

411

was said in this room is all deniable."

Flynn stared at Drake. "There's no way you can move fourteen thousand tons of platinum out of the basement before I lead the marshals to it. Try denying *that*."

"Since the platinum was legally acquired, possession of it is not a felony," Drake said. "Not even a misdemeanor. You are not required to report it, so, under the terms of the agreement you negotiated with Ms. Chadwick, you can't mention it to anybody."

"And our settlement offer to the Asterbrooks will include a substantial bonus if they agree to keep secret the details of this case," Warshovsky said, looking at Wendy to make sure she understood what he expected of her.

The Company, however, had other secrets besides the platinum. "I guess the two of you will be able to stay free for a few weeks," Flynn conceded, "until I find your polymeth lab."

Warshovsky exhaled loudly. "There is no polymeth lab!" he said in exasperation.

Flynn couldn't resist smiling. "Oh, yes there is. I caught Drs. Yamaguchi and Dornhoeffer with a sample the other day, remember? And Emilio Vasquez, the late polymeth addict, wouldn't have come out here if he hadn't known he could get it from you."

"He was making his own in our ultrabaric chamber!" Warshovsky blurted. Drake shot him a warning glance, his usually expressionless eyes turning cold and sharp for an instant. Warshovsky looked back at Drake and said, "Well, it can't do any harm to tell him now!"

Flynn wasn't buying it. "Nice try, but I happen to know that you can't make polymeth in an ultrabaric chamber."

"Computer simulations say you can't," Drake agreed. "However, the computer programs that were used to prove that the Wing-Guggenheim reaction—the one that produced the first traces of polymeth at Cal Tech—can't be modified to produce more polymeth, do a poor job of predicting complex chemical reactions at very high pressures. The people in our Ceramics Lab don't trust them. Vasquez was getting his dope someplace, he was using our ultrabaric chamber regularly, and inquiries on planet three revealed that he had left his position at a hospital in Utah and moved here when that hospital had sold its ultrabaric chamber, so I had Yamaguchi and Dornhoeffer run some *real* experiments."

"When we encountered them in the airlock on Charlie," Wendy said softly, looking at the lump of platinum on Warshovsky's desk, "they had just discovered that, at twenty-four hundred atmospheres, the ingredients used by Wing and Guggenheim yield forty percent polymethyl two four. They made twenty thousand dollars worth of polymeth from thirty dollars worth of reagents in a glass flask." She looked at Flynn. "That's what I had promised to tell you as soon as I could." She glanced at Warshovsky and Drake. "Which was supposed to be when the authorities had checked out the two dozen or so ultrabaric chambers in the solar system and learned which of those were being used to produce polymeth."

"While we speak, the authorities are closing in on the entire illegal polymeth industry," Drake said. "One of these days, hundreds, maybe thousands of people will be arrested system-wide."

Flynn looked from Wendy, to Drake, and then to Warshovsky. He shook his head. "I'm not buying it. Everything I've read says there's only one way to produce significant quantities of polymeth."

"Computer!" Warshovsky said sharply. "Connect me

with Dr. Yamaguchi!" The manager of Jupiter Station looked up from the display and said to Flynn, "I don't know why Mr. Drake thinks you're so smart . . . Ah! Dr. Yamaguchi! Someone in my office needs a chemistry lesson. It's okay to tell him about the polymeth."

Warshovsky turned the display so that the others could see Yamaguchi, who was standing in what Flynn took to be his laboratory on Satellite Charlie. "Mike Flynn!" the chemist said. "Did they finally let you in on what we discovered?"

"They told me, but I don't believe them," Flynn replied. "I've read that the synthesis of polymethyl two four takes a room full of expensive equipment and a long, complex process. They claim that you—and all the drug dealers—made the stuff in a glass flask and an ultrabaric chamber. I can understand that there might be more than one way of making polymeth, but if it can be made easily in an ultrabaric chamber, why is that complicated procedure I read about considered optimum?"

Yamaguchi chuckled. "The proper name of that process you're thinking of is optimal *sequential* synthesis. Molecules are created atom by atom in a specific *sequence* that is optimum in some sense. The procedure is readily automated; algorithms have been developed that enable chemists to enter a chemical structure diagram into a computer and the machine spits out the process. But atom by atom synthesis is slow and complicated. If you take the constituents of the original Wing-Guggenheim reaction—with about fifteen percent more alcohol—up to twenty-four hundred atmospheres, some of the amino-acid precursors in the brew get to their triple points. You get a phase change in which literally thousands of atoms bond into their correct positions. Optimal sequential synthesis can't create reactions like that." Yamaguchi paused. "My advisor in grad school will get a laugh out of this when it becomes public. He always said that computer simulations—and sequential synthesis in particular—were a major obstacle to doing good chemistry."

Flynn chewed his upper lip. He knew just enough chemistry for Yamaguchi's explanation to sound reasonable. "Thanks, Doc."

Warshovsky broke the connection. "Satisfied?"

Flynn started to reply, then had a disturbing thought. "No. If you knew that Vasquez was making his own drugs, why did Wofford think they were in that shipment? Why did he try to kill Wendy?"

Warshovsky looked at Drake, who answered, "We didn't tell Wofford. He was so desperate to earn a transfer back to Earth that we feared he'd call a press conference and tell the whole system that *he* had discovered how illegal polymeth was being manufactured. We had Company HQ inform the drug-enforcement authorities in Washington directly. And since we had bypassed Wofford, we couldn't tell you—if word ever leaked that we had let you in on the secret while keeping the marshals in the dark, our long-term relations with the Marshals Service would have suffered greatly."

Flynn looked disgustedly at Drake. "What did you think I was going to do? Dance into Wofford's office singing, 'I know something you don't know'?"

"You've been known to drink to excess on occasion," Drake replied.

Flynn had heard enough. He put his arm around Wendy's shoulder as he turned toward the door. "Let's go."

Wendy waited until they had left Warshovsky's outer office before she asked, "Do you think the Asterbrooks will accept a settlement that requires them to keep the platinum secret?"

"No." Chadwick had been afraid of that, but she was unprepared for what Flynn was trying to say. "They don't want your money. The only reason they hired me was to assure themselves that their son hadn't been doing something illegal when he was killed. Once they learn that he hadn't been breaking the law, they won't tell anyone about the platinum. They'll keep it a secret because their son died trying to keep it secret."

Wendy hesitated, unwilling to believe what she had heard. "You mean, we're going to get away with it? The cover-up, the lies, the numerous felonies?"

Flynn pursed his lips. "The bad guys win this one." He grunted. "What's really ironic is that the Asterbrooks wouldn't have autopsied their son's body. If the Company had just stored it for them, while they came out here and picked it up, they would have gone home contented. They wouldn't have noticed the missing journals. Drake and Warshovsky were too damned distrusting for their own good."

Wendy took a deep breath. "When I became a corporate attorney I never thought I'd wind up representing a bunch of criminals."

"So, are you going to resign?"

Chadwick was slow to respond. "I should, but somebody has to keep an eye on Silvanus Drake."

They had reached the escalator that led to the lobby of the Company offices. "I really tried to persuade them to tell you about the polymeth last Saturday," Wendy said. "I had Warshovsky convinced, but then Drake whispered something in his ear and Warshovsky changed his mind."

Flynn stopped walking. He looked straight ahead. "I

wasn't supposed to be told until the authorities busted the polymeth dealers, right?" He pointed back the way they had come. "Warshovsky just said, 'It can't hurt to tell him now.' Why not? The only thing that's changed is that we discovered . . ." His voice trailed off as he gazed through the front doors of Company Headquarters at the waterfall in the Company Plaza. "He played me like a violin," he said softly.

"Huh? Who?"

"Drake, of course," Flynn said disgustedly. He glanced at the security camera that monitored the corridor. Its red light was glowing. "Bet you that Drake has those cameras rigged so that he can watch you without the red light showing. He was watching me more closely than I thought he was. As soon as he learned I was looking for a polymeth lab, he wanted me to *keep* looking for a polymeth lab, because as long as I was thinking about polymeth I wouldn't be thinking about platinum. I might even have found Vasquez's source of supply for him. He probably dropped little bits of evidence from time to time to keep me suspicious." Flynn remembered the rapidity with which the library had found polymeth citations for him. That had been a gift from Silvanus Drake. The detective clenched his teeth. "He *knew* we were following Dornhoeffer and Yamaguchi to Satellite Charlie last Saturday. He could have had the Security computer tell everyone that the satellite was closed while its air processor was being purged; the shuttle wouldn't have stopped at Charlie and we would have concluded that Dornhoeffer and Yamaguchi had gone someplace else. But he let us get into Charlie's airlock, and made us believe we were being given the run-around. He *wanted* us to be there when they left, *wanted* us to see the bottle of polymeth. We wasted the entire afternoon searching Charlie's basement for a polymeth lab, and every day of the Asterbrooks' money that I wasted brought closer the day when they'd call off the investigation—Drake's ultimate goal. His whispered argument to Warshovsky that convinced your boss not to let me in on the secret? He told Warshovsky that he wanted to keep me thinking about polymeth. Warshovsky told me today because I'd discovered the platinum; there was no need to decoy me anymore. Oh, he played me like a violin, all right."

"That's a very intriguing choice of words," Chadwick said. "Drake really does play the violin. I haven't heard him play, but people who have say he's quite good."

Flynn grunted. "He's good at fooling people, too."

"But you still outsmarted him," Wendy pointed out. "You found the platinum."

"I found where they were hiding their secret," Flynn corrected. "They had to tell me what it was. Not for a moment did I think it was a precious metal."

Wendy glanced at her wristwatch. "Come on," she said, tugging at Flynn's arm and pulling him onto the escalator. "I promised to cook dinner for you, remember? I have a beef roast in my refrigerator."

Flynn looked askance. "A beef roast? But Wendy, all that fat!"

"It's a very lean cut," Chadwick assured him.

They crossed the lobby and Flynn pointed up San Francisco Boulevard. "Let's go this way. There's a liquor store up there; I'll get us a bottle of wine."

Wendy smiled. "You don't need alcohol to break down my resistance, Michael."

Flynn shook his head. "The wine is for dinner. To break down your resistance, all I need are my good looks, wit, and incredible charm." He put his arm around her shoulder and they started up San Francisco Boulevard.

About the Author

David Michael Drury grew up in Casco, Wisconsin, twenty miles east of Green Bay. He received a BSEE degree from the Milwaukee School of Engineering in 1972 and a Ph.D. from Marquette University in 1978. He spent three years with Motorola in Schaumburg, Illinois, and for nine years was a Member of the Technical Staff in the Radar Department of Sandia National Laboratories in Albuquerque, New Mexico. Since 1987 Dr. Drury has been a member of the faculty of the University of Wisconsin—Platteville, where he is a professor of electrical engineering. Dr. Drury enjoys hunting, fishing, and target shooting, plays golf and the guitar, and used to play a fairly good game of chess. He flies his own plane, Grumman Tiger N53GT. Dr. Drury is single and lives with Midnight Sky and TC, his little pet cats.